Strong Hollow

Strong Hollow | a novel

LINDA LITTLE

GOOSE LANE

Edited by Laurel Boone.
Cover photographs: *Winter Beach* © copyright Margot Metcalfe, 1993, Digital Imagery © copyright 2001 PhotoDisc, Inc. (*Violin,* Thomas Brummett). Cover design by Julie Scriver.
Printed in Canada by AGMV Marquis
10 9 8 7 6 5 4 3 2 1

Canadian Cataloguing in Publication Data

Little, Linda, 1959-
Strong hollow

ISBN 0-86492-308-2

I. Title.

PS8573.I852S77 2001   C813'.6   C00-901792-5
PR9199.3.L557S77 2001

Published with the financial support of the Canada Council for the Arts, the Government of Canada through the Book Publishing Industry Development Program, and the New Brunswick Culture and Sports Secretariat.

Goose Lane Editions
469 King Street
Fredericton, New Brunswick
CANADA E3B 1E5

For Joel

PRELUDE

JACKSON BIGNEY HADN'T FAILED a single grade all the way through school. Not one. Now his graduation loomed. Six more weeks of classes, then two of exams. He stacked his notebooks neatly, patted them even between his palms and slipped them into the garbage can at the end of the high school hallway. He felt the weight of them evaporate as they tipped over the edge, through the orange plastic trap door. The green garbage bag smell rose into his nostrils as his scribblers landed with a puff. He flattened himself against the concrete block wall and glanced around. No one looked at him. He sidled to the door, felt the metal crash bar cold beneath his palms, leaned his tall, scraggly body into the bar. It yielded, releasing him.

His mother slammed his dinner down in front of him with a force that nearly broke the plate. "What a sin. A sin and a waste. Why? Can you at least tell me why? With only a couple of months left till graduation!"

Jackson speared a bean with his fork, pressing the tines hard against his plate to keep his hand from shaking. These were the moments that terrified him, before he decided for certain that he wouldn't speak, when expectation enveloped him and barbed wire eyes pinned him rigid in mid-air. His windpipe closed over, and a raw, acid pain squeezed his stomach.

"No use talking to that one, Gert," his father said through a mouthful of dinner. "Just as well talk to the friggin' pump in the yard as talk to that."

It was true. Jackson wasn't going to say anything. Once he knew this for sure, the fear subsided, the pain dissipated, his breathing returned to normal. He was safe. His mother railed awhile, then turned away.

Later she cornered him by the woodpile. "For heaven's sake, Jackson. You can still go back. Write your exams. You know you'll pass. It's not like with Matthew or any of the others, God bless them. It would be easy for you. Grade twelve! You could do anything then!"

He turned to the woodpile, ran his palm along the bark of a junk of maple, pressed his skin hard into its rough armour until his hand hurt, until he was sure it would bleed, until his mother finished with her words and the silence wrapped around him. Such a sigh came out of her.

CHAPTER ONE

JACKSON BIGNEY WAS TOLD to pull the carrots and sort them, piling the good ones in the wheelbarrow and tossing the small ones on the ground between the rows. So he did that. Then he picked a carrot off the top of the pile and strolled to the farmhouse with it, leaving the wheelbarrow where it sat, at the end of the last row in his mother's garden. The porch boards sagged a little under each footstep. He had to press his shoulder to the kitchen door, which stuck a little more each year. He had lived in that house for every one of his nineteen years, lived with his mother and father and swelling and receding tides of brothers and sisters. Now he was the oldest of the four left at home. He stooped over the kitchen sink, watched his long thin fingers rub dirt from the carrot. He had to be so careful where he allowed his mind to wander. He could think back or up or sideways, but he couldn't think forward. He'd left school a year and a half ago, and he couldn't think about what to do now. So he waited.

Jackson turned on the cold water tap, rinsed his carrot, his hands, splashed his face and rubbed it dry with his sleeve. The phone rang, then rang again. He leaned back against the counter, bit off the end of his carrot and chewed. After six rings he crossed the kitchen, picked up the receiver and held it out from his ear.

"Yeah? No, he's not here. Yeah. Okay."

He held onto the phone a minute after the caller hung up, listening to the dial tone, before he replaced the receiver on its cradle. His mother bustled into the kitchen with two pails brimming with undersized carrots.

"Dr. Yardley wants to see Dad. He missed his appointment, the girl said."

Gert Bigney clamped her lips together and shook her head. "He never told me he had another appointment. Too busy hiding from work to visit the doctor, I guess. Don't leave that load of carrots sitting out there. Get them into the bin in the basement."

Jackson picked his cigarettes off the kitchen table and tucked them into the pocket of his quilted shirt jacket. He would take a break, stretch his legs. He leaned in the kitchen doorway while he lit his smoke, then sauntered out across the farmyard, trailing his finger along the side of the old pickup truck, exposing a line of blue beneath the dirt. He wandered up the MacIntyre Road.

Jackson needed to relieve himself. If he hadn't, he wouldn't have walked over to the side of the road and looked down. The slope of the ditch wall and the ragged remains of ditch grass obscured the body from casual view. But there was no mistaking his father's beat-up, cut-off rubber boots. The body was sprawled, twisted, face down. Jackson rolled him over. His father's eyes stared out from nowhere, like the eyes of all the cattle, all the pigs he had ever slaughtered. His skin was cold to Jackson's touch. He had been dead for hours. Jackson sat by the corpse and finished his smoke. Then he flicked his cigarette butt onto the gravel, got up and continued along the road ten feet before pissing into the ditch. He glanced back at the corpse. "Don't say I never did anything for ya," he whispered.

After his father's last stint in the hospital, the doctors had made it perfectly clear that with the state of his lungs, and especially with the state of his liver, he had to make major changes in what they called his "lifestyle" if he was going to continue living. It was unlikely that he had even considered the idea. Jackson hefted the body onto his back and shoulders and lugged it the quarter-mile to the farmhouse. He flopped it onto the old car seat on the porch, watched the head roll backwards and clack against the clapboard. His mother emerged from the house and brushed by with two empty pails.

"He's dead."

"What?" She turned, dropped the buckets and let out a shriek, or three-quarters of one, before she muffled herself. "Oh my God in heaven." The pails rolled to the edge of the porch and clanged down the step. She knelt in front of the corpse, patting his hand as if she expected to revive him. "Oh heavens. Oh Vernon." Her head snapped sideways towards Jackson as if reality had slapped her across the face. "You can't leave him here! The kids will be home from school any minute. Jackson, for goodness sake, take him inside."

"To the kitchen?"

"No! The couch in the parlour."

"He's pretty dirty."

"On the floor then. No! Not on the floor. He's your father, for goodness sake!"

"Plastic?"

"A sheet. Oh for heaven's . . . I'll get a sheet. Where's your brother? He'll help you move him. Matthew!"

Gert charged into the house. "Mat*thew*!"

Jackson laid his father out on the couch, on the sheet his mother brought down.

"Call someone, Jackson. The doctor."

"Doctor? I don't think —"

"The police then! I don't know! Where's Matthew?" She sat on the edge of the couch, her husband's shirt-tail crumpled in her fist. "For heaven's sake, Vernon." She said it just like she always said it — for heaven's sake, Vernon, stop acting the fool and come back to life.

"You want me to shut his eyes?" His mother's shoulders shuddered as if she had choked or sneezed. For a second Jackson thought she might cry. "Go," she said, and he backed out of the room.

Matthew, a year younger than Jackson, appeared in the kitchen, wiping his hands on a grease rag. "What's going on?"

Jackson sucked a deep drag of cigarette smoke into his lungs and jerked his head towards the parlour. "Old man's dead." He picked up the phone.

Gert heard the roar of the school bus and the slam of the kitchen door and came out, white-faced and shaking, to meet her two youngest kids, the last of her brood of ten. She put one arm around Margie and the other around young Tommy. Matthew, following her, placed his hands on her shoulders. "It'll be okay, Mom." He kissed the top of her head. Jackson wandered back out onto the porch to wait for the cops.

When the Mountie showed up, he viewed the body and called the medical examiner.

"You better show me where you found him."

Jackson walked him up the road to point out where his father had died. "They'll have to do a post mortem," the Mountie said. Jackson nodded.

Gert Bigney phoned her oldest, Kate. Jackson was immediately dispatched the fifty miles to collect her. Kate left a note for her husband and packed her two toddlers into the cab of the farm truck. She fidgeted with the diaper bag, tugging lamely at the half-closed zipper, and finally stuffed it between her feet on the floor of the pickup. She pulled her youngest onto her lap. Jackson sat behind the wheel idling the engine, lighting a smoke. "Go!" Kate commanded.

By the time they reached MacIntyre Road, the body had been taken away. Gert sat at the kitchen table, clutching a mug of tea. Young Tommy sat beside her, stirring his Nestlé's Quik around and around in a tall glass, trying not to look terrified. Margie, at fifteen, looked more ill at ease than usual, miserably searching people's faces for clues to how she should act. "I'm not sitting on that couch again, I can tell you," she said. She squirmed in her chair, drew her knees up to her chest, then looked out the window and burst into tears.

Kate tugged the jackets off her kids. "What happened, Mom?

Where is he now?" Kate's little boy called out, "Why is Grampie dead?"

"We have to call the other kids," Gert said. "Oh my. I've got to talk to Vernon's people. We have to make arrangements."

Everyone looked tipsy, Jackson thought. He leaned against the window sill, took his whittling out of his pocket and examined it, then tucked it away again. He stood up, sat down, lit a smoke, stubbed it out.

"Oh my," his mother sighed. "What a sin. I should have been there. Oh my."

Jackson slipped out to the barn, for once grateful he had chores to do.

With four kids at home and now Kate beside her, Gert had her five remaining children to gather in. Mary lived in Hamilton, where her husband worked for Dofasco. They had a new baby and a split level house with three bathrooms and a room in the basement where Mary ran her own hairdressing business. Then there was Delbert, who had just left his wife and two kids and moved in with another woman in Guysborough County. He had married too young, everyone had known that at the time, but what can you do? Rebecca lived in Digby Neck and was eight and a half months pregnant with her second child. If her husband wasn't fishing he could bring her home to the farm. Donny was on probation (God help him) in Halifax, where he worked, on and off, for a construction company. Shirley was somewhere in British Columbia. No one knew exactly where or why. How would they reach her?

"What time is it in Ontario?" Gert asked Kate, her finger poised above the phone.

The next morning no one showed up in the barn to help Jackson with the chores. Vernon's chores. Jackson took his time. When he went in for breakfast he found that Matthew hadn't gone to Nelson's Garage as usual to talk cars and girls and maybe get an hour or two of work. Instead he sat at the breakfast table, his cigarette trembling over an ashtray, tea cooling in a mug in front of him. In the days before Jackson came to hate the barn, he and Matthew used to play there. How old had they been the day the pigs got out? Six and seven? Seven and eight? He remembered Matthew tugging open the gate of the pen, remembered running to stop him, then standing, petrified, as a squealing wave of pigs stampeded towards him. One knocked him off balance, and he tumbled through the river of their bodies. Sharp trotters dug into his bare legs, his arms, chest, dug at his face as they charged over him, snorting and squealing.

His father exploded, cursing, into the barn, grabbed Matthew and lashed him with a rope. Matthew screamed and twisted in their father's grip. Jackson knew he would be next, but he didn't move. He remembered looking up to see Vernon towering over him, his eyes wild and dark. He remembered that huge hand descending, clamping his arm that was so tiny it barely interfered with the closing of his father's fist. He remembered so clearly his father's fingers, with their knobby joints, deep creases, a thin arc of black crowning each cropped fingernail, the dark, lonely looking hairs growing out of the back of the hand. Jackson knew he had been beaten then, with a rope, but he didn't remember it.

He certainly knew the details of the pig roundup, how Delbert had dragged a pig by its tail all the way across the farmyard while Shirley had held a bucket over its head, how Gert had ended up in the cows' trough, how a pig had led them up and down between the rows of corn in the garden, about the lasso and the wheel-barrow and the pig trapped in the baler. His father loved to tell the story.

But his father never told the next part. How he had taken him and Matthew to Scotch River the next day, and they waited in the truck as he filled the gas tank, disappeared into the store. When he came back he carried two Oh Henry bars in gleaming yellow wrappers. His face smiled, though somehow not his lips.

"You might as well have these," he said. He winked at Matthew and tossed him one. Then he glanced across at Jackson. His father's face flashed, quick as a light switch, from on to off. The lines in his face sagged, his eyes dulled, he stretched his lips across his teeth in what he must have thought was a smile. Then his eyes shifted away. Jackson knew then, at that moment, that things were never going to change. It wasn't the pigs. It was everything Jackson was. There was too much wrong with him. His father tossed him his bar but missed his lap because he looked away so fast. Jackson had to scuttle under the dashboard to retrieve it. Jackson sat there holding his candy, staring at it, trying to think of funny things so he wouldn't cry. He tried concentrating on his luck, how he had a whole Oh Henry to himself and no one else had one but him and Matthew. Everything was fine. Everything was good. The bar was proof of that. Proof.

Matthew tore open his bar. With his mouth full and jaws battling the caramel, Matthew jabbered and bounced up and down on the truck seat. Jackson took the corner of the wrapper between his teeth and tugged it open. He sucked on the end of his chocolate bar, but nothing would go down. When a peanut came off in his mouth he chewed and chewed, afraid he would spit up. He stared out the truck window all the way home, concentrating on the peanut, willing it to go down. They left the village, crossed the bridge, turned off the pavement and started up the dusty track of MacIntyre Road. The bar disintegrated in his grip. Vernon pulled the truck into its spot by the baler and climbed out, releasing Matthew, who tore off across the farmyard. Vernon stared at Jackson's mess, turned away in disgust.

"Well, feed it to the pigs then, if you don't want it." He slammed the truck door behind him, leaving Jackson sitting alone in the cab, shivering with the reverberation.

Either Gert or Kate was on the phone all the time. Between calls they gave orders. Jackson was sent to the Halifax airport to meet Mary's plane. He squinted at every young woman coming through the doors, afraid he might not recognize his own sister. But when she appeared, lugging a stroller and a shoulder bag and jiggling a screeching baby, there was no doubt.

"Here," she said to him, dropping the bag off her shoulder at his feet. She handed him the stroller, took her baby in both arms, and tried to get it to take a soother. "It's her ears. The plane's hard on them. I've got a suitcase to pick up."

The baby's screeching simmered down into steady fussing once they got loaded into the truck and out onto the highway. "She's hungry," Mary said. "How's Mom?"

Just past Stewiacke Jackson spotted his brother Donny up ahead, shoulders hunched and thumb stuck out. Jackson slowed and pulled onto the gravel shoulder, watching in the rear view mirror as Donny jogged along the highway towards them, his dirty green knapsack bouncing on his shoulder. Mary dragged herself over and tried to settle herself and the baby around the stick shift.

"Jeez, what fucking luck!" Donny's grin filled the cab. He slid in, slamming the door. "Fucking luck, eh? Service right to the door." He pulled a pack of cigarettes out of his pocket and set one between his lips. "How's my big sister Mary, down from her mansion in Upper Canada? You got the maid in the back of the truck there? I didn't notice."

Jackson kept his eyes fixed straight ahead. Things could go either way.

"I'm fine, thank you, Donny," Mary answered, weary but civil. The baby hushed a moment and stared at Donny with blue saucer eyes. He reached over and touched the tiny cheek with his index finger. Then, suddenly shy, Donny drew back. He turned to stare out his window as Jackson pulled onto the highway. "So, I guess that's it for ole Vernon, eh?"

By the time they got back to the farm the oldest of the boys, Delbert, had arrived and settled himself into their late father's chair. "There used to be a hundred head on this place, one time," he was saying. "I could turn this place around in a year." Gert stretched out her arms to Mary's baby. Rebecca would be here with her little girl and her husband by suppertime, she reported.

"I talked to her," Kate told Mary. "She's eight and a half months along, says she's big as a house."

They couldn't find Shirley. They called anyone they thought she might have been in touch with, but no luck. "I wish she'd call," Gert fretted, looking at Donny. Shirley and Donny were twins, had grown and formed into human beings around each other's heartbeats. Gert was sure Donny could pick up some kind of message from her if he tried. She badgered him until he shouted, "How would I know where she is? I haven't even seen her for three years for Jesus effing sake!" When Gert turned away from him quietly, with no comment on his language or manners, he stepped back, frightened, and stomped off outside.

Jackson shuffled with embarrassment. Donny had to act angry because everybody knew he had slugged their father. Cold-cocked him. Laid him out. If no one had known, Vernon could have covered it up, said he got caught by a cow swinging her head, hit his head on a beam, made something up to explain the wound. Then they would have been in it together, Vernon and Donny covering for each other. They would have fumed in silence for a while, then Vernon would have cocked his head as he always did when extending a clandestine invitation to one of the other kids. Out in the barn Vernon would have pulled out a bottle, they would have had a few drinks, dragged up old stories about other people's failures, ridiculed everyone in the village until they both felt invincible. Silently they would have agreed that it had never happened. It was true that Jackson had seen the fight, but they didn't know that, and he wouldn't have said anything. He knew what was shameful and private and not to be mentioned. Everything would have been fine if Margie hadn't also seen it happen, hadn't run sobbing to their mother, hadn't wailed until everyone came running. Once everyone knew, there was nothing they could do. Donny had to claim his victory, Vernon had to kick him out. Now Donny had to act the injured party, let people know Vernon had deserved it.

"Yeah, I could really get this place going," Delbert said. "Just got to get those lazy bums off their chairs." He tilted his head towards Matthew and Jackson and reached across the table for Jackson's cigarettes.

"I should have been there," Gert said.

"There was nothing you could have done, Mom," the girls chorused. Jackson thought maybe it wasn't about doing anything. She was cheated. She read the whole book and Vernon ripped out the final page. She turned her back for a moment, and he wandered off to die in a ditch.

The six-room farmhouse (seven-room if you counted the bathroom built into one end of the TV room) groaned with the weight, the mass, of fifteen people. All five brothers were crammed into the boys' room upstairs. Jackson and Matthew shoved their things up against a wall as if they were preparing for a flood. Kate's kids got the little nest in the hall closet where Tommy usually slept. Kate and Mary and Mary's baby piled into the girls' room with Margie, who had had it to herself for years. Rebecca and her family got the parlour. Jackson couldn't walk through the house without stepping over things, couldn't find an empty nail to hang his jacket on, couldn't find a chair to sit in. The air was saturated with opinions, with elbows and knees, with motion. Margie kept jumping up and running off to her room in tears — even more often than usual. Everywhere were tea mugs, crayons, other people's cigarettes, piles of sweaters and jackets and caps. Outside it poured rain. He wanted to sit in his chair by the window and work on his whittling. He wanted to ignore them all. He was carving a scraggy twig with several jerks and bends and two tiny wooden buds by a single delicately veined leaf. When Gert called Tommy away to try on a suit jacket, Jackson slid into the vacated chair. But still he couldn't get comfortable with people so close to him, felt awkward taking out his carving with such a crowd around, too self-conscious to lose himself in the work. The racket of their shouting, scraping, demanding, jostling would deafen him, he was sure.

Kate wanted to get into the drawer of the cabinet behind him.

Jackson, keeping his head bowed, tried to shuffle over a bit and bend out of the way without spilling all the wood shavings in his lap. His chair bumped his brother's, the corner of the opened drawer hit his shoulder blade, a dusting of tiny wood chips floated to the floor.

"For godsake." Kate clicked her tongue at him in disgust. "And he's carving a stick! He's making a stick out of a stick. Why don't you do something nice? Do a duck."

Jackson's cheeks reddened. Kate drew a fat envelope of photographs out of the drawer, past his ear. Jackson glanced at the package and looked away. There were so many more now than there had been that first time he discovered and explored the stash. Now there were fuzzy snaps of wedding receptions: Kate's, Mary's, Delbert's, Rebecca's. There were babies in frilly pastel dresses propped up against couch cushions and toddlers with chocolate pudding faces. Jackson wasn't interested. He tucked his whittling into his shirt pocket, pawed through the coat hooks to find his green plaid jacket and escaped from the kitchen. He strolled off across the farmyard in the rain. The line of trees dividing the farmyard from the pasture offered at least a little protection from the rain, so he ducked into the hedgerow and sat on a stump. He rested his elbows on his knees and stared back at the farm, the chilly rain slowly soaking through his jacket.

On the day he first found that brown envelope of photos there were maybe two rolls of film taken over four or five years. He was eight years old and afraid he might get in trouble. He wanted to see, though, so he pulled the three small envelopes out of the larger one. The first two held colour pictures of his brothers and sisters dressed up for school and squeezed into tight lines on the porch, all lunch boxes and book bags. Sometimes a sliver of his body or a blur at the end of a line would prove he had been there with them. He would disappear into thin air, his mother claimed, at the sight of a camera.

In the third, smallest envelope were five square black and white pictures bordered in white. Jackson liked these best. They were from another time, another world, a fantastic reality caught in a thousand shades of grey and glued shut. Two of the pictures were of people Jackson had never seen before. In the third picture their father, looking young, leaned against a tree, arms folded across his chest, smirking. Jackson just managed to recognize his mother as the girl in the print dress who stood a few feet away, her hands folded in front of her. "Vernon and Gertrude, 1956" was scrawled across the back.

Jackson clutched the next black-and-white. Four kids perched on the broad back of a workhorse. And there he was, first in the row of kids. He tingled with joy at seeing himself in a picture that was serious and important-looking, not sloppy and chaotic like the colour snaps. Jackson stared at himself until he could almost remember sitting astride that old horse, light-headed from the height, his legs aching from the stretch across its massive back, the gentle odour of the barn around him. He knew he had never been on horseback, that he was making it up. But here was proof. He stared at the picture of himself and the strange children. I used to be at an orphanage, he told himself. Here I am at the orphanage with other kids. At the orphanage we had a horse, and I would ride him up and down the streets. The horse's name was . . . Alexander. And I would feed him carrots and apples every day.

Then Matthew, who would have been seven, discovered him and his pile of pictures. He jerked the photo away, calling to their mother, "Why is Jackson on a horse? I want to go on a horse, too!" Their mother took the picture in her hand and snorted. She plunked it face down on the table. The pencil scratch on the back was barely legible: "Norman, Bob, Elsie, Vernon. On Doll. 1938."

"That's your father when he was little. She flipped the photo again. "Uncle Norm's there, too, see? And Aunt Elsie. Bob died, God rest his soul. Now who would have taken that shot, I wonder?"

In the last photo Jackson stared at himself standing on the running board of an old pickup truck. The orphanage's pickup truck, of course. He'd had a growth spurt and his pant legs hovered above his ankles. He stood off to the side of the picture, an afterthought. The picture was really of the two smiling young men in Royal Canadian Navy uniforms who leaned confidently against the cab of the truck. Jackson struggled to memorize the details of the picture. Since he was eight years old in real life and more like thirteen in the photo, this would be him in five or six years. In the future. Back at the orphanage. He read the inscription on the back: "Norm, Bob, Vernon. 1944." The words meant nothing to him.

Vernon. Jackson tried to think about his father, even though it turned his stomach. Down at the house they would be looking at the colour pictures again. Vernon as father of the bride. The big lazy smile and the slap on the back. Their father never hit the girls. He roared and bellowed, ranted and threatened, but he never touched them. He never touched their mother, either, as far as Jackson knew. Jackson frowned and ran his finger up and down the smooth surface of his half-carved twig. Of course he "touched" her. In the dark hollow of the night where everyone is something else. Jackson blinked, trying to stop the image from burrowing into his mind. Another chore for her? A chore for him? In the daylight, like·oppositely charged poles, they rolled off each other six feet apart. They never brushed up against each other, never fought either, just offered up comments to the world in general. They treated each other like the weather, grumbled, complained, cursed. But there is nothing anyone can do about the weather. Sometimes it ruins your plans, even causes disasters, but it's where you live. You can't live without the weather.

At supper the din was suffocating.

"Dad's not gonna like the idea of being back in church."

"I don't think we'll hear any complaints."

"Remember that time the vet brought Dad home? Back before the new guy, when it was that old fellow? And Dad was off in Pictou and so drunk the only phone number he could remember was the vet's? So he called and the vet went out and picked him up? And then the next month it showed up on the frigging bill — one delivery!"

"You were too young to remember that."

"I was not!"

"Get off Dad's back, why don't ya. This is supposed to be his funeral."

"I'm not on his back. I'm just saying, you know, he used to take a drink from time to time, eh?"

Mary snorted.

Delbert laughed. "Jesus, Dad used to get you runnin', Jackson. You were always sneaking up on him, hiding right near him, like you wanted to touch him or something. He'd pretend he didn't know you were there, then all of a sudden he'd take off after you, barking and snapping like a dog. Jeez, what a laugh. You'd've run clean through the walls, you were that scared! Screeching, bawling."

Jackson blinked.

"What a laugh he was."

"He frigging-near beat me to death. I remember that. The old bugger," Donny added.

Kate glared at Donny. "If you can't talk decent at a time like this, you can take your dinner outside." She stood up like she might have intended to remove him bodily.

"It's not like you didn't deserve it," Delbert added.

Their mother sighed. "Nobody's saying he didn't have his faults."

That's true enough, Jackson thought.

Jackson had stolen a poster off the wall in his classroom in grade four. He stole it at morning recess, and his palms sweat for the rest of the day, smudging his scribblers. He tried not to stare at the empty square on the wall where it had been, jumped and turned red when the teacher called on him. The poster had a handsome, smiling dad wearing a cabled sweater and a baseball glove. He was down on one knee in the grass and had his arms around a laughing boy, squeezing him in a bear hug. The boy leaned into his father's embrace, his head thrown back. Their teeth shone white as paint.

Gert had to go to the funeral home to see about arrangements. Arrangements, Jackson said to himself. Like, they don't know where they're going to put him?

Gert was barely out of earshot before Mary's voice sailed over the general uproar. "Women aren't pall bearers!"

Kate's voice rose to meet her sister's. "Don't be ridiculous. You can carry a box, can't you? There are only five boys and Tommy's too small. You want them to drag the thing down the aisle? Rebecca can hardly move, Margie's too young, Shirley's not here. There's only you and me."

"I'm not carrying the old bugger out. I told you!" Donny butted in.

"You are. Because we need a man on each corner."

"Tom can do it. He's not a fucking cripple."

"He's just a boy, for heaven's sake. He'll barely be able to reach it, let alone carry it."

The phone rang for the twentieth time that day. Jackson closed his eyes.

"Jack*son!*"

"Eh?" Who wanted him?

"Phone. It's the cop."

Donny leaned into the open fridge. "We need more beer."

"You need more, you mean. You're as bad as Dad ever was."

Jackson picked up the phone. "H-hello?"

Margie hung on his sleeve. "Is it that cute cop?"

"What's Shirley doing out in BC, anyway? Is she fuckin' stunned, or what?"

"Watch your language, asshole."

Jackson strained to hear. "Yeah, okay. Yeah. Bye." He held onto the phone after the cop hung up, listening to the empty buzz, unable to let go.

"Hang up!" Margie hollered in his face. "Hang up the phone!"

"Margie, for heaven's sake."

"Well, he always *does* that! He just sits there like a big zit, listening to the blank phone after someone calls. It's like living with a *re*tard!" She was near tears.

"Yeah, well," Delbert drawled, "he didn't flunk out of school like *you're* doing."

Then they all stopped, all looked at Jackson, waiting for him to speak. "He didn't drown, eh?" he managed. "It was his liver."

"Poor Dad."

"Anybody got a smoke?"

Mary gave everyone haircuts. The suit at the back of the boys' closet fit Donny well enough, but Matthew needed a new suit for the funeral.

"Here," Gert said to Jackson and led him into her bedroom. Lying across the bed was Vernon's old suit, the one he had been married in. It was black with narrow lapels and would be, Jackson calculated, thirty years old. A yellowing pocket square still poked out of the breast pocket. Jackson gave it a tug — three folded cotton peaks sewn to a cardboard card. He dropped it in the garbage. The suit fit Jackson exactly as it had hung on his father: a tad short in the sleeve, lots of room around the middle, trousers hanging loosely over narrow hips. He looked as if he might have stepped out of the wedding picture in the parlour.

"Oh my," Gert sighed.

Jackson ran his fingers along the seams inside the pockets, searching out the corners. The spitting image, people said. Or, the apple didn't fall far from the tree. Men would wink and say, "At least that one's not the mailman's, eh, Vernon?" His father always looked a little uncomfortable, as if the worst of himself was on display.

Delbert hung in the doorway. "You're gorgeous, That One."

"That One" was the only thing Jackson could ever remember his father calling him. Of all your kids, That One's the queerest. What's That One looking at? Who does That One think he is?

His earliest memory of his father was when Vernon had fallen out of the mow and lay convalescing in the parlour, a mess of casts and tape and bandages. Jackson was four. He heard the older ones talk, knew parts had broken. When he asked if there were pieces missing, they only laughed. He had searched the barn but found no extra body parts. He had to see if all the bits of his father's body were still there, if he had been put back together right. If he was going to look just like his father and his father had a leg where an arm should be, would he grow up like that, too? He peeked into the parlour, stared across the room at his father's closed eyes. His heart pounded. He slipped silently into the room, trying to keep one eye on his father's eyelids while examining his body. It was hard to see with all the bandaging. He had to get closer. An eyelash fluttered. Jackson held his breath. Nothing happened. He took another step, stared at the arms and legs, everything was where it should be. He tried to count fingers, four there and . . .

"What?"

Jackson jumped. Thrown off balance, he tottered backwards, hitting the corner of the end table and jostling the lamp. He heard it wobble. His palms found the wall behind him, and he flattened himself against it, petrified. He couldn't speak.

"*What?*"

Jackson's brain screamed, but nothing came out.

"Jesus! What do you want? Answer me!" Vernon groped for the half-full beer bottle on the floor beside him and flung it across the room. It bounced off Jackson's jaw and fell with a thud. Jackson stood stock still and watched it roll, foaming onto the lino, a yellow puddle growing gradually around it as pain engulfed his face.

His mother bustled into the room, shepherded him away, returned to tend to his father. "That One's always looking at me," Jackson heard his father complain. His mother's reply was low and muffled. He remembered rubbing his jaw and finding his cheeks wet.

Jackson watched his sisters washing dishes, preparing a tubful of potato salad. They stood so close to each other their arms touched whenever they moved. They seemed to take turns brushing Margie's hair until it glistened in a dark river down her back. They rocked their babies, each other's babies, offered their babies to Gert, passed them from hand to hand. "Here," they said to each other, "you take the baby." Rebecca stroked her swollen belly almost constantly. And they talked.

"Don't put so much onion in that."

"That's not a lot."

"Dad loved lots of onion."

"Well, he's not going to eat it, is he?"

"He'll be able to smell it even where he is if you don't stop."

"Quit saying stuff like that!" Margie was off again.

"Here, you take the baby."

"Lemme braid that hair, Margie. God, mine'd be frizzed out to here if it was that long. Sit down now."

The night before the funeral, Jackson sat on the edge of his bed unbuttoning his shirt. Matthew stood by the window picking the dirt out from under his fingernails, and Tommy lay asleep in the other bed. Delbert and Donny argued as they climbed the stairs. They bumped into each other in the doorway like the Stooges and shoved each other trying to get through.

"You? That's a fucking laugh. When did you ever shovel shit? You didn't know how to work a frigging manure fork. I was the one who —"

"You move two hundred pounds of shit every time you take a step."

Tommy stirred then sat up, rubbing his eyes. "What?"

"Jeez. Leave the kid sleep, would yez?" Matthew said.

"Yeah, fuckface," Donny said. "Shut up. The kid's sleeping." He turned away and kicked at the baseboard.

"That's all he ever does is sleep. I was running half this farm when I was his age."

Matthew stripped down to his underwear. He climbed past Jackson into the bed and rolled over next to the wall.

"Like old times, eh?" he said, but not as if he wanted an answer.

Jackson and Matthew had shared that bed for years, when they were little boys and the room had been crowded with brothers. Matthew and Jackson were born ten months apart. Nine months and ten minutes, was the joke. No one ever asked if they were twins. They're like chalk and cheese, their mother said. Matthew was sturdy and solid, all wrenches and grease and funny stories. The kind of boy people liked. The kind of boy their father liked. Matthew leaned on one elbow, punched his pillow a couple of times. His eyes look tight enough to crack open, Jackson thought. He looks like he's bleeding, you just can't see where it's leaking out.

Donny refused to share a bed, so he slept on the sofa cushions on the floor. "Nighty-night, fairy boys." He made gross kissing noises with his lips.

"Who'd touch you, ya fucking asshole," Delbert growled.

Jackson held his breath, held the cells of his body rigid, but Donny said nothing more. They turned out the light.

Jackson woke during the night, panting from an airless, suffocating dream. Matthew lay warm and solid beside him. He could lift his hand and lay it on Matthew's shoulder and know the smooth resistance of his body. But he didn't. He never had. Even as little boys, only Matthew had had the courage to reach out. When little Matthew had woken with nightmares, he had rolled over and pressed against Jackson. "I'm sleeping on your side of the bed, 'kay?" Jackson had never answered, just lay there while Matthew nestled in, weight of leg against leg, body by body. And Jackson imagined them fighting side by side in the-war-between-the-states, before he even knew what that was. They wore the uniforms with the front panel that buttoned up the sides, and Matthew had been wounded by the enemy, and he had dragged him back behind the line and fixed him up, and now Matthew lay here beside him, sleeping. At dawn their father would find them here in the hospital tent. He'd sit beside the cot on a chair, resting his forearms on his knees, and nod at Matthew's dressed wounds. He wouldn't say anything, but he would reach into his tunic pocket and hand Jackson a small box containing a gold medal for bravery. For saving his son.

They weren't kids anymore. Matthew wasn't going to roll over tonight and whisper, "I'm on your side, 'kay?" Jackson stared into the dark, listening. Donny's breathing rose from the floor beside them. Jackson recognised the irregular rhythm of it. In utter silence, Donny was crying.

The Anglican minister intoned his remarks with convincing sincerity. "Vernon Bigney was a farmer, a steward of the soil, a loving husband and father of ten children. He loved a good time, loved life. He lived much of his life on MacIntyre Road, was well known in the community, made many friends . . ."

Jackson concentrated on remaining upright in his pew, standing and sitting when he was supposed to. The muscles at the base of his neck knotted into a fist. It was three years since Jackson had uncovered Vernon's secret stash of rum in the barn. He had been nipping a swig when Vernon appeared out of nowhere, caught him in mid-swallow. With one swipe Vernon grabbed him by the hair, yanked his head back and forced him to his knees. Jackson tried to cry out, afraid his skull would snap right off. He gulped for air, tried to swallow or spit, but the rum was trapped halfway down his throat.

"You wanna drink your daddy's rum?" Vernon held his face directly over Jackson's, spat out "daddy" like he meant "turd." Sparks of spit flew off his lips and landed on Jackson's face. "You wanna be just like your daddy? Eh? Eh? You wanna drink?"

With every question he jerked Jackson's head back, cracking his neck, holding him off balance. Jackson's arms flailed, his eyes wide with fear and helplessness.

"Here, then!" Vernon tilted the flask into Jackson's gaping mouth. Jackson gagged, sputtered. Rum rushed down his windpipe, scalded his nasal cavity, gurgled out the corners of his mouth. He couldn't breathe, couldn't cough. His father was strangling him, drowning him. Just when he knew he would die, his father shoved him onto the hay, where he gasped and hacked and finally retched. His lungs burned, pleaded for oxygen between coughing fits. Puke filled his mouth, and his eyes ran with tears. Through it all his father bellowed at him from above, "Is that what you want? Answer me! *Answer me!*"

A buzzing hum rose in his ears so loud it drowned out the

organ. Everyone stood. Adamant hissing cut through the buzz. "Hang up the phone!" Mary jabbed him, hard, in the ribs.

"Huh?"

"I said, stand up and go!"

Jackson stood. They filed out of the pew and took their positions around the casket, Delbert and Donny, Kate and Mary, Jackson and Matthew. They carried their father down the aisle and out into the churchyard. The fresh earth smelled, for a moment, like spring. Jackson felt his father's coffin hit the bottom of the grave.

The day after the funeral everyone packed up. Delbert sat at the head of the kitchen table. "You gotta have a good bull, see? The bull is half your herd."

"No, that's okay, Mom, I can take a bus into the city from the airport," Donny was saying. "No sweat." Gert went for her purse. Jackson drove Donny and Mary to the airport, where Mary would board her flight to Toronto. Donny patted the pocket where he had put the bus fare their mother had given him, winked at Jackson and hitched into Halifax. When Jackson returned, Delbert was gone. So was Rebecca. Kate was sweeping the floor, waiting for her husband to come and collect her and the kids. That night everyone got their beds back, and Tommy reclaimed his mattress from the girls' room and dragged it back to his little nest in the hall closet. In the morning Matthew went back to hanging around Nelson's Garage in Scotch River. Margie turned her attention to staying out of school until she could really quit on her sixteenth birthday, two months away. Tommy returned to his desk at the back of the grade five classroom. And Jackson found himself standing alone in a barn full of cows.

Vernon's chair at the end of the kitchen table seemed unusually large. Holes opened up in the air. Gert cooked all Vernon's favourite foods, the same amount she always had, and while the family ate, the leftovers sat, waiting to be scraped into the slop bucket for the pigs. Silence bloomed in startling places in the middle of the day. When Jackson brought Gert back from grocery shopping and she unpacked the food, no one commented on the brand of cereal, on the Pop Tarts she bought for Tommy's lunches, on the colour of the cheese. She lifted Vernon's chocolate marshmallow cookies out of the bag and set them on the table, the stiff cellophane crinkling, filling the kitchen with plastic static. Jackson smoked silently, staring out the window. No one touched the cookies.

Jackson didn't know if Matthew noticed the extra socks and underwear and T-shirts that appeared in their drawers on the next laundry day. Neither of them said anything. Gert tucked Vernon's work pants in between Jackson's two pairs of jeans on the shelf in the boys' room. Matthew could never fit into his father's pants; he was built more like their mother, shorter and stockier. Burly. Jackson could slip right into them, though. Jackson waited for Gert to say something about Vernon's farm chores, but she didn't. She began sending Tommy out to help him every evening and weekend, and when Jackson came in from the barn she bustled around, prodding Margie to get the food on the table. At dinnertime Jackson always found his chair stacked with laundry or a bushel of onions or pails of turnips. His mother set his dinner down in Vernon's spot. The day she cashed the cream cheque she tucked fifty dollars under his plate like she always had for Vernon. When Jackson found it there, he could have cried.

Vernon hadn't been a good farmer, but he had at least managed to scrape from one year's end to the next. He had known when his cows had been bred or needed to be, and he had known how many bales were piled up in the mow. He could pull the tractor apart and knew where to find the used parts to put it back together. Jackson managed to get the separator together, run the milking machines, shovel shit. He could do what he was told. But he couldn't farm. To farm you have to pay attention, look ahead. To farm you have to care.

Jackson did the chores and turned the cows back out onto the pasture. He stood in the empty barn in his father's clothes with his father's fifty dollars in his father's pocket. His skull pressed in on him until he thought he would faint with the pain. The pressure wrung water from his brain and squeezed it out his eyes. Already people were looking at him, saying his name. Expecting. He grabbed a post to keep from sinking into the gutter. He steadied himself. Then he drove into Scotch River and spent his father's fifty bucks on a forty-ouncer of Lamb's Navy Rum and a pouch of Player's tobacco. Just like his father would have. He retreated to his stump in the hedgerow and started in on the bottle.

They weren't his goddamn cows. If he could just sit in the hedgerow forever, things would be fine. From his stump, everything receded: the barn, the cows, the farmhouse, his mother, the fading shadow of his father, everything moved away, outside of him. He returned to his orphanage. "Them," he thought, looking back at the farm. "Them. Me." His headache subsided little by little, leaving only an emptiness. He took a few swigs from his bottle, then a few more. As the emptiness pushed inwards, the rum pushed back, protecting him. He felt a kind of suspended animation. I could live here, in this empty space, he thought. He twisted himself around on the stump, turning his back on the farmhouse, and stared off into nothing. In front of him the pasture was growing up in alders and weeds. I could live here, he thought again, but this time the sentence settled into a clear, clean idea. Right here, he thought, behind this hedgerow. I'll build a cabin. I'll live right here.

CHAPTER TWO

JACKSON DIDN'T KNOW what to say to his mother, so he waited until she was into one of her long phone sessions with Kate before he grabbed the chainsaw from the shed and disappeared into the woodlot with the tractor and trailer. Later in the day he rumbled back with a load. He waited until Gert left the house before he called Duffy's Mill to see about getting the logs sawn into lumber. They worked without cash — bring them two trees, they'd keep one and mill the other for you. Jackson waited until Gert returned to the house before he hooked the trailer to the pickup and drove down the MacIntyre Road with his load. He returned just in time for supper.

"Up here," she commanded and led him, with a heaping plate, past his chair to Vernon's spot as if she was luring a cow to slaughter.

"Where were you going with that firewood?" Gert asked.

"Saw logs."

"Well, saw logs, then?"

Jackson said nothing.

Gert repeated, "Where were you going with them?"

"Duffy's Mill."

"What for?"

"Lumber."

"What for?"

"Lumber."

"Yes. I heard you. I mean, why are you carting saw logs to the mill?"

"They saw it on the halves."

"I know they saw lumber on the halves! What do you want lumber for?"

Jackson poked his fork into a mound of potato. "I'm, ah building a c-cabin."

Matthew jerked his head up. "What for? What kind of a cabin? Where?"

Jackson tilted his head to the south.

"Come on, man. What are you doin'? Come on."

"Behind the, uh, hedgerow."

"And . . .?"

"And?"

"What are you going to do with a cabin?"

His mouth went dry. "I-I'm going to m-move out there."

"Live there?"

Jackson nodded but didn't raise his eyes from his plate. He waited for his mother to speak.

"You gonna sleep there?" Tommy asked.

He nodded again. Tommy would be scrambling to figure out what would be up for grabs, what he stood to gain. Jackson felt the corner of his mouth twitch a little.

"I don't see the point in all that fuss." Gert's voice was thick. "A sin and a waste if you ask me." When Jackson didn't comment she pushed on. "What do you want to live in a cabin for? What's wrong with the house?"

Jackson shrugged.

"Well?"

He said nothing more and eventually Gert gave up. He would have to keep on with the barn chores for now. He didn't know how to quit. Once he got his cabin he would be able to think. He was sure of that. He would build his cabin and everything would be all right. He would stop waiting for his father in the barn, stop cringing in expectation, stop cringing altogether. He would have a place of his own, and no one would bother him. Everyone would leave him alone. Then he would be able to tell his mother he wasn't going to work the farm. He just had to get his cabin built.

The Bigneys' woods trailer was small, so Jackson figured it would take five trips to the sawmill with the wood for his lumber and that many trips again with the wood to pay for the milling. Matthew made himself scarce when Jackson tramped off to fell trees, but he reappeared magically when the trailer sat brimming in the yard and Jackson was struggling to load a few extra logs onto the truck bed.

"Hey, all ready, eh? Awright! I'll drive. No problem. You go on back to the woods for the next load." He slid in behind the wheel.

Jackson could picture Matthew driving the laden truck and trailer into the mill yard — the window rolled down and his elbow stuck out, swinging down out of the cab and greeting the guys at the mill, leaning against the truck and shooting the breeze. Jackson stood back from the truck and let Matthew roll off out of the yard. It would be such an effort to stop him.

Listening to Matthew at supper, anyone would have thought he had spent twenty years trucking in the big rigs instead of taking three trips to the mill in a pickup truck. A guy at the mill, he said, had railroad ties for sale at three dollars each.

"I don't know where you think the money is coming from for all this nonsense," Gert said. "I'm not putting gas in that truck for you to be running back and forth over those roads all day."

On Thursday Jackson hoisted the cattle box onto the truck and loaded the one animal that belonged to him, a little Angus-Jersey steer. Matthew bounded out into the yard.

"Hey, we going to the sale?"

"Yup."

All the way to Truro Matthew talked about the great ideas he had for the cabin, where they could get windows, how they should build in a bedroom, which led to his speculations about Mandy White, who had started hanging around Nelson's Garage with her cousin, Calli. Mandy, he said, seemed to like him all right.

At the sale barn Jackson unloaded his steer. Matthew bought them both burgers and fries, and they climbed up into the stands surrounding the ring to watch the bob calves, heifers, cows and steers, one by one, being prodded around the ring. They chewed their hamburgers while the auctioneer called out for bids. When Jackson's steer came out he followed the numbers, eighty cents a pound, eighty-five, ninety, and did the math in his head — $549 minus four percent commission. They waited around to collect the cheque, then Jackson cashed it at the Scotiabank in town, filled the gas tank and drove home with cash in his wallet.

"How about a case of beer?" Matthew asked, as they neared Scotch River. It was clear he meant Jackson was buying. Jackson bought a dozen Keith's and a flask to tuck into his jacket pocket. They drove home the back way, bumped across the old culvert at the base of the field and slipped up by the hedgerow. Matthew sat on the stump.

"Yup," said Matthew, "there she'll be. Party cabin. Right there. When are you starting in on 'er?"

A surge of panic swept through Jackson. No one had ever followed him to the hedgerow before, no one had ever sat on his stump, filled up his space. He drank a beer straight back and then another one. The third he took a bit more slowly. Gradually he began to feel better, or, more specifically, he began to feel less. He regained himself, didn't mind Matthew so much. He didn't mind anything. They sat there while it got dark and their mother's calls to supper became increasingly terse. It occurred to Jackson that she didn't know exactly where they were. He abandoned the rest of the beer to Matthew and pulled the flask from his pocket. It was way past chore time when Tommy, who had been sent out to search, stumbled over them.

"Mom's real mad. You guys missed supper. Mom wants yez right now."

Matthew snorted. He grabbed Tommy by the arm and pulled him down onto the ground, got him in a head lock and pummelled him with make-believe punches. Matthew had been wrestling with Tommy several times a day since their father died. They twisted and shoved and held their bodies against each other, sometimes until

Tommy dissolved in tears, but he always came back for more, never passed Matthew without poking or punching him.

"Quit it! Quit it!" Tommy flailed at Matthew and kicked out at the air. "Mom says you guys gotta — owww! Lemme go!"

Matthew released him carefully, holding Tommy's hands behind his back to prevent a counterattack. "Why don't you go back in and say you couldn't find us?"

"You guys are drunk! You guys are in trouble." Tommy wriggled free of Matthew's grip and ran over to Jackson. "You gotta do the chores right *now*!" he yelled into his face.

"They're not my goddamn cows," Jackson answered evenly and tipped another swig into his mouth.

"I'm telling!" He aimed a kick at Matthew, but Matthew caught his foot and Tommy landed on the ground. Tears sprang to his eyes, and he ran off into the dark to hide them. "I'm telling!" trailed off behind him as he headed for the house.

The older boys waited, Matthew laughing into his beer, Jackson staring at the night. But Gert never came for them. About fifteen minutes later they saw her striding towards the barn, flashlight beam bouncing along the path. Jackson heard her open the barn door to admit the lowing herd. He was glad he felt so far away.

The next morning, Jackson awoke early and scared. They're not my goddamned cows, he had said. Saying things always led to trouble. He tore out of bed. In the kitchen he left lots of clues so his mother would know that he was up and in the barn, that there was no need for her to come out.

When he came in again his mother plunked a bowl of oatmeal in front of him.

"I hope everyone had a good time last night."

Gert always said this whenever Vernon got drunk and neglected his duties and she had to trudge out to do his work. Now she was saying it to him. His whole body writhed in confusion. Doing the chores, not doing the chores, both nailed him into his father's skin. But soon he would have his cabin. Things would be different. And when the cream cheque came, someone else would get the fifty dollars. Jackson welcomed the figure into his mind, juggled it around to calm himself. Fifty dollars a month was six hundred dollars a year. To earn a thousand dollars would take twenty months — that was one and two-thirds years. If he worked the farm for forty years, that would be . . . $24,000. Lifetime earnings. Lots of people earned that in a year, he knew. He couldn't block out Gert and Matthew's arguing.

". . . you had plenty of money last night, I'd say, why . . ."

"I never! And you owe me twenty bucks from Tommy's . . ."

"That money was . . ."

They weren't fighting about him, at least. So that was eighty-two cents for every bout of chores, or about fifty-five cents an hour.

Tom came downstairs in a T-shirt, holding a bright plaid cotton shirt out in front of him. "I hate this shirt. I'm not wearing this shirt. Mo-om, I hate it." Gert turned to him with her hands on her hips.

Jackson swallowed the last of his tea, pushed his chair back and headed for the door.

Over the next week Jackson staked out his cabin. He bought railroad ties for his posts and sills and stacked them at the site. Then he started digging. He set his posts, squared and levelled his sills, waited for his lumber.

When Jackson's two-by-fours and floor boards were ready, the guy from Duffy's Mill phoned, but Matthew took the call and then called Nelson's Garage and recruited a whole party to help load. It was all settled by the time Jackson heard about it. He sighed, but he didn't feel like discussing it. Matthew spun off with the truck, in a high mood.

While Matthew was gone, Jackson dug the pit for his outhouse. They got the bathroom in the farmhouse the year he turned ten. He was afraid Matthew would tell the kids at school. Matthew always boasted about the wrong stuff, and when things didn't go as he imagined, he ended up in a fist fight, and then it was up to the principal's office and a note home, where he caught it all over again but even worse because there was no law against using the belt at home. Jackson remembered trying to explain to him why he shouldn't say anything.

"If you tell that we got a bathroom, everyone will know we had an outhouse before. Only poor people have outhouses."

"So! Now we have a bathroom it proves we're not poor!"

"No. We're even poorer now. Because we had to pay for the bathroom. Just don't say anything, okay? Pretend we always had one."

But you couldn't change Matthew's mind.

"Hey, you figured out how to use the toilet yet, Bigney?" Jackson blinked in remembered embarrassment. Shh, his brain warned him. Shut up. Shh. Be good. He hated how stupid stuff like this could still make his stomach tighten after all this time.

Mrs. Patterson, the grade five teacher, called his name out over the heads of everyone. "Jack. Son. Big. Knee." Four distinct words. "I want to be able to read your work next time. Look at this, class, little mouse scratches. We have a little mouse in the class." He tried to force his pencil to fill the massive space between the lines on the page but he couldn't keep it up. The more she hollered at him, the smaller his writing got. "Jack. Son. Big. Knee. I have eyes in my head, not microscopes!" Everyone giggled. She held his paper out at arm's length, between her thumb and forefinger, and everyone watched as she released it to float slowly downwards and settle into the wastebasket. Be good, his brain admonished him. Shh!

When he heard Matthew returning with the truck he slipped through the hedgerow and down into the tool shed, where he hid in the dim light, sorting through nails, waiting for Matthew and his friends to unload and leave.

Margie came by and sat on his stump, chewed her gum and watched him nail the decking in place.

"I can't believe you dug an outhouse. God, talk about gross! Mom says it's ridiculous to be heating two houses when there's tons of room at home. She says you'll still expect to be waited on hand and foot, that's for sure."

Matthew brought his friends from the garage around to check on progress. The guys stamped their feet on the deck as if to test it for strength.

"We're going to have a window here, bedroom along that side, stove over there. I got that window in the village — ten bucks," Matthew told them.

"Cool," said Mandy, smiling at Matthew.

Tommy and his friend who lived down on the paved road charged in and out through the studs. Once Jackson hung the door they slammed through it about twenty times, making jokes about locking it when they could walk right through the walls. When they got bored they swung on the studs, trying to pull them over and accusing Jackson of building the walls crooked.

As they walked away Jackson heard Tommy telling his friend, "There's going to be a loft up in the rafters. We can sleep over whenever we want."

Margie came back when he was framing the windows. One tiny slot of a window, mainly for ventilation, he built high up along the back wall facing the farmhouse, and one larger one on the opposite wall, next to the door. "Aren't ya going to put a window on that side? But that's going to be so ugly. You need more windows than that!" She took a sip of his beer and made a face. "Mom says it's prob'ly good you're making the cabin. She says since you're doing the farm work now, since you're grown up, you oughta have a room of your own." She pulled a weed and began plucking the leaves off it. "I don't know why she thinks you're so grown up when she treats me like a freakin' baby half the time."

Jackson finished his framing. He wondered if he should call the mill about his sheathing board. It ought to be ready. He would set up his stove first, while he was waiting. A pot-bellied stove had been sitting in the back alcove of the barn for years. There were other things in that alcove, too: old bikes, parts of stanchions, waterers, piping, an old treadle sewing machine. Jackson stared at the loops of wrought iron that formed the base of the sewing machine. He picked the feed bags and chicken feeders off it and tugged it out into the open. There was no actual sewing machine there, just the curving, flowing wooden cabinet on wrought iron supports, four small drawers sculpted into the gentle roll of the wood. He remembered it sitting in the kitchen when he was a little boy, but how come he had never noticed its beauty? He sank to one knee in front of it, ran a finger along its edge, following the swerving outline. He rested his cheek in the hollow, closed his eyes. Suddenly his body froze rigid, froze as if his blood had been shot through with ice. Liquid nitrogen pulsed at his temples. His throat closed over until he couldn't breathe. He lurched to his feet, hugged the sewing machine to him and stumbled, trying to run out of the barn with the stand banging awkwardly against his legs. He struggled towards his cabin, still running, praying no one would see him. Safe in his cabin, he clung to a stud, his hand on his heart, scared and waiting.

"Fuck," he whispered. "Shit."

This wasn't the first of these attacks that set his heart racing. Now he struggled to get his expression back to normal, quick, in case anyone had noticed him and came up to see what he was doing. He tried to call up the image of Guy Nelson loading hay last summer, standing on the wagon, tossing bales to the top of the load. He concentrated on a section of Guy's back, where the tanned skin disappeared behind the waistband of his jeans. He held the image until his panic simmered down into a dull dread he could easily hide, then he shut the image off. Shh. Be good. Be quiet. He needed a bottle. He drove to Scotch River.

"When are ya going to finish that stupid cabin?" Tommy asked him after supper Friday night.

"Whenever my board's ready."

"Oh, yeah. The mill called," Margie tossed over her shoulder.

"When?"

"I don't know. A few days ago. I don't know."

Jackson twitched his eyebrow in annoyance.

Matthew lit into her. "Nice goin', dumb-head. We're waiting for that, you know! They're all gone home by now! Can't get it till tomorrow, if they're even working then."

"Well, don't yell at *me*!"

Jackson shut down his ears, pulled his whittling out of his shirt pocket. When he surfaced, Matthew was poking him in the ribs and they were alone in the kitchen.

"Come on, man," he was saying, "Calli really likes ya. Mandy told me she keeps asking why you never come out. She really wanted to know if you'd be there tonight. I'm serious. She's hot for you."

"Who?"

"Fuck, man! Calli! Calli Joudrie. Mandy's cousin? Who was up here two days ago looking at the cabin? Who kept looking at ya? Saying stuff?"

"Oh."

"So . . . so she's hot for ya. Big time."

"What does she want *me* for?"

"Fucking Jesus, man. What d'you think? You saving yourself for the fucking priesthood, or what?"

"Why would you care?"

Matthew leaned over until their foreheads nearly touched. "I'll tell you why," he hissed. "Because those two, Mandy and Calli, they're like that." He shook his crossed fingers under Jackson's nose. "I just get started with Mandy and it's, I got to get back to Calli, Calli said not to leave her alone. Calli this. Calli that." Matthew sat up straight. "Just come, okay? It wouldn't kill ya to have a couple of laughs, would it?"

Jackson shrugged and went back to his carving. They sat in silence for a minute.

"Okay, then. Forget the girls. Forget 'em. Just come. You an' me. We'll have a few beer, eh? It'll be a blast." Matthew stood up and, from behind, clamped his hands tight down on Jackson's shoulders, close to his neck. He leaned over to growl into his ear, "I know where we can get some great weed."

Gert walked in and Matthew broke the huddle.

"Mom, tell Jackson to come to the party with me."

"Go, for heaven's sake. No point moping around here all night. Go. Keep your brother out of trouble."

"See, buddy? Even Mom says. Come on. You and me."

Jackson folded his jackknife into his shirt pocket.

"Awright, there we go!" Matthew slapped Jackson's head in triumph. "He's just getting cleaned up there, Mom, getting a clean shirt. Then we're off."

Margie barrelled into the kitchen. "What if people stare at me, Mom? What if they think I'm bad for going to a party when Dad's only been dead for, like, a month? My hair's a mess! I can't find that little plastic brush, and I want to make French braids! What if everybody stares at me?"

Gert clicked her tongue. "Oh my. Your father — just a minute." She brushed by Jackson and darted into the bathroom before him.

Margie turned and faced Matthew head on, hissing. "I'm going to Joudrie's later on with Courtney. And if you embarrass me, if you come on to just *one* of my friends, I will tell Mom *three* of the top ten things you don't want her to know."

Matthew had no time to answer before Gert returned with the brush Margie wanted.

"No one's going to stare at you. Oh my. You're young for heaven's sake. It's been three weeks. Go, Jackson. Get ready. Go. Here, Margie, how are we doing that hair?"

It wasn't too cold a night for November. People flowed in and out of the house, around the bonfire, behind the sheds. Jackson found Calli had more questions than he could have thought possible about a simple twelve-by-sixteen-foot cabin. He offered her a beer and she seemed really excited about that. He sat on one of the logs by the bonfire for a long time and saw no sign of Matthew. Calli's voice blurred into the atmosphere like the shimmering heat rising off the flames.

"I've nearly got her," Matthew kept saying on the way home. "I'm that close. Great tits. Tasty, I'm telling ya. And she loves it, too."

It seemed to Jackson that there wasn't much time between when they got to bed and the morning chores. And most of it he spent listening to Matthew whacking off. His head throbbed.

After chores and breakfast Jackson sat over his tea. He had to buy tar paper, rolled roofing and insulation for the ceiling while he still had a bit of money. He drove into Scotch River for the building supplies, stopped at the liquor store for a couple of cases of beer, then the garage to fill the gas tank and buy a pouch of tobacco. That was the end of his money. He would have to finish the cabin with what he had.

Matthew was chomping at the bit when he got home, waiting for the truck.

"My sheathing board's ready," Jackson said.

"Yeah, I'm just going for it. Soon as you get your ass out of the truck."

"There's two loads."

"Yeah, yeah. Move it."

Jackson barely got his materials out of the back before the truck disappeared in a cloud of dust.

Jackson waited for his board. He waited. And waited. And waited. Finally a truck turned into the yard. But it wasn't Matthew, it was Guy Nelson. Guy's father owned Nelson's Garage, and he and Matthew chummed around a lot, always pulling parts out of this car and sticking them into that one.

Guy leaned his head out the window. "Hi there."

"Uh, hi."

"Springs went in your truck," Guy said. "Up the end of the road."

"My board?"

"I got half here." He jerked his head back towards the truck bed. "Where do you want it? Matthew's back with the rest."

"Oh, uh, yeah. Over there. He t-took it all in one load?"

"Yeah. You should see your truck, man." Guy laughed. "I wasn't carrying all that in *my* truck."

Jackson rode with Guy back up MacIntyre Road, over the hill

and down to where the road joined the labyrinth of gravel roads that stitched the county together. They found Matthew sitting on the pile of lumber, smoking a cigarette and grinning. The bed of the Bigney truck sagged pitifully, practically dragging on its tires.

Jackson spoke directly into his brother's ear. "You're paying for those springs."

"I am not! It's your wood. I was just doing you a favour."

"I said *two* loads."

"I could get it all in one. No sweat."

No sweat? Jackson didn't say anything.

"Mom'll pay. It won't be much. I'll get new springs in 'er tonight. There's tons of used springs down at the garage, eh, Guy?"

"Yeah. It shouldn't be too bad."

Matthew jumped up and started helping Guy toss the load into Guy's pickup. The two of them climbed into the cab.

"Take it easy on the way home with that truck, eh?" Matthew called over his shoulder.

Jackson leaned against the Bigney pickup and tapped a smoke out of his pack. The middle of fucking nowhere. If MacIntyre Road could be said to lead anywhere, it was here. Archie Strong's old derelict farm, abandoned before Jackson was born. Strong Hollow, it was called back in the days when every intersection had a name. He finished his smoke and climbed in to nurse the poor limping truck home to the farm.

That evening Jackson and Matthew rattled down to Nelson's Garage. Matthew wanted to work on the truck there because it was Saturday night and that's where the party was. Guy's father left Guy to close up the pumps around nine or so, but he let them all hang around out back afterwards with the music blaring while they boasted and laughed and tinkered under hoods.

No one was in a hurry. Every time someone new joined the party they all had to take a look and hear the story and give their opinions. Even the girls had opinions. Jackson wanted to go home.

After an hour they'd got as far as choosing which sets of springs they were going to put in. A few people said hello to him: Guy Nelson, Calli and Mandy. Chester Duggan nodded at him.

Matthew could hardly take his eyes off Mandy. He talked loudly and swaggered a lot, but he avoided actually going under the truck and leaving her to talk with other guys. When Jackson tried to take the wrench so he could move the job along, Matthew bristled like a cat defending his freshly killed rat. Jackson backed off.

Another hour passed and the springs got replaced on the driver's side. Matthew tossed Jackson another beer and winked. Interest in the springs waned, and everyone wandered over to inspect the dump truck which had been at the garage all week for transmission work and a new clutch. It was fixed now and waiting to be picked up. They opened the hood and chewed over every bit of work done on it. Matthew had changed its oil, and he talked a lot about that. Jackson sighed and went to take a leak. When he came back Mandy had a grip on Matthew's belt and a smile on her face.

". . . so take me for a ride in it, then."

"Yeah, right."

"You said you knew where the keys were."

"Well yeah, but . . ."

When Mandy turned back to her girlfriends, laughing, Jackson's heart sank.

One of the guys climbed up the side of the dump truck and jumped down into the steel cavern. The thud of his boots echoed around and around, and his laughter bounced back and forth until he made a party all by himself. "Me and Mandy in the back," he shouted over the side. "Come on, Mandy!"

"In your dreams, buddy!" Mandy shouted back.

"Hey, pass me that chair. I'm setting up my office in here, now. Pass up the beer."

"Hey, I'm coming too." A second boy scrambled up the side as if the truck were a tree house and he was afraid to be left out.

"Hey. Pass the beer in here!"

One of the girls climbed up and over, and the beer followed. The inside girl shrieked and laughed. "Owww, that's gross!" The boys laughed. The others forgot about the transmission and ran to scale the truck wall. Before Matthew could join them, Mandy rushed at him, tugging on his arm, laughing, bending her knees to pull him away with her weight.

"Come on!" She jerked her head for him to come, she had something to whisper in his ear just as soon as she could stop laughing long enough. One of the buttons on her blouse had come undone.

Mandy wrapped her arms around his neck to get close to his ear but then kept laughing and pulling him off balance, so they ended up leaning against the truck, arms around each other, laughing into each other's necks. From where Jackson was standing he could see one of Matthew's hands cupping a cheek of Mandy's bum. The other hand, at the small of her back, had disappeared halfway into her jeans. They exchanged what must have been a very funny secret. He tried to keep his stomach from fluttering like it always did when people laughed privately in front of him. Mandy broke away and ran towards the garage office, Matthew following close enough to keep one hand on her. When they came running back with the keys, Jackson forced himself to the cab door.

"Don't," he whispered to Matthew.

"Jeez." Matthew brushed him out of the way as if he were a cat. "Fuck off, would ya, ya wuss."

Mandy squealed, hanging off the open door of the dump truck cab as if she couldn't possibly make it up to the seat without Matthew's help. When he tried to help she squirmed and thrashed and held on to him. When she ended up lying on her back on the seat with Matthew on top of her, she squealed again as if she hadn't set the whole scene. For a second Jackson thought Matthew might fuck her right there, but she pulled away, laughing and playing indignant.

Jackson shrank back against the wall of the garage, closed his eyes and waited out the long, bleak seconds until the engine roared to life, exhaust fumes filled his nostrils and cheers rose from the dump.

"Hey! Matthew, my man! Take us on a tour."

"Jesus, I'm not . . ." one of the girls tried to protest but then dissolved into giggles.

"Awright!"

Guy Nelson called out in concern, then in alarm, then in a stream of curses and threats. His head and arms kept popping up over the edge of the dump as he tried to climb out, but the others, like crabs in a tub, kept grabbing him, pulling him back down, laughing. Jackson knew Matthew was sitting up there in the cab with a hard-on so stiff it hurt, but whether that was from the girl or the truck he couldn't be sure. The gears clanked and the ground shuddered as the truck lurched out of the lot, around to the front of the garage and onto the road. Jackson slipped along the garage wall and watched Matthew turn onto the highway and drive about a hundred yards to the intersection. Matthew was trying to turn down towards the ocean. The truck wheezed and gears ground as he grappled for the right gear. Hoots and jeers from the back of the dump truck filled the air. A small blue car, coming from Scotch River, slowed behind the dump truck, waiting for it to make the turn. Matthew found his gear, and as the truck lurched onto Peninsula Road, someone tossed a beer bottle out the back. It sailed through the air in a high arc, bounced off the hood of the car and smashed on the road. Jackson couldn't see whose car it was, but it turned around immediately and drove back into Scotch River.

Jackson couldn't watch. He staggered back to their pickup truck and slumped into the seat, forehead resting on the steering wheel. He couldn't think of one reason why that car would have turned around except to go call the police. Matthew would be tearing down the road now. He'd probably end up spinning donuts in the sand at the beach, rolling the truck, tossing people out onto the rocks. There would be no end to the trouble.

The steering wheel pressed a shallow trough into Jackson's

forehead as he waited five, ten, God knows how many minutes.
He could hardly believe it when he heard the roar of the truck
returning, heard its huge tires crinkle the gravel of the garage yard
as it turned in. Maybe nothing bad would happen after all. He
looked up. Matthew rounded the corner into the back lot a little
too fast. The brakes squealed, there was a sickening crunch, the
tinkle of broken glass, and the truck bounced to a stop. Matthew
and Mandy jolted forward, then back in the front seat. The cargo
cursed. Matthew hopped down and inspected the damage. He
had driven into the light pole, just nicking the corner of the cab
and smashing a headlight.

Guy Nelson leaped out of the back, screaming. "Look what
you did, you idiot! My dad's going to kill you! You're outta here!
That's it. You are fucked!"

"Take a pill, Guy, Jesus."

"Yeah, what's the big deal?" Matthew laughed. "One headlight. That's nothing."

"Oh, Gu-uy! I'm writing my na-ame in the dust on the side of
your precious tru-uck!" one of the girls sang out. Everyone laughed
hysterically.

"Hey, Chester says he's not coming out. He says it's too nice in
there. He just needs more beer."

"He fuckin' *is* coming out! Right now!"

Matthew climbed back into the cab with Guy clutching at his
leg, trying to pull him back, but Matthew kicked him away, sent
him sprawling. "Party's over, Chester." The hydraulic hoist made
a terrific racket, groaning and clanging as the dump rose into the
night like an awakening dinosaur. In the midst of the squeals and
hoots, a police cruiser pulled into the back lot, lights flashing.

Matthew looked up in surprise. "Fuck."

"You're fucked now, Bigney. That's theft, damage, dangerous
use of a . . . of a . . . a dump truck." Spit bubbled at the corners
of Guy's mouth, his face bright red.

The Mountie walked towards them. "We've had reports of a
disturbance on the Peninsula Road."

In the back of the truck Chester's grip gave way, and with a melodramatic cry he rolled out and flopped on his back at the cop's feet. Beer bottles rained down on top of him.

The Mountie crossed his arms over his chest. "Who was driving this truck?"

"He was!" Guy was screaming. "Drove 'er all the way down to the beach and back. There was no way he had permission to do that. No way!"

"Aw, come on, I just . . ."

"You were the driver of this vehicle?" The cop stepped up to Matthew. "I want to see your license, registration, insurance." Matthew looked over at Jackson and Jackson looked at the ground. "Come over to the squad car and blow into the tube."

Late the next morning Jackson began sheathing his cabin. Matthew sat cross-legged on the floor, smoking and scowling.

"Fucking asshole. It was probably Guy who called the cops anyway. Fucking asshole. No way we would've got caught."

Guy was trapped in the back of the truck the whole time, Jackson thought, how could he have called the cops? But he knew Matthew didn't care about that.

"I did all the work on that dump truck — replaced the clutch, fixed the transmission, everything! Why shouldn't I take it out to test the gears?"

Jackson kept his eyes on his work. All Matthew did to that truck was change the oil, wash the windshield and break a headlight.

"I never even got paid for that work!" Matthew ground his cigarette butt into the floorboard. "Guy *would* fuckin' squeal. He was always fucking jealous. Shit, Guy couldn't fix a trike. He's hopeless, a fucking hopeless asshole. Nobody will take anything to that garage now. They're fucking done for now that I'm fired."

Fired? You have to have a job to be fired. Matthew had been banned. Jackson stared past Matthew at their farm truck, now sadly lopsided, with one set of springs installed and the other set abandoned in the bed of the truck. Why couldn't they just have stayed at home and fixed the springs and everything would be fine now? The truck would be finished and there would be no trouble.

"You gonna fix those springs?"

"Let's have a beer." Matthew tugged open Jackson's case of Keith's.

Jackson felt a sudden surge. "That's mine. Two bucks each." The words were out before he knew where they came from. How could he charge his own brother for a beer? But once he'd said it, it seemed like a brilliant idea. This way he could get Matthew to pay for the new springs like he should have all along. Jackson sat down on the case of beer, punctuating his point.

"Fuck off," Matthew said in disbelief.

Jackson shrugged.

"Come on. Fuck off. Jesus. Come on. Fuck, man."

Matthew always started with pleading. Jackson needed something else to think about. The dump truck. A person, alone, could lie in there, coated in gravel dust, surrounded by solid metal walls and a view of the sky, the smell of steel and rock and gasoline enveloping him. He imagined the floor, hard and cold and slightly rounded beneath him. Nothing else. Space and walls, hidden, protected, alone. But it hadn't been like that for Guy, of course.

". . . and I drove all that wood in, you fucker, picked up all that lumber. And now you start acting like an asshole, and I . . ."

Jackson tried not to listen. Even so, he knew part of him heard because his body tightened into a cringe. No. What was he thinking about? Guy Nelson. Guy had jumped into that truck with his friends, as one of them. But they had turned and torn into him, grabbing bits and feeding on him. Suppose there had been just him and Guy, alone in the truck with no one else around, and Guy leaned up against the wall of the dump and smiled a bit, off to the side, a little shy and not like he was when everyone else was around, and the moonlight shone down enough to bring out the blue in his eyes, and because he was a little nervous he lifted his arm and kind of rubbed his chest . . .

"Here, then, ya cocksucker." Jackson jumped six inches when Matthew's hand smacked down on the case of beer he sat on.

When Matthew lifted his hand a two-dollar bill fluttered in the spot. Jackson trembled. He'd missed the make-up part where Matthew quit ranting and turned to him as if he and Jackson stood together against the world. That was when Jackson was supposed to get up and hand him a beer, or do his chores or his homework, or forge their mother's signature or lend him a twenty they both knew he'd never see again. Then Matthew would bob his head and give him that wink that said, no matter what, they were brothers forever and never alone. And in that moment, Jackson would believe him, believe that Matthew would never turn on him, and all those times in the past were special cases, exceptions, insignificant trifles.

This time Jackson had missed his cue, sitting and thinking about Guy when he should have been listening to Matthew. With quivering hands Jackson stuffed the two dollars into his pocket, got up and handed Matthew a beer, not looking at him, not speaking. He wouldn't make Matthew speak to him now.

"Thanks a lot, you cheap fucking son of a bitch." Matthew shoved over a stack of boards with his foot, and Jackson watched them splay across the ground.

Jackson hung his head, looked away, started back to work. He left the case of beer open on the floor between them and hoped Matthew would help himself to the next one, which would mean Matthew had forgiven him. He hated himself for feeling like this. But in a few weeks he'd be on his own, moved into his cabin, and all that would be over with. Matthew had paid two bucks. That was fine. He had the money so he could put it towards the truck springs Matthew should have paid for anyway. It was a good idea. He should be glad. He chugged a beer.

Matthew's friends began arriving, and Matthew hailed them up to the cabin. They sprawled on the floor deck, propped themselves against the studs.

"Could you believe that fucking Mountie?"

"Did you see the look on Guy's face?"

"Oh, man, I thought he was going to pop a vein for sure."

Jackson felt himself shrinking away. More and more people

arrived: Chester and Calli and all of them. Only Guy Nelson was obviously absent. And Mandy. Jackson continued with his measuring, sawing and hammering, gradually closing them all into the cabin.

In no time at all they'd polished off the six-pack Chester had brought, and one of the boys turned to Jackson's case.

"Hey-hey. That beer belongs to my big brother, and he's not letting anybody have one unless they pay two dollars. Isn't that right?"

Jackson's brain snapped to attention, freezing his face so it showed nothing. Matthew wasn't going to let him back out.

"Yeah," Jackson answered, "that's right."

"Fuck that. I'm going to buy my own."

"It's Sunday, Einstein."

"Oh, yeah."

"What a prick, eh?" Matthew said, urging them all on.

"I didn't know you were setting up in business." Chester pulled out his wallet, fat from his first unemployment cheque after the richest herring fishery in years. "You could at least of waited till you got the walls up on the bar."

Everyone laughed. "Yeah, then you could put up one of those nice calendars with the girls on it."

"Hey, a table, maybe, and a couple of chairs wouldn't hurt, would they? For beer at that price?"

Chester handed twenty bucks through the wall studs to Jackson. "Give us a round, there, my man." He snapped his fingers like a movie star. "And make it snappy."

Jackson set down his hammer and began passing the bottles through the studs. The sharp ridges of the bottle caps pressed into his fingers. Chester hadn't sounded annoyed at all, and no one else seemed to mind once they had a beer in front of them. Jackson sneaked a quick peek at Matthew, who glared at his beer and lit into Guy Nelson again with renewed fury.

The party grew raucous. Jackson sheathed the back of his cabin. No matter how loudly Matthew talked, the conversation kept straying away from Matthew's exploits and back to tales of the party in the back of the dump truck. Calli only shrugged whenever Matthew asked her where Mandy was or why she hadn't arrived. Matthew slipped away from the party a couple of times to try to phone her but came back frowning each time. Before long Jackson dug into his case of beer and was surprised to find only a few empties flopped over on their sides. Jeez, he thought. He pulled his second case out from under the cabin's floor. Chester and his cousin were arguing about who should buzz into the village for chips and Doritos. Neither wanted to leave the other there with Calli, who had clearly given up on Jackson.

Jackson sheathed the east end of his cabin, the party climaxed and headed into decline. Calli rolled her empty beer bottle across the deck, and Chester and his cousin simultaneously jumped to attention. They each ordered two beer. Jackson had to tell them there were only two left. Everyone turned to watch as they bid each other up, glassy eyes narrowing. Calli struggled to stop giggling, to look smug and demure. Chester won out. He and Calli got the last beer. Jackson pocketed sixteen dollars.

Once the beer was gone people began to drift away. The temperature tumbled in the late afternoon sunset. Jackson set down his hammer and left Matthew sitting alone in the dark, half-sheathed cabin. He climbed the stairs to their bedroom in the farmhouse, closed the door and sat on the floor with his back against it. He drew out all the money he had been stuffing into his pockets all afternoon. There was the price of two cases of beer, the price of the truck springs and twenty-eight dollars more. Plus he had had his afternoon beer as well. It wasn't satisfaction or happiness or hope or excitement that Jackson felt. It wasn't anything, really, except cold, logical reality. The key was to have beer when no one else did. He could do that. Absolutely no sweat.

CHAPTER THREE

THERE WAS NO SINGLE DAY or time when Jackson finished his cabin, no moment when his new life ought to have begun. Matthew and his friends stopped complaining about the cold when Jackson got the walls closed in and the stove installed. He laid his leftover lumber across the rafters for a loft floor and got about a third of the space planked in before he ran short. No one seemed to mind when he climbed over their heads to stuff his fibreglass batts between the rafters. The afternoon he wrestled the little cot down from the attic in the farmhouse and crossed the farmyard with the thin mattress propped over him like a tent, he noticed a faint humming in the marrow of his bones. It may have been happiness, he wasn't sure. Don't, his brain warned. Shh! Be good.

"Well?" Gert said to him after breakfast the next day. "Are you going to invite your mother up to see your new house?" She untied her apron and hung it on the peg behind the door. She glanced in the mirror, her hands automatically jerking upwards to pat her hair. Jackson could tell by the tone of her voice that she wasn't mad, but she wasn't exactly happy, either. He couldn't put his finger on it, but if it had been anyone else's cabin, he would have guessed she sounded a little proud.

"Sure," he heard his voice say.

They walked across the meadow together. "This is the back," he said as they came upon it, and he saw how plain it must look to her. Twelve by sixteen, with a low pitched roof and a stovepipe out one end. It was swathed in black tar paper held in place by strips of lath. He led her around to the front, past the window and through the scavenged wooden door.

"I'm gonna paint that door," he mumbled.

In addition to the pot-bellied stove and the woodbox beside it, the cabin was furnished with three milk crates and a couple of bench seats from old cars that Matthew had found. Vernon's old chair from the workshop sat in one corner, and beside it the sewing machine stand. His cot was pushed up against one wall. He was going to tell her about the wall he planned to build along the end of the cabin to make a bedroom and how he thought he might even bring in water and electricity later on. But her gaze had come to rest on the old sewing machine stand. He had patched the top and kept his kerosene lamp on it, and he used its little drawers to store his tobacco fixings, his whittling knives and (he was hoping she wouldn't look) an emergency flask of rum.

"I-I-I found that in the barn." It was hers, of course. He hadn't thought to ask about taking it.

"Who'd've thought there'd be use in that old thing yet," she said. She looked around at the walls. "You might get cold, later on in the winter."

"I can get shavings from the mill to insulate, soon as I get some chipboard, eh? I just got to get some money together."

"Well, you've got your spot now, like Vernon and his old workshop. And you've still got your chores and your meals and laundry and such. You should get a bit of peace, anyway. A quiet fellow like you needs something of your own to tide you over until the house empties out."

She dusted off her hands as if she'd just set the bread to rise. Then she nodded at him and walked out the door.

The bud of hope growing in him froze, turned black and shrivelled.

Jackson noticed the handmade Bristol board sign and ventured into the United Church Women's pre-Christmas rummage sale, where he bought a pot and a frying pan for two dollars and a can opener for a quarter. That night when he didn't show up for supper Gert sent Tommy out searching. Tommy found him in his cabin hunched over the pot of Chunky Soup he'd heated on his stove.

"Tell her I already ate," he said.

Jackson tried to avoid Gert over the next few days, but she turned up at his elbow when he was separating the cream, hovering, hesitating as if she didn't know exactly what she wanted to say to him. He didn't have to look at her to feel the chill.

"You got no place for a razor in that cabin of yours? Or you forgotten what it's for?"

Jackson hadn't shaved since his father's funeral, and half his face was now hidden behind stiff dark hair. He'd seen her looking at his beard, but she hadn't said a word about it until now. The edge in her voice cut through him. He set the milk pail down and walked back to the cows.

He stood between two Jerseys, leaning against them. He remembered missing school with the flu when he was a boy, and Gert had bundled him up and coaxed him onto her knee even though he wasn't a baby anymore. They had sat in the rocking chair listening to its rhythmic creak, Jackson burrowing into the warmth of her body with the weight of her arms wrapped around him, her soft dough and woodsmoke smell enveloping him. Just him and her. "Oh, my Jackson," she'd whispered to him.

At the end of the week Jackson showed up at the farmhouse after chores, looking for his winter jacket. Gert stood back from the wood stove, her hands on her hips, beaming, and crowed, "Well, look who's back scrounging around for one of his mother's home-cooked dinners."

Jackson found his jacket upstairs in the closet and left with it under his arm, closing the kitchen door behind him. He didn't say a word.

Twice a day, morning and evening, Jackson worked his way along the line of cows' rumps with the milkers, scrubbed the separator parts and hung them up to drip. Twice a day he slopped the hogs. His panic attacks subsided, not on their own but because Jackson worked out when to distract himself, how to flatten himself against the trepidation, where to walk to avoid the shadows of the beams, where to focus his eyes. He stopped pretending he was going to tell his mother that he quit, started pretending he didn't mind the barn, the sour tingling it brought to his stomach, the dread that lurked behind him. He learned when and how much he needed to drink.

Jackson would have one beer when he woke up in the morning. Sometimes he'd have a second if he really needed it. After that, he held out for the rest of the morning. He'd do the barn chores, then work on his cabin. He built a little counter to set against one wall and installed a shelf to hold his cans of soup, his jar of peanut butter, his loaf of bread. He walled off a four-by-eight-foot cell in a corner of the cabin for his bedroom. He fetched himself a supply of firewood, split it, stacked it and eyeballed a site just outside his door for a little woodshed. Every day, around noon, the tightening of his flesh just beneath his skin became too intrusive to ignore. Then he took up his seat in the corner behind the stove and pulled his whittling knives from the top left drawer of the sewing machine table. With these he could hold the mounting pressure at bay, buy himself another hour or so.

Acorns, maple keys, bits of bark, a field mouse, a bottle cap, a leaf. These were the sorts of things Jackson carved. He simply dropped them on the ground when he was finished, and they melted into their surroundings and disappeared. Sometimes he would do a pencil or a fork or a spool of thread and then toss them into the kindling box. Later he would use them to start the fire. He sat and whittled and considered which can of soup he would open for his dinner, or if he would have the beans for a change. Sometimes, no matter how hard he tried to prevent it, his brain would form a renegade thought which bounced around from one corner of his head to another, unable to find a way out or a way in.

He held out for as long as he could, until his chest started to crumple under an irresistible pressure like an empty beer can in a closing fist. Before it caved in completely, splintering his ribs, he would set his knife back in the drawer and draw a case of beer out from under his counter. Drinking was like pouring water into that collapsing can, filling the vacuum, packing substance into the void, relieving the pressure.

On his way back from chores on the morning after the first dusting of snow, Jackson stopped dead as he passed the workshop. Inside, Matthew and Tommy were laughing together. Through the single grimy window he could make them out, standing over Matthew's sack of snares and traps, sorting them out, pulling them apart where they had become tangled. Matthew had never let anyone touch his traps before. Matthew and Vernon used to go off into the woods together for rabbits and, if prices were up, get a few beaver pelts or coyote or fox. Matthew and Vernon. Donny might go deer hunting with them, but only Matthew and Vernon trapped. Jackson watched his brothers silently for a moment, then continued on his way back to his cabin. It wasn't long before Matthew and Tommy passed the cabin window side by side, each with a small pack slung over his shoulder. Jackson watched Tommy's eyes, first trained intently on Matthew's face, then turning towards the woods where Matthew was pointing. They disappeared into the trees together.

"Jeez, where's the tea, man?" Matthew and Tommy, red-cheeked and grinning, stomped their feet at his doorway. Matthew stirred up the fire, tossed on another stick and placed Jackson's little pot of water on to boil. "Tons of rabbits this year. All over the place."

"I want hot chocolate," Tommy said.

"There's none here."

"I want some. I hate tea."

"Go home, then." Matthew shrugged.

"No."

"Well, shut up then."

"Is there sugar?"

"Right in front of ya, look."

"Oh yeah." Tommy sat silent for a second. "We're gonna get tons of rabbits, eh Matthew?"

"Yeah, bud."

Jackson tossed tea bags into mugs. Tommy reached across the table for Jackson's cigarettes. "I'm having one of these," he said.

Matthew smacked his hand. "Smoking's bad for ya."

"You do it."

"So?"

"Come on."

"Piss off, you little faggot. Go home. I want to talk to Jackson."

"So talk to him then. I don't care."

"I said get lost! Get ta hell out of here or I'm not taking you trapping anymore. To hell with you!"

Jackson turned away. The noise went on a little longer. Finally the door slammed, shaking the cabin, and Jackson heard Tommy's boots pummelling the earth as he bolted for home.

Matthew flew to the door, flung it open, yelled after him, "Suck mine!" and slammed it again. He lit a cigarette and smoked the whole thing silently, leaning against Jackson's window. Finally he said, "We gotta get him something nice for Christmas. He's all upset, eh? 'Cause of Dad."

The following week Matthew and Tommy went off for the Christmas tree. Gert talked all the time about who was coming home for the holiday and who wasn't. When she gave Jackson his cream cheque money, he kept enough for a can of tobacco and passed the rest back to her.

"Get something for the kids," he mumbled.

On Christmas morning he had to show up in the farmhouse parlour. There was absolutely no way he could avoid it. His palms sweat like crazy, like they always did when he had to open a present. He would wait until Tom began opening the package with the brand new .22 rifle, then he would do his gift real quick while no one was looking and get it out of the way.

Play Doh, he had said. Play Doh, Lego, anyone could see it had been just a mistake. His mother hadn't really been angry with him. Anyone could see that now. She had only been frustrated, disappointed, after trying so hard to get some half-decent things for far too many kids with far too little money. And she could have got the right thing, too, if only he had said it clear enough. Play Doh was a lot cheaper than Lego, after all. She never would have known if he hadn't cried. There had been no need of him saying anything, making a fuss, ruining everything. He didn't know she would be mad. He thought it had been Santa Claus, after all, but as soon as he had said it, he knew Donny was right. There was no Santa Claus. Even through his tears he couldn't have missed the look on his mother's face. Play Doh, Lego, what difference did it make? He was lucky to have got anything. Shut *up*! his brain yelled at him. For godsake shut up and be good. But it wouldn't shut up.

The next year he found the hidden pocket knife with the three different blades and the little scissors. He was so happy to be getting such a thing for Christmas, and to *know*! Now if anyone asked he could say, "I want a pocket knife." He knew the right answer. He was all ready. He was prepared. It would be perfect that year. Thank God no one had asked him. Thank God Donny had opened the knife first, before he got to his own present. Thank God no one could see his stomach constrict when he saw how stupid he had been, how close he had come to repeating his mistake. He had been so confident he had almost said to his mother the day before, "I hope I get a pocket knife." He had started to say it but had been interrupted — that was how close he had come.

Shut up! Shut up!

He couldn't stop his hands from trembling, ripping the gift wrap. It was a tea kettle for his woodstove. It was over, thank God, for another year.

All through Christmas week people washed up at the cabin to drink and talk and laugh. People brought friends and family who were home for the holidays, sometimes people Jackson didn't even know. Even when the liquor store was open he would usually sell a beer or two to someone without the money for a six-pack or who couldn't be bothered going out to buy one, but most of his business was after hours. Jackson ploughed every cent of his profits into keeping his stock up. Sometimes people would come and bring their own drink. Then Jackson sat in his corner, tapping his foot in the air and wondering how to stop them.

Eighty percent was what he had heard — eighty percent of the cost of alcohol goes to the government in taxes. Even allowing for some exaggeration, he should be able to undersell the liquor store, then maybe people would stop bringing their own. So early in the new year Jackson bought his first beer kit. Best Cellar it was called. It wasn't the cheapest on the market, but it was at the lower end of the price range. Jackson liked the label. It was nice and simple — a monk and a keg alone in a basement. He hauled water up to his cabin to make the beer, sloshed the buckets down to the milk room in the barn for bottling, clanked the bottles back to his cabin and hid them in the rafters until they had aged a full three weeks. He bought a clear plastic Kool-Aid pitcher and a pack of disposable beer glasses. He waited until late Sunday afternoon, when the crowd was thickest, then he decanted a quart, poured himself a drink, and waited. At a dollar a glass there was no way anyone could lose.

Before winter ended, one cow died from milk fever, a newborn calf drowned in the gutter before anyone found it, and a case of mastitis got out of hand and ran down the line until half the herd needed penicillin shots morning and night. Two calves died of parasites. Only those cows most obvious and insistent about their heat were bred, so by early summer a quarter of the herd stood with empty wombs and flaccid udders.

By early summer, it was clear that Jackson's homebrew would

be a success, and he began digging the trench to bury the pipe that would carry running water into his cabin. He installed a kitchen sink and thought about the possibility of building in a little bathroom. That summer Guy Nelson and Mandy were married. That summer Matthew met Rosie. That summer Marsha Nelson and Rick, her boyfriend or husband (Jackson wasn't sure which), came home from Brampton and started visiting his cabin. They were the first ones to ask for hard liquor and the reason Jackson began keeping a couple of bottles of rum and a bit of rye whisky around the place. A couple of times Rick came by without Marsha. And once, Marsha came by without Rick.

Now, from what Jackson understood, there were two ways to fuck a woman. The first, the missionary position, was with her lying on her back on the bed with her legs spread and the man on top. The other way, called doggy style, was with her bent over on her knees with her ass in the air and the man going up from behind. Up her cunt though, not her ass. She would probably scream if you got it in the wrong hole. That's what Jackson understood.

Of the two ways to fuck, it was probably the woman who chose, he supposed. At least on the morning Marsha showed up at his cabin half lit, that's how it was.

"God," she said, "it would be something to have a real man for a change." She pressed her palm flat against his chest, against the little mound of muscle dotted with a nipple which would be a tit in a woman but which had no name he knew of in a man.

He stared past her silently, his arms hanging at his sides as she rubbed his crotch slowly, up and down. The feel of hands other than his own, even through denim and flannel, surprised him. They were only tiny hands, but still . . . his cock twitched and started to stiffen.

She kept talking, but he couldn't concentrate on what she was saying. She was antsy as hell, and her eyes kept flitting around the room. He followed her in behind the board wall that cut the bed off from the rest of the cabin and watched as she stood beside his bed taking off her clothes, just as if she were alone. She sat down and removed her socks and sneakers, then struggled briefly with a button on her shirt before clicking her tongue, annoyed, and tugging the shirt off over her head. She stood up and stepped out of her jeans and underwear together. She was almost as skinny as Jackson, with ribs that, while not individually visible, telegraphed their presence by the sag in her body between the bottom of her ribcage and her pelvic bones. Her breasts weren't a presence the way they were with the women in Matthew's magazines, they were little more than puddles of flesh capped with large dark coins of skin, seemingly held in place by rigid, push-pin nipples. A bushy fistful of pubic hair interrupted the flatness of her body and clung above the space between her legs as though liable to topple off and fall to the ground. She lay back on the bed with her knees drawn up part way and flopped open.

"Well," she said. "Take off your clothes."

It was, well, slipperier than he had anticipated. And it turned out she wanted a whole bottle of rum, for free, afterwards.

In the days and weeks following, Jackson found himself thinking about sex a lot. After years of shaving his fantasy life to the bare minimum, down to the stark bones of necessity, Jackson inched forward with caution. The most remarkable discovery had nothing to do with the act itself but with the fact that no one knew he had done it. Obviously Marsha hadn't told anyone, certainly not Rick. People sat drinking and talking in his cabin, just as they always had. Even when Marsha and Rick showed up together, Marsha never even glanced at him. In fact, it was only a few weeks after the incident that she and Rick left for the west. So no one knew. And as long as no one knew, it meant nothing. He could think anything he wanted.

He started out with a few words, considering what he liked. The word cock he liked. And hard. And fuck. He liked fuck-rod even better, but only when he actually had a hard-on. It sounded stupid otherwise. Semen was a word he had learned in high school, and it stuck with him because it made him think of sailors and tall wooden ships. He liked the word cum because of its simplicity. Cock, hard, fuck, semen, cum, he repeated to himself.

Marsha had said fuck, but she used dick instead of cock. And she hadn't said semen, didn't refer to his juice at all. He didn't like the way it had disappeared into her.

The best thing about doing it with someone else was the magical feeling of getting off without touching yourself. Also, there was the feel of the legs, the skin sliding against his thighs. Anyone would have to admit, though, it wasn't as good a rush as normal, not as good as doing it yourself. When he really thought about it, there was an awful lot to be said for jerking off as opposed to sex. For instance, he didn't know what to do with her afterwards — after he came. He hated that part. He heard a joke once: the definition of *forever* is the time between when you shoot and when she gets up to go home. At least he knew that part of him was normal. And he didn't like the smell that crept into the air and stung him at the very back of his nose. But maybe that was just Marsha. There was something mushy and spongy about the whole thing, something he didn't trust, like a rotten floor board.

And there was something else. With her, he missed seeing the gush. When he pumped himself he always resisted closing his eyes at the final moment. That he could produce something so lush and abundant amazed him. He didn't like the idea of giving it away.

Jackson had expected that "doing it" would have given him more answers. He had expected to be more certain about the jokes. He could still never be sure when people were really kidding and when they were just sort of kidding. Like about the blow jobs. Jackson wasn't sure this happened very much, but it was clearly something the guys thought about a lot. They would grab them-selves, shake the bulge in the front of their jeans at someone, "blow me," they would say, or "suck mine," and everyone would laugh. It meant fuck off, or go to hell. It meant, you're not going to get what you want.

Or like when Matthew and his friends were working outside on Chester Duggan's new motorcycle. Matthew picked up the wheel wrench, one of the heavy old ones shaped like a cross with a socket at the end of each of the four arms. When Chester bent over to examine the headlight connection, Matthew sneaked up behind him and shoved one of the arms of the wrench between Chester's legs. Chester jumped in surprise and grabbed at the nub of steel at his crotch but only managed to pull the cross-piece tight to the back of his legs. For a second he found himself stuck, tugging on the rod while the rest of them howled with laughter. Chester turned bright red.

"Fuck ta Jesus off!" he yelled.

"Oooh, he loves that!"

One of the others thrust his pelvis forward and cried in a falsetto, "Oh, harder, harder!"

They laughed like maniacs.

Chester wasn't exactly drunk, but he had had too much beer to be nimble. He stumbled trying to move forward and had to regain his balance. He freed himself and grabbed the wrench in his fist. He swung it over his head like a club. Jackson shrank back, sure Chester was going to brain someone with it. But Chester caught himself, interrupted his own fury. He tossed the metal cross into the dirt and mumbled, "Morons."

But they never knew when to quit. "Oh, why don't you show us your rod again!"

"Why don't yez all shove one of them spokes up your asses, and I'll twirl yez all around like a friggin' windmill."

Jackson heard them laughing behind him as he ducked inside his cabin. There were only three others besides Chester. He was the fourth. He didn't like being included even in the most peripheral way. He didn't like being noticed. He didn't like — didn't like the way his hands were shaking. He swigged a few shots of rum from his personal stash.

They were always doing stuff like that.

Time began to slide for Jackson. One day bled into another, this week into the next, summer became fall became winter. Matthew, now preoccupied with Rosie, didn't come by so much. And when he did come by, he either had Rosie with him or he would come late at night and lean forward, his eyes glittering in the lamplight, eager to confide his adventures with Rosie. Jackson did chores, brewed beer, visited the liquor store. He drank, and, when he could get it, he smoked marijuana. Mostly he kept the world at bay, but on days when the emptiness threatened to crush him, he would roll a joint and sit on his bed in his windowless cubicle and stare at his father's wedding suit.

He kept the suit together on a single hanger, the trousers hanging straight from the waist, the white shirt brilliant against the black wool, the tie slung around its collar. The suit jacket topped it off. After his father's funeral, after he had built his cabin and driven the nail especially for it, Jackson had carried the suit across the yard draped over his back, his index finger curled around the hanger hook, the clear dry-cleaner plastic shimmering out behind him like a ghost. The wedding suit hovered at the foot of his bed, waiting. A couple of times a year he dusted the plastic covering, but he had no need to disturb the suit. Then, after two and a half undisrupted years, he was required to put it on four times within six months.

Margie's wedding was to be held in the huge stone Presbyterian church in New Glasgow. Margie fussed constantly for a month about how much she was "showing." Just a little wedding — just the family, Ronnie's mother kept saying, strained and doubtful. But Gert had to sell two cows to pay for the bridal gown and the flowers and something to wear herself and a wedding present that wouldn't look pathetic beside the things that piled in from Ronnie's side. Ronnie's family was paying for everything else including, according to rumour, an open bar at the reception. Ronnie's father was a doctor. Jackson sat in a pew on the bride's side of the church, next to Matthew and Rosie. Later, at the reception at the golf club, they all sat at a long, white-clothed table waiting for dinner. Jackson blinked at a red concoction which a uniformed waitress set in front of him. Someone said it was shrimp. Dinner was chicken. There was something in sauce and no stuffing.

"Don't put that suit away," Matthew whispered in his ear later that night when they escaped to the country club balcony with big glasses of Dr. MacLean's rum. The frigid April wind felt homey next to the stretched smiles and gelid politeness of the MacLean family. "Rosie's got one in the oven." Matthew winked broadly at him. "It's a secret till she tells her mom. We're gettin' married. You're the best man."

"Eh?"

"No sweat, buddy. Ya just stand there till I jab you in the ribs, then you hand me the ring." Matthew laughed as if he would be happy even without an open bar.

But before Matthew and Rosie could think about arrangements, Jackson had to don the suit again. A sudden freezing rainstorm whirled in off the ocean, coating everything with slick, clear ice. The storm caught Kate's husband returning from somewhere he never should have been in the first place. The driver of the oncoming semi-trailer survived. He said the car had fishtailed, spun completely around before the impact. No one had any control. The funeral took place on a day so dazzlingly warm and sunny, who could believe the accident had been real? Certainly not Kate, who stood at the front of the church with her new baby and her two little ones, her face frozen. Jackson tapped the flask of rum hidden inside his suit jacket.

Kate didn't want to be left alone. She moved her young family into the farmhouse. After a couple of weeks she began walking a few hundred yards up MacIntyre Road and then a few hundred yards down, staring at the land while traces of her old look crept back onto the edges of her face. There was insurance money. She called a contractor. By fall she had moved into her new bungalow, just up from the farmhouse.

Matthew and Rosie put their wedding off until August. On the chosen day, Jackson stood in his suit, staring past the minister at the sunflowers gushing out of their vase on the altar while Matthew and Rosie got married. Their party was a pot of chili and a barbecue at their tiny, half-built house across the road from the farmhouse. At Matthew's insistence, Jackson donated a keg.

In September Jackson needed his suit again. The legal aid lawyer told him to wear it, and to trim his beard and to speak up when he was on the stand. They didn't have a tight case, his lawyer said, they had only managed to subpoena a few reluctant witnesses. The worst of them claimed the case of homebrew under his arm was his own, and he had been taking it over to his brother's to celebrate the completion of his brother's new duck pond. He claimed the money he was paying Jackson was for a prize turkey Jackson had raised for him to eat at that very occasion. He claimed the turkey had been of a rare breed (hence the extraordinary expense), that he had to pay for special feed for it, that he couldn't raise it himself on account of his wife's allergies. On and on he went, recounting fantastic details that brought laughter and hoots from the gallery and sharp rebukes from the judge. Mostly it was the Mountie's testimony. Mostly it was the stash of liquor, the three kegs of brew, the jar of small bills and the tab. Mostly what got him was that lousy piece of paper with the names of all his customers and the amounts they owed. The one with "Drinks Tab" printed neatly across the top in tiny letters.

Guilty. His lawyer admitted that they really go after the guys who manufacture — even beer. The fine cost him all the money he had and all he could expect to make for months and months.

But the news travelled fast. He had only served a small circle of Matthew's friends and acquaintances before, only earned enough to pay for his own drinks, his tobacco, his few groceries. Now all kinds of people began to stop by. Everyone wanted to contribute to the "turkey fund." Everyone wanted to laugh about it. In three months his clientele broadened to include the fathers and uncles and neighbours. Vernon's old drinking buddies became regulars. His business tripled, then kept on growing, slowly, steadily. Jackson did away with the milk bottle full of coins and bills he used to set in the middle of the table and began palming the cash into his pocket and then sliding it into one of the dozens of carved-out hiding places around his cabin and woodshed. He became more discreet about his stashes, more inventive in hiding them. Most of all, he did away with the written credit list. Three times every morning he recited the names and amounts in his head. It was no problem at all.

Margie and Ronnie had a baby girl, Matthew and Rosie had a baby boy, Tommy got his choice of bedrooms. As soon as the frost was out of the ground the following spring, Ronnie and Margie, sick of bill collectors and eviction notices, bought a mobile home and set it up on the land just below Matthew's. The down payment on the trailer was a loan, Margie said, and the last money the MacLeans would shell out.

As the number of families on the farm grew, the number of cows dwindled. When the marketing board started talking about doing away with cream quotas altogether, offering cream shippers a chance to sell out, Gert jumped. The cows and calves went first, then the hogs, leaving pens with doors swinging and dirty bedding to sink into permanence. Jackson had numbed himself to the barn for so long that he couldn't muster even a breath of relief. Time was disrupted. He sat at his table with his tea and smokes for the few extra hours each day. By the end of the week he couldn't imagine that he had ever done barn chores.

The more customers came by, the more they crowded the tiny cabin, the less they noticed him, and the less he was required to speak. Soon the sound of his own voice unsettled him, and he avoided using it. Making the connection was such an effort anyway. He concentrated on his business. He bought wine kits and sold the finished product at six dollars a bottle. He turned an easy profit on bottled spirits (though stock was expensive), and he kept up his mainstay of homebrew and bought beer. When Matthew's bar tab reached a thousand dollars, Jackson suggested they could make a deal if Matthew could find him a serviceable pickup truck. Jackson ended up with a little Ford S-10, and Matthew got his first-ever liquor credit. Matthew also looked forward to years of service and maintenance on the truck, which would earn him drink without diverting scarce cash from his young family. Every two weeks Jackson would head off to a different liquor store, to a different outlet where he could buy beer malt, so he could spread his business around and not arouse suspicion. He also learned that care and attention served him as well in marijuana production as it did in bootlegging. He learned how to sex his plants and when to harvest the buds, and he never tried to bulk up the product with weak, ineffectual leaves. He kept the quality good, information about supply tight to his chest and the price high. Jackson turned twenty-three and then twenty-four. His brothers and sisters kept having baby after baby. He ran a wire to the cabin so he could have a light and a hotplate. He turned twenty-five. Ronnie gave him a tiny apartment sink and toilet that he salvaged from a renovation. Jackson walled off the corner by the bedroom and hung a slender board door to make a little bathroom. He installed the bathroom sink. The toilet would require more work, digging a hole, a forty-five gallon drum, more rigorous plumbing. So he just set the toilet in the corner and stacked beer bottles on it, figured he would hook it up later. He turned twenty-seven.

A new Mountie was stationed at Scotch River. Constable Townsend parked the cruiser on the side of the MacIntyre Road, walked up the back lane to Jackson's cabin and knocked on the door. Considering the size of the cabin, a long time passed before Jackson eased the door open a few inches. Jackson glanced at him and looked away. This new cop was a lot younger than the other one.

"We've heard some guys were jacking deer out along here. I was wondering if you might have seen anything?"

Jackson shook his head. He could feel the cop staring over his shoulder into the cabin, taking in a dim, sparse sliver of his life.

"You're Jackson Bigney?"

Jackson jerked his head to one side in an ambiguous affirmative. This fellow's voice was quieter, too.

"That's quite a stack of kegs you got there."

Jackson didn't answer.

"Give lots of parties?"

"Yeah."

They stood quietly a minute, Jackson leaning in his doorway staring down at the Mountie's ankle where the yellow stripe met the black boot. Jackson was afraid his cabin might smell of dope. You don't notice a smell like that so much if you live with it all the time. There was no jacking going on and no talk of it either. It was far too early in the year.

"Okay then. If you hear anything . . . about the jackers . . ." The Mountie took off his cap, studied the yellow band around it, ran his fingers through his cropped hair and fitted the cap back on his head. "You can give me a call, eh?"

Jackson bobbed his head without lifting his eyes.

CHAPTER FOUR

THE SMELL OF BACON FRYING prodded Jackson awake. He wasn't alone in his cabin. He didn't care to think that through immediately. He buried his face in his pillow, eyes still closed, and took stock of his body. At nearly twenty-nine years old, it held up well to abuse, recovered quickly. He wasn't too bad. He shuffled himself around so he could lean over the edge of the bed and grope through the case of Keith's he kept under there. When his hand located a full bottle he sat up in bed, punched the pillow behind him and sipped back his hair-of-the-dog. It was Lori, he remembered, who was frying the bacon. She had stayed over last night. They had probably fucked, he didn't bother trying to remember. He finished his beer and staggered out of bed.

When Jackson sat down at the table Lori set a huge plateful of food in front of him. He frowned, trying to bring into focus an idea he had been working on yesterday. He picked at his bacon, gradually moving it onto the toast to build a sandwich. His eggs had all the whites cut off them, three golden buttons, cooked all the way through so they didn't run. He blinked in embarrassment that Lori knew this about him. The old Surge milking machine! That was what he had been thinking about. And copper piping looped around and around through cold water in that sink. His eyes shone out from beneath his scraggly bangs.

"I always look a fright in the morning," Lori giggled.

He had wine nearly ready. He could start with that, as a test, move to a cheaper mash later on. He licked his lips.

Lori giggled again. She sauntered over to him and wriggled her way onto his lap. "You were terrific last night."

Jackson noticed her there on his lap. He mumbled, as always, into his beard. "Uh-huh." Her chest was so close he had to turn his head to finish his toast. He could heat the mash on the hotplate, no problem.

"I cleaned up the cabin a bit," she said. "This is not a bad place. It's so cool that you built it yourself. I used to go out with this other guy, I mean like years ago, and he was so useless you wouldn't believe. He got a flat tire once, and *I* had to change it for him."

Jackson was thinking about soldering.

Since the cows and pigs had gone, pigeons had taken over the centre of the barn, dropping long furrows of shit onto old hay beneath the beams. Piles of junk had grown up. Jackson hadn't been in the barn in ages. He stood and stared, then tentatively stepped inside and began picking through the junk. Soon he came across the main part of the milker, a large, round, stainless steel container with a plate-sized hole in the top where the cover fit. The search for the cover stretched into an hour, but finally he pulled it out of a jumble of feedbags, hay rake tines and barbed wire. Fitted together, the milker looked like a huge silver curling stone.

By eleven o'clock, as usual, Jackson's ribcage had hardened into a tin cylinder, his breathing had become laboured. It was the pressure against the emptiness. There was nothing inside. Nothing. Whenever he tried to speak to other people now, it was like climbing up out of a well. It was hard to focus on them, they were so far away, at the wrong end of a telescope. He had to put them together in his mind, piece by piece. He had to strain to hear them over the rush of nothingness. The muted mumblings he produced required great effort, as if he were shouting from far below, shouts usually lost in an echo before they reached anyone. It was too much work.

He left his milker in the workshop and headed back to his cabin. The seashell drone in his ears had become a roar. He drew himself a pitcher of homebrew from the keg and drank it straight down. Lori perched on the edge of a chair, filed her nails and chattered away a mile a minute. Then she looked at him expectantly, waiting for a response. He twisted his lips into a vague smile, hoping this would pass as an answer. He drew off another pitcher. Since Lori had washed all the glasses that had been lying around, he had to search the shelf for some. He poured them each a beer.

She giggled, uncertain, rickety. "What's that smile supposed to mean? Do you want to get married or not?"

Jackson slowly took in the words he had heard. He understood that she was talking to him, about him. About them. But it was like overhearing a conversation in a parking lot. He took another long drink, then picked up the pine cone he was carving, turned it over in his hand. Lori said something more.

The roar of an unmuffled engine rolled into the air between them. Jackson peered out the window to see the Everett boys' pickup bouncing to a stop. Lori stamped her foot. She was yelling at him. "I'm not hanging around while that crowd gets pissed and drools all over your floor! I'm going to Rosie's to call my sister to come and pick me up." She was leaking tears now. "Oh Jacky, I love you!" She lunged at him and hugged his neck.

Jackson, confused, let his hand fall to her waist. He could see, dispassionately, how he could have bedded her all those times. Doggy style, he thought, and the expression brought a tiny smile to his lips. He said nothing. She grabbed her things and fled.

Jackson stooped over his work in the tool shed by the farmhouse, forming a length of bendable copper piping, curling it around and around in perfect, even loops. While he worked he forced himself to think about Lori. It was like doing a school math problem, completely apart from him. Academic. It made no sense that she would want to marry him, but she did. It didn't make any difference to him. Nothing did. He didn't want to upset anyone. If it would make her happy, why not? He had no experience with this kind of thing. And he wasn't fond of metal work. Soldering and welding made him feel far from his hands.

He didn't notice his six- and seven-year-old nephews until a little fist curled around the pipe.

"Jackson's making a giant-size Slinky!"

Matthew sauntered along behind his boys. He leaned on the door post, watching progress. "Never you mind that, old man," he said to his son. "And don't you two get into any trouble or I'll whop yez both." The boys paid no attention.

"I'll give you a hand with the solder later on if you want." Jackson nodded at his lap. When he heard receding footsteps on the gravel he looked up and watched his brother stroll off, shoulders swaying gracefully on his stocky frame.

Matthew showed up for the soldering and the inaugural run. When they finished tinkering with the joints, Matthew held the milker while Jackson poured in the wine. Soon the still had settled into operation, and they sat back to wait and watch.

"Good thing it's you and me, b'y," Matthew crowed. "'Cause brandy's too good for that regular crowd you got around here."

Jackson looked across the table at his brother, saw the way his hair twirled in a cowlick above his left eye, the tiny scar beside his nose where he had been hit as a kid with a snowball filled with ice. He looked, for just a second, into his eyes. He couldn't remember the last time he had looked into the eyes of another human being, and the intensity of it stung him. He gathered himself up, forced his voice to form words.

"Lori wants to get married."

"Jeez. Is she pregnant?"

The question had never occurred to Jackson. Now that he thought of it he supposed it was possible.

"I don't know."

"Well, you better ask her, buddy! Jesus, Jackson, sometimes I think you're thick like that." He rapped on the wooden tabletop with his knuckles.

Jackson got up and checked the connections in the still.

"Married. Christ, I remember before me and Rosie got married, when we were going out. What a time we had! We went out to that barbecue in Crooked Harbour. Remember I told you that time ole stunned-arse Clifford was selling hash in the parking lot? And he went to put it back in the glove compartment of his car, and Rosie was standing there, so she opened the door of the next car over for him, and he was so lit he never noticed it was really the minister's car and not his car? And the minister and his wife came back and drove off, and Clifford took off running down the road after them, cussing a blue streak? Rosie hates that fucker Clifford. She near pissed herself that day, she laughed so hard.

"And remember that time Chester was working for Lloyd Harris, and he got fired cause he fucked off and never fed the pigs? And he was wild because he never got his last day's pay? So we all rattled over there in Chester's old truck in the middle of the night and stole those piglets and ran out of gas, and the Mountie came up, and Rosie had to convince him we're home late from the sale? Home from the cattle sale at three o'clock in the fuckin' morning! She was beautiful. I didn't care when she got pregnant. I was glad. I'd've married her the first day I met her."

The still chortled and hissed.

Matthew looked out the window. His voice turned oddly warm and delicate, not much above a whisper. "Make damn good and sure you love her. Or you'll both be fucked."

The first bright drop of shine slipped out the end of the copper piping, pinging into the waiting pitcher.

Lori didn't visit him the next day or the next. Jackson could have just let it go. Most things will go away if you ignore them. His father had always said that, but Gert would slam or bang something and proclaim that that was *not* true of the bills. He tried to recall everything he knew about Lori. Her father was one of his steady customers. Her hair was brown. She had taken a couple of his carvings home with her once. It had probably been about a year ago that she, well, he didn't know exactly — one night she was there when everyone else had gone, and they were both very drunk. Now that he thought about it, she had been around quite a bit lately. How had he managed to get into this trouble? Of course it wasn't really his trouble. Unless she was pregnant. That was the question that kept coming back, that caused a dislocated vibrating in the air around him, a buzz from the other side of a wall. If she was pregnant, then he would be a father, even if he never saw her again or if he never saw the baby. Even if no one knew, he would still be a father.

The following morning he drove to the public telephone outside the Quik Mart in Scotch River. He looked up Lori's father's number in the phone book, dialled and asked to speak to Lori. After a moment he heard the receiver being passed over with a whisper: "It's a man!"

Lori answered with a question. "Hello?"

"Hi."

"Jackson!"

"How are you?" He had reminded himself to ask this, practised it.

"Good, Jackson. I'm really good. Gee, I don't think you've ever called here before. This is great. I was just doing my toenails. Geeky, eh? It's that really bright red shade I had on a couple of weeks ago? Wild. I was going out later, just to the store, I mean. You're lucky you caught me. How are you?"

"Okay."

Then Jackson wasn't sure exactly what was the polite way to ask a girl if she was pregnant. "I was, uh, wondering. 'Cause you said you wanted to get, uh, married? I . . . just wondered if you were . . . pregnant or anything."

Jackson waited. He wondered if maybe she had put the phone down and gone off to do something. He wasn't sure if he should say something else. This had been a stupid idea. He was just about to hang up and go home when he heard her voice.

"No. I'm not pregnant. Or anything."

"Well, uh, that's good."

"Yeah. Thank God, eh?"

"Yeah. So . . . I guess you don't need to come around like before." There was silence. She was waiting for something.

"You're, um, not mad, eh?" he asked.

"No."

"Okay then." He hung up.

Matthew and Jackson recovered from the first batch of shine just as the experimental potato mash was ready for the still. Jackson set up the machine, and they sat back in their chairs, watching droplets form on the cooling pipe that poked above the water in the sink. Jackson felt a shrug of feeling deep in his chest, a kind of gurgle bubbling up through the beer — not something bouncing off him from outside, but something rising inside him. It was strange and frightening after all this time. Matthew had helped him out. Not that he had said anything great, just that he had answered. For a second he imagined he could reach over and touch him. Jackson swallowed. The bubble grew almost painful.

"Matthew," he said. The word pierced the air between them, sharp with expectation. Jackson cringed at the intimacy of it. Matthew looked straight at him. Jackson felt a bit dizzy and had to gulp a breath.

"Oh, jeez, uh, this is, uh, going to be a great batch," he said.

CHAPTER FIVE

ON THE FIRST DAY OF JUNE Jackson began a new whittling project. Lately he found himself branching out a bit. His last carving was of a spark plug with a faint but clearly recognizable image of Matthew's face worked into it. Jackson had sort of liked it and had carried it around in his pocket for several days before burning it. Now he was beginning a set of onions, hollowed out and lidded so the larger ones would hide the progressively smaller ones inside, like the little Russian dolls Mr. Scarth had brought into their grade six class when they had studied the USSR. Matryoshkas. He remembered his amazement that a particular toy, a thing you might never come across in your whole life, had its own name. He practised that name, making it his own — a word no one else in his family would ever know. He remembered Mr. Scarth placing the cool, rounded wood in his hands, remembered taking apart the calm, quiet-looking lady on the outside and uncovering the worried face on the doll beneath. Then the surprised face, then the happy one.

He glanced up from his chair in the corner when Matthew shuffled in, slumped down at the table and nudged empties out of the way with his elbow so he could rest it on the sticky table top. "Just pull me a light one, there, Jackson. I'm driving Mom in to the doctor's in a few minutes."

Jackson set down his first rounded block to draw a glass of lager for his brother from one of the kegs. He turned Matthew's words over in his mind and squeezed the meaning out of them.

The message was odd. Their mother had been to the doctor eleven times in her adult life — for ten children and one miscarriage. At fifty-nine years old, she wasn't pregnant. That was for sure. He drew himself an ale from the adjacent keg and joined his brother at the table. He stared into the bare wood grain of the tabletop and rubbed it with his finger.

"She's got this pain. Kate found her doubled over yesterday. Mom says it's nothing. It's all right for her to haul us off to the doctor's, but you know what she's like when it's her that's sick."

A sin and a waste, thought Jackson.

"A sin and a waste," Matthew clucked, then laughed and drank down half of his beer in one go.

Jackson drank more heavily than usual that afternoon. An itch tickled the base of his stomach, and he tried to calm it. He was waiting, he realized, for Matthew to return. When Matthew did return to the cabin for another drink, it was so late Jackson suspected Matthew had been home in bed and then got up again when he couldn't sleep.

"Tests, boy. All kinds of tests. They want her in Halifax, first thing Wednesday morning. Jesus, Jackson, they're not saying anything, but it don't look too good."

Jackson tried to focus on what his brother was saying. He'd drunk too much, though, too much to work on his carving, too much to be chasing after words, trying to pin them flat, stare down at their patterns, search for meaning. He poured himself one last shot of shine, slugged it back and stumbled to his bed. He left Matthew fidgeting at the table, staring into the bottom of his empty glass.

The next morning Jackson found himself in rougher shape than usual. He struggled into his jeans and wandered outside to relieve himself. The loneliness of early morning came upon him slowly, wrapping itself around him. He became excruciatingly aware of himself, a thin, sallow creature, head bent, face hidden behind a wild mane of hair, one hand around his penis, spilling golden water onto the earth.

Jackson knew there was something to be afraid of. Matthew had come by with bad news about their mother. Jackson sat on the bench by his cabin door and smoked a cigarette. He crossed and uncrossed his legs. He got up and went back into his cabin. He found his knife and gouge and returned to the bench to start hollowing out his first onion.

"Cancer," Kate declared. "It's in the lymph nodes for sure. Liver, too. They don't know what else. They can't operate. Chemotherapy. That's what they say. She has to go in to Halifax for that, stay overnight. Then she comes home for two weeks or three. It depends on blood work. Then she goes in again for another dose, up to five." Their oldest sister had summoned them all to the farmhouse. She stood at the kitchen table lifting folded clothes out of a small suitcase, shaking them out, then folding them again. A nightdress, a sweater, a housecoat. She packed and unpacked the case four times during her speech.

"I want her to come up to the bungalow. But she won't, of course. Wants to be here in the farmhouse." Her voice snapped, clipped below the quick.

"Matthew will drive Mom and me to Halifax, and we'll stay with her. My Peter will go to Rosie's, my Emma and my Charlie will stay in the bungalow. Ronnie will keep going to work as usual. Jackson will have his truck here in case anyone needs a ride. I've phoned Mary and Rebecca, and Margie phoned Shirley. Matthew is tracking Donny down. I talked to Delbert last night."

Gert Bigney hobbled into the kitchen.

"Sit here, Mom." Kate continued to dole out instructions. "Mom wants her bed moved downstairs to the parlour, so you boys should do that today."

"They say you get quite sick with this chemotherapy business." Gert spoke matter-of-factly. "There'll be no running up and down those stairs tending to me, I'll tell you that. Especially for you girls now." Margie and Rosie were both pregnant again.

Jackson glanced up through the hair dangling over his forehead, sneaked a peek at his mother. It was a shock to see her so old and tired. When had she begun to look like that? He couldn't have guessed. It had been years since he had really looked at her. His brothers and sisters and in-laws, all their kids, looked strange to him. Like people he passed on the street. Strangers. His mother could have been a neighbour. He knew it was wrong. He should put his hands on his mother's shoulders like Matthew did. He should do something useful like Kate or say something nice or at least sniffle into a Kleenex, but instead he stubbed out his cigarette and skulked back to his cabin for a drink.

The first treatment happened as Kate had decreed. And Gert suffered as predicted. When she wasn't in bed, she sat more than she stood and almost never ventured as far as her garden. School let out and the place swarmed with kids. Week after week Gert was sent home from the hospital with failed blood tests. Faces grew grave. Jackson finished carving his second onion and started his third. Gert's blood cell counts struggled upwards to the point where the doctor agreed to a second chemo treatment in late July. Determined optimism deteriorated into icy doggedness. Jackson finished his third onion, then lost heart and hid the project away in his sewing stand drawer. August bumped into September, which bled into October. The blood tests got worse.

When the hospital sent Gert home with the morphine pain pump, Kate called them all to the farmhouse again. She doled out more orders, then added, "Delbert phoned yesterday to say he and Darlene and the four kids are coming home to help out. I said we had enough help and didn't need more kids running up and down and in and out, but they're coming anyway."

Tom jumped to his feet. "Not here, they aren't! He better not expect any of his kids to sleep in *my* room."

The day Delbert and Darlene and their four kids were due to arrive, they didn't show up. The following evening, well after dark, they wheezed into the farmyard, their sagging station wagon weighed down with a laden roof rack. Jackson, just back from the village after buying groceries for Kate, paused on the farmhouse porch and watched them all emerge from the car. Kate met them at the door.

"Mom's sleeping," she told them. "Go have supper at Rosie and Matthew's. You can unpack later." She pointed them across the road. "You go, too," she said to Jackson, then muttered loud enough for him to hear, "Probably hasn't had a decent meal all week."

Everyone squeezed through Rosie's kitchen and into the cube of a living room.

"Delbert, my man," Matthew slapped his brother on the back. "How's things in Saint John?"

"Oh my, the trouble we had!" Darlene collapsed onto Matthew and Rosie's couch while her kids swirled around her.

"Mom, I gotta go."

"Me too. I gotta go real bad."

"I'm hungry."

"We gonna sleep here?"

By the time Jackson adjusted his ears to the noise level, Darlene was well into the story of the trip.

"So then we had it towed to Moncton, and we got stuck at this garage with this Frenchie trying to sell us who-knows-what. They always pretend they don't speak English so they can rob you blind 'cause they hate anybody English. So Delbert just told him right off — said he wasn't dealing with any frigging frog, and they better get someone who could make some sense. Then this other guy . . ."

Margie had seen them drive in and waddled over to help Rosie prepare food for everyone. Jackson heard her asking Rosie why Delbert and Darlene had so much stuff and how the two oldest kids could miss so much school.

". . . so Delbert told him we're not paying for a brand new alternator and that's it, so they can just get on the phone and find us a used one . . ."

Jackson eyed his oldest brother.

"God, I can't wait to get these kids to bed."

Tom stormed into Jackson's cabin, kicked over a chair, then righted it, slamming it hard back into its spot.

"He's got his kids moved into my room, for chrissake! Him and the wife are set up in Mom's room. Go sleep in the closet like you used to, he says. I'm twenty-one years old, man. I'm not sleeping in the fucking closet!" Jackson watched his little brother sitting there with his head in his hands, near tears, and he felt nothing. Jackson picked a loonie off the table and filled Tom's glass. "Sleep downstairs on the couch, he says to me. But I can't. Mom . . . talks. She says stuff at night. She's *not* going to die."

"I'll stay with her." Jackson shrugged. "You sleep here." His brother nodded but didn't seem much happier.

"The parlour" was a very fancy name for the downstairs room where Gert Bigney's bed had been set up. The ivy on the wallpaper had turned yellow around the edges, as if the plants themselves were shrivelling with age. Jackson sat on the arm of the couch, his elbows on his knees, his sock feet on the cushions, staring out the window. It was quiet here in the old farmhouse in the middle of the night. The moon shone, nearly full and bright enough to light the edges of the clouds moving across the sky. Jackson felt eerily free-floating — away from his cabin, sitting in his childhood home with his mother breathing quietly in the silver dusk several feet away.

He had thought she was asleep, that he had slipped in without disturbing her, but after a while she began to speak. Her voice sounded odd in the dead quiet, ethereal, the way something will look completely different if you pull it out of one background and set it against a different one. Maybe that was true for sounds, too, for voices or music. Maybe this was her true voice, and he didn't recognize it in the silence. At first Jackson assumed she was just talking, but gradually he realized she was talking to him. He didn't know why, but she was.

"You wouldn't remember Maggie Hopewell, of course. You were a babe when she left. Just two years she lived here, out on the paved road in that big yellow house by the corner, but I felt like I'd known her all my life. She'd come by here just to help out. Whatever I was doing, laundry, gardening, cooking, anything. She said she got bored in that big old house all by herself. The kids all loved her.

"I remember one afternoon, it was hot as Hades. It was July because I was eight months gone with you and big as an old sow. I remember I was trying to get those twins trained and out of diapers before you came along. I'd been putting up peas, and I'd just finished and was thinking I should soon be starting on the dinner, when there came Maggie driving into the lane. She walked right into the kitchen with a brown paper bag full of orange Popsicles. Come on, Gert, she says to me, it's time for your summer vacation. I remember her handing out those Popsicles to the youngsters like they were the luckiest kids in the world, sitting them out on the porch like a line of crows. Then Maggie unrolled a blanket under the oak tree, and we sat there in the front yard with our legs stuck out in front of us. I could have been the Queen, lying back there with the weight off my feet, a nice breeze chasing the heat out of my skin, Maggie chattering away beside me. Maggie pulled her hair back in the summer weather and tied it up. I thought it looked lovely, showed off her face so nice."

Gert trailed off then, and Jackson climbed down from the couch's armrest, unfolded the blanket lying there and stretched out on the cushions, staring up into the dark. Before he could drop off to sleep she started up again.

"Now Gert, Maggie says to me. There wasn't a quarter of what she said was anything but pure nonsense. She'd come up with all sorts of crazy notions. She'd make you laugh, though. I'm reading this book, she says, all about the Scots and the Irish and where they came from and all. Now it turns out the 'Mac' part of all those names means 'son of.' And the other part, well, tells you who your ancestor was. Like MacDonald means the son of Donald. Now, you were a MacShay, weren't you? So, 'son of Shay,' I don't know who that would be. Could be short for Seamus, I suppose. Which is James. Like Jack, y'know. So your name would be Jackson. Translated from the old Gaelic, I mean. Gertrude

Jackson. She laughed at that. When Maggie laughed it made me think of kids turning somersaults in the grass. I thought the name was handsome. Awfully handsome."

Jackson felt something shift inside him. He lay motionless. Although he never asked, he imagined he was named for the Johnny Cash song, "I'm Goin' to Jackson." He imagined it came on the radio when they were filling in the forms. It was handy. It would do.

"The night before you were born I had a dream. I'll never forget it. It was so beautiful. Me and Maggie were strolling along a beach like they do on TV commercials, fluttery skirts like nightdresses flying in the wind, flowing hair, the sand hugging our bare toes. I don't know where the kids were, but I remember I wasn't worried about them, and I remember my waist, so tiny, like a girl's. And there we were, Maggie and me, dancing on the beach, free and easy and nothing to do but call our names into the wind and listen to them float over the sea. Ger-trude, Mag-gie . . . we started to laugh, and I called out Jack-son. I turned around and didn't see her, but that's because she was kneeling in the sand, kneeling in the sunshine, holding my hand and smiling up at me, and my name came floating back over us from the sea — Jack-son. Then I was pregnant again in the dream, and Maggie put her hands on my belly, feeling you move, and she rested her head on my belly and kissed me, kissed you. Her lips, I remember, were so soft. Her hands . . ." She paused. Jackson thought she might have said all she was going to. Then she added, "I wanted you to be a boy so I could give you that name. That bit of peace."

Jackson stared across the dark to where he knew his mother lay. A black fear rose up inside him and sat in his throat. He pulled his blanket around him, curled into the couch. No. He didn't want the name, didn't want the gift. The expectations nearly choked him. You know what I'm like, he thought, his cheeks hot with embarrassment, so leave me alone.

In the morning Jackson woke to the crying of a baby and the stomping of feet above his head. He made a pot of tea and brought it in to his mother. Then he picked up his just-emptied

Keith's bottle. He had brought the beer down with him the night before. He wouldn't have been able to sleep without knowing it was there waiting for him.

Delbert's booming voice tumbled down the stairs. "You'll shut your trap or I'll shut it for ya!"

His mother stared at the bottle. "You're the spitting image of your father," she said with a reassuringly familiar edge to her voice. Daylight brought everything back to normal. "Drink, drink, drink. Bootlegging, for heaven's sake. I don't know. I don't understand it. I'm glad I won't be around to see you drink yourself to death. Like your father."

This was nothing he hadn't heard a hundred times. It led into complaints about his brother, Donny's troubles with the law. Did they want to break her heart? People probably thought her kids were never taught right from wrong. But they were. You bet they were. Jackson left the tea and drifted back to his cabin.

With Delbert there, Jackson knew he would no longer be required for errands at the farmhouse. Traffic through his cabin intensified. It was impossible not to overhear developments. Donny arrived home that morning, fought with Delbert and left. Matthew dropped in with rumours of Shirley's arrival and specu-lations about Mary and Rebecca. Jackson put down another batch of beer.

Jackson waited in his cabin until very late at night. He could hear Tom snoring quietly in his bed before he tucked his morning beer into his jacket pocket and crossed the meadow to the farmhouse. He padded through the house in his grey and white work socks and stretched out on the parlour couch with the extra blanket again. When his mother spoke, her voice carried the same floating quality, the same searching, wandering cadence it had the night before.

"Maggie left when you were a baby," she said. "I couldn't believe she'd only been my neighbour for two years. I couldn't see how I'd get on without her. She said we'd have to have a night on the town, a lobster dinner in a decent restaurant, she said. I didn't want to go at first, but Maggie said I had to. Said she couldn't leave unless we had a proper goodbye. That's what she called it. I said

I'd just feel silly, and Vernon wouldn't allow it, and I couldn't leave you kids, and it was a foolish waste of money, and I'd nothing to wear anyway. But she wouldn't hear no, so in the end off we went. Two girls alone together in a car. My goodness. Out to dinner. And, oh my, it was so fancy! Candles, white tablecloths, sparkling glasses with long handles, everybody smiling at you. Would you like this, can I help you with that, everybody so nice. And the lobster! I swear even it looked happy to be there. They cut it open for you and laid it all out in a great big smile there on your plate. With lettuce all around and bits of tomato, everything just so. Maggie paid for the whole thing. Wouldn't take a nickel.

"She left for somewhere in Ontario. I don't know where. Her husband got a better job. That's why she had to go. I never told anyone this, but I cried. Just like a little youngster. Every time I went to the outhouse I'd cry while I had the chance. I remember having you in there with me, sitting, holding you and crying for her. I cried more then than I ever did for your father. That's a sin, I know, but it's the truth.

"You were always so quiet, even as a baby. Quiet and sad. Like you were full of secrets. Mine, yours, Maggie's, everybody's secrets. Sometimes I thought I made you like that. It's not natural for a child to see his mother cry."

Jackson wanted to say it wasn't her fault. He wanted to apologize, to say he wished the child she carried had been better, not such a disappointment. He was glad she couldn't see him in the dark. He wished she had had a better life. He wanted to ask her something, but he didn't know what. I'm sorry, he wanted to say. The night silence closed in around them, and soon he heard her breathing slip into the steady pattern of sleep. And he hadn't said anything at all.

The next day Mary and her husband and two children flew in to Halifax, rented a car and arrived at the farmhouse with armloads of hothouse flowers. Matthew said they had booked a suite of rooms in a New Glasgow hotel for a week. Matthew also had details about how obnoxious Darlene's kids were and how Kate seemed to think God had made her the boss in His absence. Tom said Kate could shove a pickle up her arse, and Delbert could shove the whole friggin' bottle and he'd volunteer to help push it up. Jackson left his cabin only to buy tobacco and, since he was there, a licorice pipe.

At night Jackson returned to the farmhouse and stood by the parlour window, watching the moon, smoking a cigarette, his back to his mother.

"Vernon," his mother said softly. Jackson stood still. "Vernon." He turned towards her, revealing the bushy beard that hid the resemblance.

"Oh Jackson. I thought you were your father. In the moonlight like that. For a moment I couldn't remember if I was dead and we were both in heaven, or if I was young and he was still alive. My goodness." She closed her eyes again and lay still.

"Vernon Bigney. He'd get up to anything. You never knew what he might come out with. It's funny, you'd think I would have thought about your father more. When he died I expected the earth to open and everything to get swallowed up. But the only thing that got swallowed up was him. I suppose I missed him. But I'm not sure I really need to see him again. I know that's a sin. Together in heaven forever, they say. We were together thirty years on earth. That was long enough."

And I'm the spitting image, Jackson added to himself. His throat filled with phlegm.

"It drove your father mad that you wouldn't speak up. He thought he could make you talk, but all he could do was make you stubborn. And you'd fade away to nothing, right in front of his eyes, like you just walked out of your body, left him standing there yelling at a scarecrow."

Jackson felt as if he had swallowed a fist. He thought he had finished feeling like this. He thought the emptiness had pushed it all aside. He didn't want to hear about his father. He wished she hadn't laid this silence at his feet.

"Why did he hate me?" Jackson felt his cheeks flame scarlet in the dark at the boldness of his question.

"He didn't." She went on as calmly as she had before. "You

scared him, I think. So he scared you right back. He didn't know any other way. He hid things, too, just like you did. Just like you hid all those beautiful drawings you made as a little boy. When I found them crumpled at the bottom of your school bag, you said it wasn't you who drew them. They weren't yours. Beautiful pictures in coloured markers and crayon, hidden under your mattress. Your little school papers, all As and Bs, sneaked into the stove before anyone could see the good in you. Tiny carvings hidden at the back of your drawer. Never let anyone near. Such a gift. But you treated it like a curse, a shame. You kept making things, though. So much beauty in you it had to get out. But you'd burn them if you thought anyone had seen them. Never gave me even one. I never understood that. Sometimes I think it must have been my crying that made you so afraid of beautiful things."

The night silence enveloped him so profoundly he touched his own cheek to make sure he was still there. "I . . . I'll give you one," he finally managed.

"Good."

Kate was already in the farmhouse kitchen by the time Jackson woke and straggled out for his mother's tea. She stood there talking to his sister Shirley. He had heard Shirley had arrived from somewhere far away, but he had forgotten.

"Mom needs someone with her all the time," Kate said. "I'm going to start spending the night in her room."

Jackson, sitting there waiting for the water to boil, wondered if she even knew that he had been sleeping there. That that was *his* place. A deep sadness stirred in him. Not the flat, hollow sadness that lived inside him every day, but one jagged with teeth, with currents of anger shot through it, one with a source somewhere far beyond him.

"I sleep in Mom's room at night," he said.

Kate glanced over in surprise. She and Shirley exchanged a look. "Well, she might need help now," Kate said flatly. "So you go back to your cabin."

Jackson frowned. He lit a smoke, shifted in his seat, stared up through his unruly bangs at his sister's back, watching her shoulders dip and sway as she kneaded the mammoth mound of bread dough on the counter. He didn't know what to do. He had never wanted anything badly enough to fight for it.

"*I'm* staying with her at night," he blurted out.

She didn't respond for so long that Jackson wondered if he had said the words out loud or just in his head. Then she stopped kneading, hung her head and leaned heavily on the counter on strong, straight arms. She turned to stare out the window. For a moment Jackson thought she might cry, but she folded her arms across her chest and sighed deeply. "I don't need this right now, Jackson," she said.

Their mother called out from the parlour. Kate ran to her, rubbing bits of bread dough off her fingers with her apron.

After the nurse's visit that afternoon, Kate declared their mother would be going into the hospital. Her voice sagged with defeat. The kitchen shuffled into life as people began packing clothes and food, finding things and putting them away, arranging for drives, straightening things, shaking out coats. People preparing for something, anything. Except the inevitable. Jackson went back to his cabin to carve the tiny central onion for the heart of his set.

Gertrude Bigney lived two more weeks in the hospital, where she was intermittently conscious. Then she died, and the family buried her in the cemetery in Scotch River beside her husband. Jackson layered his wooden onions inside each other, sealed them all, and hid them in his mother's casket. It was November fifteenth. She was fifty-nine. All ten of her children made it to the funeral, six with spouses, her four oldest grandchildren, three of her sisters and two brothers, Vernon's sister and her two daughters, and several neighbours. Jackson identified each face. No mysterious strangers. No one left over at the end to be Maggie.

People heard of her death. No one came by the cabin to buy bootleg liquor. All night long Jackson dozed and woke. He lay in the darkness trying to understand what it would be like to be dead. He often did this — had for years. He lay very still, slowed his breathing and imagined the emptiness inside him evaporating. He grew numb, chilled, remote. It scared him this time. Death looked clearer, cleaner from far away than it did up close. It was bigger than he had supposed, more powerful, insidious. He rolled out of his blankets, dressed, slipped out of his cabin and escaped down the road in his truck.

He drove slowly out on the road along the ocean's edge. In the faint grey light before dawn Prince Edward Island lay barely visible across the choppy expanse of the Northumberland Strait. Just beyond Scotch River he turned down to the water. The beach stretched out, eerily empty, dream-like. Jackson parked his truck and peeled off his boots and socks, rolled his jeans halfway up his calves and walked out onto the strip of freezing sand. He hugged himself warm inside his green-and-black-checked jacket. The sand, rigid with cold, grated against the soles of his naked feet. So cold. He concentrated on the sharpness of it. He concentrated on the restrained pinkish-yellow glow that seeped across the sky as dawn broke, the first cries of waking birds, the moist salt on his lips, the whitecaps flinging themselves onto the shore, spraying over the pebbles, embracing the sand, sliding back into the ocean. When his soles began to numb, to accept the cold, he walked to the edge of the beach where the sand rested in sodden ripples. A wave rolled up and broke around his legs, enveloping his bare flesh. He gasped, winced from the cold, but held his ground. The next wave rolled in, forcing tears of pain from his eyes. He backed out of the surf, backed over beach rock and sand, beyond the shifting line where wave water bubbled into creamy froth and disappeared. He hunched down on the spray-dampened sand and wrapped his arms around his legs, pressing the warmth of his hands hard into his numb feet. He fixed his mind on the warmth, felt it penetrate his skin, followed its progress deep into him. He rested his cheek against his knee and wept.

The day after the funeral Delbert announced that he and his family wouldn't be returning to Saint John but would be living in the farmhouse from now on. It turned out he had just declared personal bankruptcy and needed a place to start fresh. Tom put his fist through the farmhouse wall. Delbert's voice sounded like their father's when he yelled, Jackson noted.

"Who do you think you are, waltzing into Mom's kitchen like you own it?" That was Margie. Rebecca sat on the porch weeping, and Kate declared she had had enough, walked up the road to her bungalow and locked herself in. Donny and Shirley screamed at each other for hours. Their mother used to hate to see the twins fighting, and the sound of it would always bring her running. She had been silly about the twins, superstitious. Like it was some kind of sin when they fought.

Jackson sat on the bench in front of his cabin in the cold, smoking and listening to their voices rising from the world behind his back. We're all orphans, he thought. They can act up all they want. She's not coming back to calm things down, put things right.

"You've got your fucking nerve, man!" That was Tom.

"You've been sitting around here for years on your ass. Why don't you look after yourself? When I was your age I had . . ."

Matthew's voice cut in over Delbert's. "How'd you like your head split open, ya dumb fuck!"

Jackson didn't bother getting up to look, but he was fairly certain Matthew was wielding some metal tool in the air. Next he would hear the women intervening or he would hear the crack of bone.

We'll all drown in this, Jackson thought. They'll drown each other down there — he chugged several more swigs of shine — and I'll drown myself up here.

The ruckus carried on for two more days until Kate emerged from her bungalow and began straightening up. No one had the energy to resist. All ten kids were to choose something from the farmhouse, but although Jackson walked through every room in the house twice, staring at every individual thing, he left empty-handed. Kate collected all their mother's personal things, all her dishes and cake pans and baked Plasticine ashtrays and plastic flowers and pictures off the wall, and she and Margie divided them amongst the five girls. They passed a few useful things on to Rosie as well.

Kate arranged for Tom to follow Mary to Hamilton. Mary's husband would be able to get him into some kind of casual work at least, and he could stay in the extra room in their basement.

"You'll have opportunity," Kate told him.

In Jackson's cabin Matthew bought Tom a pitcher of beer and hooked his arm over Tom's shoulder in a half headlock, half hug. "Ontario. That's where the money is. Give it a try, buddy. If it don't work out, you can always come home, stay with Rosie and me and the boys, eh?"

That week, Tom boarded the bus for Hamilton, Rosie gave birth to her fourth son, and Margie had her fourth daughter. It began to snow. And snow. And snow.

CHAPTER SIX

THE FIRST WEEKEND OF MAY the sun came out strong and hot and full of bravado. After the coldest, dirtiest winter in twenty years, celebrations spilled over from Saturday into Sunday. Jackson's business hopped. Customers laughed and shouted, hilarity bouncing off hysteria.

Harold Sutherland's old Impala rolled up to the cabin and disgorged its passengers: Harold, two of his regular drinking buddies and his twenty-two-year-old son, Ian. They milled in the sunshine before ducking into the dim cabin, greeting the crowd and calling out for drinks. Revellers came and went. Harold kept standing up and swaying over the crowd, ringing out like the town crier that his boy, Ian, had just graduated from St. Mary's University in Halifax.

"Not stupid like his old man," he crowed, laughing himself into a wheezing fit. "And he plays the fiddle, too. Like an angel!" Everyone knew this because when Ian was a boy he used to play every year in the Scotch River fiddling contest. Won it, in fact, several years running. "Play the folks a tune, Ian."

Ian rolled his eyes and carried his beer out into the sunshine and sat on the bench outside the door.

Jackson drew pitchers of homebrew from his kegs, sauntered off to fetch bottles from the firewood pile in the woodshed, the tank of the toilet he never got around to hooking up, the planks on the rafters. He shoved twenty-dollar bills into his pocket, added to and subtracted from personal tabs. In the first brief lull he stepped out to join the cats in the sunshine. He settled himself and his beer onto the vacant end of his bench. He folded his hands over his crossed legs and sat quietly, looking away, preoccupied.

Beside him, Ian said, "Hi. You're Jackson, right? I went to school with your brother, Tom, for a few years."

Normally Jackson didn't speak. No one expected him to. But today that coating of tin he carried inside his ribcage seemed thinner than usual. Lighter. Not suddenly, but as if it had eroded gradually over the winter and he only noticed it now in the brilliance of daylight. He felt reckless.

"Hi," Jackson said.

Ian smiled, slightly drunk. "This is my Dad's idea of throwing me a graduation party." Winter pallor made Ian's long, angular face almost glow in the sunshine. His nose and cheekbones stood out a little sharply, not softened by his straight brown hair. "Yeah, Dad's a real party animal."

Ian looked around. "Sorry to hear about your mom . . . still fairly young and everything." His eyes, even a bit glassy from drink, offered a pale, flannel-grey comfort. Jackson shifted on the bench. None of his customers had mentioned her since a week after the funeral.

"I bet you miss her."

Jackson felt a wrinkle of vulnerability under his ribs, then a ripping yank, like tearing off a Band-Aid. He hoped he hadn't gasped. He glanced at Ian. No reaction. Safe. He nodded. He stretched out his legs, felt the sun's heat soak through the denim to his skin, radiate through his body. "She loved the sun," he said. The strength of his voice surprised him.

Ian smiled a little in response and bobbed his head. He pulled a pack of Player's out of his breast pocket and offered one to Jackson. "That's good," he said. Jackson felt he meant it. That's good that your mother loved something. That's good that you miss her. That's good.

"I remember when my mom had to have surgery that time, and chemo after . . . I was shit-baked. We all were. She was lucky, though."

They were silent for a minute, then Ian began again. "It's really weird being here, in Scotch River. I've hardly been back, only for Christmases really, since I moved to Halifax. But I'm totally stinking flat-out broke. I got no choice. I'm looking for a job. Christ. Stuff doesn't change that much around here, does it? Everything goes on exactly the same. When I was little my dad used to drink with your dad. Now he drinks with you."

He drinks *at my cabin*, Jackson corrected in his head.

"I wish I could've stayed in Halifax. At least there's stuff going on and I have friends and that, eh? I'm glad exams are done forever, though. I get so up-tight, like I'll fail and everybody will find out I'm really dumb after all. You ever get those dreams where suddenly you look down and discover you're naked?" Ian snorted. "Then you wake up and you're way more scared than you were in the dream."

Jackson felt a tingle at the base of his skull.

"Oh, jeez. Sorry. I don't usually talk so much. I guess I'm a little drunk." Jackson looked up. Ian's face flushed slightly, his smile sheepish. Ian's eyes pulled Jackson's into them. A couple of seconds passed before Jackson could tug his gaze away. He tried not to panic.

"N-no," said Jackson. "Tha-that's okay. That's good." He wanted him to keep talking, all afternoon and all night. He wanted to say something to make him come back here to this bench, again and again. But Harold Sutherland and all his crowd were standing there in front of them, and they were piling up a stack of bills and shouting out orders.

"A case of Keith's to go, there, Jackson."

"No, two!"

"Okay, that's two cases of Keith's and one of Oland's."

Jackson had to get the beer, load it into the trunk of the car. He saw the back of Ian's head disappear into the back seat, then glimpsed his face through the car window. "I'll come by." Is that what Ian said through the glass? The car drove off. Jackson found he had followed it ten feet down the lane. Is that what Ian had said to him? I'll come by?

Jackson had the rest of that Sunday and Sunday night and then Monday and Monday night to put everything back to normal. The sweat at the back of his neck and his armpits was from the heat, though the temperature was really only fourteen degrees. The headache was from something funny in the wine, though he had made it himself, the same as always. That constricted feeling that made it hard to breathe was indigestion. The tremor in his grip every time he heard a car engine was the DTs. The ideas — the ideas were just foolishness. Why would Ian want to come by here?

Late Tuesday morning, while Jackson was refilling his empty kegs, Ian Sutherland knocked and walked through his door. He carried his fiddle case in his left hand.

Jackson hadn't even thought of what he would do. "You came," he said.

Ian smiled. "They drive me crazy over at home. I hear your beer's cheap."

Jackson drew him a glass and drew one for himself as well.

"You ever have trouble with the Mounties coming by?" Ian asked when they had settled themselves around the table between the empties and the hubcap ashtray and the odd puddle of beer spill.

Jackson swirled his homebrew around in his mug. "Mostly they buy at the liquor store," he said. Ian's laugh made Jackson think of a bucket of rubber balls being tossed into a room. It bounced off the walls, free, chaotic, uninhibited.

"I practically had to prostrate myself to get a couple of bucks out of the old man this morning," Ian said.

Jackson had no trouble at all listening to Ian's voice. Ian didn't talk very long, though. He was hardly there ten minutes when Old Angus MacCarron's Dodge truck, parts practically shaking off it, rattled over the back culvert and humped up the lane.

Old Angus thumped in on his cane and lowered himself down at the table. He peered at Ian, rapped the crook of his cane against the table top. "Who are you, now? One of Harold Sutherland's, I'd say, to look at ya. Ha-ha-ha. What'll I have now? A nice neat bit of rum, that's what. A pint of beer and a neat mick of rum to carry home. And look here," he poked the fiddle case with the butt of his cane. "What's this now? A fiddle, b'y. A fiddle, I'd say. Ha-ha." He slashed his cane through the air like Zorro, then pointed it directly into Ian's face. "You're the one that plays. Harold Sutherland's fiddling lad. We'll have a tune, so we will. Give us a tune. Ha-ha-ha."

"Go on," Jackson whispered. "I'll give you a beer."

So while Jackson set a glass of ale in front of the old man Ian hauled out the fiddle and played "Tickle Cove Pond." Jackson disappeared to fetch the rum. When Ian started in on "St. Anne's Reel," Old Angus pulled himself to his feet and managed a dozen dance steps before he settled down to banging his cane on the floorboards to keep time.

"Ha-ha-ha. That's the spirit. 'St. Anne's Reel.' That's the spirit." He pulled a wad out of his jacket pocket and peeled off a stack of one-dollar bills whose design declared them to be at least twenty years old. Then he tucked his rum flask into the pocket beside the remaining money, downed the rest of his beer and clumped across the floor to the door. "I knew an Anne once, but she weren't no saint. Ha-ha-ha. Good for a reel or two, though. Ha-ha."

Jackson and Ian watched from the cabin door as Angus hobbled back to the cab of his truck.

"Christ," Ian whispered.

"You should have seen him last fall. He broke his hip and needed a walker. Tossed it into the back of the pickup — took it everywhere."

The truck sputtered, coughed, then roared and rolled off, clanking and shuddering out to the MacIntyre Road. Ian raised his fiddle to his chin and, smirking, played a few bars of the *Beverly Hillbillies* theme.

As Old Angus disappeared down the back way, Matthew barrelled up from the farmhouse in the souped-up go-cart he was working on. He had welded up a little wagon to hitch behind it, and in it, screeching with delight, sat his four-year-old son and Margie's two preschool daughters.

"Hey-hey!"

The kids raced indoors to the shelf where Jackson usually stored a large bottle of Coke.

"Thirsty work, this babysitting." He punched Ian on the shoulder. "How's Mr. Sutherland?"

They followed him into the cabin, where Matthew doled out Coke to the kids and Jackson poured the beer. Once Margie's Annie had secured her ration, she planted herself in front of Ian.

"Play the fiddle," she demanded.

Ian played "London Bridge" and then tumbled directly into "The Devil Went Down to Georgia." Everyone laughed. The kids begged him to go on. Half an hour later Margie showed up, baby on her hip, looking for her girls. She frowned but sat down for a tune or two. She didn't ban her children from Jackson's cabin like Kate did, but she didn't approve — it only encouraged her husband to waste his time here. Two of Matthew's friends showed up looking for a car battery but shifted their focus to homebrew when they found the party.

Ian just kept playing. "Hey, you guys know this one? 'Great Big Sea.'"

Jackson sat in his corner trying to remember if he had ever spoken to Ian when they were growing up. He could remember Ian's sister from school, but Ian was seven or eight years younger — he had been a little kid.

Down on MacIntyre Road the school bus dropped its load of youngsters and turned around. Soon the cabin was overrun. Two of the "regulars," Rolly and Frank, stopped in for a beer and stayed for three or four. Rosie arrived and asked Ian and Jackson to her place for supper.

Ian dropped by the cabin every two or three days. He would peddle over the back way on his mountain bike with the fiddle strapped to his back. People began cocking their ears, listening, peering up the road for signs of him. Kids would keep an eye out for the bike leaning up against Jackson's cabin. Most days ten or fifteen minutes could elapse before Ian's presence was discovered. Much more than the increase in his business or the music, Jackson loved those private intervals when he could sit and listen to Ian's voice wafting across the table. Whenever Jackson looked up Ian's eyes were always waiting for him, asking for something or offering it. He couldn't tell. He found himself wondering all the time when Ian would arrive. His heart would quicken when Ian appeared in the doorway.

"Hey, Jackson," Ian would say, as if they were old friends. Then he would draw up to the table and in a confidential tone he would report his troubles with his father, his frustrations over looking for work, his desperate financial straits. Or he would reminisce about his life in Halifax. If Ian had managed to scrape together enough money for a pack of Player's, they would sit together and smoke them. If not, they would smoke Jackson's home-rolled cigarettes. Jackson kept their glasses full and rolled a toke from time to time.

Jackson loved the way Ian spoke to him, all sad and serious, but as soon as anyone else showed up he would laugh and play the fiddle and pretend to be happy. Jackson felt chosen. Chosen to share a secret. This knowledge straightened his shoulders.

"You got a girlfriend?" Ian asked him one afternoon.

Ian had never mentioned girls before. Jackson stood up and headed for his keg even though his glass was still two-thirds full. He stood at the tap as long as possible with his back to Ian.

"No," he said.

The next question hung all around them, thick and stringy, clinging to every movement, every breath, like years of spider webs, like old nets drooping from a boat shed's rafters. His brain wouldn't allow him to put the words in order. Stop! it kept shouting. And deep in his ribcage something hot and sharp stabbed at the emptiness.

Ian said nothing more.

That night Jackson had to get up, as he often did, to tend to a rowdy crowd tumbling through his door. This time it was the Everett brothers who were out on a tear. He poured them a round of ale and sat in his corner while they argued about the price that could be placed on their lobster fishing license if they ever wanted to sell, which they didn't. They drank three rounds, then Jackson sold them a bottle of shine. After they had gone he returned to his cot, where he sat with his knees drawn up to his chest and his head resting on his arms. Alone in his room he thought easily of Ian, but in that unreal, detached way he thought of the men he picked out from the videos he sometimes watched at Matthew's house; Tom Cruise and Brad Pitt were obvious choices, but also Robin Williams, Grizzly Adams, the Indian chief from *Dances with Wolves*, the Kris Kringle from that kids' movie. Guy Nelson or Mel Gibson — they were equally unreal to him. Bodies without flesh. Nothing he thought about in that room had anything to do with the world outside it. A person can think anything at all. No one knows. It makes no difference. He got up and strolled back to the main room. The overhead light shone far too brightly, so he lit his old kerosene lamp and set it on the table.

He leaned on the back of the chair where Ian always sat. He floated back to his bed, picked up his pillow and hugged it to his chest, carried it out to the chair, where he sat rocking for a moment. He wandered back and forth between the dark cocoon of his bedroom and the glow of the lamp on the table. Finally he stopped halfway and lowered himself to the floor in the bedroom doorway, still clutching his pillow. He leaned against the jam, one leg in each room and closed his eyes.

Several hours later he woke in the darkness, his neck stiff and his back aching. His lamp had burned dry and fizzled.

Ian arrived at noon, grey-looking and agitated. He didn't sit down. He lit two cigarettes and passed one over to Jackson.

"Get out a bottle, Jackson. I'll need something stronger than beer today." While Ian paced around the room Jackson retreated to the bathroom for the rum, then reappeared with the bottle. He stood quietly, scratching at the label with his fingernail and sneaking glances at Ian.

"I've got to find a job. I can't hack it much longer at home. They're all so . . ." Ian bounced the toe of his boot against the base of the wall in an angry rhythm; one, two, three, four. "Christ! It's such a fucking *farce*!" Jackson stared at Captain Morgan's over-tall leather boots. Every sound that Ian made filled the cabin. Every kick exploded in Jackson's ear. Blam, blam, blam. Bop. Nothing. Bop. The kicking petered out, finally punctuated by a heavy sigh and silence. Then Ian's footfall of the floorboards several feet away, two feet, one foot away. Could he hear Ian's breathing?

"Look . . ." Ian's voice melted into a soft peppermint tobacco cloud, teasing Jackson's nostrils. Jackson flushed at the heat of him standing there, beside him, the hot dust of MacIntyre Road in his pores.

"I'm sorry," Ian continued. "I'm . . ."

Their thighs, through two layers of denim, touched. Jackson didn't move away. He wanted to look up, find in Ian's eyes everything he had imagined. But fear paralysed him. Then Ian raised his arm and wrapped his hand around the bottle, enveloping Jackson's fingers. Neither moved.

Either one of us could step back right now, Jackson thought, and nothing will be said. Nothing will have happened.

The pressure on his thigh increased. He felt his body leaning into Ian's.

Ian whispered something so low Jackson couldn't make it out, although Ian's lips practically brushed his ear, disturbed the hairs of his beard, making his entire body quiver. Then, the gentle pressure of a hand hot on the base of his neck. When he lifted his head Ian's lips covered his and there was nothing he could do but stand there concentrating on the bottle, suddenly leaden and slippery in his grip, Ian's hand firm over his.

Ian set the rum bottle on the table and their bodies pressed into each other as though all along the bottle had been the only thing keeping them apart.

Then Ian jerked his head up, pulled them back against the wall of the cabin. "The window," he mumbled. They kissed again, deeply this time. Jackson felt a tongue strong and rough against his own, Ian's body pressing against his, Ian's palms, firm on the bare flesh of his back under his T-shirt.

"Hey!" They both froze. Kids' voices.

"Hey, Jackson!" They jumped apart just as the cabin door flew open.

"Hey, Jackson, Mom wants ya!" Matthew's two oldest boys ran across the floor of the cabin. "Mom wants you over to get some dinner, 'cause she's got this big bunch of stew."

"Yeah," the older boy lowered his voice to imitate his father, "a big frigging vat of bone-boil." Both boys laughed.

"Git down there or she's coming over to drag ya back. That's what she said!"

Jackson and Ian exchanged looks. "I'll be over in a while." Jackson hoped he wasn't shaking, hoped his arousal wasn't obvious. "Go tell her that." He held the door open for the boys to run out again, then to be sure, followed them to the corner of the cabin and watched them run back down towards the farmhouse. Behind him, the tin-pan clanging of Old Angus MacCarron's truck rose in a crescendo. No, he prayed, please don't let it be him. But it made no difference what he prayed, the truck rattled towards him.

By the time Old Angus heaved himself through the cabin door, Jackson and Ian were settled at opposite sides of the table with cigarettes lit and half-full glasses of brew in front of them.

"Ha-ha-ha. That's the lad with the tunes. Dancing time. Ha-ha. A grand tune'll keep you young. That's the truth. Come on now, lads!" He stomped his cane on the floor.

Ian winked at Jackson and hauled out the fiddle.

"Sure, Angus. How about 'My Bonny Laddie'? You know that one?" The cabin filled, swelled, overflowed with lament. Jackson had to turn away.

The next day when Jackson drove to Truro to buy beer malt and wine kits and bottle caps, he took Ian with him. They pulled off onto a logging road and jumped out of the truck. Ian's hands clutched Jackson's beard, tugged at his belt. Jackson shook with urgency, overcome by the rush, the clouds of black flies and mosquitoes. Ian knew exactly what to do.

On the way back, Jackson pulled over in a different spot. The bugs were even worse. They stayed in the truck this time, fumbled around the stick shift and bucket seats. That night Jackson lay alone in his bed, a mass of fly bites, feeling his breath, the newness of his body, the memory of skin on skin, a breeding, billowing, marvellous fear bursting through his ribs.

They were afraid to be seen together too much. Ian restricted his visits to the cabin to every two or three days. When he came they stole moments to kiss, to stroke each other's bodies, but mostly they sat amidst the drunken company and the constant flow of kids and family. Everyone swarmed to the cabin. It was such fun when Ian played the fiddle. No one would leave while he was there. His jigs and reels cut through the air at a manic pace. His laments pierced the depths of disappointment and personal tragedy. Jackson pretended there was nothing but the air and the music and him and Ian.

Jackson's ears strained constantly for the click-clunk of a bicycle gear, the sigh of a tire on the path, the knock of handlebars against the shed. It was nearly noon when Jackson jumped to his feet, dropping his carving knife. Ian slipped in the door and they both leaned back against it. They slid their hands inside each others' clothes and kissed.

"I got us a place in Halifax this weekend," Ian whispered. "My friend says his roommate will be out of town. We can use his room."

Jackson nodded and they kissed again. An impatient rattling of the door knob pulled them apart. Jackson braced his shoulder against the door and motioned Ian over to the table. Then he opened the door with a jolt. "It sticks sometimes," he said to Matthew.

Leaving Matthew to look after things at the cabin was like appointing a fox to the chicken marketing board, but Jackson wasn't going to pass up the chance to spend a night in bed with Ian. He had left Matthew in charge before but never on a weekend. In the past ten years he had been away overnight on three occasions. Once he had to drive Kate to Digby to visit their sister Rebecca. They stayed overnight and came back the next day. Once Ronnie asked him to go to Margaree to help build a dock at his parents' cottage. They were gone four days and three nights. Once his mother sent him to North Sydney to meet the ferry from Newfoundland to collect his sister Shirley. Jackson had left after midnight to be there when the boat docked in the morning.

Jackson waited to get Matthew alone.

"You, uh, wanna look after things this weekend? I gotta go, um, visit somebody. I might not get back Saturday night."

"Sure. No sweat. What's up?"

"I . . . well . . . I heard Murdock's been down to the States again. So, y'know, um, he might have something to sell."

Matthew snorted. "Save your gas. You heard wrong. Murdock's in the frigging hospital. Fell off a scaffold two weeks ago." He laughed and took a long draught of his beer. Jackson fidgeted and Matthew's eyes narrowed. "You don't need all night to visit Murdock anyway. What's going on?"

Shit! He had heard about that accident but forgot. "I . . ." He felt his cheeks turn pink beneath his beard. He started to sweat, twisted in his seat, gripped his cigarette so hard it crumpled in two between his fingers. Don't panic, he told himself.

"I might know, I got a chance . . ." He leaned closer to Matthew but kept his eyes averted, dropped his voice even lower. "I saw that weird guy, you know, who lives up the mountain?"

"That guy's a bastard."

"Yeah. Well, he knows these people, in Cape Breton, I, uh, might be able to get some hash. Real cheap."

Bingo! Matthew's eyes lit up.

"Oh yeah?" Then he said, "I thought you wouldn't touch that stuff. I thought you said only home grown. No dealing."

"Yeah, well." Jackson shrugged.

"Awright!"

Jackson got up and left the cabin. He shut himself in his outhouse, where he stood hugging himself and trembling. He could hardly believe he had done it.

In Halifax they had to stop by the hair-stylist shop where Ian's friend worked to pick up the key to the apartment. They didn't have the apartment to themselves, just the bedroom, Ian explained.

"But don't worry about Byron," Ian said. "He's gay, too."

Gay. The word stuck like a bean in Jackson's ear. All the way to the apartment building and up in the elevator it worried at him, then dissolved into thin air when the bedroom door clicked shut and he found himself alone with a double bed and Ian grinning at him.

Jackson could have spent the next thirty-six hours locked behind that door, but Ian had plans. When Ian heard his friend at the apartment door he rolled out of Jackson's arms where he had been resting and started searching for his clothes.

"I'll help with dinner," he said. "Come on and meet Byron." Ian pulled on his jeans and disappeared. Jackson took his time getting up, getting washed and dressed, hoped maybe Ian would come back, but he could hear him yakking away, talking and laughing in the next room. Jackson leaned against the bedroom wall, trying not to feel anything. He chugged one of the beer he had brought with them, but he wished he had a flask.

"Hey, Jackson! What are you doing in there? Come on out here." There was silence for a second, then a low mumble, and Jackson knew Ian had whispered something about him. Jackson stashed the empty beer bottle and opened the bedroom door just wide enough to slink out. Ian patted the cushion beside him on the couch.

"Here he is. Jackson. Not bad, eh? And this is our gracious host and patron, Byron Seymore."

Jackson bobbed his head without looking up. He didn't know what Ian meant by "not bad," and he didn't know how long he was supposed to sit there on the couch staring at his own fingernails. Byron was a faggot. He waved his arms around when he talked, and he rolled his eyes a lot. His stories went on and on and didn't seem to have a point.

"So he's here all afternoon, sniffling into his hanky, going on about how deeply he's been hurt, and I'm patting his shoulder and tut-tutting all over the place. Honest to God, dear, if I'd have draped a dishtowel over my head you wouldn't have known me from Mother Teresa. So then he starts in on how he's tired of the whole shallow scene and how he's been defining his goals vis-à-vis his personal relationships. I swear he used those exact words. That night, *that night*, mind you, he's at the club wriggling his tush all over the place and leaves — wait for it now — with Jory Dean. I mean, puh-*lease*! This guy's cock has attention deficit disorder."

Jackson figured this was some kind of joke because Ian and Byron laughed.

Then Byron folded his hands in his lap and asked, "So how are things out in the wilds?"

"Don't ask," Ian replied. Suddenly Ian shuffled closer on the couch, threw his arm around Jackson's shoulder and began running his fingers through his beard. Jackson's body went rigid, his cheeks burned, his heart pounded. "God," Ian said to Byron, "don't you love this beard. I thought it could stand a trim along here," he said, "and down by the neck. Give it a bit more shape, you know? What do you think, Byron? You're the pro."

"I thought you'd never ask. And there's just time before dinner. What a coincidence."

Jackson didn't know what to do. So he did what Ian said, sat on the stool, suffered the towel clipped around his neck.

Jackson wasn't sure about his "new look." The shorter hair and more sculpted beard gave his face startling definition, a definition that scared him when Ian wasn't by his side. So he stayed by Ian's side. Dinner was impossible. He could never eat when he was nervous, never in front of strangers. He kept pushing his food around the plate, willing it to disappear, chewing and chewing each bite, praying that eventually his stomach would accept it. After dinner, to his immense relief, Ian took him back into the bedroom.

But at ten o'clock Ian jumped up again. They had to get ready to go out.

"Why don't we stay here for the night?"

Ian looked at him funny and tossed him a T-shirt. "Wear this," he said.

The bar was louder and darker than any bar Jackson had ever seen. It wouldn't have been so bad if Ian hadn't kept wandering around — down by the pool tables, over to the dance floor, back to the bar, out to the centre of the floor. Jackson stayed close, afraid he would never find Ian again if he lost sight of him. Ian kept greeting people he knew, hugging them. It was shameful. Then Ian would introduce them, but Jackson couldn't hear their names, and he didn't care who they were. Ian took him by the hand and led him through the crowd. He wanted to draw his hand back, but he was afraid. Jackson knew where they were, what kind of a place this was. They ended up on the dance floor. Ian laughed and motioned for him to dance. Jackson stood there, sick with fear, people jostling all around him. He backed out of the crowd, keeping his eye on Ian, who showed no sign of following. He leaned against the wall, out of the way, where he could watch Ian writhing to the seamless and endless soundtrack. Blinded by the flashing lights, deafened by the pounding music, petrified by the strange world swirling around him, he held himself still, blocking everything out. He focused on Ian and thought of nothing.

The next morning Jackson woke with a splitting headache. He found a bottle of aspirin in the bathroom and washed several down with a beer before returning to bed. When he started to feel better he propped himself on one elbow and watched Ian sleeping beside him, remembering their walk home from the bar, Ian's exuberance, the flash of his teeth in the dark, how their bodies, shaking with anticipation, had electrified each other when they finally melded behind the bedroom door. He wished Ian would wake up. They didn't have much time left. He reached over and held his hand so close to Ian's cheek he felt the heat rising from the skin. He drew his hand back.

Ian woke, groaned, then looked up at him, blinked and grinned.

"Hi," Ian said, and rolled on top of him. Instantly everything was perfect.

It seemed like no time at all before they were up and on the streets. Ian took forever looking over the magazines on the newsstands, stopping at all the store windows, sipping at the coffees and then the beer they ordered in the cafés. Ian borrowed another twenty bucks from him. Everything was so expensive. Jackson didn't understand why they didn't take their last six-pack and go back to their room.

"Quit nagging, for godsake."

Jackson fell into silence.

On the way home, after they turned off the Trans-Canada, Ian reached over for Jackson's hand. He held it for a long time.

"I'd go crazy without you, Jackson," he finally said. "You're the greatest."

"No," Jackson said. "You are."

At the River Road turnoff Ian said, "I'd better hitch from here." Jackson checked the mirrors, pulled over and let him out.

It was only a couple of days before Ian arrived at the cabin with a new scheme.

"I got friends with a cottage in Parrsboro. We can use it next Tuesday — all day, all night. Free. Nobody there but you and me!"

Jackson's heart raced.

Jackson kept his head down, worked hard on the carving he was making as a gift for Ian. He knew he would have trouble asking Matthew to tend the business again so soon, but he had no other choice.

"Again?" Matthew frowned. "Cape Breton?"

Jackson nodded.

After a long silence Matthew grinned and said, "You fucker. You never got the hash down there, but you got a girl, didn't ya? That's why you been so different lately. Who is she? Do I know her?"

Jackson stared straight ahead, said nothing.

"Come on. Do I know her?" He smirked and rubbed his jaw. "I bet she's a hairdresser."

Instantly Jackson's cheeks flashed scarlet, and with his beard trimmed right back and his forehead exposed he felt completely naked. Matthew roared with laughter.

Jackson was sure he would remember the events of the second week in August for eternity. Monday was his thirtieth birthday. Ian unhooked a gold chain bracelet from his own wrist and pressed it into Jackson's palm. Then Ian led him out behind the shed and, in broad daylight, sank to his knees and brought him to exquisite climax. The heart-pounding danger of it, their success, their victory, left them both feeling bullish.

Tuesday morning Ian told his parents he was meeting a friend from school for a camping trip, and he and Jackson escaped for a glorious twenty-four hours in the Parrsboro cottage. From Wednesday afternoon to Friday they each recovered at home. On Friday afternoon Ian burst into the cabin, panting, his face shining from more than exertion. Jackson looked up from his whittling, Matthew stopped counting his change and Old Angus interrupted the complicated tale he was recounting to his pitcher of beer.

"I got a job!" Ian cried. He ran directly over to Jackson, grabbed him by the shoulders and cried again, "I got a job!"

Matthew was on his feet and at the keg in an instant. "This calls for a drink! On the house, eh?"

"Can you believe it? Can you fucking believe it! I got a job!"

Jackson tried not to grin too hard. Now Ian could get his own place, somewhere out of town, somewhere private, and they could see each other whenever they wanted. Jackson's mind flashed to long leisurely nights and early mornings, waking together in groggy bliss..

"Toronto, buddy! I'm off to TOR-ON-TO! I am out of this stinking hillbilly backwater. Forever!"

Everyone stiffened.

No, Jackson said to himself, he is mistaken. This is not true.

Ian came by early the next morning, trying for a more graceful goodbye.

"Thanks for, you know, everything."

Jackson stood rigid as the Tin Man. He could hardly respond. A lonely "too much to lose . . ." trickled out of him, barely audible.

Ian looked away, then back at Jackson, then down at his shoes. His voice slid to the edge of defensiveness. "You've got more now than you ever had before." He bounced the keys to his father's car up and down in his palm. He glanced around the empty cabin as if, for once, seeking an interruption.

"You're a great guy. It was fun."

Jackson gave no response. Ian leaned over and kissed his cheek, turned and walked away.

Jackson drove into Scotch River and bought a lock and key for his door and a sliding bolt for his bedroom. He installed them both, answering no questions. Gradually, quietly, surreptitiously throughout the afternoon, he transferred all his moonshine, his wine, all his purchased beer and liquor out to his woodshed and stacked it there, unprotected. He drove out to the shore and stood for what may have been minutes, what may have been hours, staring at the sea, watching the whitecaps crash onto the rocks. Back at his cabin he tried to make himself a cup of tea, but his hand shook too much for him to get the mug to his lips. Before the sun began to set he collected every forty-ouncer of rum he had and set them by his bed. There were six of them. He tacked a sign that read "Gone to Cape Breton" onto his door, drove his truck up the

MacIntyre Road and hid it in the bush off a logging road. Then he walked home through the woods in the falling dusk, sneaked into his own cabin and locked the door behind him. He nailed the window shut, slipped into his cell of a bedroom and bolted its ill-fitting door.

He sat on his bed, staring straight ahead of him into the dark, suffering beyond endurance. For years he had felt nothing. Nothing at all. Then a twinge for his brother, Matthew. Then a crack that leaked sadness and slid into grief when his mother died. Then Ian. Ian. The weakened armour fell apart. Lacy with rust, anyone could have punched a fist through it. Ian.

Tears rolled down his cheeks. He felt like a boil swollen to bursting from years of hoarded pain. Now the blister had been lanced, oozed everywhere. The air stung him, his existence reduced to pure, infinite pain. He twisted the cap off the first bottle and began pouring it down his throat. He'll drink himself to death. Just like his father. He'll drink himself to death. A sob choked him, forced a mouthful of rum across the room in a spray, droplets dotting his father's suit, the larger drops sliding down the protective plastic. Drink, he told himself, drink it straight down. He finished one bottle and started on the second, praying for the numbing that would never end. Silent convulsive sobs overtook his body. He cried, drank, cried himself to exhaustion.

"What ta fuck . . .? Where ta hell . . .?" The rattle of the doorknob, the lock tested and cursed, the window pushed and pulled. Silence while Matthew struck a match, read the note, discovered the goods in the woodshed. Laughter, the clinking of bottles being carried away. Jackson's ears picked up the racket outside the cabin, tried to send the information to an unwilling brain. He hadn't drunk enough, not fast enough. He could easily find his bottle in the dark if he could lift his heavy bones off his bed. He managed to raise a shaking hand to his chest and found it damp, soaked. He wondered for a moment if it was blood. Then Ian rose up before him in a razor slice of pain. He found a bottle, downed it, found another one. He drank until he fell back on his bed and lay there as wave after wave of pain flooded over him.

Sometimes he cried. Sometimes he didn't. He drifted in and out of sleep, in and out of stupor. His dreams leached into delirium. Disparate images swirled around him, large drunken hands, the wood box behind the old kitchen stove, his mother zipping his little red nylon parka up to his chin, the hay mow, his father's suit hovering above the bed. He'll drink himself to death. Just like his father. Delbert slamming him against their bedroom wall, a bloody rat crawling across the barn floor. Faggot. He's gay, too. He'll drink himself to death. Just like his father. Ian. Ian. Then nothing.

Three days after Jackson had left the note on his cabin door, Kate's Peter came running home, breathless. "Mom!" he cried. "Mom! Jackson's truck is in the woods!"

Kate put down her Windex and her paper towels and listened to Peter's description of where he found the truck, how it was parked, how the keys were in it, how Jackson had lied about going away. She thought a moment before a flash of horror hit her. She buried it with matter-of-fact resolution.

"Is Jackson's new lock a padlock or a key?"

He hesitated. He was not supposed to visit the cabin. "Key," he answered slowly.

"You stay here with Charlie and Emma. I mean it. You stay here. Emma! Watch Peter. I want everybody watching TV."

The kids would have laughed at this command if they hadn't seen the look on Kate's face. She would need to break the window. She grabbed her rolling pin and her gardening gloves and set off for Jackson's cabin.

He came to consciousness panting, blurry, desperate for air, choked by the stench of puke and piss. And desperate for water — so thirsty, but his skin had evaporated. Nothing to hold the water in. Ian smiled at him, tossed back a drink, turned away. The rum. There was still another bottle there, just there, on the floor.

The aching nausea, the cracks of light, the desperate need for water — these sensations settled into identifiable reality. The cracks of light? Half dreaming, he floated towards them, crashed to the floor, stumbled to his feet, moved towards them. His hands grappled with metal. Something gave way. He lost his balance toppled, somewhere, blinded by light. Things, strange yet familiar, swam around unbound by gravity. He felt a great sense of direction, of knowing beyond himself, of effort, tugging. His muscles screamed for something, at something. The air cleared and for a second he remembered. I'm sick, he thought. I need to . . . then dizziness overtook him. Confusion. Everything fuzzy. But his hands felt wood, gripped wood. I know this wood, he thought. I need to . . . what? So sick. His fingers found a cool metal knob.

When Kate rounded the corner of Jackson's cabin she found him on his knees, clinging to his open door, blinking in the sun. For a moment she stood staring. "Oh Jackson," she whispered. He blinked harder. She dropped her rolling pin. This was a man in bad shape. Just a man in rough shape. Lord knows she had dealt with this situation enough in her life. She helped him to his feet, led him back into his cabin, sat him down on a chair. She brought him water and held it to his lips. She stripped the fetid clothes off him, wiped his face and hands and dressed him in dry pants and a shirt. She opened the door, pulled the nails out of the window and opened that, too. She brought him more water.

She took him by the shoulders and spoke directly into his face, "Did you eat today?" Jackson shook his head. "Yesterday?" He shrugged. He had no idea. "Soup first," she said, like she was listing chores for a child. "Then bath and a hair wash. Then more soup." He let her help him out of the cabin, down the path to her house.

For two days Jackson stayed with Kate, following her orders, not saying a word. He was careful how he moved, how he stood. Everything inside him lay exposed, tender as a fresh burn. Outside he sat on the porch and inside on the couch. He hobbled a short piece up MacIntyre Road, testing his legs. And he went through everything in his mind: what had happened, what he had done, why he had done it. He had fallen in love with a young man who had left him. It sounded impossible but it was true. He had fallen in love.

When he returned to his cabin he went through everything in his mind again. He closed his eyes and remembered Ian's embrace, how he had felt Ian all around him, on his skin, in his ears, behind his eyelids, seeping into the vacuum in his chest, blooming, growing. For the first time in his life he had felt brave. Terrified, yes, but also brave, strong, manly. He had lived in anticipation, felt hope, excitement. Most of all he had felt Ian's need, Ian's desire, and he, Jackson Bigney, had satisfied him.

It was his own fault. If he hadn't let Ian in, nothing would have been disrupted, nothing would have been yanked away, and he wouldn't be in such pain right now. He could go back to the way he had been, he knew that. He could stop the hemorrhaging, seal himself back up, fill the cavity with booze again. He sat quietly on his bed staring at his father's suit, his suit, running his hand through his shortened hair, over his narrowed, trimmed beard. He had carved for Ian a tiny fiddle from a block of pine. He had nestled it into a bed of fine shavings packed into a little box printed with the words "Red Bird, 250 matches." Ian had slid the box open, he had been delighted, amazed, awed. He had reached up and hugged him. "Thank you," he had said. "It's beautiful." He had kissed him. "You're beautiful, you know that? Beautiful. Don't ever forget that." Jackson was surprised to find he still had a few tears left.

Jackson placed his five-gallon brewing buckets under the spigots of his kegs, opened the taps and drained every drop. He lugged the pails out behind the cabin and dumped them onto the ground. The stock he had left in his woodshed had been ravaged, but he poured out the few quarts of wine, the remaining vodka and moonshine. He was working his way through the only remaining case of Molson's when Matthew showed up. Matthew's jaw dropped as he took in the scene.

Jackson looked at him, then looked away. He returned to his

task. It wasn't so hard a job. You opened the bottle, you poured it out, it disappeared. He rocked back on his haunches, bounced a few times.

"Christ, man, what are you doing?" Matthew stammered. "Jesus, don't . . ."

Jackson took a deep breath and concentrated on speaking clearly. "You had your share," he said to his brother. "This is mine." His hand pressed an empty bottle gently to his chest, felt the wound beneath it, the tender spot where he meant to grow his heart.

"This is mine," he repeated.

CHAPTER SEVEN

TALL TREES AND WINDING PATHS confused him, but he wasn't afraid, just impatient. Ian's fiddle called out to him through the treetops, and he followed the trail of notes. There, in the distance, he glimpsed Ian's back and the flashing of his bow arm. He was sitting on a bright yellow picnic table, one leg propped up on the bench, facing away. Jackson broke into a jog. As he ran trees obscured his line of vision, then opened it up again; he saw him, then he didn't. Though he ran harder and harder, the distance between them barely diminished. Then the music stopped, Ian tucked his fiddle under his arm and stood up to leave. Jackson, now breathless and leaden with exhaustion, called out in panic.

Jackson woke. He groaned, crossed his arms over his face and held himself still. When he thought he could stand it he told himself, "He's gone." When he thought he could stand it he leaned way over the edge of his bed as he had almost every morning for the past decade. He reached out and touched the lighter, dustless square on the floor where he used to store the six-pack from which he would pull his morning beer. He hung there for a minute more while the blood ran to his head. He was built upside down. That's what his mother used to say. Always running away from things the other kids would run towards. He remembered her staring down at him in the kitchen, trying to get him to say what kind of a cake he wanted for his tenth birthday. He didn't know. Matthew always answered for him, but Matthew wasn't there. She was waiting. "Well?" she said, "Chocolate or white?" He knew she would be angry in a minute. Where was Matthew? He remembered the sweat turning his palms clammy, the pain spreading through his bottom lip as he chewed it. He bolted, hid under the porch, lay there with his heart racing.

Jackson hauled himself back onto his bed. Built upside down. In the country songs people started drinking when someone walked out. But how could he have known? Who would have believed someone could want him? And who could have known that he, Jackson, would be able to want in return?

He kicked his legs free of the covers and crawled out of bed. He pulled on his jeans and a T-shirt, lurched through the doorway, made tea and smoked a cigarette. He dug into the pocket of his jeans and pulled out the gold bracelet that Ian had given him, fingered the links, his thumb pulling the chain across his forefinger one link at a time. He sat and ate Shreddies, one at a time, from the box, like popcorn. His hands shook a little but not too badly. He found a bottle of aspirin in the bathroom and swallowed a couple. His reflection in the mirror startled him. He hadn't shaved for days and stubble was overtaking the clean lines of his Halifax beard. Shaving seemed an easy place to start, so he heated some water and picked up his razor.

When he finished he sat back down at his table and wrestled a thought out of his sadness. "What now?" He looked around at his unpainted walls, tacked-together cupboards, dripping faucet, hubcaps overflowing with cigarette butts and ashes, dirty board floors and scavenged furniture. The empties go first, he decided. He smoked another cigarette, then got up and collected and boxed all the beer bottles in the cabin and woodshed and scattered on the ground outside. The take was considerable. After he stacked them in the truck and cashed them in at the liquor store, he stopped at the Co-op and bought a new broom with a dust pan and Lestoil, Ajax, Windex, paper towels and a scrub brush.

kson worked slowly and methodically, spacing his cigarette breaks exactly one hour apart: every hour on the hour, five minutes each. All day long nieces and nephews, then siblings and in-laws ran in and out of the cabin laughing at the spectacle.

"Come and do mine when you're done!" the women kept saying.

"I lost twenty bucks in here once," Matthew said. "So if you find any money at all, it's mine."

Rosie laughed. "Jesus, I love to see a man on his knees!" She told him to come over for a proper dinner that evening — to keep his strength up.

Kate offered the assistance of her two oldest kids, Charlie and Emma. Her kids who had always been forbidden to set foot anywhere near his cabin. Jackson shook his head. He wanted to do it himself.

Delbert sat himself down at the table in the middle of the cabin. "You can't scrub back and forth like that. You've got to go in a circle. That's how you get all the dirt. Otherwise you just get half. You gotta be crazy to pay for that Windex stuff. Darlene came home with that once and I sent her right back with it. Use vinegar and water. It's twice as good." He smoked Jackson's cigarettes, and when the kids left he said, "Roll me a joint. That friggin' cleaner's giving me a headache."

Jackson barely heard him. He gripped the scrub brush hard to keep from shaking. Ian was gone, the drinking was over, his bootlegging business was closed. Everything he touched seemed sharp enough to cut him.

He worked all day and through the evening. When he didn't show up at Rosie's table for supper, Kate sent her Emma up to the cabin with a plate of dinner and a huge slab of blueberry pie. Emma set the foil-covered pie pan on the table apologetically.

"Mom says you gotta eat this. She says she's not spending the rest of her life scraping you off the floor because you're too stubborn to swallow a few bites."

He didn't look up, just kept scrubbing until his watch showed exactly seven o'clock. Then he stood up. Emma still sat there, leaning over the paperback novel spread open on the table in front of her and sucking on a strand of her straight brown hair as it fell over her face. She was a bulky, graceless girl with errant pimples pushing through her puffy skin. Jackson was surprised at how close she seemed, how sharp and clear and real. With a quick calculation he figured her age at fourteen. He knew nothing about her, except that she was smart and that Kate was absolutely determined to see both Emma and Charlie at university. Emma looked up when he sat down and immediately got up to fetch him a fork.

"Are you really giving up drinking?" she asked when he peeled back the foil and stared at the enormous pile of beef and potatoes and turnips and gravy.

"I guess."

He stuck his fork into the meat. An ancient dread began to well up in him. He heard his mother's voice. *You'll eat every last bite of that. Look at you, you're the size of a starved cat. It's not decent.* She hadn't known Vernon would take over, haul him off his chair, tearing the T-shirt off him to show everybody his ribs. "I wouldn't waste milk on a calf skinny as that one."

Jackson must have sighed out loud because Emma looked up at him. He was poking his potatoes. Her voice slid across the table, small and kind.

"If you can eat half, I won't tell Mom you didn't finish."

Jackson looked away then back at her and felt the corner of his mouth rising in a fraction of a smile. He pushed the slab of pie over to her. "You eat this," he said.

"I can't. Mom would kill me for sure."

"Then I'll know for sure you won't tell."

Emma giggled. He grinned. Emma went for a second fork and dug into the pie. For a minute they each worked on their plates in happy conspiracy.

"If Mom comes in, we're dead!" Emma whispered. Her laughter made him hungry enough to get one more slice of beef down before he pushed the plate away and lit a smoke.

Jackson returned to his cleaning. About midnight he emptied his bucket and hung up his rag. Immediately his hands snatched up the carving he was working on, a rather frightened looking little rat. He smoked three cigarettes before he could face his bed.

In the middle of the night Jackson's door crashed open and drunken shouts spilled into the cabin. Jackson tumbled out of bed, found his jeans, and dragged himself through his bedroom door. Disoriented and vaguely sick, his own irritation confused him.

Rolly MacDonald tripped over the threshold and sprawled across the floor. His neighbour, Frank, collapsed in laughter.

"Jackson!" Frank gasped for breath. "Look. He's that desperate for a bottle — he's begging you on his knees!" He brayed with laughter.

"Aw, fuck off." Rolly managed to climb to his feet.

Jackson stood there blinking, running his hands through his hair.

The two men slumped down at his spotless table. "We'll have a round. Then a quart of rum."

Jackson rubbed his face. "I'm not selling anymore."

"Fuck off. You are so."

"No." He nodded in the direction of the shelf that used to hold the row of homebrew kegs.

Rolly slammed his fists into the table and shoved it crashing down on its side. Jackson and Frank jumped out of its way, the ashtray landing upside down, dumping ashes and butts onto the scrubbed boards.

"I came here for a fucking bottle and I'm not leaving without one!" He kicked at a table leg, missed, and nearly lost his balance. "I'm getting my fucking bottle. I can tell you that much!" He stumbled off through the door.

Frank laughed all the louder. In his head the incident had already jelled into another of his huge collection of Rolly stories to recount down at the gas station.

Jackson waited for Frank to follow Rolly back out to the car and away. But before that could happen, Rolly filled the doorway again, brandishing a .303 rifle. Frank stopped laughing.

"You're a fucking liar! That's what you are! My old lady told you not to give me anything. Didn't she." It wasn't a question. He swung the rifle by the barrel around his head. With a great sweep he cleared off a freshly washed shelf of clean beer glasses, which hit the floor, sending splinters of glass in all directions.

"Jesus, Rolly, cut it out. Let's go." Then Frank turned to

Jackson, "Don't ya have at least a micky of something? Anything? Jesus, look at him. Put the gun down, Rolly."

"I'm not gonna . . ." Sentence formation was beyond Rolly now. He managed to get the rifle turned around into firing position but couldn't hold it still. Rolly's finger fluttered over the trigger. Jackson's blood pounded at his temples. Neither he nor Frank dared move.

A shot exploded. Glass shattered. Rolly tottered to the floor. Jackson rocked back against the door frame, Frank against the wall. No one moved. The night silence gradually closed over the reverberations. Jackson looked around. He was alive. They all were. No one was bleeding. Several ragged teeth of glass bit into the empty space where the window pane had been. Frank retrieved the rifle and laid it on the counter, and he and Jackson lugged Rolly, now subdued and half limp, into his car.

Frank laughed nervously. "I guess we'll be off now," he said, revving the engine and drowning out the end of his sentence. Frank bumped down the lane towards the dark end of MacIntyre Road.

Jackson sat bare-chested and bug-eaten on the bench outside his cabin, longing for sleep. Matthew showed up groggy and annoyed. "What happened?"

"Visitors. Horsin' around."

"Jesus Christ. I told her it was nothing."

They both headed back to bed.

It was barely first light when persistent pounding on his door hauled Jackson out of his sleep again. He pulled on his jeans and opened the door to Constable Townsend.

"Morning, Jackson."

"Uh."

"Mind if I come in?"

Jackson stepped aside, noticed the shards of smashed glass sprayed around his bare feet. The table still lay on its side and, in full view, the .303 rested on the counter.

"You might want to get some shoes on." Townsend waited a

moment, but when Jackson didn't move he continued. "We found Rolly MacDonald's car sitting in a treetop just down the road. No sign of him, though. Wondered if he might have been through here?"

"In a t-tree?"

Townsend strolled across the room and stared down at the rifle. "By that steep gully where the creek runs under the road. Looks like he drove off there and the trees caught him before he hit the ground." Half a grin leaked onto his face. "It's quite a sight."

Jackson wanted a smoke.

"I'd like to speak to Mr. MacDonald as soon as possible. Get some information on where he was last night, who with, what state they were in. Rolly's not supposed to be driving, eh? No licence."

Townsend ran his gaze pointedly over the upturned table and shards of glass, then tapped his forefinger loudly on the countertop beside the rifle butt. "You have a spot of trouble here last night?"

Jackson said nothing.

"This your rifle?"

"No. It's, uh, my father's. I was, um, cleaning it up. Didn't check for, uh . . ." He nodded towards the window. "Kinda stupid."

"They didn't drop by here? Rolly and . . ." He peeped into the little bathroom and eyed the bedroom door. "May I?" Jackson waved his hand, and Townsend, a question lodged between the creases in his forehead, checked the rest of the cabin. It was impossible not to notice the empty space where the liquor had once been stored, the absence of dirty beer bottles. Even through the disarray the new cleanliness shone through.

Jackson followed the Mountie outdoors, hung in the doorway of the woodshed as Townsend ducked inside. Townsend leaned against the pile of empty beer kegs Jackson had stacked there.

"You're not giving parties here anymore?" Townsend's voice was quiet, his left eyebrow raised in a gently inquisitive expression. Jackson shook his head. For a full minute they stood there in silence before Townsend whispered, "Well, best of luck then, eh."

Townsend stepped back out into the sunshine, regained his voice. "Sure would help if I knew who I was looking for."

Jackson scratched at his mosquito bites.

"You're looking at major violations as far as the proper storage of a firearm. With all the kids around here we don't want a tragedy."

Silence.

"I better take that rifle with me."

Jackson shrugged.

Townsend slipped the rifle into a plastic bag and carried it out to his cruiser. Jackson watched him open the trunk. Townsend's hair circled the tops of his ears in perfect curves, came to the same little point at the neck that Ian's had. Ian's hair was a little longer at the back, quite a bit longer in front. When Townsend bent over to lay the gun in the trunk, his summer uniform shirt, tucked in neatly, stretched into a fan of wrinkles rooted at the small of his back and spreading like giant fingers towards his shoulder blades.

Jackson hugged himself, conscious of his skinny chest.

Townsend shut the trunk and slid in behind the wheel. He opened his mouth as if he was going to say something but changed his mind. He looked straight at Jackson. "If you see him, give me a call, okay?" He pulled away from the cabin, heading back down to the road.

Jackson didn't feel too bad. He tugged on his boots, lit himself a smoke, swept up the glass, righted the table. The clarity of his early morning thoughts came as a surprise to him. He eased into them gingerly, like a kid venturing out onto a newly frozen pond. He would replace the pane first, then continue with his scrubbing, buy some paint and do the walls. The floor, too. He could build cupboard doors, maybe even get some clapboard for the outside of the cabin. He recalled Townsend's voice, his uniform. Trevor, he remembered, it was Constable Trevor Townsend. He could cut in a second window, maybe even a third, let a bit more light in. Today he would have to start thinking about how he would manage without his bootleg income. He had to plan.

He made himself a pot of tea and allowed himself a few minutes to think about Ian. When the pain grew too sharp he veered off and remembered the fiddle, the ebb and flow of Ian's tunes floating through the air as if he was singing to him in a secret language. He got up and began his scrubbing again. He would paint these floor boards with that light grey floor paint left over from the farmhouse stairs.

Over the next few weeks Jackson did more work on his cabin than he had done in all the years since he built it. The new windows altered the light in the cabin in ways that continuously surprised him. He put together a makeshift septic tank and installed the toilet. Fresh paint gleamed everywhere.

The grain ripened well that year, and by mid-September the farmers began preparing to get it off their fields before the weather turned wet. Jackson thought about where he might find a bit of work. Lloyd Harris sometimes hired an extra hand if he could find anyone desperate enough to work for him.

Lloyd Harris was an austere Presbyterian who spoke entirely in statements or threats, in what was true or what would soon be true if one were not vigilant. He frowned and nodded when he looked up to find Jackson standing in his farmyard, kicking at the dirt with the toe of his boot. A loosened pebble skittered across the ground and bounced under the harvester.

"Y-you need anybody to, um, work?"

Lloyd looked doubtful. He turned back to his combine with his wrench and grease gun. "You're just looking for your unemployment cheques. Something for nothing, that's what all the youngsters want now. Well, I'm not fooling with all that paper work."

Jackson shook his head. "Cash."

A long pause followed. "We won't have no alcohol on the place, and that's it!"

Jackson nodded.

"We work a full day here. Start at five o'clock in the morning. You're here for the chores or you don't bother coming. I don't like my help lying in bed with a breakfast tray."

Another nod.

"You'll get no work if it's wet."

Another bob of the head.

Lloyd sighed as if he had done all he could, and now it was up to the Lord to judge.

"You'll go hungry if you don't tell Elsie to set another plate." Jackson turned towards the house and patted his pocket for his cigarettes. Lloyd called out after him, "That's *five* tomorrow! Not ten past!"

Jackson was waiting in Harris's barn the next morning when Lloyd switched on the lights. He helped milk the cows, then Lloyd pointed him to a great pile of firewood behind the kitchen which could be split and stacked during his idle moments. As soon as the dew was off, Lloyd had his harvester in the field, and Jackson began trucking oats from the combine to the granary.

Elsie beamed at him at dinnertime. "Isn't the weather wonderful? A couple of weeks of this and everything will be tucked away cozy as toast, won't it, Lloyd?"

"God willing and no rain."

"Sit here, Jackson. I hope he's treating you all right out there. Have some of this rhubarb pickle with your meatloaf, Jackson. Don't be shy with those potatoes. There's lots. It's lovely to have someone young on the place again, isn't it, Lloyd?"

Lloyd grunted but didn't look up from his plate.

"Go on and finish up those beans now, Jackson. We don't see enough of the young people. There's only us two old fools left, now our girls are all married with kids of their own. We've six grandchildren now, don't we, Lloyd? Pass Jackson the butter, Lloyd. Those are the grandchildren there." She pointed behind him to a narrow set of shelves squeezed into a corner. The few knick-knacks on the shelves had been pushed out of the way by a bustle of photographs. But on the very top shelf — Jackson's throat dried to sandpaper. If he had known it was there he could have prepared himself. He could feel his fingers starting to tremble. It was just that he hadn't been expecting it. Most of the time he felt like a china cup balanced on the edge of a shelf. He couldn't manage the jolt of surprise. Sometimes he was afraid he might start to cry and not even notice until his cheeks glistened and everyone stared. Oh please, he prayed, don't let me cry.

Elsie followed his stare. "I found that old fiddle at an auction years ago, thought maybe one of our girls would take it up. Nobody here ever did, though."

He couldn't tear his eyes away. It's okay, he told himself. It's only an old fiddle.

"Do you play, Jackson?"

"No."

"I just love fiddle music, don't you?"

"Yes."

"Maybe you should give it a try. Maybe you'll learn it. No one here will miss that old thing. Sure, you give it a try." She scuttled around the table and had it off the shelf before Jackson could think of what to say.

"No, I don't . . ."

"Go on. I'll just get something to put it in."

She set it on the table beside him. He couldn't help reaching out to touch the shiny finish, stroke the smooth grooves in the head. When Elsie came back with a plastic bag Jackson didn't stop her from packing it up.

"Now, there's apple crisp here. You'll have ice cream with yours, won't you, Jackson?" She cocked her head to one side as though she were judging a new calf. "The size of him, eh, Lloyd? I'm afraid we'll lose him through the cracks in the barn floor."

Jackson drove the truck, shovelled oats and drank a lot of ginger beer. They worked until daylight utterly abandoned them. Then Jackson drove his pickup home in the dark, the fiddle resting on the seat beside him.

The first time Jackson tightened the bow the way he had seen Ian do it and drew the hairs across the strings, the screech rattled his bone marrow. The next squeal drilled down through the roots of his teeth. He lightened his touch, gained a little control over the volume, but he couldn't make the noise any less annoying. He stashed the fiddle under his bed.

The good weather held. When Jackson woke to a clear, starry sky he felt a rush of grateful relief that he had another day's work to keep his hands busy. People still came by the cabin all the time, walked in and sat down. It did no good to say he had nothing to sell. They were waiting for him to change his mind so things could get back to the way they had been before. They still woke him in the night, looking for a drink, like they always had.

One night Jackson arrived home tired. He found Matthew sitting at his table with a six-pack in front of him. When Jackson stared at the beer, Matthew growled, "It wouldn't kill you to keep a couple of beer around, for chrissake. But you're too good for that now, I guess."

The old emptiness rushed in on him again. He turned and walked out of the cabin, drove to the shore, hid in the darkness at the edge of the ocean. The vastness of the sea eased the pressure a little, as if dropping the hole inside him into the sea made the emptiness insignificant or at least bearable.

Behind him and off to the east the herring fishermen were returning to the wharf, chugging from the blackness into the pool of light that spilled generously over the piers and planking. Amid the roaring and putting of engines a few voices called out, there was laughter, the smell of fish and rope, diesel fuel, gasoline and men. Matthew had crewed on a lobster boat one season, but boats terrified Jackson. He got to his feet and followed the beach away from the wharf, walked until an outcropping of rock blocked his path. He leaned against the rock and concentrated on the deep breathing of the waves as they exhaled on the shore. He needed to be home in bed, but he couldn't face Matthew's disdain. And there was no way he had the strength to face that golden six-pack. Then he had an idea.

The following night when the Everett boys showed up, Jackson picked up Elsie's fiddle and began sawing away, shooting shrill and painful off-notes into the tips of their nerves. They hollered at him to knock it off, but he didn't stop. Finally they left. Who could stand it? Jackson reminded himself to go searching for his chainsaw ear plugs in the morning. From then on, at the first sound of an engine, the first sight of a body in the doorway, Jackson reached for the fiddle. Finally, the stream of drunken intruders thinned to a trickle. Several nights in a row he slept without interruption.

Then Rolly MacDonald arrived again, roaring drunk, with Frank small and sorry in the background.

"What ta fuck did you do with my rifle, giving it to the stinking cops?"

"He t-t-took it. I, ah, said it was my father's."

"Well, he knew it wasn't cause it's fuckin' registered! To *me*!"

"He told them it was his dad's, Rolly," Frank pleaded. "Let's go now. He can't stop the cops from taking a gun."

Jackson said nothing. He was tired. He tightened the bow and took up the fiddle. He settled himself at the table and began wringing out the usual moans and squeals.

Rolly didn't seem to notice. "And you know why it's registered? Because my bitch of a wife phoned it in. Signed 'em all up. Every goddamned popgun on the place! She thinks she can fuck off and do whatever she fucking well feels like! Register *my* goddamn guns? I make it clear to her she is to mind her own business and keep her filthy holes shut, and she goes running to that cunt Townsend. Next thing there's two of them pussy-boy Mounties, with those yellow stripes running down their legs, standing on *my* porch telling me what I can do to *my* goddamn fucking *wife*!"

He snatched the fiddle out of Jackson's hand. "And they take my guns!" Jackson's eyes never left the fiddle as it floated upwards in Rolly's fist, jerked back and forth through the air like a teacher's pointer.

"Come on, Rolly, let's go," Frank repeated.

"They got a list of every single one of 'em! They take every one of them except that .303 because they already got that one, even though I left it in your precious fucking care!"

The instrument hovered, hovered, then descended — *crack* — on the edge of the table. Jackson felt the crack in his own ribs, and the blow knocked the wind out of him. He watched as the neck bent back in slow motion to a sickening angle. The fiddle bounced off the edge of the table onto the floor, where it shuddered once with the impact and rocked twice. Jackson gathered the instrument to his chest. When he finally looked up he was surprised to see Rolly swaying in the open door. In those seconds, Jackson had utterly forgotten about him. Frank had Rolly by the arm, and even Rolly seemed to have forgotten why he was here.

"If you ever so much as touch my wife I'll fuckin' kill ya," sifted through to Jackson before the door slam, the engine roar and the tire squeal.

He wrapped the fiddle in a towel and laid it under his bed, then he fell back into bed himself and lay there, eyes closed, his fists vices gripping handfuls of bedclothes while an electrical shimmer vibrated through the cavern of his chest. He waited for the dead weight of sleep.

Outside it began to pour. All night and all morning it poured. There would be no work now for days. Jackson huddled on his cot and knew he wasn't going to make it. What was the point? Ian had never cared about him. Matthew hated him. All his old customers hated him and wanted him gone so they could use his cabin again. I would, too, he thought. I'd want me gone, too. Everything was too loud, too bright, too sharp, too big, too close. How had he even thought he could go on like this for the rest of his life? He didn't get out of bed that morning.

At noon the careless slam of his door roused him, and he lay listening to Matthew putting the kettle on. Matthew poked his head into the bedroom and laughed.

"Get up, ya lazy frigger." His voice was light and friendly. "Look," he called, whizzing something rock-like by Jackson's head. "The apples are ripe." When Jackson sat up a perfect red Mac rolled off his pillow towards him.

"Get out here and listen to this." Matthew was already laughing. "You know that woman who crewed on with the Everetts, just for the herring, eh? Hey! You getting up? I want you to drive me in to the garage. Guy's got an axel there for me."

"Uh . . . yeah." He staggered into the bathroom.

"Yeah, so anyway, the Everetts thought it was pretty funny having a woman fishing with them, and they kept making these jokes about her dressing up like a mermaid and everything? And they're always trying to grab her when she bends over and stuff, or that's what she says, anyway, and I guess they had this big fight, 'cause then she's fired or quit or whatever. No problem. But when they go down to their boat yesterday, you know their boat, eh, the *Blazing Star*? Well, the name's totally painted over. *Flaming Arsehole* it says now. I seen it last night." The room shook with Matthew's laugh. "Christ. Get dressed, will ya, tea's ready. The *Flaming Arsehole*. Ha-ha. She got that right, eh, buddy? She got that right."

Jackson dropped Matthew off at Nelson's Garage and stopped in at the Co-op for a few groceries. Feeling tender and battered, he kept his eyes on his boots as he walked across the parking lot. He was right beside Rolly MacDonald's car before he noticed it, before he saw Rolly sitting in the passenger seat scowling and chewing impatiently on a stalk of straw. Jackson blushed and looked away.

Inside, across the aisle from the canned spaghetti and the Chunky Soup, Rolly's wife, with her right arm in a cast, had a job to keep her cart rolling along straight. Rolly's wife. He didn't even know her name. She kept her eyes to herself. He could have stood there all day staring at the purple bags under her eyes, the fading bruise on her jaw. She wouldn't look up. He knew that. They both knew how to keep their eyes in, close to their bodies. Don't look up, don't say anything. With her good hand she tried to reach the cheapest jars of strawberry jam on the top shelf, but she was too short. He watched as she calculated the second least expensive jar and raised her hand toward it. This loneliness would devour him for sure. For a decade the booze had protected him. He hadn't needed to see anyone. Now people pressed up against him everywhere — no space at all. Don't cry. Jesus, don't cry! He blinked, gulped twice, drew in a deep breath and rubbed his face, hard, with his hand.

He glanced around to make sure they were alone, then he crossed the aisle and reached down a jar of the first-choice jam for Rolly's wife. She started as he offered it to her, then bobbed her head in quick thanks and disappeared down the next aisle.

When he got home he pulled the fiddle out from under his bed and stared at it. The neck had come loose and a split had opened up along the fiddle's back. The strings dangled obscenely, two of the pegs had fallen loose, and an ominous rattle came from inside the cavity. But the sides weren't broken and neither was the neckpiece, really, or the top. Maybe I can fix it, he thought. Maybe it isn't so bad. It's made of wood, fixing it must be possible. He just needed . . . he wasn't sure what he needed. Maybe they made parts for fiddles. Maybe.

There were, Jackson knew, music stores. He drove to town in the rain and parked outside a shop where posters and drum kits filled the front window. Inside, guitars covered the walls except for the furthest corner, which sheltered a banjo, a fiddle and a couple of things Jackson couldn't put a name on.

"I-I don't know," said Jackson when a middle-aged man offered help. "I, uh, need to fix a broken f-fiddle . . ."

"Oh. I don't do that. You won't get anyone around here to do that. Is it badly damaged? They can be extremely expensive to repair. If it's damaged at all badly, look, I've got a couple of violins here. Now, this one is a very reasonable price."

The shop overwhelmed him. He couldn't focus on what the man was saying except to recognize that it had nothing to do with him. His eyes wandered. On a massive rack at his shoulder, rows and rows of large, soft-covered music books ran down the wall. A line of thicker, heavier books were stacked along the floor at his feet. They looked as if they were being stored there, out of the way. On the top of the far pile he read the title: *Building Your Own Guitar*. He knelt and began flipping through the stacks. There at the bottom of a pile sat an ancient volume with a dusty blue cover: *Violin and Cello Building and Repair*, stencilled in small gold print.

"I'll take this." Jackson stood and turned towards the cash. The proprietor's sales pitch trailed into the air as he followed him to the cash and rang up the sale. Jackson stood clutching his book, staring at it.

"You want a bag for that?"

Jackson shook his head. Before he could think about it, before he could stop himself, he blurted out, "What's a sell-oh?"

"What?"

Jackson pointed to the word in the title. The man looked at him in disbelief. "Cello," he said, pushing the *ch* through his teeth. "It's like a violin, but bigger."

"Oh."

"Here." He pulled a business card out from underneath his cash register and slid it across the counter. "This guy does repairs. If you're in Halifax. It's not cheap."

Jackson tucked the card into his breast pocket and left, holding his new book tight to his chest.

Jackson read the entire book from beginning to end. He didn't understand it all, but he kept reading. He learned that the top or "belly plate" of a violin is glued in place with only half the amount of glue used to secure the back plate so the belly can be removed in case repairs are needed. He learned that the rattling inside was probably only the bass bar come loose. He learned that the sides were called "ribs." He learned the names of the strings and how they were put on and taken off. So he removed the strings, labelled them, and looped them into little circles and hung them on a nail by his bed. Then he worked the point of his knife into the seam where the belly met the ribs and slowly, gradually, ever so gently, began inching the blade around the perimeter of the belly plate, easing it away from the ribs.

After what seemed like hours of probing, coaxing, wriggling and gentle prying, he finally set down his knife and lifted off the loosened top. He jerked backwards, terrified for a split second at the magnificence of the instrument, at his own brutality. For a moment guilt pierced him. He had exposed this terrible vulnerability. Then, overwhelmed by the beauty, his eyes filled with tears. He reached out to stroke the smooth, rounded corners, edges, surfaces. He caressed the perfect hollow sculpted inside the ribs, delicate but so strong they withstood Rolly's bashing. He laid his hand inside the instrument and rested it there until forgiveness seeped out of the wood and into his fingertips, spread through his hand and up his arm and washed over his body.

Jackson began to read his book again, this time with the exposed fiddle at his side. He examined the linings, the bevelled slots where they fit, the corners where the ribs met, the blocks, the hills and hollows of the plates, the notches cut to hold the neck in place, and he could see with perfect clarity how it all fit together. With sandpaper and glue he set to work.

At first Jackson was elated with the restored fiddle. Then self-doubt crept through cracks, around corners, rolling over him, swarming him like a plague of earwigs, crawling everywhere. What did he know about violins? Nothing. How would he know if it was okay? He had probably ruined it.

He took the fiddle back to the music shop. He waited outside in the truck until the only customers, two scraggly teenagers, got bored with poking the guitars and left the shop empty except for the man who had sold him the book. Jackson slipped into the shop with the instrument nestled in the crook of his arm.

"I-I put this back t-together, but I can't play. So I don't know . . ." He held it out to the surprised shopkeeper. "Is it okay?"

The man took it, turned the fiddle over and over in his hands, squinted at Jackson. He plucked a string and began screwing the pegs tighter until he had tuned it to his satisfaction. "I don't really play, either," he admitted. But when he pulled the bow over the strings, it sounded to Jackson as though he did.

"First rate."

Jackson shook with excitement all the way home. He would tell Elsie there had been an accident with the fiddle, but it was all right now. He would show her his work. It was nothing to have fixed it. Nothing. He wanted to build a fiddle all his own. He wanted to start from nothing, shape a fiddle around the air. He wasn't sure why, exactly, but it had to do with that swelling feeling inside him. He loved the strength of construction that looked so fragile, the knowledge, as the book said, that "the music arises from the play between the outside and the inside. The wood and the space around it come together as equal partners."

It was true. He loved the way the fiddle moulded hollowness into powerful music. The thought of it made him shake — the thought of dipping his hands into all that beauty. He had to shut himself in his room where he could cry.

CHAPTER EIGHT

JACKSON KNEW THE BLOCK OF PINE he had chosen for his fiddle's mould was perfectly dry because he sawed it off a board which had been nailed across his rafters for a decade. The book said to keep it above his stove for a week, though, so he did. He cut it to size and planed it until it sat perfectly square and true. One and a quarter inches thick by eleven and three quarters inches wide by seventeen and a half inches long. Every day before he left for Harris's and every night when he got home, he ran his fingers over the surface, caressed the edges, pressed his T-square up against its angles over and over, searching for a fault he could right. Then, like the book said, he tapered the top of the block into a gentle slope, three-sixteenths of an inch over its length. Every day for a week he measured and remeasured, planed, searched for flaws, terrified by its perfection, terrified that he might find a blemish. Was it really dry? Should he leave it longer? He wanted to leave it longer, daunted by the fear of sinking a saw blade into the perfect block. Still, an ominous urgency shoved at him from behind, as if he was holding up a line, as if it was his turn to jump off the branch into the river below, and the kid behind him kept pushing and shouting, "Go!" He had to jump or he would fall.

He lifted the pattern from Elsie's fiddle. He traced the outline and cut a template. Then carefully he transferred the silhouette to his pine block. He scored inside the shape with his own homemade compass, to get an exact but smaller copy, five thirty-seconds of an inch inside the original line. This was the correct size for the ribs.

"Five thirty-seconds of an inch," he whispered to himself. One notch past one-eighth of an inch. No big deal, no harder to measure than any other distance, but the sound of it both scared and reassured him. It needed to be exact, but if he got it right it would be perfect. The book told him precisely what needed to be done. "Five thirty-seconds of an inch," he repeated.

He sharpened his fret saw until its teeth gleamed like a cat's, then slowly, painstakingly, began to cut along the sweeping outline — one rounded shoulder, the tight C-shaped bite in the first side, the sweeping curve of the base, the matching bite on the other side and the final shoulder. He tapped the sawed block apart, liberating the solid pine shape of a fiddle from the mould. He gazed at the solid fiddle shape, ran his fingers over its curves and hollows. He loved the warm sawdust smell, brought the pine to his nose, closed his eyes, pressed the smooth grain to his cheek. When his lips responded with a kiss, it startled him. He stepped back, embarrassed at himself.

He dropped the solid fiddle shape into the stove's firebox. The nest, the hollow shape left in the pine block, was the useful part. This space would give form to the ribs. Gingerly his fingers explored the cavity. He set the mould on his table and stared at it.

The book said anyone could build a bending iron. So Jackson did. It was simply a pipe with a heating coil — a cylinder hot enough to make a drop of water sizzle. But the wood — the book was specific about the wood: sycamore, maple or pear, Swiss pine cut on the quarter and sold in specially sized blocks and strips. He could probably find a good dry slab of maple for the back and a bit of pine for the belly, and maybe he could even cut the strips for the ribs himself. Maybe it didn't make much difference . . . what did he know about it? He had to do exactly what the book said. He wanted to do what the book said.

The afternoon they finished harvesting the corn, Lloyd Harris handed him a plain white envelope with his pay so closely figured that coins rolled along the bottom of the packet. Jackson spent the change on licorice pipes and curled the bills into a tight cylinder and hid them in the hole hollowed into the top of his bathroom door.

In the drawer of his sewing machine stand, where he used to hide his personal flask, he kept the business card the music store man had handed him. Every day he read the card. Folkard's Music Store. The card folded out to list all sorts of things they did — music lessons and instrument repairs. There was another long list of things they sold, among them, at the bottom, "supplies for instrument building and repair." He had to go to Halifax.

Jackson wasn't sure how to get Matthew to go with him. Fact was, he had never asked before. It was always Matthew who decided on trips — where they would go, who they would take, what they would do. He found Matthew in the shed by his house, sorting through brake pads, looking for a pair less worn than those on his car. Jackson shifted his weight, kicked the door frame lightly, lit a cigarette.

Finally he asked, "Wanna go to the city?"

"Halifax?"

Jackson nodded.

"What for?"

"Uh, you know, uh, shopping. Trip."

"Jesus. That's all I need. Shopping trips. You're going a bit mental since you gave up the drink. You know that? Look at these goddamn brake pads. I gotta get this friggin' car inspected this week."

Jackson leaned in the shed doorway, smoking his cigarette and waiting, but Matthew never mentioned the trip again. He turned back to his cabin. He could go on his own. He had been to the city before, for chrissake. If only Ian were here. Shut up. *Shut up!* He would be better off without Matthew. Matthew would just want to spend the afternoon in a bar anyway. He had that inset map of Halifax. He sort of knew where Queen Street was. Sort of. And he knew how to get in over the old bridge and turn down Gottingen Street. It made him nervous, though: the toll booth with the gaping basket, that empty cop car they left sitting there, the merging traffic, the way the land fell away and the city rose up out of the sea. The last time he parallel parked was for his driving test fifteen years ago. He picked up his mould and ran his fingers along its curving walls. He drew a wad of bills from the crevice cut into the bottom of his window sill and the business card from the drawer, his heart pounding in his chest. He counted eight quarters out of the jar hidden up under his sink — three to get over the bridge, three back, and two extras, in case he missed his shot. He didn't tell anyone, he just left. Quick, before he lost his nerve.

So many people. So many cars. He had trouble paying attention to everything. His hands shook from the first traffic light until he crossed the bridge and escaped into a parking lot at the far end of Gottingen Street. He left the truck and continued on foot, weak with relief. He stopped and lit a cigarette to calm himself, fingered the business card nervously in his jean jacket pocket. It took forever to cross the streets in Halifax, they were so wide. No one stared at him, no one even noticed him. He was surprised to come across Queen Street so much sooner than he had expected, relieved when address numbers indicated he was walking in the right direction and almost amazed when he saw the sign for Folkard's Music Store. It was so ordinary.

A little bell tinkled when Jackson entered. It startled him, embarrassed him. He slunk towards the back of the store. Like the other music store, this one had a few electric guitars, blacks and reds and silvers, but mostly there were cowboy guitars gleaming with polished wood, banjos and a smaller, rounded instrument. Mandolin. The name surprised him, jumping out of his brain like that. There were various styles of small drums and all kinds of flutes and whistles. Fiddles hung high up on the walls.

The saleswoman chatted with one of the other customers, who must have been a friend of hers. In the back corner, not in a separate room but in a little nook, stood a tall, slim case where Jackson recognized the sycamore and pine slabs he had seen depicted in his book, the strips for ribs and linings, the blocks for moulds and necks and a half carved scroll. There wasn't a lot of wood, just one or two of everything. In a glassed-in cabinet beside the shelves were the smaller supplies, purfling veneer, tailpieces, patterns, fingerboards, bridges and pegs. A twinkle caught his eye. On the top shelf of the cabinet sat a row of brass thumb planes, like golden eggs sliced flat along the bottom, their little blades regulated with tiny thumbscrews. The smallest of the three was only three-quarters of an inch long from one perfect glittering end to the other, the largest about two inches. Involuntarily his hand reached out to them and pressed against the glass. He pulled his hand back and shoved it in his pocket, but his fingerprints remained, smudged on the glass between him and the golden temptations.

The saleswoman appeared so suddenly at his side that he jumped.

"Hi, there!"

"Uh, hi."

"Can I help you?"

"Uh."

"Are you making an instrument?"

"F-fiddle."

She opened the cabinet while he examined the wood. And she began chatting, just like she had with the other customer. Her name was Brenda, what was his, where was he from, she hadn't seen him in the shop before, had he been making fiddles long? She talked about Albert, who did repairs part-time in the back room, and she showed him a fiddle Albert had made. He didn't mind her talking, really. Her voice bubbled, reminded him a bit of Rosie. He didn't have to say much himself. He bought sycamore for his fiddle's back, ribs and neck, and pine for the belly and linings. He bought all three of the brass violin planes. He couldn't remember ever spending so much money in one spot before in his life.

"Thanks, Jackson," she said as she handed him his change. "Good luck! We'll see you later, eh?"

Jackson walked as quickly as he could back to his truck, manoeuvred out of the lot and out of the city, over the bridge and home.

His heart beat faster when he held the wood in his hands. The fine strips of sycamore for the ribs he was to square perfectly and cut to length, then plane to an even one-sixteenth of an inch thickness. One side, the side which would face outwards, he must sand to a perfect sheen before he could begin to fit the pieces together. He set his tools out before him on the table and began. His mind enveloped the task, pushed everything else aside, until peace, the first real peace since Ian announced his leaving, seeped into his lungs and dispersed slowly through his arteries.

When Jackson heated up his new bending iron and pulled a dampened sycamore strip across it, butterflies fluttered in his stomach. The wood curled into the hot cylinder at the slightest encouragement from his fingers. He shaped it, bent it, and slipped it into the mould, where it nestled into its new shape.

The first two strips began at the top of the mould where the fiddle's neck would eventually join the body. They curved gently from this point outwards along the line of the mould like shoulders. The two middle ribs arched sharply inwards in C shapes, as if two bites had been chomped out of a tiny guitar. The final two ribs swooped downwards in a broad arc, meeting at the tail. Where the ribs met at the neck and tail their butt ends joined on the same plane. Where they met at the "corners" of the fiddle, the top and bottom of the two C-shaped cutouts, they formed points. Jackson bevelled the joints so they fit as though they had grown together. The detailed work drew him right into the flowing grain of the wood. The closer he got, the more control he had, the more he became a part of his work, drawn out of the larger world and into the microcosm of grain and pith. The concentration left no room for anything else. Not alcohol cravings. Not even Ian. For the first time since Ian had left, no, for the first time since he could remember, he sat still without alcohol and without fear of being crushed. Before he knew it, the ribs completely lined the inside of his mould.

For the six points where the rib pieces met — the top, the tail and the four corners — he sculpted intricate fine-grained pine blocks to nestle against the ribs to hold them in place. Thin strips of pine, called linings, had to be measured and planed to a sleek slope on one side, forming a long, snaking wedge. They were glued along the top and bottom rims of the ribs, wide edge up, to provide enough surface area to glue on the back and belly. Jackson bent over the supporting blocks, as slender as the tip of his little finger, carving tiny slots in them to hold the ends of the linings. He didn't hear Matthew come in and didn't notice him at all until he leaned on the table.

"I said, what are ya doin', boy?"

Jackson lifted his head. It took a moment for his eyes to adjust to the scale of the objects around him.

"Oh. I, uh . . ."

"Jesus, what is that?"

"It's . . . I thought I might try making, you know, a fiddle."

"What for?"

Jackson shrugged.

"You better not be thinking about playing it, like that other one you had. Fuck. I'm fucking burning it if you do. Ever since Ian Sutherland, its been nothing but fiddles around here. He was okay, but fuck, you give a guy nightmares."

Jackson bent his head over his work again. Matthew chattered on a while. Then he must have left.

Jackson kept the mould where he could see it every time he looked up. Inside its sweeping curves the ribs, blocks and linings sat clamped, their new shape settling into permanence, gaining strength and stability with every day.

Jackson prepared the wood for the back plate of the fiddle and cut out the shape. The outside of the back had to be rounded in a gentle hill, dipping slightly at the base of the slope and rising out into a narrow flat plateau bordering the edges. Early in the morning he began gently scooping wood away with his gouge, then with his planes. Modelling the back, shaping it, seemed a job that had been waiting for him to discover it. Each stroke led to the next. Shavings spilled onto the table top. Working from left to right, top to bottom, Jackson began to expose the roundness hidden in the block of wood. When light began to fade he looked up, annoyed, and found the day had passed, the sun had set, and darkness had overtaken the cabin. He switched on the overhead bulb. He hadn't eaten since breakfast, and hunger clawed at his stomach. He didn't want to set down his tools. I'll just finish this bit, he said to himself, then I'll heat up some dinner. But another two hours passed before he could force his hands to comply. He wolfed down a peanut butter sandwich while he waited for his tea water to boil. He worked late into the night. A gentle hillock emerged from the slab under his hands, an elongated mound, surprisingly steep in the middle where the fiddle's shape tucked in, more gradual at the ends. When he finally set down his tools, his eyes watered from strain and his shoulders ached, but even as he crawled into bed his hands itched to get back to work.

Jackson recognized the need. But this time it wasn't the emptiness that pushed in on him. It was everything else. It was as if he had pulled his finger out of a dike. He couldn't control what came through the hole. He was afraid he would be swept away, drowned. The fiddle kept everything at bay. So in a way it was like drinking. But in a way it wasn't. The liquor had filled the void, but the fiddle preserved it, kept it dry, gave him a chance to think. Now, when he felt strong enough, he could pick thoughts out of the back of his mind and mull them over. He could set before himself the facts of his life.

Ian hadn't loved him. The surfacing of this knowledge caused barely a ripple. He accepted it so calmly that he suspected he had known all along. But Ian had liked him, wanted him, turned to him, trusted him. Ian would have gone crazy without him to talk to, that's what he had said. Ian had needed him. They had lain together in bed with their skin pressed close. Ian hadn't cared that Jackson's body was too skinny. Ian had stroked it, kissed it, held it, fucked it, nestled into it, opened his own body to it. Ian had whispered to him, purred into his ear. And Jackson loved Ian. If it hadn't been Ian, though, it might have been someone else. Part of him denied this, part of him accepted it calmly, but the largest, loudest part just wanted Ian back. The planing, stroking the hard-wood surface of the back plate to its ideal thickness and perfect smoothness, required his very close attention. Ian hovered above him, close enough for Jackson to feel his own longing but not so close that he collapsed inside the loss. Sometimes his yearning for a drink pushed Ian right out of the picture. And as mid-November drew nearer, increasingly it was his mother who stood over him.

When he finished the outside of the back plate he flipped it over to begin sculpting the graceful series of pools in the wood which would eventually cup the notes it received, shape them and offer them back to the ear. He worked steadily with his planes, callipers and sandpaper until the back plate answered the book's speci-fications on every point: five thirty-seconds of an inch thick along the centre, gradually narrowing to three thirty-seconds at the outside edges. He sanded the wood until it glowed.

Kate's Emma dropped by the cabin every few days. She leaned across the table to get a good look. "Wow. You're really building a fiddle, aren't you?"

"Yeah."

"You got any Coke?"

"A bit." He dipped his head in the direction of the shelf. Emma poured herself a tall glass, then returned to sit at the table and watch him.

"How'd you learn what to do?"

"Book."

"You gonna learn to play it, too?"

"Nah."

"Too bad that Ian guy left, eh? Remember that guy who used to come around last summer? He could've played it."

"Um."

"Mom says Uncle Ronnie ought to get you on a job with him. Now that you're not drinking anymore you should be a real carpenter. You should earn some money, she said, and add on some extra rooms and build a proper foundation and stuff. So you could get married and everything. Prob'ly get a half-decent wife, she said, especially now you've got your hair cut a bit. She was talking to Uncle Ronnie about it, finding you a job, I mean."

He didn't respond.

Emma drained her glass.

"I gotta go do my homework or Mom will kill me."

As the first anniversary of Gert Bigney's death approached, tempers on the road snapped, flared, sputtered, exploded again. The slam of the farmhouse door carried all the way across the meadow and through the walls of his cabin. Jackson wondered if he hadn't felt the earth shake a little. A second later Darlene's voice cut the air. Jackson didn't get up to look. He knew she would be standing there on the porch shaking her fist.

"Don't you set foot in my house again, and you keep those brats of yours away from here!"

"It's *not* your house. This is *my* mother's house! Don't you ever lay a finger on one of my girls again or I'll call the cops!" That was Margie.

Jackson completed his fiddle's back plate and began on the belly. He planed his softwood slab and cut the outline. He arranged his gouges and planes in a row in front of him and began to work. Delbert was the first to retreat to Jackson's cabin to catch his breath. He yanked a chair away from the wall and slapped it next to the stove, where he sat and glared at the cabin door as if daring someone else to come through it.

"I come out of the bathroom, and Margie's kid's standing there, wallpaper all over the place, and she's holding on to the end of a big strip of it! Torn right off the wall! Christ. She's got the whole fucking place torn apart! A hundred and fifty bucks worth of wallpaper! We just did that room a year ago. Brand new wallpaper. I told Darlene that kid better not show up at our house again."

Not long after Delbert left, Ronnie arrived with his baby girl in one arm and Annie, his five-year-old, hanging off the other. He sat uneasily in the corner. Although Ronnie drank very little, he looked naked without the excuse of a beer to account for his presence.

"Delbert's all over us again. What's wrong with that guy?"

Annie stuck out her chin and planted her hands on her hips. "Ya know what? Ya know what he did? I had to go to the doctor and everything! Me and Chelsea were playing, and it was Chelsea's fault anyway, and it was a *ax*ident!"

Ronnie frowned. "He went after her with a belt, twisted her arm right around. I took her in to the doctor, just to check, you know. Make sure it wasn't dislocated or anything. Gee. She's just a little girl."

Ronnie stayed until the baby got too fussy and they had to leave.

Matthew was the next to show up.

"That Delbert's a fucking case, and so is that fucking bitch of a wife of his! He wants fucking trouble, he'll get it!" Matthew hurled his words across the room so hard Jackson could almost hear them splat against the opposite wall. Matthew's eyes blazed with an anger so sharp it hurt Jackson to look at him. "He wants trouble? No problem!"

Emma arrived the following afternoon and dropped her body gracelessly into the chair across from him. She shoved a large cookie tin and a loaf of bread over to him.

"Aunt Margie was over at our place crying and everything. Mom says none of them have the sense God gave a goose. Mom said you're supposed to eat this gingerbread." Emma plunked her elbows on the table and her chin in her hands and stared glumly ahead of her. "I think you better, or she'll be up here with a poker. You should see her, she's been cooking like mad. I got terminal dishpan hands. It's just like when Nana died. Remember?"

"Um." He remembered. The gouge he was staring at, using to scoop slivers of pine onto the table in front of him, was the same one he used to carve the onions he made for her. He tried not to think about it. He tried to think about Ian but couldn't get him to stick in his mind. Even the night they spent together in the cottage when they had lingered over each other's bodies for hours, kissed and stroked every curve and hollow, even that memory kept slipping away from him. He couldn't distract himself from the sharp stones grinding away in his belly, from the images pushing in on him.

He remembered crossing a street in town, his red-mittened hand tucked inside hers. She wore no mitts or gloves, and the sleeve of her coat was brown. He had felt a rush of excitement at the miracle of being there alone with her. The white diagonal lines of the crosswalk had disappeared from beneath his boots, and he remembered stepping up onto the curb. When his mother turned he bumped gently against her side. She smelled of woodsmoke and every kind of soap. He remembered his mother saying, "This way, Jackson." Her voice was so quiet it floated into his ear and hung there, cradled in a cloud of his own breath.

But no, he had thought then, she wasn't his mother at all. She couldn't keep him any more, and so she was bringing him back to the orphanage. Around the next corner would be the huge stone building with the spiky wrought iron fence all around it. The chain would clang against the metal and release a great whiff of rust as they waited for the gates to be opened. They would walk, hand in hand, up the cobblestone pathway and mount the stairs to the massive wooden doors. She would kneel in front of him so her face was level with his, and she would fumble with the collar of his coat. I can't keep you, she would say. There isn't enough money. You be a good boy, now. He would nod his head. And he would, in that moment, make a vow to himself that he would work hard and return to her when she was an old woman and living alone in the rundown farmhouse, forsaken by all her children. He would be rich by then and knock on her door in a storm. She wouldn't recognize him, of course, but she would take him in and give him a bed and a meal, and in the morning he would reveal his identity as the orphan she had returned to the orphanage so many years ago. She would throw her arms around him and beg his forgiveness and say how he, although only an orphan, was better than all her real children who had deserted her. Then he would take her off to the city, where they would live together in his fancy house with a statue of a lion on each side of the front door.

Jackson jumped as the top of the cookie tin hit the floor and wobbled loudly on its rim before collapsing with a final clang. He must have looked fearsome because Emma blanched and scampered to retrieve the lid.

"Sorry," she said through a mouthful of gingerbread and disappeared out the door.

Disoriented, he was suddenly unable to remember if the nights his mother had spoken to him about his birth and his name and about Maggie Hopewell had been real or if he had made that up, too. That same quiet voice came back to him. He stared at his hands, now idle and trembling, trying to steady his mind. No. He hadn't made that up. He had really carved those onions for his mother. He had trouble with the lip of the second one and thought he might have to start over. He changed from pine to maple to carve the tiny central onion. That part was real. He remembered the hardness of the maple and its fine swirling grain, how its colour and density set it apart from the three softwood layers covering it. Yes, the stories she told him were true.

He set down his gouge and buried his face behind his fists. For the first time he wondered if his mother had ever woken at night and thought of Maggie Hopewell. He wondered if they had ever held hands like schoolgirls and if they felt that swelling inside and knew they wanted something more. What about the night he had been conceived? What if his mother had been thinking about Maggie while Vernon grunted on top of her? What if Vernon had suspected and pushed himself farther and harder into her, trying to get her back, get her attention, forcing her to make a baby boy. A boy who looked exactly like him, a boy she would have to attend to for years and years so she could never leave him, never forget her duties. What if Gert had loved Maggie Hopewell all along? What if there had been a desperate kiss, an urgent whispered plan? What if his mother had tossed a few things into the old hound's-tooth cardboard suitcase and hid it behind the woodpile, risen in the middle of the night and waited in the dark kitchen in her coat and good shoes, with her new baby wrapped tight in a blanket, straining to hear an approaching motor, glimpse the sudden spears of headlights in the night. What if everything had been different?

No. That would have been impossible. His mother never thought of leaving. "You always have your family," she used to say. It was him, not his mother, who had yearned and whispered and groped in secret lust.

He got up to wash his hands and face. His fingers ached with tension when he forced his fists open and revealed a line of arcs across his palms where his fingernails had dug into his skin. His face was ridged with red blotches where he had forced his knuckles hard against his cheekbones. Fresh water splashing against his skin was all the sensation he could bear. He returned to his planing, burying his mind deep in the grain of the wood.

Over the next six weeks Jackson kept himself close to his fiddle. He finished the belly plate, modelling its hollows and hillocks with the same precision and intensity he had used on the back. He measured the exact positions for the sound holes and traced their narrow and graceful S-shapes onto the wood. He started each sound hole by drilling a hole through the bottom circle, just like the book said, then undercutting all the way around the outlines with his fret saw and trimming them with a knife. He finished the edges with a file and finally sandpaper. The pair of matching, swirling slits balanced the belly plate so beautifully that Jackson's chest tightened when he sat on his bed at the end of the day beholding them. He smoked a joint and imagined the fiddle's body swallowing the sound waves, rolling them around and around into notes before setting the perfect music free to float upwards through the slits and into the world.

The din of his family grew deafening. He had to shut down his ears. Emma stopped by the cabin almost daily now. Her voice was quieter than the others, so he took in the news she brought him. Delbert and Darlene were mad at Margie and Ronnie because of the ripped wallpaper. Margie and Ronnie were mad at Delbert and Darlene because they twisted little Annie's arm and strapped her. Kate was mad at Ronnie because he hadn't found work for Jackson. Matthew was mad at Delbert for acting like he owned the place. Kate thought Matthew should never come near the cabin if he had been drinking. Rosie thought Kate should stand up to Delbert and not always let him have his way. Delbert was talking about getting his other two kids, the ones from his first marriage a long time ago, to come to the farmhouse for Christmas for the first time ever. Darlene said they should come because their own mother was hopeless, so it would be good for them to get out, but Emma thought Delbert might have told Darlene that she *had* to like the idea. Emma had begun to study for her Christmas exams; she thought English was a cinch and geography was boring and math was boring except for geometry, which was fun, and science wasn't bad except that the teacher this year was putrid.

Just the facts. It was so easy for things to get out of control. "Gay," he said to himself as he planed, squared and then tapered the strip of pine for the bass bar. Gay. Gay. Gay. The bass bar was to govern the vibrations of the two lower strings and had to be painstakingly shaped to fit exactly against the inside of the belly plate. Everything had to be exact or the tone of the instrument would suffer. Gay, gay, gay. Once the bar was glued in place it was supposed to bring the plate to a perfect D, which meant that a bow drawn over the narrowest point on the plate would produce a D note. Gay like Ian. Gay. Like him. Jackson would never to be able to tell if the note was true, he could only follow the directions and hope. Gay, he repeated.

Jackson squared and planed his final piece of wood, the piece which would form the neck and head of the instrument. He began with the peg box. He measured in five thirty-seconds of an inch from the edges of the neck. The space between these two "cheeks" was to be hollowed out like a blunt-ended canoe to make room for the pegs, which would hold the strings. The book said the trick to the peg box was to cut the wood rather than levering it. Jackson felt his knife sink into the grain, severing the fibres, watched his hands as, bit by bit, the hole opened up. He knew it was hard for people to like him. It wasn't their fault. He never knew what to say. That was what his father had hated most: that he would cower silently, a little Vernon-shaped shell, hollow, helpless and silent. A wuss. A faggot. Vernon had probably known all along.

Christmas loomed. When Matthew arrived with Guy Nelson and a dozen beer, Jackson kept his eyes on his work. The pssst of the bottle caps, the warm clank of the bottles, the yeasty smell of the hops, the malt, set him on edge. But he knew he wasn't going to drink. He was going to finish his fiddle. Carving the fiddlehead scroll was the most delicate job of all. When making his template and tracing the design onto each surface of the wood, he had to keep translating from two dimensions to three and back again. The book showed him where to make the four saw cuts that got him started, but after that he had to ease along from the outside to the centre eye, coaxing the flowing scroll shape out of the block. He left his cabin only for tobacco, sandpaper and a few groceries. His supply of money was dwindling. Christmas came and went. He finished the head and neck.

He thought a lot about Folkard's Music Store. There was something exhilarating about knowing people that no one else knew, not even Matthew. He thought about Brenda, the saleswoman who had sold him the supplies, and wondered about Albert, who worked there and had made that fiddle he had seen. He couldn't put his own fiddle together until he knew his plates were right, that the back would produce a C note and the belly a perfect D. Maybe his plates didn't sound anything like they were supposed to. Maybe they were a disaster. Still, disaster or not, he had to know. He wrapped the pieces in towels and tucked them into a plastic grocery bag. He would leave in the morning.

This time he drove right down Brunswick Street and parked at a meter. He lit a smoke to settle his nerves. As he headed to the shop, the plastic bag turned slippery with the sweat of his palm, and the heat of embarrassment rose to his cheeks. The shop door felt extraordinarily heavy when he pushed into it, and he steeled himself for the tinkle of the bell.

"Hi!"

He glanced around. Brenda smiled at him.

"You're the guy from Scotch River. Oh, gee, don't tell me, the name is common but not . . ."

"Jackson."

"Yeah! Jackson. Great name."

"It was my mother's." Jackson could hardly believe he had said that. It was only half true. He hadn't needed to say anything. "I made the pieces for my, uh, but I . . . I don't know how they sound. I can't . . ." Suddenly he couldn't remember the words the book used to describe the process. He set his bag on the counter. Brenda pulled the beautifully sculpted belly from its wrappings. "Oh, look at this!"

Jackson's stomach constricted. He concentrated on a spot just behind the counter, trying to control his rising panic. She unwrapped the neck with the elegant scroll carved into the end. He covered the belly quickly with the towel and tried to stuff it back into the bag.

"Go on back and show them to Albert. Through there." She pointed at the doorway at the back of the store. "Albert!" she sang out.

Albert's room measured about eight feet square, two walls covered in tools, strings, fingerboards, moulds and instruments in various stages of disrepair. A work bench with a vice sat beneath the large window, which offered an abundance of light and a clear view of a parking lot. Sprawling stacks of paper covered both the table and the filing cabinet pushed up against one wall. The air swam with the rich smell of wood chips and fine sawdust laced with an intoxicating whiff of glue. Jackson stood in the doorway clutching his plastic bag, staring at Albert's back. Albert seemed to take up what little space was left in the room. His almost spherical body perched on a stool like a ball on a stick; his scalp peeked through scarecrow-straight greying hair. He glanced over his shoulder. His face was as round as his body, his cheeks jowly and his forehead deeply creased. His eyes were lively, and when he raised a bushy, curly eyebrow, Jackson thought of a *Sesame Street* puppet that Matthew's kids played with.

"Uh, what? Oh." Albert gestured towards a second stool pushed halfway under the bench and covered with a copy of that morning's paper. Jackson stepped forward.

"I don't know why that girl sends people back here. It's not the tourist association." His voice was gruff but not unfriendly. More as if he and Jackson were sharing a common complaint. Albert set aside a mandolin, then stood up and turned to Jackson. "What did you want?"

Jackson set his bag on the table and unwrapped the back plate of his violin. He handed it to Albert. Albert took it with kind, practised care, turned it over, glanced up at Jackson, crooked one of his large eyebrows,

"D-d-does it make the right note?"

"Looks like," he said, examining it closely. Albert screwed it into the vice on his bench, protecting it between thin shims. He glanced around the table, patted a spread of papers and finally drew a bow out from under the pile. "Why ask me?"

"I can't . . ." Jackson touched his ear.

He watched as Albert drew the bow over the narrowest part of the plate, releasing a melodious hum. The skin all over his body tingled. It wasn't a note like a piano would make, or a fiddle string, but a note nonetheless. Like a warm-up, a promise. Was that the right sound, he wondered. He realized he had stopped breathing. Albert nodded.

"It's easy. You're looking for a C. Listen." He slid open a drawer built into the work bench and picked a pitch pipe out of a velvet-lined box. He blew a single note. Then he drew the bow across the fiddle again. One made a thin vibrating sound, the other a moan.

"See? Perfect."

Jackson could detect no similarity. He nodded vaguely.

"Let's see the other one."

Albert set the belly in the vice and slid his bow across it. He wrinkled his nose slightly, picked a violin plane off the window-sill, tilted it towards Jackson. "Okay?"

Jackson nodded again. Then he turned to the fiddle resting on the stack of paper at his elbow. He bent over it, studying the inlay that ran around its edge. Purfling, he knew it was called. Albert fussed for a couple of minutes, slipping minute slivers of wood off the bass bar. He bowed again, and unscrewed the plate from the vice.

"Yup." He unwrapped Jackson's carved scroll and turned it over and over in his hands, staring down the length of its corners to check the straightness of its lines. He raised his eyes to Jackson. "Do I know you?"

"No. I just, um, Brenda said . . ." If only he could stop himself from turning so red. He should never have trimmed his beard, he felt so exposed.

"I mean, you haven't brought fiddles in here before?"

"No. This is my first."

Albert's eyebrow lifted again. He set the piece down on its towel and rewrapped it tenderly. "Your first, eh? Well, bring 'er in when she's done. I'm here Mondays, Wednesdays and Friday mornings."

Yeah, I will, thought Jackson. He packed up his pieces.

"And get a decent case for that thing, will ya?"

The corners of Jackson's lips flickered. He liked Albert.

Jackson walked back out to the front of the store and bought pegs, strings, purfling inlay, everything he needed to finish his fiddle and all the wood he needed to get started on his next one. Brenda showed him a magazine just for people who make violins. He bought one. He bought a special tool called a post-setter, which struck him as ludicrously over-priced for such a cheap piece of tin. Brenda chatted happily as she helped him. "Tons of great fiddlers up by Scotch River! I was up to the Pictou Lobster Carnival last year. Oh my gawd! Party! We spent the whole day . . ."

By the time he finished, Jackson found he had spent all his folding money. His arms were full, though, and he still had enough pocket change for a pack of smokes. When he stepped out of the store the city didn't seem so overwhelming. He walked to the corner and turned up Spring Garden Road towards a drug store.

On his way back to his truck with the cigarettes he remembered the bridge toll. He had eighteen cents in his pocket. He stashed his parcels, fished the violin makers' magazine out of his bag and walked the two blocks back to the store. Albert was leaning on the counter.

"I-I need my money back," he told Brenda, setting the magazine on the counter in front of her. "Forgot about my bridge toll."

Albert hitched up his pants, dug into his pocket and set a token on top of the magazine.

"Just till next time," he said and walked back through the shop to his workroom.

Jackson picked up the token and the magazine and left without a word.

CHAPTER NINE

JACKSON BEGAN JOINING HIS FIDDLE TOGETHER. After the weeks of gouging and shaping and planing and sanding, progress seemed swift. While he worked he considered his immediate situation. He had no money, none at all. He had been sloppy about his business since he met Ian, twice leaving it in the hands of Matthew. He had laid in a big stock of liquor just before he gave up drinking, and he had lost all that. He wasn't going to be selling marijuana anymore because he didn't want people coming around. So he had harvested only a few of his buds, barely enough for himself and the remainder were long dead from frost. All his savings and all the money he made working at Harris's was gone — spent on fiddle supplies. He checked and rechecked every secret cubbyhole cut into his cabin studs, doors and boards. No forgotten packages turned up. He had ten cigarettes left, about a gallon and a half of gas in the truck and two cans of stew on the shelf.

It was years since he had been flat broke, since the year he was charged and had to pay the bootleg fine. He might be able to sell a few loads of firewood, earn enough to tide him over until spring, maybe. He kept an eye out his back window, watching the farm-yard through the naked hedgerow. It was a fine day, though cold. Not much wind. He could see Matthew puttering around the farmhouse tool shed. When Delbert wandered out into the yard, Jackson set down his tools, tossed on his jacket and followed the snowy path through the line of trees and across the field to ask him about using the tractor.

"I was, uh, going to get, um, a load or two of wood."

"You got lots of wood up there."

"I-I-I need a few bucks."

"You're not fucking selling *my* wood, buddy-o."

"Eh?"

Matthew stopped sorting through bits of wire.

Delbert raised his arm and leaned against the shed wall, trapping Jackson between his massive bulk and the shed. "I pay the taxes on this place, you know. I don't keep that tractor running on air. I get Kate's wood in every year. I don't see you lining up to help with that."

Jackson's throat tightened. The year he turned ten he got a card with five dollars in it, a blue five-dollar bill with Sir Wilfred Laurier gazing out at him, calm and confident. He rolled it up into a little telescope and smoothed it out again. He folded it in half and then in half again and carried it around in his pocket. The bill grew a soft, linty surface in no time because he kept pulling it out of his pocket, unfolding it and staring. He slept with it tucked in his pillowcase that night. The next day Delbert cornered him in the barn, backed him up against the wall. Delbert would have been sixteen then. "Hand over the five bucks." Jackson started to sweat. "I don't have it on me." But his hand moved instinctively to the front pocket of his jeans. Delbert laughed. He easily twisted Jackson's arm behind his back, held him useless, unable to move. Jackson stood on tiptoe trying to climb out of the pain. Delbert slipped his hand into the pocket and pulled out the bill, waving it briefly in front of Jackson's eyes before it disappeared. Jackson remembered crying out, swearing he would go to their mother. But Delbert said he wouldn't. Delbert yanked at the zipper in Jackson's jeans, jerked them to his knees. He folded his hand around Jackson's privates, held them for a moment. That money belonged to the farm, he said, to help pay for all the food Jackson ate, the room he slept in. Jackson felt Delbert's damp, sour breath hot on his ear, the rough scratch of his pants against his naked bum. Delbert released Jackson's twisted arm but held him in place with one hand to his chest, the other stroking, caressing him, massaging him gently. Who pays for brats who never do a lick of work, Delbert wanted to know? Then he closed his fist, crushing Jackson's balls, shooting a flame of pain up through his body, and dropped him. Jackson doubled over, groping for breath in the dirty hay on the barn floor. He had lain there writhing at Delbert's feet, his jeans at his knees.

Jackson slid along the shed wall trying to ease away.

Delbert followed. "I bust my ass to keep this place up, and you waltz in grab whatever you can, whenever you want? Is that it?" Delbert's face hovered six inches from Jackson's. Jackson could say nothing.

"Christ, Delbert." Matthew spoke up behind him. "It's not your goddamned farm, you know. You're sitting there, rent free, scared the couch'll float away if you get up off it. Don't get any fucking ideas. That wood's not yours. He needs a bit of cash. Give him a break."

"He gets lots of breaks. I need that wood."

"Well, I don't exactly see you at it night and day. Look at your own goddamned woodpile — a puddle of bark and a dead leaf. Rosie was over yesterday, and Darlene was trying to bake a batch of bread with your old Christmas tree, for chrissake. Why don't you get off your ass . . ."

Jackson backed away. Why was every little thing so hard? He wasn't fighting Delbert for wood, that was for sure. He wasn't fighting Delbert.

It was January, the middle of winter. What else was there to do? Carpentry jobs dried up this time of year. Ronnie had just filed for his unemployment. It would be at least three months before there would be even the chance of a few days shore work for the lobstermen, and then maybe a bit of spring work for Lloyd Harris again, fencing, disking.

People owed him money, probably around a thousand dollars all told. When he was in business he used to run through his accounts every day in his head, but after he dumped the liquor he just wanted to be clear of it all. He dismissed those debts from his mind. Now he had a few vague ideas but no exact amounts.

The trouble was, as long as people kept drinking, they kept paying. Now that he wasn't serving anymore they wouldn't be so anxious to hand over scarce cash. Still, it would be worth a try. He didn't see any other choice. He slipped his gold bracelet, the one Ian had given him, out of its hiding place behind a wall stud and tucked it into the pocket of his jeans for luck.

Rolly MacDonald lived out on Division Road in an old farm-house surrounded by a cluster of precarious outbuildings. Rolly's laneway gleamed with a thin layer of hard-packed snow. Jackson parked his truck behind Rolly's little Topaz. Rolly was without a driving license, he remembered. A dog barked ferociously, and when Jackson stepped out onto the icy lane, he heard it lunging against its chain. The whack of an axe on wood encouraged him. Rolly was home, and he would be able to speak to him outside, not have to go up to the door. When he rounded the corner, though, it was Rolly's wife standing at the chopping block. She looked up at him. He couldn't turn and go now. The dog's barking rolled in and out of a deep growl. The cast he had seen on her wrist a couple of months ago was gone.

"Is, uh, Rolly around?"

She shook her head. Jackson looked at the ground. How's your wrist, he wanted to ask. The splitting probably hurt her arm. He wished she would hand him the axe so he could finish it up for her.

"You, um, know when he'll be back?"

"No. Sorry." She wasn't friendly but she wasn't not friendly either. They took turns glancing at each other, looking away. The toe of his boot kicked a little hole into the shallow snow.

"Does he owe you money?"

Jackson was surprised by the shy kindness in her voice. How's your wrist, he thought again. "I, uh, sorta really need it."

"How much?"

"A hundred," Jackson lied. Two hundred would have been a more reasonable guess. "I-I kind of need it," he repeated. "Or, uh, what you can spare?"

She set down her axe and began loading split junks onto her arm. "I'll see what I can find."

Jackson nodded. He waited until she struggled into the house with her armload before he took up the axe. He set a junk on the block and split it with a swift blow, then raced to set up another. Then another. There was only about a quarter of a cord left.

She returned in no time. "Just a twenty. Sorry. Come back when Rolly's here."

Jackson had to stop splitting to take the bill. He bobbed his head. "Thanks."

"I can do that." She held her hand out towards the axe.

"J-just this bit here," he stammered. "Your . . ." He indicated her arm by holding his as if it was broken. He looked away, turned red and dove back into the work. She gathered up another armload and disappeared into the house. He raced through the remainder of the pile, his back growing clammy with sweat.

After he split the last junk he escaped down the lane, exhilarated by his success. He had twenty bucks! Now there was Frank Vasser, a mile down the road. He owed over a hundred bucks for sure. And there were a couple of Matthew's friends, the Everetts and Chester Duggan. The list unfolded in his head. More and more names came back to him. There were a couple more guys out this way. Ian's father, Harold Sutherland, ought to be able to come up with fifty bucks. He tried to imagine himself driving up to the house, standing in the porch, talking to Ian's mother. The thought made him queasy. He would start with the others.

By the end of the day Jackson had collected a grand total of ninety-five dollars in cash and another hundred and seventy-five in wandering-gaze promises. He stopped at Nelson's Garage and bought a pouch of tobacco, a pack of papers and ten dollars worth of gas. The remaining money he folded into his wallet. The early winter darkness settled around him. He was glad to get back to his cabin and stuff a few sticks of wood into his firebox. He looked down at his almost-completed fiddle and felt calm. Even tentatively happy. Definitely hungry. For the first time in ages he walked back out to MacIntyre Road and up to Kate's back door, where he kicked the snow off his boots. He stepped in onto the mat. The bungalow glowed with warmth from the woodstove, the blue flickering light of the TV, the smell of fresh bread and meat and cooking onions. Kate glanced at him over her shoulder and tugged open the silverware drawer so abruptly the cutlery rattled.

"Well, he may not starve after all," she said to the air.

Jackson sat at the table and watched her moving about her kitchen, stooping to pull a roast of beef out of the oven. She's pleased, he thought. Pleased I've come. He gulped back a twinge of panic, looked away, took several deep breaths. It's okay, he said to himself, looking down at his long, chilled fingers, rubbing them together. It's okay. I'm pleased, too.

In the days that followed, Jackson cut the bridge for his fiddle, fitted the fingerboard, fastened the tailpiece, inserted the pegs. He strung the instrument, winding the strings tight enough so they didn't sag. After hearing his plates singing under Albert's bow, Jackson was curious to hear his fiddle played, but not anxious. Mostly he found himself content to gaze at it. He set it on the shelf where he could look at it and where it could absorb the sunlight. The book said it was best to play it for a month or two "in the white" before varnishing. Jackson was glad of that. He would have a while to admire it, just as it was, naked and unprotected, before the varnish declared, it is finished, nothing more can be done.

Matthew arrived at the cabin with three of his boys in tow. They all had pop and chips, all giddy with their good fortune, prodding and goading each other, each sneaking glances to see who might still have a few chips left once his own bag was empty.

Jackson frowned. "Isn't it a school day?"

"In-service. Two in a row. The fun goes on and on."

Matthew took a seat and Jackson put on the kettle. He glanced over at his table to see what tools he had left out, what the boys could get at. Matthew's Troy finished his chips and waved his grease-shiny fingers. Jackson saw him eyeing the shelf where the fiddle sat, leaning back against the wall on display. The fiddle hadn't looked precarious before the boys arrived. Jackson started towards it. The boy raised his arms and curled his glistening fingers around the end of the shelf. Jackson wanted to call out but couldn't. He was nearly there.

"Hey, Dad, watch!" Troy sang out. He took a step back and jumped up to grab the end of the shelf like Tarzan swinging for a vine. Jackson lunged for the fiddle. The little metal shelf bracket buckled and bent under the boy's sudden weight, dumping awls and gouges and files forward in a shower onto the floor. Jackson saw his fiddle tip onto its belly and, in slow motion, start the diagonal slide along the board and out to its edge. He couldn't move any faster, he was already in mid-air. He could only watch space and time and gravity playing out between his reaching arm and the sliding instrument. A finger touched wood, then another, his hand pressed the fiddle against the collapsing shelf, then his other hand appeared underneath to catch the fragile weight. He had it. He had it.

"Jesus Christ, you frigging Indians!" Matthew hollered. Troy lay on his back on the cabin floor, crying loudly. His older brother berated him. "Look what you did, ya stupid idiot." The youngest brother backed away from the commotion, leery of blame. Matthew advanced on the guilty son and lifted him off the ground by the arm.

"Pick this stuff up," he yelled at the boys. "All of yez!"

"I'm not picking it up. He knocked it down."

"You friggin' are. All of yez." He smacked the sobbing boy on the shoulder. "There! Cry for that."

Jackson backed away from the noise, cradling his fiddle close to his chest. No one had even noticed the near-disaster. Matthew kept yelling at them to pick up the tools that had bounced onto the floor. Jackson just wanted them to go. He set his fiddle carefully on the table and returned to retrieve the tools.

"Leave them be," Matthew shouted. "These animals will get them." Matthew and the oldest were yelling at each other now. Jackson collected the tools as the oldest stomped across the room and sat heavily in a chair, shoving the table. A half-full can of Coke tipped over and fizzed in a trail across the tabletop towards the instrument. Jackson sprang up, grabbed his fiddle again, but not before the sticky bubbles dampened a penny-sized spot on its back.

"Look! You got Coke on Jackson's fiddle, now!" Matthew grabbed the boy by the shirt collar. "Clean that up!"

Jackson desperately scanned the room for a cloth, tugged out his shirttail and held it under the tap. He wiped the spot clean, backing away from the others, up against the wall of his cabin. He rubbed the spot with fine sandpaper. He knew he looked ridiculous, huddled there coddling his fiddle like a frightened little girl with a baby doll, like a wuss, like a pansy. He wanted them gone but didn't know what to do. Something wild and powerful threatened to burst up through him. The voices of MacIntyre Road overran his brain. Get ta fuck outta here, piss off, drop dead, get lost, get ta hell out of my face, fuck off, fuck off. Fuck off!

"It's *okay*!" The fury in his own voice startled him. "I'll clean up," he added, scared and contrite. But the wildness fought back. It jerked his head towards the door. Matthew glanced at the door, not understanding, then recoiled and looked away, embarrassed.

"He spilled my Coke!" the youngest whined. "I want some of his."

"He made me, the little faggot."

"You're the one who . . ."

Matthew grabbed the closest boy. "We're outta here!" The two remaining boys clambered after him, batting blame back and forth.

Jackson closed the cabin door behind them, his cheeks burning. He leaned his back against the door and listened to their voices grow distant. The fire in him melted his embarrassment. He turned and his fingers sought out the lock. The only time he had ever used that lock had been the weekend after Ian left. And yet it had been sitting here in his door the whole time. All he had to do was turn it to the right. He clicked it shut, felt the deadbolt side into place. He wrapped his fiddle and hid it under his bed.

He needed to get busy. He needed to start in on his next plate, focus on work, distract himself. His hardwood slab sat planed and ready for the pattern, but Jackson couldn't find a pencil, and once he found one he sliced the lead off it twice trying to sharpen it. He couldn't hold his template still, couldn't hold his hands still.

What the hell is Matthew doing, dragging his kids over to my cabin and letting them run wild? He didn't even notice they nearly wrecked my fiddle. Why would Matthew care, anyway? A smile and a slap on the back and what's your problem? And Delbert. He makes things up the way he wants them to be, and everyone else has to go along with it. He bullied his way into the farmhouse, and now he thinks the whole place belongs to him because he paid a couple of hundred bucks in taxes. He doesn't own the place. And Delbert doesn't take Kate her firewood for nothing. That's guaranteed. Kate is always fronting money to Darlene at the end of the month before the cheques come. And fuck that Rolly MacDonald. What kind of a man takes a nice quiet woman like his wife and breaks her bones, turns her black and blue? She should leave him, that's what she should do. Let him look after himself, the fucker. Why doesn't she? And Harold Sutherland. Doesn't bother paying his bills. No, don't bother with that. Expects me to go looking for it. Expects me to walk into his kitchen. Probably got pictures of Ian wearing his graduation robes smiling from stand-up picture frames on the mantel in the living room. Our son, we're so proud, living in Toronto. Yeah, well, I could tell you something about your son you don't want to know. A slash of rage ripped through him like lightening.

"You bastard," he whispered under his breath. "Ian, you fucking bastard. Take what you want, then bugger off. To hell with what I want. To hell with me. Ian Sutherland, you first-class prick." He slapped his T-square onto the table. Fear and rage foamed over, each feeding the other. His anger scared him. His fear made him mad. He couldn't tell them apart, and he couldn't separate himself from his father's rage or Delbert's or anyone else's. Rage flooded over him. He couldn't breathe. He was drowning.

He had to do something fast. He fought with his lock, sprinted out of the cabin and down to the barn, to the pile of old sashes, where he grabbed a window. That one wouldn't do, too much rot in the wood. He hurled it aside. It shuddered against a hay bale but didn't break.

"Fuck! Oh, Jesus, fuck!" He grabbed the next two sashes without even looking at them, tore back to his cabin. He was going to make a cabinet to store his fiddles in. A cabinet with a glass front. No problem. He needed lumber. He tossed his crosscut saw onto the planking overhead and pulled a chair underneath a rafter. He hauled himself up to the loft floor and began sawing pieces off it. He didn't stop to measure anything, couldn't stop. One length fell to the floor and he sank the saw teeth into a second cut, but he pushed too hard, kept bending the little teeth, jamming the saw.

"Fuck you! Fuck you!" He kicked at the saw with his boot, sent it clattering to the floor. He jumped for the rafter and swung to the floor so fast he didn't know if he had jumped or fallen, really. He ended up on his hands and knees. He crawled across to the toolbox under the sink and grabbed his hammer. He pulled Ian's bracelet out of his jeans pocket and threw it on the floor, began pounding it, missing it, hitting it.

"Fuck you, you bastard! It's all your fault, you fucker!" The bracelet ricocheted off the ball of the hammer and flew across the cabin. Jackson hurled the hammer after it. The hammer hit the wall, split the chipboard and lodged there. Struggling to stand, he tripped over the window sashes and kicked one against the stove, where it smashed to bits. The second one he stomped on, put his boot right through the glass. The shards clung to his ankle, trapping it in the wooden frame. He thrashed about, trying to shake it free, finally pulling the frame apart with his hands. Wielding a piece of the frame like a club, he lunged at his cabin's smallest window. The explosion of glass urged him onwards like applause. He grabbed Ian's bracelet off the floor and flung it through the broken window. Then he turned to his new window above the sink, grabbed a wrench and shattered the top pane, hacked at the lower pane but caught it wrong and only cracked the glass. He jumped onto the counter for a better shot and fell into the pane.

It gave way, he caught himself, lost his balance again and fell back onto the counter and then onto the floor. He crouched there on his hands and knees, panting. Sweat stung his eyes. He shook his head wildly, sending droplets flying from his forehead. As he watched, splotches of burgundy dripped onto the pale grey floor paint. The fire inside him fizzled and died. Slashes of physical pain welled up across his shoulder and down his shin. He was bleeding. Suddenly he felt small and ridiculous. Only drunk people get away with acting like they're crazy. Only crazy people act like they're drunk.

Loneliness and self-pity overwhelmed him. He sniffled, crawled across the floor and locked the cabin door again. He didn't want anyone to find him like this. He curled up into a ball in the corner. All this raging, this crashing, gushing eruption, it was too much. He wanted everything back the way it had been, back before the fiddles, before Ian, back when his mother was alive, when he drank every day. He tried to calm himself, clutched his limbs in to his body so tightly his knuckles hurt, his wounds hurt.

"These are the things that are wrong with me," he whispered, "I'm a faggot, I'm too skinny, I don't talk enough, my hair's ugly, I'm an embarrassment, I never speak up, I'm a coward, I sound like an idiot when I talk, I'm not very bright, I need cock, I can't even fix my own car, I have no friends, I'm just like my father — I'm the spitting image — I act like a retard, I let men fuck me, my cabin's pathetic, I can't say anything without . . ." Eventually his heart stopped pounding and he slid into the black comfort of the familiar.

When Jackson finally got to his feet he blinked at the mess and limped into the bathroom. He stripped his blood-soaked clothes away from his wounds. There were cuts on his hands, several gashes on his right shin and arm and a deep slash at his shoulder. He bound the shoulder as best he could with a towel. Wind whipped through the glassless windows. He shut off the water to the cabin so the pipes wouldn't freeze in the night and went to bed.

Eight inches of snow fell silently overnight. Jackson woke in pain. He didn't take any aspirin. He lit a roaring fire in his stove, made tea. He swept up the broken glass, burned the broken sashes, mopped up the blood. In the corner by the door was an ugly stain where the wall boards had soaked up his blood. He sat looking through his one intact window and tried to hold his mind as calm and white and silent as the world around him. He hadn't unlocked his door from the night before, so when Emma showed up she had to rattle the knob and call to him. He got up and let her in.

"Jeez, what's wrong with your door? How come it's freezing in here?"

Jackson didn't answer, but he set out another mug on the table for her.

"Hey, your back windows are all . . ." She stared into the sink where Jackson had left the bloody towel, watched Jackson pouring the tea with his left hand. The hammer still hung embedded in the wall. She sat down at the table and quietly chewed her lip. In a tiny voice she asked, "Who busted the windows and stuff?"

Jackson blinked and pawed at his eyes, but it was hopeless. He was crying. "Me," he said.

Emma sat perfectly still. Finally she whispered, "I'd do that too some days if I could."

Jackson nodded.

"I could look at your shoulder. Just check that it's cleaned out okay. Get some iodine. It's still bleeding a bit."

Their eyes met for a second. Jackson turned his back, tried to dry his tears.

"Yeah. That'd be good," he said.

She didn't get up right away, just sat there in her chair swinging her legs and chewing her lip. "I won't tell," she said.

Jackson replaced the glass in his windows. He gave his shoulder a couple of days to heal before he took out his new fiddle-back and traced the pattern, cut the shape, began coaxing from it the gentle knolls and valleys.

Jackson prepared to return to Halifax as soon as he finished carving his second set of plates. He chose a Friday morning so he would be sure to catch Albert at the shop. He had pushed Rolly and most of his other debtors for a little more money. Only Harold Sutherland he avoided. He collected enough to buy varnish, but he wouldn't be able to buy fittings and strings for his second fiddle and wood for his third. Not even close. He packed his finished fiddle into the wooden box he had made for it. He would still have to rely on a grocery bag for the plates.

Brenda remembered his name right off this time. He didn't mind so much that she latched on to his homemade fiddle case and coaxed him to open it, let her see his progress, marvelled over his finishing it so quickly, gushed over its beauty. He still blushed. He still backed away. But he didn't feel the tightening in his chest or the panic pushing out from behind his eyes.

"I n-need to buy some violin varnish, a brush, a tailpiece, four pegs."

"You need a fingerboard, too, eh? Strings? A chin rest?"

"I-I don't think . . . I'll have to see."

They collected the supplies, and Brenda carried them up to the cash.

"Albert in?"

"Oh, yeah. He's back there. But I tell you, he's in some mood today."

He had no time to worry about it because Brenda had already backed into the hallway and called down to Albert's room, "Albert. Com-pan-ee!"

Jackson packed up his fiddle and headed for the little room. Albert sat hunched over his work, but not an instrument this time. He had a form spread out in front of him, all lines and boxes and shaded areas in blue and grey. Jackson coughed quietly to announce himself.

Albert glanced around at him and grunted. "You any good at these things?"

"What is it?"

"Eh?" Albert looked at him as if he were stupid. "Income tax."

"I never . . . paid . . ."

"You mean someone else fills in your forms."

"No. I never paid tax."

Albert set down his pencil and twirled around on his stool. "Course you have. What kind of work do you do?"

Jackson turned his head away, stared at a tiny file hanging on the wall. While his brain considered what he should say, he heard his voice answer, "I used to, uh, drink, and I used to, uh, sell a bit on the side."

"Bootleg?" Albert sounded impressed. Awe-struck, even.

Jackson nodded.

"So you've never, ever filed a return? Paid a cent of tax?"

Jackson shook his head.

Albert started a chuckle that rolled into a full, round laugh. "Jesus," he said. "I like that. Oh, I love that." He was still chortling when he reached out for Jackson's case. "Let's see how you got on." He opened it and carefully lifted out the fiddle. He held it up, turned it over, ran his eye along the edges, inspected the bridge, sound holes, neck. He tucked it under his chin, plucked the strings and, with a deep frown but no comment, brought them into tune.

"Where's your bow?" He reached a hand out to Jackson.

"Uh, I never . . ."

Albert picked one off a nail on the wall. He laughed again. "With the income tax, eh?" He found this extremely funny.

When Albert drew the bow across the strings, the fiddle awoke. He whipped up and down several scales. Jackson stood gripping the counter. The sinews in his body, his muscles and nerves, sang as though they were the strings, vibrating under the arching bow. And yet another part of him pulled away, not believing he could have had anything to do with creating such brilliance. Albert dove into a chorus of "Donald, Where's Your Trousers?" and then emerged into something Jackson had never heard before but knew must be classical. He blinked a few times, closed his eyes, but the sensation threatened to sweep him away, so he opened them again and stared at a rasp on the wall in front of him. Albert played pairs of notes, sets of notes, listening carefully to the way they rose from the wood.

"Well, that's a fiddle," Albert finally declared.

Jackson wished he would keep playing. He didn't know what to say. "I have plates, too." He fished them out of the plastic bag. Albert checked them each in turn, nodding his satisfaction. "You buy this wood here?"

Jackson nodded.

"Don't. That's all stuff from kits. Ordered in from the States. You don't need to pay those kinds of prices. You need wood, you come out to my shop."

Jackson could barely follow his words. He was still back with his fiddle, still listening to the memory of it resonating off the walls. He didn't know what Albert was talking about, could barely hear over the lingering notes. He knew he must look like a moron. He didn't move.

"Look." Albert sat back down in front of his tax forms and grunted. "I'm here till noon. You want to come out to Eastern Passage with me, you come back here then."

Come back here by noon. Jackson picked up his things and left.

He walked down towards the water. Gradually he began recognizing the streets, the businesses he and Ian had visited the weekend they spent together. He recognized the magazine shop, ducked inside. It had amazed him how Ian could float around, not caring who saw him, not caring what anyone thought. He knew where the dirty magazines were. He knew he could stand by the computer magazines and see over the central rack to where they were all laid out. Naked women stared out across the store, but in behind them were the men. *Mandate. Torso. Stallion.* No one avoided the area. People looked as they passed by. Some stopped, even. A couple of young men flipped through the rack, and one of them picked something out. When he went to pay, the cashier just put it in a bag with another magazine, didn't look at him funny or snicker or anything. Real casual. Just like it had been when Ian had bought stuff here that time. Jackson was sweating like mad. He looked down at his hands, at the magazine he held — a jumble of computers fought for prominence on its cover. He glanced around. No one was in the least interested in him. He set the magazine back on the rack and began moving towards the other side of the store.

He didn't linger. He chose a *Blueboy* with a handsome brown-eyed man unzipping his jeans on the cover and a smaller book showing two shirtless men with their arms around each other. At the cash he kept his eyes to himself. But when he heard the young woman behind the counter say $14.94, he had to look up. He couldn't believe she was talking to him. He completely forgot to check the prices. How could they possibly be that much? He wasn't going to put them back now. He wasn't going to say anything. All he could do was pull the last twenty out of his wallet and pay.

Immediately he headed back to his truck and hid the bag under the driver's seat. Dirty pictures. When Matthew was fifteen their mother had discovered his stash of magazines. She cornered Matthew in the kitchen, her face blazing red, her eyes sharp and hard as spikes. "Filthy," she yelled at him, swatting him over and over with the rolled-up magazines, beating him around the head. "Disgusting!" She wasn't a tall woman, but she was wide and strong and sturdy, and even though Matthew was nearly full-grown, he cowered. "That's sick," she cried, "sick!" She was panting from exertion when she finally stuffed the offending material into the firebox. Jackson remembered Matthew lowering his arms from protecting his head and watching the magazines being stuffed into the stove. Jackson could tell Matthew was wondering if the fire could consume all that glossy paper at once, if maybe he would have a chance to rescue the remnants later. Their mother must have known what he was thinking, too, because she dropped the firebox lid and chased Matthew out of the house, brandishing the poker. She never hit them with the poker, only chased them with it. Then she returned to the stove and stood there muttering and poking at the flames, lifting up the magazines, making sure the fire did its cleansing work. He remembered his mother's anger and Matthew's ludicrous beating, but what had he been doing? Just standing there. Watching. He hadn't laughed then. But he laughed now. Dirty pictures!

He didn't head back down to the water. Instead he turned towards Citadel Hill. This was where the men met in the city. Even he knew that, so how much of a secret could it be? He followed a path up the hill and joined the pavement which ringed the old fort. He had been here on Citadel Hill once before, on a grade seven field trip. He remembered only the canon they fired at noon and feeling far, far away. Now he could see old Halifax, down at the harbour, and where modern Halifax had grown around it, on top of it, and sprawled out in all directions. He could see how this hill had been meant to protect the town below. The wind off the water blew chilly and damp, and Jackson felt exposed, standing there blatantly on the barren summit. It's an odd place to keep a secret, he thought. He stood at the edge of the twenty-foot deep trench that surrounded the fort. It looked cozy down there, out of the wind, but you would die or at least break your legs jumping. He remembered that the enemy would have had to climb down on ladders, race across and climb up the other side in order to reach the fort. And behind those slits of windows on both sides of the trench walls, soldiers hid, muskets loaded, setting up a deadly crossfire.

He turned his back to the wind to light a cigarette, cupped his hand to shelter the struggling match flame. Eventually he strolled back to his truck to get warm. At noon he returned to Folkard's store. Albert saw him coming and met him on the sidewalk.

"That's my car," he said, nodding at a battered grey Tercel. "Where are you parked?"

They drove out of the city, Jackson tailing the Tercel as closely as he dared. They turned off the highway and followed the coast. Eventually Albert signalled and turned into the driveway of a small lot crowded with buildings. On their left sat a white bungalow, to their right a small mobile home and directly ahead a third building, half garage, half something else. It was this third building that Albert led him to.

"Come on into the workshop."

Jackson paused in the doorway. He had never seen such a workshop. Heated, probably insulated, windows and doors trimmed out, lots of room for a table saw, a band saw, drill press, joiner, hand tools, power tools, everything Jackson could imagine. Wood of all kinds stood sorted and stacked to the ceiling along one wall. A door led to a second room, three large windows along the back wall looked out towards the distant ocean. Jackson watched to see if Albert would stop to take off his boots. When he didn't, Jackson followed him in.

"This here" — Albert was talking to him — "this here is black birch cut near Musquodobit, back about forty years ago. Should be nearly dry now, eh? You can use this for the back. It polishes up beautiful. This is a nice piece of pine here . . ."

Jackson struggled to pay attention. "Y-you build other stuff, too?"

"Huh?"

"Not just, uh, fiddles?"

"God, yes. I'm not independently wealthy — yet."

Albert packed a tailpiece and several lengths of purfling into a bag. He carried three or four chunks of wood under one arm. "You should play. Never knew a fiddle-maker who couldn't play. I've got an extra bow here, now Jesus where . . . it's over at the house." Albert started to leave. Jackson didn't want to go to the house. He stood dumbly, watched Albert walk away. "Come on," Albert ordered. Jackson followed him across the little yard, in the back door of the bungalow and up a few steps.

"Sit." Albert motioned him towards a shoddy veneer table with four equally shoddy chairs around it. Albert fiddled with a coffee maker and poured water into it, then he flicked the radio on to a country station and disappeared down a hallway.

Jackson wasn't sure if Albert's wife or someone would appear. He practised what he would say to explain himself. Soon Albert reappeared with the bow. "This is a loaner. You make one from that maple I gave you. You can play with this till then." He stopped and frowned. "You don't play at all?"

Jackson shook his head, blushed. "Can't," he managed.

"Humph." He set the bow down on the kitchen counter, not on the table by Jackson. Jackson wondered if he should go over and pick it up. Albert rummaged in his fridge for a moment. "You had lunch?"

"No, I . . ." Jackson shook his head because he hadn't, but then he realized he should have said yes because the question was like an invitation, and now he had to stay when all he wanted was to get home. He needed a cigarette. He took the plastic pack of home-rolleds from his shirt pocket and offered Albert one.

"No. Thanks. I had to give them up. But you go ahead." Albert pulled ham slices and mustard out of the fridge. Then suddenly he said, "Beer?"

"Uh, no. I had to give it up." Then Jackson added, "Y-you go ahead."

Albert twisted the top off a bottle of Moosehead and tossed half a loaf of bread onto the table beside the pound of butter that sat there, its blue foil pulled back to expose carved out valleys and ridges of toast crumbs. Albert handed him a knife, then turned back as though he just remembered something and brought two small plates from the cupboard. He sat down opposite Jackson. "Might as well have a sandwich since you're here." The few times Jackson looked up, Albert was looking somewhere else. "I got cheese, too," Albert said uncertainly. "You like cheese?"

"No. No, this is good." He hated eating in front of strangers. Ashes dangled dangerously from the end of his cigarette. He cupped a hand under the precarious tailings, glanced at the sink. Albert saw him, got up and routed in a cupboard, pulled an ashtray off the top shelf and set it in front of Jackson. "The kids made me give up the smokes."

Kids? Jackson followed Albert's lead and began putting a sandwich together. "Your wife?"

"Divorce."

Jackson didn't know what you were supposed to say to that. Albert didn't say anything more about it. He rolled up a slice of ham into a little telescope and bit the end off it.

"You go to Folkard's pub?" Albert asked after a long silence.

"Eh?"

"Folkard's pub. The Journeyman's Joy."

No answer.

"You know Jim Folkard. He owns the store. Cut the ends off three of his fingers with a radial arm saw five years ago, so he can't fix instruments anymore. So he bought the pub. Spends most of his time down there now. Hired me half-time in the shop to keep up that end of the business. That's why I'm there, eh?"

Jackson concentrated on chewing his sandwich. "I can't buy that wood today. I, uh, I'll get a bit of work in the spring."

"That wood's not dear. You gonna sell?"

"Eh?"

"Those fiddles you're making and can't play. You intending to sell them?"

The thought had never occurred to Jackson. What *did* he intend to do with them? "They're not good enough for . . ."

"Sweet Jesus. You're a fiddle-maker, son, a natural. Know that?" Albert got up and poured coffee into two mugs and brought them to the table. "Milk?"

"Yeah."

Albert opened the fridge and checked the dates on three cartons of milk. "This one's good," he said, plunking it down in front of Jackson.

"You'd get about six hundred and fifty dollars, I'd say. Since it's your first. Just varnish 'er up. She's sold."

"It needs a few months of sun . . ."

"That's just for colour. You can do that as well with varnish as with light. You want me to show you, you just come out."

Jackson finished his coffee in silence. This new possibility distracted him. When he stood up to leave he found much of his nervousness had fallen away. Albert pressed him to borrow the bow.

"Try," he said. "And this stuff" — Albert handed him the wood and fiddle parts — "pay me later." It was probably about two hundred dollars' worth of materials. Jackson didn't want to be in Albert's debt, but if he accepted it he could finish his second fiddle and start on his third. He hesitated, then took it with a bob of his head and turned towards the door.

"I want to see a fiddle from that stuff, now." Albert's tone made him sound sort of like a teacher, but not exactly. "Call me at the store — Monday, Wednesday, Friday morning."

CHAPTER TEN

EMMA PULLED OFF HER TOQUE, unzipped her parka and flopped into the chair opposite Jackson at the table.

"Guess what. Aunt Margie and Uncle Ronnie are taking me and Amber and Annie and Alison to a movie. They've got matinees for March break, eh? They're not taking anybody else, just their own kids and me."

"Uh-huh."

Jackson bent over his fiddle, measuring and adjusting, carving out the notch in which he would set the neck. He was on the verge of finishing his second fiddle, and his satisfaction bubbled over into happiness, escaping from him in a thin whistling under his breath. He felt almost gregarious.

"Boy, you really gotta be careful doing that, doncha?"

"See this? The top of the fingerboard down here has to sit twenty-three thirty-seconds of an inch above the belly."

"Wow." She sat quietly and watched him for a while. "Twenty-three thirty-seconds. They couldn't just say three-quarters?"

"Nope."

"Wow."

Eventually Emma continued. "Douglas is coming to live at the farmhouse, you know. For sure, Aunt Darlene says."

"Who?"

"You know. Uncle Delbert's son from when he was married to his first wife. He was here for two days in the Christmas holidays. Didn't you see him? Aunt Margie says they can't look after the kids they have, and they have no business messing up another one."

Jackson strained to remember the boy. "How old is he?"

"Supposed to be my age, but he's like a little kid. And he's only in grade six." She snorted. She sat with her chin in her hands watching him. "Can I help?"

Jackson, finally satisfied with his work, set the neck with glue, clamped it, then looked up. "Yeah." He shook his absolutely last smoke, the one he had been saving for the celebration, out of his plastic cigarette box and set it between his lips. He lowered his eyes. "I'm out of smokes. Can you get me some from Matthew?" It wasn't really right, he knew, to send her begging for him.

"That's not what I meant."

She was a little ticked off, but she grabbed the box anyway and skulked off with it. His second fiddle was finished. He could string it once the glue had set. He sat with the instrument while he smoked. A few minutes later Emma dashed, puffing, into the cabin and threw the cigarette box onto the table. "I gotta go! Aunt Rosie's taking me to the village!" She was gone. Jackson checked the box. Nearly full. Eighteen to be exact. If he was real careful he could make them last until tomorrow afternoon. He set aside his second fiddle and hauled out the wood for his third.

Jackson was busy squaring his slab of black birch when Delbert arrived.

"I could do with a coffee," he said, reaching for Jackson's bummed cigarettes. Jackson got up and put the kettle on, watched Delbert light up. "Got my plants going," Delbert declared. "Ya gotta get 'em started early. Yup. I got over two hundred this year. Most ever. Yeah, she's gonna be a great crop this year."

Jackson spooned instant coffee into the mugs, not quite finishing off the jar. In addition to the coffee, he had the bowl of sugar on the table, the three bottles of pickles his sisters had sent up over the winter, half a box of tea bags, the scrapings of the peanut butter jar, half a bottle of ketchup and three slices of bread.

"I got a bunch of places for 'em, got 'em all picked out. I got good spots. The best. Ya gotta know how to hide 'em from those cocksucker Mounties in their choppers." Delbert rocked back in his chair.

Jackson said nothing. From behind, he watched Delbert stub out the butt of his cigarette and light another. Delbert accepted the steaming mug set in front of him and stirred sugar into it. He looked around the table.

"Where's the milk?"

"Got none."

"Jesus, you're fucking useless."

Jackson's stomach tightened. He stared deep into the grain of the birch, stroked it with his plane, watching the yellow curl emerge from behind the blade and tumble to the floor. Delbert's voice grew distant. The year Vernon crushed his leg had been one of the worst. Delbert quit school to keep the farm going. He, Jackson, was in grade six. The jam sandwiches their mother packed grew thinner and thinner, barely pinkened with jam, half sandwiches replaced whole ones, molasses replaced jam. The last wormy apples gave way to bits of raw carrot, then turnip, then cabbage. He saw his brothers slinking out of the stalls in the boys' washroom at school, crunched up bags in their fists, and knew they had been wolfing down their lunches in private, hiding from the humiliation. He didn't care that his brothers and sisters would take his lunch and divide it up amongst them before the bus arrived, not even bothering to make a game of it after the first couple of times. He couldn't eat it anyway. Then the brown bag with "Jackson" written on it appeared in the line with all the other bags and lunch kits there on the shelf above his coat hook in the cloakroom. He stared at it the first day, afraid it might be a joke, but his teacher, Mr. Scarth, placed it silently in his hand. Every day after that Mr. Scarth watched to make sure he took it. Mr. Scarth never said anything. It was a secret. There were sandwiches on store-bought brown bread, oatmeal cookies in crinkly packages, butterscotch pudding in tins with pull-tab lids, bananas or apples or oranges.

Once there was a Baggie with a bunch of green grapes. He had never tasted a grape before, and when he plucked one off its stem and cautiously eased his teeth down through its skin, tangy juice exploded over his tongue, filled his mouth, slid down his throat and made his skin tingle. It was like magic, a little capsule delivering special powers all through his body. Pop, now you are brave. Pop, now you are the orphan who fell off the school roof trying to save the entire kindergarten class from fire. You are lying crumpled on the ground. Pop, now you're being carried off by Steve Austin, Six Million Dollar Man. Pop, you're in the operating room. Pop. He'll never make it, doctor. Pop, pop, pop. Yes. We have the technology. Pop, pop. Two arms. Pop, pop. Two legs. Pop, here you are back in school, the bionic orphan. They all depend on you now. Jackson, says Mr. Scarth — pop — even a bionic orphan needs a home, you must come and live with me. Pop. There were six grapes left. He hid them in his desk for later, for when he needed strength.

The cabin door slammed, snapping Jackson back to the present. Emma ran in waving an envelope. "You got a letter!"

Delbert had been talking since he sat down and kept talking as though she weren't there. "So when Douglas comes here to live she can shut up about the money. I've had it listening to that bitch harping at me for child support."

"Eh?"

"Darn right. Fuck her. She can pay me for a change." He lit a third cigarette.

"Look!" Emma waved a small white envelope at him. "Jackson Bigney. It came in our mailbox. Open it."

The only other piece of mail Jackson had received in his life was a summons. He frowned deeply.

"Come on!" Emma thrust it into his hand. "Mom wants to know what it is." Delbert stared at him, waiting. Jackson glanced at the envelope and knew instantly whose handwriting it was. Blood rushed to his cheeks, leaving his palms clammy and his face beet red. He turned his back and pried open the envelope, hoping to get a chance to read it before they grabbed it away from him. A cheque. A message on a small piece of notepaper folded over. He read it, folded it and stowed it safely in his shirt pocket. The cheque was for eighty-five dollars. Jackson had completely forgotten he had loaned him money, but he had, in dribs and drabs, in Truro, Halifax and Parrsboro.

"A cheque," he said to Emma. "Somebody repaying a debt."

"Let's see, let's see. Oh! Eighty-five bucks," Emma said, impressed.

"Ian Sutherland," Delbert said, half a question, half a threat.

Emma plucked the note out of his pocket before he knew what was happening. "Let's see the letter. 'Hi. Sorry to take so long getting back to you about the loan, but it's taken me a while to get on my feet here. Toronto's great! Ian.' He was the fiddling guy, right?"

Jackson nodded. He shoved his hands in his pockets to hide the trembling, tried to force the colour out of his cheeks but only made things worse. The note said nothing. Nothing. But he couldn't look at Delbert.

Emma lumbered off. Delbert pushed himself back from the table and pocketed Jackson's cigarettes as though he were innocently mistaking them for his own. Jackson was going to say something, but Delbert looked straight at him from underneath pitched eyebrows, stared right through him. "Moneybags," was all he said.

Delbert's son, Douglas, arrived at the farmhouse on the last weekend of March. April Fool's Day was Douglas's fourteenth birthday. Darlene made a big pot of chili and summoned everyone to the farmhouse for birthday cake. Except for Margie's family, of course. Jackson did as he was told. He followed the path across the sleeping meadow from his cabin.

The wind whipped garbage around the farmhouse yard, and it began to rain. Ice pellets. There would be no slipping outside to escape the crush. Jackson stood at the farmhouse door watching Matthew and his family approach. Rosie carried a massive casserole dish covered in foil. Matthew had his infant son on one arm and the other arm curled around a dozen beer. Their three older boys, bouncing around them like popcorn, dispersed into the mob of kids at the farmhouse door. Kate had already arrived and busied herself sawing thick slices of bread off a loaf, while Emma piled stacks of dishes and cutlery on the table. Jackson patted his jacket pocket, double-checking for his cigarettes.

It wasn't hard to spot Douglas, a head taller than the others, a gawky kid, scrawny for fourteen, with shallow, narrow features and a slash of desperation through his eyes that made Jackson want to turn away. Douglas struggled to keep his new Gameboy above the crowd, showing it off without letting anyone touch it. Jackson squeezed into the corner by the little cellar door, trying to stay out of the way. He watched Margie's oldest daughter sneak in and hide at the fringes of the action. But in no time at all war erupted in a screaming tumble of fists and hair and sobs. Delbert burst into a booming laugh. The women jumped up to quell the riot, but Darlene arrived first, grabbed the interloper and dragged her, screeching, to the door.

"Brat," she said, under her breath but loud enough for anyone to hear who wanted to.

Food was heaped up, doled out, squabbled over. Tumblers of Kool-Aid were poured and tipped over, yelled about, mopped up and poured again. Jackson tried not to stare at the beer. He crouched in the corner with his dinner balanced on his knee. The hoppy smell mingled with cigarette smoke, dried his throat. He gulped a huge mouthful from his glass, swallowed and winced at the searing sweetness of the iridescent green Kool-Aid.

Douglas forced his voice above the din. "This is great. I never had a party before. My mom never ever made me a birthday cake."

Darlene fluffed her feathers. "Yeah, well, around here if it's your birthday you get a cake."

"Ya get fourteen lashes, too." Matthew grinned widely as he flicked Douglas with a dish towel whip. "Hey, Douglas, you ever hear the story about when your dad took the buggy whip to school when he was a young fella? Oh man! See, the principal's kid was a little prick, eh, used to squeal on everybody. So this one day

Delbert slips the old buggy whip out of the barn and hides it in the bushes at school. Come recess, he takes off after the kid, chases him across the field, buggy whip just a-flailing. Runs him right out of the school yard and down the street past the Co-op and the bank. That kid's hollering and screaming like he's on fire, a stream of teachers running after, half the frigging school dashing around behind like a frigging parade." Matthew shook with laughter. "Remember, Jackson?"

Jackson remembered the trouble: the phone calls and shouting, the police, the fear in his mother's eyes.

Everyone finished laughing at Matthew's story. Jackson wished he couldn't see Bertie, Delbert's oldest son from this marriage, glaring at Douglas, sneaking quick, fearful glances at his father. "Me and Dad," Douglas kept declaring. Me and Dad — the men of the family — we'll get things going. "And I'm gonna drive the tractor, eh, Dad?"

Bertie's eyes darted between his mother and his father. He swaggered over to the birthday cake and drew his finger through the little ridge of icing at the base of the cake, where it met the plate. He stood there glowering, slurping the chocolate off his finger. Douglas sneered at him. "I say how much icing ya get, kiddo! It's *my* cake! I get all the corner pieces if I want. Me and Dad get the most."

Bertie stuck his finger into the chocolate icing on the top left hand corner of the cake. He dragged his finger diagonally across the cake, through the looping "Happy Birthday" written in thick green icing. He sucked the icing back before Douglas could bound across the room. By the time he got there Bertie was ready. He hurled his little ten-year-old body at Douglas, fists flying.

"Jesus-Jesus-Jesus!" Darlene advanced again, hand raised to Douglas.

Delbert smirked. "You better get those kids sorted out," he said to her.

In the midst of the shouting, pulling and punching, Jackson slipped out. He drew cold, damp air into his lungs. He wished the beer didn't bother him. It was all he could smell, though, and all he could think about. Except for Douglas. Part of the family but not part of the family. "You've always got your family," his mother used to say. Well, he wasn't so sure about that. Some people are born on the outside.

Jackson saved the bending and fitting and moulding of his third fiddle's ribs for when he was ready to think about Ian again. He loved this job. An ordinary strip of wood dipped in water and exposed to heat would bend into a new form at his touch, flow into something different while remaining the same, retaining its beautiful grain, all its natural qualities. If he held the strip flat he could snap it between his fingers, crumple it in his fist. But set it on its side and try to bend it, alter it in any way, and it stood strong as cast iron. He's built upside down, his mother used to say.

He tried to think about his nights with Ian, but he couldn't. He hadn't been able to for a couple of weeks now and had thought maybe moulding the ribs might help. He couldn't force Ian into the same category as all the other men he thought about, part of a perfect fantasy, as if Ian had nothing to do with real life. The Ian who wrote the note, who had made him so angry he had punched the windows out of his cabin, was real. Ian wasn't perfect and he wasn't a fantasy. Ian was the one who held him, moaned at his touch, the one who made him feel so strong and able. Back before Ian, he used to think that nothing mattered if he didn't say anything or do anything. But it did matter what he thought. Jackson waited until he got his rib safely tacked in place before he finished his idea. It did matter what he felt. His vision blurred. He waited a moment before he picked up the next rib.

He bent a middle rib and matched its delicate bevels precisely to its brothers in the mould. You were always so afraid of beautiful things, his mother had said. He was afraid; he knew that the past could close over, and he could lose, not just Ian, but everything that had happened, all that he was. Some days the past seemed fluid, as if it could float away from him. He didn't trust himself.

He needed something real to tack it all to. If one other person knew . . . Jackson frowned. That was not possible.

By Thursday of his first week at the farmhouse, Douglas's routine solidified like quick-dry cement. Each day the school bus delivered him home at 4:05. By 4:25 the ruckus from inside the farmhouse reached such a pitch that it cut across the field and penetrated Jackson's peace. By 4:30 Douglas was perched on the captain's chair in Jackson's cabin, his knees pulled up tight to his chest, his arms wrapped around his legs as if he were holding himself together, rocking gently and talking non-stop.

"Me and Dad are driving to New Glasgow tomorrow. Dad's gonna get me a trail bike. Maybe me and Dad should both get trail bikes. We can go off camping and stuff."

Jackson simply kept his eyes on his carving.

"This weekend me and Dad are going into the woods. I'm driving the tractor. Dad said. 'Cause I know how. I'm hauling out the firewood. Me and Dad are splitting it. Me and Dad are going to plough up that whole back piece of land for garden this summer. I'm driving the tractor. We're going to sell stuff, eh? To the stores and that. We'll make tons of money. Couple hundred or a thousand maybe. We'll go away on a trip somewhere, Dad and me. Maybe Disney World. My sister went there with her boyfriend who was working in Fort McMurray. It's cool. There's this ride called the Tower of Terror and you drop, like, straight down from this cliff. Ever been to Disney World, Jackson?"

Jackson shook his head.

"That's where we're going. Me and Dad. This Saturday I'm driving the tractor."

Saturday morning Jackson sat working on his belly plate. He cringed at Delbert's bellow, imposing even over the roar of the tractor's ancient diesel engine.

". . . you're not getting near it . . . when you quit acting like a little prick . . . not *touching* that tractor, boy . . ."

When they finally set off for the woods, Jackson stood up to look out his window. Douglas and Bertie clung to opposite ends of the woods wagon, bumping along after Delbert on the tractor. Jackson heard them return at lunchtime. Later, he wasn't surprised to see Douglas trudging back and forth between the wagon and the splitter, the splitter and the woodpile, stacking firewood. Delbert and Bertie were nowhere to be seen.

Monday afternoon Douglas showed up after school, right on schedule.

"Me and Dad are gonna sell firewood. Fifty bucks a load. I'm gonna drive the tractor. We can go into business now that I'm here to help out. Bertie's way too small. Dad's gonna get me my own chainsaw. He's gonna show me how to start the tractor. You wanna buy a load of firewood, Jackson?"

"Nah. I get my own."

"Yeah, but this stuff is good. Me and Dad are going to haul out another load soon — block 'er up, split 'er, everything. I'm driving the tractor this time. Fifty bucks a load. This is way better than when I lived with my mom. She called yesterday. Dad told her to fuck off. I laughed. She's so stunned. I wouldn't've talked to her anyway, even if she hadn't hung up." Douglas rocked himself quietly for a minute.

"Know what else?" Douglas glanced to the left and the right like a TV spy. "I'm helping Dad with his . . . you know . . . plants."

"Hey. Don't tell people that."

"I'm not! I just said it to you." Douglas pouted a second. When Jackson said nothing more, he couldn't resist the silence. "I water them, carry them in at night. I know how many there are. Dad's letting me drive the tractor tomorrow. I wish I had my own room. I hate sharing with those little kids. Bertie's so stupid. Darlene gives him whatever he wants. What a spoiled brat. Dad thinks so, too. Did you have your own room when you were growing up?"

Jackson arched an eyebrow. But when Douglas actually sat quiet, waiting for an answer, he said, "We were ten kids in that farmhouse you live in."

"So did ya? Have your own room?"

"No."

"But you do now! I should get a cabin like yours. This is cool. Me and Dad are going to build a cabin like this. Just for me. And him. No one else can come over unless I say."

Then Delbert sauntered into the cabin. "I told you to clean up the yard."

"I picked up all that stuff around the back of the house. See that, Dad?"

Delbert grabbed Douglas by the ear and lifted him out of the chair, thrusting him towards the cabin door. "Get at it!" he roared, barely glancing at the boy. He nestled himself into the empty seat and reached for the pack of cigarettes on the table.

Douglas turned at the door, spitting, stammering and utterly helpless. "I'm not cleaning up Bertie's stupid shit!" he yelled before he slammed the door so hard the walls shook.

As soon as the frost was out of the ground, Lloyd Harris told Elsie to call Kate who got Emma to run up to Jackson's cabin and tell him there was work for him. He spent several days swinging a maul above his head pounding fenceposts. Then it rained, and Lloyd sent him home until it was time to start the planting. He took his first fiddle out and, with his pristine bottle of violin varnish, his new brush and the sketchy instructions in his book, he began tentatively, carefully applying varnish to it.

Jackson started only a dozen marijuana seeds that spring. There were so few that tending the seedlings was no trouble at all. By mid-May they were coming along well in their little plastic pots, and he took a walk through the woods to choose the spot where he would plant them out. They were well hardened off, but the nights still veered close to frost. Maybe next week, he thought, after the full moon. He stood at his cabin door and looked past his woodshed. He could put in his own little vegetable garden if he wanted. It wouldn't take much to get a little patch worked up with a fork. He walked over to the spot, trying to picture neat rows of beans and tomato plants. He started to pace off a square when a sparkle caught his eye, and he bent to uncover Ian's gold bracelet, his gold bracelet. This wasn't where he had chucked it two months ago. Some animal or some kid must have dragged it around the cabin. He picked it up and examined it closely. Two of the links were bent, and it was chipped in several places. He rubbed it against the front of his shirt to bring up the shine, picked some of the dirt from between the tight corners in the links. It was a beautiful thing, heavy and masculine. He glanced down towards the road and over his shoulder, then slipped it on his wrist, feeling the weight and strength of it against his skin.

If he was going to plough up a garden patch, he would have an excuse to use the tractor and give Douglas a chance on the stupid machine, put him out of his misery. Jackson felt a twinge of resentment. He hated metal and gears and diesel fumes. He hated dealing with that tractor.

When Jackson returned from Scotch River with his groceries and a little paper bag of vegetable seeds, he passed Douglas poking at the ground in the meadow behind the farmhouse. Douglas leaned on his shovel and waved him over. Jackson looked the other way. But Douglas persisted, yelled out to him, flung his arms about like he was bringing down a 747, ran towards him. There was no way out. Jackson stopped his pickup in the rutted lane and strolled across to meet the boy.

"Me and Dad are planting the early potatoes. We're putting all this in potatoes." He waved his hand down four impossibly long furrows. The sod lay turned over, thick tangles of root mass exposed, brown weed stalks and dead grass peeping out from under the slices of earth. It hadn't been tilled or broken up at all. Douglas had a tub full of eyes beside him, obviously trying to bury them in the pathetic trenches. "You need new ground for potatoes, eh? 'Cause of the potato bugs. Dad ploughed this, but when I get the tractor I'm gonna do all that part there." He waved his hand vaguely at the western half of the meadow. "Me and Dad."

"Where's Delbert now?"

"He took the tractor back in for wood. I'm getting a start on the garden. That's the last wood we're doing. Me and Dad are going . . ."

Jackson kicked at a furrow, searched the clouds for signs of a weather change, lit a cigarette. The drone of the tractor emerging from the woods, headed for the farmhouse, overtook Douglas's endless chatter. Douglas stopped in mid-syllable, blanched to a sickly white. There on the seat, hands on the wheel, driving the tractor, sat Bertie. Delbert rode on the tow bar, looking over Bertie's shoulder, both of them beaming.

Douglas dropped his spade and wobbled towards the farm-house, slowly at first, as if he was sleepwalking, then faster and steadier, breaking into a run as the tractor slowed to a halt and Bertie climbed down from the seat. Without a second's hesitation Douglas grabbed Bertie by the hair and punched him square in the face, sending him sprawling across the ground. He threw himself on top of his squirming, screeching half-brother, pounding away on him. Delbert straightened up from unhooking the trailer and lumbered into the fray. He lifted Douglas by the scruff of his neck and the seat of his pants, held him flailing in space for a moment, then tossed him through the air a good fifteen feet onto the packed earth at the end of the driveway.

Jackson grunted as Douglas hit the dirt, hard. Jackson tried to look away but couldn't. The earth quaked beneath his legs. Inside him, pieces shook loose and tumbled away into a chasm. He fought to keep himself upright.

The next thing Jackson knew, the entire family had crowded onto the rough deck at the door of the farmhouse and stood staring down at Douglas's sprawled body. Douglas moved a little, swimming in slow motion in the dirt. Above the storm of noise Delbert's voice boomed, *"And if you don't like it you can fuck to the road! Just fuck to the road, Douglas."* He ordered everyone inside. God, Jackson wanted a drink. He was afraid to move in case he moved towards a drink. He sank to the ground, knelt there, watched Douglas drag himself up to a sitting position. Douglas didn't get up, didn't move. Where did he have to go? Jackson held his ground. He waited. Maybe five minutes, six, fifteen?

The family emerged from the house, the kids dressed in fresh clothes and scrubbed for town. They crowded into the car, whispering, elbowing each other and stealing glances at Douglas sitting cross-legged and tear-streaked in the driveway dirt. Bertie crawled into the front seat, into the coveted position between his parents. Douglas lurched to his feet and staggered towards the car as Delbert revved up the engine and pulled away. The younger kids rolled down the back windows and called out, "brat, asshole, faggot . . ." Douglas stood in the empty yard, staring after the cloud of dust blowing up from the retreating car.

Asshole. Faggot. Jackson suddenly felt very ill, nauseous, as if he was spinning alone in black space. He wished that boy would go home to his mother, get away from here, stop standing out there in the open like that. Stop making them say those words. That word. His stomach cramped, heaved, and he spat bile onto the earth.

Jackson made himself a pot of tea to settle his stomach and smoked half a dozen cigarettes. His hands trembled so much he couldn't trust them to work on his fiddle. But he had to do something, think about something. If Delbert had gone to New Glasgow he wouldn't be back for a couple of hours at least. He could borrow the tractor, show Douglas the ropes, let him get a good turn at it, and have it back in the yard before they got home. They could plough a few furrows to get his garden started. If he replaced the diesel fuel Delbert would be satisfied. But he didn't know how to start that goddamned tractor. The glow plugs were toast, and the starter switch had shorted out last year. You had to spray ether into the air cleaner, he knew, and bypass the switch, hook up a battery terminal to the . . . he didn't know what. Mechanical things repelled him. Matthew usually changed the oil in Jackson's pickup, for chrissake. Of course, Matthew could start the tractor for him.

Matthew's boys were all a-buzz with the news of "the big punch-up." They weren't interested in talking about where their father might be. Jackson stuck his head into the kitchen of Matthew and Rosie's tiny home. Rosie put on the kettle.

"He's off campaigning for office this weekend," she told him. This was code for "on a binge." "Come in, come in," she continued. "I just made this cake. It'll be at least forty-five seconds before that tribe of hellions discovers it. If we eat fast we might get halfway through a piece before it's snatched out of our hands." She plunked a piece of apple cake topped with a shower of icing sugar in front of him. He wasn't sure he could manage it, but after the first bite he realized he was hungry.

"What do you want Matthew for?"

"I need the tractor," he said. "I can't start it."

Rosie always had the phone within reach. She punched in a number and spoke to Kate. Kate's Charlie, who may have been able to help, wasn't home either. Then Rosie punched another number.

"Margie got her phone hooked back up, did you know? New number." Someone answered and she handed the phone to Jackson, who blushed and shook his head, but Rosie forced the receiver into his hand. It was Ronnie.

"Oh, uh, I was thinking of ploughing, uh, I can't start the tractor, eh? Could you . . ."

"I might be able to, but I don't know. Gee, you know . . ." Ronnie lowered his voice a tone so Jackson had to strain to hear. "Margie and Darlene are at it tooth and nail these days, kids not allowed on the property, the whole nine yards. If I start poking around the White Knight's noble steed, Christ, he'll come through the wall after me."

"Sure. Yeah. That's okay. That's okay. Bye."

"Delbert's going to have to smarten up about that young Douglas," Rosie said. "It breaks my heart to see the way he's treating him. You can't just expect the boy to fit in like that" — she snapped her fingers — "not after all these years."

Rosie poured the tea. They both sat there in silence, smoking cigarettes.

"Those boys of mine are awfully quiet. They must have found

something really good to pull apart. I hope it's nothing of mine."
Rosie laughed and cut them each a second square of cake. Jackson
smiled. He felt remarkably calmed, sitting here with her.

"Cops, Mom!"

Rosie jumped to the window. "What?"

"The cops are at Uncle Delbert's! We seen 'em turn in."

"What in God's name do they want?"

Foreboding rose through Jackson, jostling the cake. "I'll go
see," he said.

When Jackson stepped into the farmhouse kitchen, Constable
Townsend, his face grey and solemn, nodded at him. Another
cop, an ox of a fellow with his arms crossed over his chest, stared
hard at Jackson. Douglas didn't even glance up. Jackson could have
been a housefly or a piece of litter blown in through the door. A
jungle of marijuana plants, quite large by now and ready to be set
out, were lined up on the kitchen table.

"Most of them are down here," Douglas said, starting for the
little cellar door under the stairs. "There's two hundred and
eighteen altogether. I know. I had to water them."

Christ! The little rat had called the cops! Jackson had heard of
this happening to people, but always as stories, far off in the
States or somewhere. Never anyone he knew, not here, not his
own brother, not right in the family. Jackson sank onto a kitchen
chair and sat there, his head in his hands, as the Mounties
followed the boy down into the cellar. It couldn't be true. Police.
Jesus.

Kids swarmed at the door, attracted but afraid. "What did
Douglas do? Is he getting arrested?"

Jackson went out on the deck to keep them out of the house.
Margie's daughters hung around the edge of the property, dancing
from foot to foot, desperate for news. "No. It's about the plants.
Don't hang around here. They'll take you, too."

They dispersed instantly, each wanting to be the one to bear
the news. Only Rosie's oldest hung back. He always got two and
two put together before the equation was on the board.

"Douglas called them, didn't he?"

Jackson looked away. "You go on home," he said and turned back into the house.

The boy knew he had the rest of them scooped.

Both cops reappeared with their arms full of plants.

"Biggest haul ever in this county," said the big one. "Good work, kid."

Townsend looked grave. "I'll call for the van. And the Children's Aid."

Jackson sat slumped in a chair while Douglas helped the cops haul armload after armload of plants up from the cellar. The foliage encroached over the floor in an advancing tide. Jackson managed a peek at Douglas every now and then. Dope rat. He turned in his own father.

Delbert's car crunched on the gravel behind the police car. Jackson counted the seconds. The porch door slammed against the outside of the house. Delbert burst into the kitchen like a mad bull, white with rage. Townsend emerged from the little cellar door beneath the stairs with his arms full of plants. Douglas appeared behind him. Delbert stampeded through the jungle on the floor, knocked Townsend sprawling and lunged for Douglas's throat. He pulled the boy by the neck into the centre of the room, holding him out in front of him, taking good aim. Jackson found himself on his feet before he could think. He threw himself in front of Douglas, against Delbert's outstretched arm. The boy skittered away. Jackson took the punch, full force in the gut. He slid to the floor, gasping like a fish, unable to catch a breath. Colours swam in his head. Feet stomped around him, a pain shot through his foot and up his shin. His body retracted into a ball.

The bellowing threatened to blow out the windows. "I'll kill you, you little bastard runt of a dog bitch. You ratting faggot . . ."

Jackson tasted dirt, he couldn't see. The floor boards vibrated with the slamming of bodies. People screamed. Above it all a voice roared, "I'll kill you, ya fucking faggot!"

Jackson braced himself for a kick, covered his head with his arms. But no blows fell. He waited, cringing where he lay. Action moved away from him. It wasn't him. It was the boy. Douglas.

Douglas was the faggot. He opened his eyes. Delbert lay face down on the floor, writhing, raging, spewing showers of dirt, abuse, plant pots and serrated leaves in all directions. He flailed helplessly, his arms pinned behind his back, handcuffs secured. The big cop still knelt over him, holding him down. Two more cops arrived. Townsend crouched by Delbert's head. "It's okay," he was saying. "Calm down now. You're okay." It had never occurred to Jackson that his brother could be subdued.

Townsend herded Darlene and the kids through the kitchen into the main part of the house. The three others muscled Delbert into the squad car. Then Townsend crouched down beside Jackson. "You okay?"

Jackson nodded. Townsend helped him to the closest chair. Then the cop opened the cellar door and poked his head through.

"Douglas? Come on up now, son."

Douglas climbed up through the little door like a zombie, a boy with no past, no connection to anything. He stood, his arms limp at his sides, absolutely solitary. He stared straight ahead, not seeing the kitchen, the cop, looking right through Jackson. He didn't respond to Townsend's questions or overtures, but he followed him out to the cruiser.

Jackson had to snip the battery cable in his truck so he couldn't drive to the village for a bottle. Alone. Douglas all alone at the open cellar door. The image haunted him whenever he shut his eyes. He hid in his room until dark, then, afraid to go to bed, paced his cabin. Eventually exhaustion overtook him and coaxed him to a chair, where he slipped, defenceless, into sleep. All his family crowded in on him. He had done something terrible. He couldn't remember what, but it was bad and now they had him.

"Faggot."

"That's fucking sick. *Sick!*"

"Hey, remember this buggy whip? Hold him still, boys. We'll stick it right where he wants it."

Jackson woke terrified, his head splitting with pain. The force of Delbert's punch sat fresh in his gut. And it made him hungry for the next one. Yes. Why didn't they all come at him . . . fists, boots, clubs, whatever they wanted. Lay him out flat and leave him. Alone. Then it would be over.

He bolted for his cabin door and ran, just ran into the woods, damp and frigid in the early dawn. He followed a deer path until the futility of running overwhelmed him. The path led him meekly back out to MacIntyre Road. There was nowhere else to go. He stood there in a daze.

Somewhere up the road a car engine laboured. He followed the noise around the next bend. Matthew, his car tipped in the ditch at a forty-five-degree angle on the wrong side of the road, sat stupidly, pointlessly spinning his tires and cursing. He was too drunk or too hung over to think of anything else to do. Jackson trotted over to him.

"My big brother!" Matthew broke into his loud, infectious laugh. He was still very drunk. "This goddamned car is fucking useless."

"Just leave it here for now," Jackson said. "Turn off the engine."

"It's fucking useless anyway."

The driver's door was blocked with mud and undergrowth, so Jackson extended his hand and helped Matthew climb out the passenger side.

"Well, big brother, ya missed the party. All over. Now it's time for a nice little nap." He flopped against the car.

Jackson wrapped one of Matthew's arms around his shoulders, and the two of them headed unsteadily down the road, Matthew leaning into him.

"Yup, jus' you an' me, buddy."

Jackson struggled under Matthew's weight. He had never felt so alone.

CHAPTER ELEVEN

JACKSON DEPOSITED MATTHEW on his own doorstep and retreated to his cabin, his heart pounding. His shirt hung damp and heavy across his shoulder where Matthew had draped his arm. More than from the chill, he shuddered from the weight that clung to him. He filled his bathroom sink with steaming water from the kettle and began scrubbing himself. He scoured his entire body twice, washed his hair, shaped his beard, put on clean clothes. He made himself a pot of tea, smoked a joint and tried to settle himself. But nothing worked. His cabin pinched him like an outgrown shell. It bore down on him. He wanted out. Methodically, carefully, he packed up his two completed fiddles, stowed them in the cab of his pickup and drove off, watching in the rear view mirror as MacIntyre Road disappeared in a shimmer of dust behind him.

An hour later he merged onto the Trans-Canada and drove south. At the Cole Harbour exit he had to admit he was headed for Albert's. Why not? He had a few bucks from his week with Lloyd. He could pay him something on the debt. Ten o'clock. Jackson hoped Albert would be in his shop, even though it was Sunday. The padlock on the shop door hung open, so he pressed his ear to the door. The faint murmuring of a radio rose in the background. He raised his knuckles to the door, hesitated and finally knocked twice, wincing at the noise. A deep voice called out, "Come in."

Albert looked up from the only upholstered chair. He had a

newspaper spread out in front of him on the huge wooden cable spool that served as a coffee table. The smell of coffee rose over the pervasive aroma of sawdust and power tools. Albert lifted an eyebrow, flashed a smile, sucked in the edges of his lips.

"Well, look! Thought you'd died."

Jackson felt a tug at the corner of his own mouth. He shook his head.

Albert poured him a mug of coffee without asking if he wanted one. "Milk, right?" He showed him a can of Carnation. "I got fresh in the house."

"No. That's great. I, um, got some money for you."

"Where's that fiddle you're supposedly building?"

Jackson tilted his head towards the driveway. Albert jutted his chin out at the door, lowered one of his eyebrows as if to say, "Go get it and look sharp about it." Jackson complied, returning with both his varnished fiddle and his white one. He set them out on the cable spool between them. Jackson stirred his coffee around and around, sipped a bit of it off the spoon and stirred it again. He watched Albert examining his finished fiddle. Albert had the same look as a farmer buying a horse. He imagined being pulled out of the queue at the orphanage by someone looking for a child. Well, he's awful scrawny, but he don't look lame. Does he eat much?

This was the fiddle that had carried him through those first months of anguish, had saved his life, really. He knew every inch of it, every sixteenth, every thirty-second of an inch of it. Albert plucked the strings one at a time, tuning it. He picked up his bow and released a wild, tumbling, racing exuberance of notes. Jackson had no idea how Albert could store all that jumble of feeling behind that pinched forehead. Albert looked away when he finished, paused briefly, then began again, slowly, with deep, round, aching notes. Jackson recognised the ballad, remembered Ian singing as he played, "In Montjoy jail, one Sunday morning . . ."

Albert lifted his chin and set the fiddle in his lap.

"Go on!"

Albert stared at him. Jackson turned scarlet.

"P-pl-please?"

Albert played one more piece, then carefully set the instrument on the table. He got up and poured himself another cup of coffee, stood by the window and looked out. "Never knew a fiddle-maker who couldn't play."

Back at his cabin with the fiddle sitting on the shelf, Jackson hadn't been able to think about selling it. Not that the idea was abhorrent, just that he couldn't seem to concentrate on the question. Now he only needed to know the fiddle would be played. Played just like that.

"Y-you keep that fiddle," Jackson mumbled, not looking at Albert.

"What? Me? Oh. No way. You'll get good money for it."

Albert stood and walked over behind the chair where Jackson sat. He gripped his shoulder and squeezed for a moment until the pressure bordered on painful. "We'll find someone good to buy 'er," he whispered.

Jackson nodded. They avoided each other's eyes. Albert rummaged for something in a drawer. Jackson stared out the window, stirred his pale coffee, glanced sidelong at his resting fiddle. When Albert came back to the table, he set down a fountain pen and several tiny pieces of paper. "You need to put your label on that."

"No, that's okay."

"Write it on that label and glue it right in there." He pointed inside the left sound hole. Jackson knew where it belonged.

"It doesn't need my name."

"Look." Albert's voice turned flat and frank. "People will be paying for that name soon. You got to put it in. And put the number in as well. Number one. Sit up here at the bench where you can write neat."

Mr. Scarth used to make him answer a different question every week. I'd like you to answer this question for me, he would say. The handwriting along the top of the blank sheet said something like, if you were flying on the back of an animal, what kind of animal would it be? Or, if you could hide inside a flower, which one would you choose? Or, if you had an invisible castle, what colour would you paint it? All through the day, the week, Jackson could feel Mr. Scarth sitting at his desk, waiting for his answer. Waiting.

Jackson sat at the bench, Albert looming behind him. JACKSON BIGNEY #1, he printed in tiny perfect letters.

Albert glued it in place. "That label goes in easier before you glue the belly on, eh?" He set Jackson's fiddle on a shelf.

"Now let's get a good look at this one," he said, picking up the unvarnished instrument. "You want to start varnishing this one today? I've got lots of sealer here, and you can take a look at some of my dyes if you want."

Sealer? Jackson's book had only very basic information about varnishing and polishing. He nodded. Albert took him into the little room off the end of the shop, which bloomed with aromas when they opened the door: turpentine, lacquer, varnishes, resins. Little bottles and boxes crowded onto the shelves, fighting for space with brushes and pots and cans for mixing. Jackson reached out towards them, didn't know what to touch.

"Here," said Albert. He selected a bottle from the front row. "This sealer has sandarac, benzoin and mastic gums." He took several tiny packages off the top shelf and laid them out. "See? Now this here is spirit alcohol, eh?"

Albert told him all about the sealer, showed him how to apply it in coats to bring out the natural colour of the wood. They set his fiddle in Albert's drying cabinet, and Albert brought out several slabs of wood with patches of different coloured varnishes on them.

"My last violin I did with the brown, like this here. You know what colour you want for yours?"

Jackson examined the samples closely and shook his head. He didn't know there could be such subtleties. Albert started mixing colours and handed Jackson a brush and a shingle of sanded wood to practise on. Albert hovered at his shoulder.

"Now, keep this thinner here in case your brush starts to drag at all. Downward strokes, then cross strokes. Not too heavy, there. Look here, that's right. Now this varnish, the old Italian violin makers, back before the nineteenth century, eh, they always used to . . ."

It was five o'clock before either of them noticed the time. Albert stood up and cracked his knuckles, began cleaning up.

"So, Jackson." He had never used his name before. "So, we're going to sell that fiddle?"

"Yeah."

"Here's what we do." Albert looked more animated than Jackson had ever seen him. "It's Sunday, so dinner's at Jim Folkard's place. His wife's a great cook, and she feels sorry for me, so we're in like Flynn." Albert winked at him. "We'll take the fiddle, Jim will have a play at it, check his list, see who it'd be good for. He'll have it sold in no time. Come across to the house. I've got to get cleaned up a little, put on a clean shirt." He led them through the shop, grabbed Jackson's jean jacket from the back of a chair and tossed it at him.

"N-no. I-I can't go . . . they don't even know . . ."

Albert snorted. "Jim wants to meet you. Grab that fiddle, will ya?" Albert walked out, leaving Jackson no choice but to follow. Jackson thought about climbing into his truck and driving away. He didn't want to go to some stranger's to eat, but he didn't want to go home either. Albert seemed to know what he should do. Albert would be with him. He couldn't explain it, but he was pretty sure Albert liked him.

They drove into the city together in Albert's Tercel. Jackson followed Albert up several steps to a bright yellow front door. Albert rang the buzzer, then opened the door and walked in. A slight blond boy of about ten stuck his head into the hall and called back, "It's Al-bert. And an-oth-er guy."

A handsome man of about forty-five appeared in jeans and a faded red sweatshirt with the sleeves shoved up to the elbows.

"Hello, hello."

Albert planted his hand on Jackson's shoulder.

"This is the young fiddle-maker I was telling you about. Jackson Bigney."

Jim grinned from ear to ear and pumped his hand. "Jim

Folkard. Welcome, welcome. Really glad you could make it. Come on through and meet Carol. We're eating out back tonight. We're bound and determined it's summer."

Folkard's back yard overflowed with people laughing and talking and playing music. It was a party. Jackson's stomach contracted. He would never be able to eat anything. He wished he had never come.

"Here's Albert."

"Hey, Albert," a teenager called out.

"Hey yourself, ya punk."

Laughter.

Nearly the whole back yard was paved with patio stones and covered with big wooden lawn chairs. Teenagers sprawled all over. Jackson struggled to pay attention to the introductions, but everyone looked so much alike. Two of the teens were Jim's, but he couldn't remember which ones. The little boy's name was Stuart. Carol was the wife. There were several members of a band that had played a matinee in the pub and a few other people not from that band, maybe twenty people altogether. They all had smiles with beautiful teeth. He sat by Albert, sweating.

Young Stuart hung over his father's chair and climbed into his lap like a baby. And Jim kissed him as if he were a baby. Jackson tried not to stare. No one made fun of them. When Albert brought out Jackson's fiddle, people swarmed around. Jim prodded the boy off his lap and said, "Run and get your poor old daddy a bow, son."

The boy smirked. "No. Why should I?"

"'Cause I'm so worn out and feeble and you're so sprightly and energetic, and 'cause you love your dear old dad so much."

"Oh, brother!" The boy rolled his eyes but ran into the house and emerged a minute later with a bow.

Jim played first. When he picked up the bow it was impossible not to notice the injury Albert had described: the top joint was missing on the first two fingers and the tip cut off the third. When Jim started in on a tune, though, Jackson couldn't imagine that he had ever played any sweeter. Jim closed his eyes and nodded.

"Congratulations," he said to Jackson.

Jackson didn't know what to say to that.

They passed the fiddle around so all the musicians could have a go. "I want a turn!" Stuart called out. His father shushed him, but a young woman finished up her jig and handed the fiddle to the boy. Jackson trembled. How could he save his fiddle again in front of all these people? With the boy's father right there? He looked at Albert, but Albert was drinking a beer, totally unconcerned. The lad tucked the instrument under his chin and ripped into "Billy Peddle." Jackson relaxed back into his chair.

Everyone served themselves from the food laid out on the picnic table. Jackson didn't recognize much, but he followed Albert, took a little salad, the thinnest slice from a loaf of buttered crusty bread, a bit of something from a casserole dish. He spread it out across his plate to make it look like more. He sat by Albert in a circle of people talking about a music video they were making. A powerful-looking man had taken up the story. The salad had something so tangy on it that it hurt his tongue. There was white cheese crumbled in it that made his eyes water.

"So the producer says what he needs are shots of all of us riding horses across a field, and everybody's standing there nodding, like, sure, great idea. So I don't say anything . . ."

The bread had a deep, rich, not-really-onion taste to it. Albert opened a beer. Jackson got up and poured himself a glass of ginger ale from the bottle on the table.

"Finally we end up with a shot of me sitting on the back of this poor old nag. I'm totally shit-baked, hanging on for dear life, sweat pouring off me, eyes popping. And the horse is just *standing* there. Beside the fence! With the little girl holding onto the reins for me."

The casserole had skinny sort-of pancakes rolled up in it with some kind of vegetable. And cheese in the sauce.

"From the highway we can see this midway set up in a mall

parking lot. So in we go, and he gets us all on the merry-go-round, and the whole shoot's done in five minutes!"

The casserole thing wasn't bad. Everyone laughed. Jackson noticed he was smiling and had to quickly cover his crooked, stained teeth. Albert went off for another beer. Jim came by and sat in the empty chair and told a funny story about another band. Stuart kept showing up, then running off, then returning to his dad's lap. Jackson didn't mind that Albert was off talking to Carol at the other end of the yard. He had finished every bite of his dinner. There was a huge bowl of fruit on the table, and he sat slowly popping green grapes into his mouth. The stories, Jackson thought, got funnier and funnier.

A line of plastic Chinese lanterns were switched on as daylight began to fade. Carol appeared by Jim's chair and tapped her watch. Jackson watched Jim whisper in his son's ear. The boy looked like a baby chimp, nestled so cosily in his father's lap, his cheek pressed against his chest. The boy frowned, shook his head, wiggled, protested. His father whispered again, stroked his hair, kept whispering. A moment later they both struggled out of the chair.

"Good night, everybody," the boy said in a practised voice. With his arm over the boy's shoulder, Jim led him into the house. A young woman took the chair.

When Jim returned about ten minutes later, he squatted beside Jackson. "I know a couple of people who will be interested in that fiddle if you'd like to leave it with me."

"Uh, yeah. Sure." Such a smile Jim had.

"It should be about a week. If you want to check in with me, my number's here, or stop by anytime." He handed him a business card from the Journeyman's Joy Pub, and on the back Jim had written his home number. "It's a good fiddle."

When people began to leave, Albert showed up at Jackson's side and jiggled his key ring on his index finger. "Maybe you better drive," he said a little sheepishly.

Back in Eastern Passage Jackson stood in Albert's driveway, the house to one side of him, the little trailer to the other. He looked straight ahead at the workshop. He struggled to situate himself, to fend off the disappointment that the evening was over. "I'll need to get my other fiddle," he said.

"Oh jeez. Are you working in the morning? You're not going home this time of night."

"Uh."

"Come on. It's not like there's a shortage of beds."

So Jackson followed him into the bungalow. Albert immediately headed to the fridge and pulled out a six-pack with one can missing. He led them into the living room, where he flopped into his easy chair and nodded Jackson onto the couch. He downed a beer in no time and opened another. Jackson lit a cigarette, got up to fetch himself the ashtray in the kitchen and returned to the living room.

"That Jim," Albert said. "He's quite a guy."

Jackson nodded. Feeling emboldened, buoyant even, he asked, "What have you got in that trailer out there?"

"Nothing. Well, I store lumber in there now. I keep meaning to clean it up. Rent it out. But I never seem to get around to it." After a moment he added, "I used to live there."

"Eh?"

"The wife and I weren't getting on so good, but the girls were still in school. I didn't want to cause too much upset. I needed my shop. They needed the house. You know. That's one of my girls there, the youngest." He nodded at a graduation photo smiling down at them from the top of the upright piano. "She's in chemistry. Master of Science. University of Waterloo. Got her mother's brains." He pointed at a framed photo on the coffee table. A smiling young woman posed with a baby girl in her arms and a young man beside her. "That's the older one there, and the granddaughter. They live in Halifax. She got herself hooked up with a no-good." A grimace creased his face and he said, "I guess she's got her mother's brains, too."

Jackson waited for him to go on, finish the story, but he didn't. Jackson knew not to push, not to pry, not to ask questions, but he wanted to know. He wanted to be able to talk like those people at Folkard's. Embarrassed but determined, he pushed his tongue to ask, "And the boy?"

"Eh?"

Jackson indicated another picture sitting on the cabinet, the only piece of furniture in the dining area that he passed through on his way to the ashtray. The family photograph was barely visible from where they sat. There was Albert, less weight and more hair, with the woman who must have been his wife, the two daughters who looked about twelve and fourteen, and a teenage boy standing tall and slim beside him.

"Oh. That's my son."

Jackson waited.

"Christopher. We didn't always get on as good as we should've."

Jackson could see Albert struggling and knew it was his fault. "I n-never got on that great with my father, either," Jackson said.

"Maybe they should get together," Albert answered flatly.

"I don't think so. My father's dead."

Albert's words grew coats of armour. "Yeah, well" — he reached for Jackson's pack of cigarettes on the coffee table — "so's my son. You mind if I have one of these?" He held his head still, didn't look up. He waited for an audible answer.

"Go ahead." Jackson had no idea what to say. Every time he opened his mouth he said something wrong.

"AIDS." Albert finally said.

"AIDS?"

"He was gay."

As easy as falling off a cliff, they say. It was exactly like falling off a cliff. Jackson suddenly found himself much closer to the edge than he expected. He could have put out a foot to stop himself, but the allure of the free fall, the cloud's laughing promise of soft landing, the clear, uncluttered horizon, the need to know one thing for absolute certain stalled his reflexes for a fraction of a second. Then it was too late. The wind rushed by his face. "I am, too," he said.

"Gay?"

"Uh-huh."

Albert lit a match, sucked deeply on his cigarette, looked off into the distance, nodding. "Yeah," he said, as if he already knew.

Jackson reached for one of the three remaining beer. "You mind if I have one of these?"

Jackson woke at dawn in a panic. He had to get out. He couldn't stop to think why, he just had to. He grabbed his jeans from the floor, where they had fallen from the chair. Desperately searching for his shirt, he got his leg caught up in his pant leg. He tottered and tipped over, catching his balance against the bedroom wall. His brain bubbled and spit. This was Albert's house. Last night they went to Folkard's, then came back here, and they talked. Said things. He drank two beer. The two beer now swelling his bladder. He tossed the bedclothes aside searching for his socks, found his shirt, fumbled with the buttons. His mind raced — one fiddle hung locked in the shop beyond his reach, the other left with Jim Folkard. It's okay, there's no reason to be upset. Futile. Those two beer fanned the flames of his panic. He could find only one sock, so he frantically stuffed it in his pocket. Boots. Boots! Please don't let Albert be up, he prayed, don't let him see me, don't make me have to talk to him. He stuck his head out the bedroom door and glanced up and down the hall. All clear. Every pad of his bare feet on the hall linoleum made him wince. Then the kitchen. Was Albert already up? Sitting there? Waiting for him? He held his breath, afraid to round the corner, afraid not to. He peeked in. Safe. His jean jacket hung over a chair, his boots stood by the door. He grabbed everything and ran to his truck. When he turned the key the engine jumped to life in what seemed to him a deafening roar. He tore down the driveway and off towards the highway.

Ten minutes down the road, he had to stop to take a leak. Panic drained from his body, and he became flustered. Why was he running? Had he done something wrong? What time was it?

His head throbbed behind his eyes. He smacked his tongue, trying to dislodge its heavy thickness, shake the sour taste from his mouth. He had to go home. He had to sort things out.

Even after the two-hour drive, shutting himself in his cabin, drinking two cups of tea and smoking a string of cigarettes, Jackson still couldn't settle. His mind jagged from one spiky corner of reality to another. He told Albert he was gay. Just told him, and now someone knew. Two people knew: Ian and Albert. And Albert told him about his son. Gay. Dead. Christ. Last night he drank two beer. He had said he wasn't going to drink again but he had. Two beer. And why? Jim Folkard and his wife were so nice, invited him back, Jim agreed to sell his fiddle. He sat in their back yard with a real band, listening to them talk. Jim's little boy, bigger than Matthew's oldest, had curled into his father's lap, been cuddled, stroked, kissed, right out in public. Jesus. He was only gone twenty-four hours.

He smoked a joint, but it did nothing to calm the jangling. He needed to ground himself, use his muscles, his arms and legs and shoulders and heart. He needed to feel breath in his lungs and sweat on his back. He slunk down to Kate's shed and carried off her spade and garden fork. In front of his cabin, beside his woodshed, he marked out a level patch twelve feet square and began slicing through the earth with the spade, cutting along the perimeter, then undercutting the roots of the grass to remove the sod. He laid the sods grass-side down in a careful square beside the bare patch. He would plant potatoes there in neat rows buried under eel grass and maybe a couple of bales of straw if Lloyd could spare them. He hadn't worked in a garden since his father died, since he moved out of the farmhouse. He spent his boyhood working in the fields or barn or garden, kept his head down and his mouth shut, never talked back. He did what he was told. He never made a suggestion or a choice or a decision. Once his shoulders began to ache he let his mind wander.

Jim's son had curled up in his dad's lap, pressed his head into his dad's chest. Ten or eleven probably, and still mollycoddled like a baby, still being put to bed, and by his father! He's his dad's boy, that's for sure, Carol had said. The little guy could have been in TV commercials, he was that beautiful. Jim had stroked his boy's hair, his sawed-short fingers looking almost normal, the tips hidden behind wisps of blond hair. Jackson had caught himself staring and blushed with double embarrassment when he realized it would look as if he had been staring at the disfigured fingers.

Vernon caught him and his mother once. Jackson was nine or ten and way too old to be held. He was sick with flu, and Gert had wrapped him in a blanket and sat rocking him by the stove in the kitchen, humming lightly in his ear. He lay there listening to Vernon's boots scuffing on the mat, the groan of the door opening and the puff of cool air as he walked in and sat heavily in his chair, scraping its legs across the floor.

"Christ, woman, that's not a baby!"

She gave him no reaction.

He remembered the blanket being torn from his face, the sudden rush of air on his skin, feeling exposed in his pyjamas, guilty of something dreadful.

"Oh, that one."

He remembered the disgust in the voice and lying there quietly waiting for the blow that never came.

"Some people seem to have a lot of time for other people's business," his mother said. But she set him on his feet and walked him up to bed.

His father held him close once. When he was sixteen, the time Vernon caught him stealing his rum in the barn. When Vernon grabbed him by the hair and forced him to his knees, his cheek grazed the worn fabric of his father's shirt, his face pushed into the hollow in his father's gut. His father's belt buckle tore his lip, and he tasted the metallic sharpness of his own blood. He remembered his father's lean stomach, the barny smell against his skin, away from the stink of his alcohol breath. Jackson gagged with the memory, gasped for breath, choked, hacked, awash in panic. Now, almost fifteen years later, the memory of his father's voice crumpled him into the garden dirt.

"You wanna drink? You wanna die? Try drinking this." Vernon

was roaring drunk. He left him but returned to pull him off the barn floor, gripped his arm and jolted him to his knees again. This time his head rammed sideways into the barrel of a .22 rifle. His father shoved the barrel right up against Jackson's mouth. "It'll be a fuck of a lot faster." The steel barrel cracked against his front tooth, pain shot through his skull. He remembered thinking he had been shot, remembered waiting for the bullet to reach his brain, but it never did. He kept kneeling there, captive, with the rifle barrel smelling of blood, dead cows, tasting of burnt steel.

But he also remembered seeing himself and his father from above, from the rafters maybe. He had seen himself on his knees, head bent back, rifle in his mouth, a dribble of blood and yellow vomit running down his chin, eyes open and staring up, up, searching for his father's face. He remembered his father's finger on the trigger, the shaking rage in his father's eyes. Then he remembered seeing his father melt like a bread bag on a radiator and turn away. His father grunted something that sounded like "Jackson" and dropped the gun onto the carpet of old hay on the barn floor, the loose stalks around it bouncing a little on impact and then yielding to its shape. And he remembered his father walking away, hunched forward, eyes crazy. How could he have seen his father's face like that? How could he have? He didn't trust himself about the "Jackson" part, either. His father never used his name. Maybe he said "that one."

Jackson picked up the gun, wiped his blood off the barrel and put it away, washed his face at the barn tap, fingered the newly chipped corner of his front tooth, rubbed the back of his aching neck. He climbed into the mow and crawled into a narrow hiding place he made by lifting two bales out of place. He curled into the prickly bed, the smell of hay, the crushing weight of humiliation pressing in on him. He lay perfectly still, trying to hold his mind blank. But he hadn't been so good at it then. What would his father say when he sobered up?

"No use talking to that one." That's what he usually said. But this was worse than ever before. Maybe this time he would say, "I guess we got a little carried away there in the barn, eh? Heh, heh,

heh. I bet there's still a couple of drinks out there. Come on, boy. We won't tell your mother." Jackson let the physical pain wash over him. He didn't mind. He was glad it had happened. He only had to wait a short while now until his father sobered up.

But his father said nothing the next day, and for the next three years his father avoided looking at him or speaking directly to him. It was as if his father had not taken his life but borrowed it, put it in his pocket, forgotten about it. For three years Jackson waited. But his father never did speak, never did reach into his pocket and give him back his life. And then his father died.

Kneeling there in his new garden plot, he sank back on his heels. His hands clutched at the soil, lifting handfuls up and letting it drop in small clumps from between his fingers. Suddenly he felt his mother there with him, kneeling beside him in the springtime garden with all the energy of the new season. "You're the spitting image," she said in that resigned way, like she had a thousand times when she was alive. "Must be like looking in a mirror." She chuckled low and deep, the way she used to in the spring when she planted the garden and made everyone believe things would be better that year. He heard her tsk-tsk and felt her shaking her head. "You'll want a good big load of manure on this poor pitiful patch." Jackson closed his eyes tightly to try to hold on to her. Just a few moments more.

"Did you find my onions?"

But she was gone.

He drove over to Harris's, and Lloyd let him load his truck with manure from their pile. He returned and immediately began digging it in. He dug the plot over once and then a second time to try to break up the clumps. He wanted a cigarette but couldn't risk setting down his fork. He had been sure the digging would calm him, but it wasn't working. No matter how fast and hard he dug, he couldn't outrun the memory. He spat repeatedly into the dirt, trying to escape the taste of metal and burnt powder, trying to blank out the suffocating humiliation of his father's disgust.

He needed a drink. What difference did it make? He drank two beer last night. He tried to quit and he failed. So what? The whole thing had been an utter failure. He needed to get ripped, blotto, pie-eyed, filthy stinking drunk. He dropped his garden fork onto the soil at his feet and fled to his truck. At the Scotch River liquor store he winced at his reflection in the glass doors. He hurried in.

"We haven't seen you around lately." The voice came from the counter by the cash register. Jackson didn't look up, just set a dozen Keith's and a quart of rum on the counter and reached for his wallet. His palm landed flat against his denimed backside. He patted his other pockets, ludicrously he knew, because he always carried his wallet in his back right-hand pocket. He had never lost it before. Never. Even when drunk. The only time it ever fell out of his pocket was at night when he hung his jeans sloppily over the bedstead or chair. In the morning he would find it on the floor, where it had clunked onto the boards during the night. Jackson felt himself blush a deep red.

"I, uh, I left my, uh . . ." Ashamed to look up, he abandoned his liquor at the cash. His wallet, he knew, would be on the floor under the bed at Albert's house.

He climbed back into the cab of his truck and rested his head on the steering wheel. "Oh jeez." It came out desperate, almost a sob. Sweat rolled into his eyes and made him blink. He licked hot salt off his lips. He was so thirsty. Matthew would have beer.

Back on MacIntyre Road he turned into Matthew's driveway. A crowd of kids swarmed the truck. One of them knocked on the window and yelled something, but Jackson didn't respond and they ran off. As soon as he opened the door he heard the ruckus of voices behind the house and the smell of charcoal.

Another wave of kids swept by calling, "Barbecue!" Bertie rounded the corner of the house stuffing the end of a hot dog bun into his mouth. Jackson followed the noise.

"Who wants this one?" Rosie speared a wiener off the grill and plopped it into a bun. "Oh look, here's Jackson. Eat this. I'm putting burgers on next."

Jackson couldn't focus. A hot dog warmed his hand. In front of him the picnic table lay covered in paper plates and plastic tumblers. Plastic spoons loaded with globs of brilliant yellow mustard and glowing green relish smeared into puddles of radiant red ketchup. Jackson spooned a line of relish onto his wiener and sat down beside Matthew on one of the large tree stumps that made up the lawn furniture.

"You into the beer?" he managed, which meant, where is the beer?

"Fuckin' Christ!" Matthew laughed, not understanding. "The time we had on the weekend! That stuff's poison. You were right to give it up, there, Jackson." Matthew winked at him. "I'm giving it up, too. Not another drop till the next cheque."

No beer? Jackson took a bite of his hot dog and was suddenly consumed with a ravenous hunger. He wolfed it down as Matthew gaped.

"Jesus. When'd you last eat?"

Jackson had to think. "Uh, yesterday, I guess."

"Rosie! You better fill up a plate for this one, we're losing the pulse on him."

Where was Ronnie? He would have beer. Margie kept him on a pretty tight rein, but this was a barbecue, for godsake. He could have a few beer. He looked around the circle, noticed everyone for the first time. His brain struggled to recall the weekend. It came back to him slowly, sluggishly. He had lived another life since then.

There sat Delbert, going over the whole story about Douglas, the cops, how he had been screwed, who was to blame for what. Darlene's list of complaints ran even longer than Delbert's.

"No one knows the trouble we had with that boy," she said over and over.

Kate kept trying to tidy up the picnic table, Rosie manned the barbecue. Margie's girls chased around with their cousins, but Margie was nowhere in sight. Probably keeping out of Darlene's way. In the house, maybe. Everyone joined in the rehashing of the story, shaving down this corner, building up that one, moulding what would become the official version. Even Matthew interjected refinements, and he was off on a binge the whole time, missed everything.

Kate set a brimming paper plate on Jackson's knee. Two hamburgers oozing ketchup and a mound of potato salad with a fork stuck in it like a flag. She handed him a large glass of pinkish Kool-Aid. His stomach jolted.

"Where's Ronnie?" Jackson asked Matthew.

"Trouble at a roofing job. He had to stay till they finished. Should be here later."

Jackson drank his Kool-Aid, picked at his dinner and waited for his brain to catch up and his nerves to settle.

"I'll fuckin' kill him if I ever get my hands on him again." Delbert ploughed on with his story. "I'd'a fuckin' killed him then if I could've."

Jackson frowned, turned to Matthew and asked, "D-did Dad ever try to kill you?"

"What?" Then Matthew laughed. "He threatened to about a million times."

"No." Jackson's eyebrows knit together in such furious seriousness that Matthew shifted uncomfortably and looked around. "I mean really, like with a gun or something. For real."

"Shit. Dad never . . . jeez."

"Once . . . with the .22 . . ."

Kate, her voice rigid with authority, cut him off cleanly. "That's enough! Nobody's killing anybody. That's enough, Delbert. We don't need any more of this talk. None. And you!" — she pointed at Jackson — "You leave Dad in his grave where he belongs." Her face had turned a tomato red and tiny bubbles of spit appeared at the corners of her mouth, now thin and hard. She turned away but stopped and whirled around. "And here's another thing, Jackson Bigney. You've got my garden fork lying in the dirt by your cabin. And I expect you to look after it and bring it back when you're done." She got up and went into the house to make it clear that no more was to be said.

"I-I just thought he'd kill me once," Jackson mumbled.

Delbert laughed. "I thought he'd kill me about a hundred times."

Jackson made his way through a hamburger, trying to clear his mind, push them all aside. He couldn't think any more. He imagined the inside of his fiddle, clean, uncluttered, empty. Maybe he could do without a beer. Maybe. Perhaps he could go home to bed. See how things looked in the morning. He stood to leave, made it nearly to the driveway before Delbert shouted over, "That pig, Townsend, was asking about you. Said for you to call him. I told him I'd call him anything he wanted, the pigfucker!" Everybody laughed.

Jackson barely found the energy to kick off his rubber boots and step out of his dirty clothes before he sank into his bed. The smell of his own pillow filled his lungs like ether, and he dropped into a heavy, dreamless sleep. Twelve hours later he woke, registered daylight and rolled back into sleep again. This time Trevor Townsend, dressed in a bright yellow short-sleeved shirt and cut-offs, handed him a wallet. Jackson took the wallet, knew it was his. He had been very worried about it and felt relieved to see it, but the identification inside was scrambled, wasn't his, or at least he didn't think it was.

"Does it look like yours?" Townsend was asking him.

"Yeah. Yeah, well, the money looks like mine." He knew he sounded like a smart-ass, hadn't meant it that way, didn't know how to explain himself. He was going to pull out the driver's licence and say it wasn't his, that wasn't his name, but then he wasn't so sure if it was or not. And then Jackson woke up again.

"It's okay," he said out loud to himself. "It's okay," he repeated as set his kettle on to boil. While he waited for the kettle he went out and picked up the fork and spade and returned them to Kate's shed. He paused for a moment, watching the bungalow, until Kate's little terrier bounded out the door, yapping at him. Kate tapped on her kitchen window and beckoned him in.

"Lloyd wants you over there tomorrow morning. He's nearly ready to start on that high field over at the old farm."

Whenever he looked away he could feel her studying him, assessing him. He thought about the two beer he drank with Albert, his humiliating trip to the liquor store, and wondered if she could tell.

"Yeah, okay. I brought . . ." He jerked his thumb towards the shed.

"What? Oh. The garden fork."

He nodded.

"I, um, lost, well, uh, left my wallet, I think." He patted his back pocket as if offering proof. "Could I, could you, for gas and smokes? Just till I get it back? Like, twenty bucks?"

"Hmpf. Not like you to mooch, Jackson." Kate barely managed to control a smile. "Darlene will be disappointed to discover you got to me first." She reached behind him to her purse hanging on the back of the kitchen door. She seemed slow to find the bill she wanted to give him, fumbling in the depths of the purse, hesitating over her wallet. "Don't you worry about anything Dad ever said to you," she said, never raising her eyes. "When men get drunk . . . but that has nothing to do with you now. Here you are, eight months without a drink. And you making those beautiful fiddles out of chunks of old wood." She snapped her purse shut, and when she looked up it was as if she had never spoken.

She handed him a twenty-dollar bill. "Now I want that back. I mean it. I'm not the Bank of Nova Scotia."

Jackson bobbed his head and ducked out.

He returned to his cabin, stepped inside and leaned back against the door. He endured the stab of guilt that came with clicking the door lock into place. He looked around the empty room, felt the breath rising and falling in his lungs. He washed and changed into his father's suit, knotted the tie around his neck, buttoned the jacket. It still fit the same way it always had. He stood in front of the bathroom mirror and stared. The hair wasn't quite right, a bit too long but not bad. The beard was wrong, of course. His father had never worn a beard. He kept his eyes on the mirror image, picked up his razor, watched as his image turned the razor over and over in his hand. He searched the eyes in front of him, the corners of the face, looking for his father. Jackson was thirty years old. He had never seen Vernon at thirty, of course. When Vernon was thirty he had a wife, two little girls and a baby boy. For the first time since her marriage proposal, he thought of Lori. What if he had married? The image in the mirror twitched, the eyebrows lowered, forehead wrinkled, eyes darkened, and in that flash of fear he thought he caught a glimpse of him.

"Vernon?"

Jesus, Jackson thought, and tears welled in his eyes. His father disappeared. He splashed water on his face, stared harder, harder. He picked up his can of shaving cream and shook it, closed his eyes, opened them again. The foam felt cold on his skin. One stroke at a time the bare skin of his face appeared. He hid things, his mother had said, just like you. You're the spitting image. His jaw line emerged out of the foam. Just like your father. That's got nothing to do with you now, Kate said. The last of his beard disappeared into the sink, then his moustache.

He stared and stared at his clean-shaven face, tried on different expressions, watching, watching. He sneered and grabbed himself by his own collar. "Answer me. *Answer* me!" Nothing. He only frightened himself, made himself feel foolish. It was all so foolish.

"Vernon," he whispered. "Who's the spitting image?" He swirled saliva around in his mouth collecting a gob. But he looked so funny he couldn't help smiling. He threatened his image with the gob, grinned, spat into the sink.

He picked up his razor again and screwed it open, lifted out the blade. He held the bare blade up close to the glass and raised his other hand to it, slit the top of the little finger on his left hand and watched the blood ooze up into a lush dollop.

"Here's a good one, Vernon." He set down the razor, picked up the can of shaving cream and shot a dab in the middle of his forehead. "Bang," he said. "You're dead." He dotted the shaving cream with blood, watched the red and white dissolve together, begin to drip. "Father, son, and holey ghost." He snorted. He wiped his "wound" away with the back of his hand, dried his hands on a towel, pushing the fabric into his cut to stem the blood.

"Hey, Vernon?" There was no answer. He saluted his own image with the can of shaving cream, as though it were a beer. "Cheers." He squirted the mirror with foam, walked out of the bathroom.

He picked up the scroll he had begun carving and pulled out his tools. He drifted back to Folkard's party. He had been nervous, sure, but not too bad. Jim seemed okay. And Albert. Albert liked him. Almost for sure. And Albert knew. He worked from the outside of the curl towards the centre eye, just like the book said. Keep going, pretend there is something hidden there, tucked underneath, deep in wood at the end of the scroll. He sat there in his good suit, behind his locked door, the morning air fresh on his naked jaw, carving his way towards the magic centre.

CHAPTER TWELVE

JACKSON KNEW he had to get his wallet back. He thought about it on his way to Harris's, all through the milking chores, and as he drove the disk harrows around and around Harris's field. The more he thought, the more unsure he became. Everything got all mixed up. Maybe he shouldn't have said anything to Albert, asked Albert those things. Albert might be mad at him for the questions, or for running off in the morning, or for giving him cigarettes when he was supposed to have quit smoking. Or because of what he had told him. He didn't want to talk to Albert, but what choice did he have?

At dinnertime Jackson found Lloyd tinkering with the seeder. Lloyd told him to do one more round with the disks and go home. He didn't need him until the next morning. On the way back to his cabin Jackson stopped at the Quik Mart pay phone with his handful of change and called the store.

"Good afternoon. Folkard's Music Store. This is Brenda. How can I help you?"

"Uh, is Albert there?"

"I'm sorry, Albert's stepped out for a moment. May I take a message?"

"Oh. Um, it's Jackson."

"Hi, Jackson! Thank goodness you called. Albert has your wallet. He didn't know what to do with it. Are you coming in for it, or should I wrap it up and put it in the mail for you? I don't mind. Just let me be sure I get the address right."

The mail? He hadn't thought of that.

"T-tell them to keep it at the post office for me." He didn't want Kate getting his package from Halifax.

Two minutes after he got home from work, Matthew strode into his cabin and stood there with his hands on his hips. "You gonna do something about that truck of yours, or what?"

Jackson hadn't been able to get his truck's stick shift into first gear for months, and then reverse started to balk. The grinding and groaning had been getting progressively worse, but things had come to a head on that last trip to Albert's. The noise was frightful.

"What do you think it is?"

"Listen to it, for chrissake! That back end's gone. Listen to it!"

"How much is it going to cost?"

"I don't know. Want me to have a look at it?"

"I guess."

Matthew spent a couple of hours under the truck and reported back with grim glee. "Differential's shot. Oil seal's gone, ring gear, worm gear, bearings, everything. You'll need all new brakes, eh? And the transmission's toast, clutch worn to nothing. Total mess. It's gonna take me a couple of weeks, I'd say. I know where I can get the parts but, still, eh? It ain't gonna be cheap, I'll tell you that now."

Jackson rubbed his face, hard. He hadn't even finished paying Albert for the wood he had, and he wanted more. He needed to buy fingerboards and tailpieces. He wanted to start making his own varnishes like Albert. Maybe Jim would sell his fiddle soon. But maybe not. Maybe when buyers got a look at the fiddle they would see the faults in it and change their minds.

"How am I going to get to Harris's, get to work, with no truck?"

"Five o'clock in the morning? Don't look at me, b'y."

Kate's oldest, Charlie, hardly ever used his mountain bike. He shrugged when Jackson stammered out his request.

"Sure," he said.

To get to Harris's on time Jackson had to leave by four-fifteen, pedalling down MacIntyre Road, the darkness surrounding him eased by a slit of a moon. Once he reached Scotch River, the village's few street lights offered a break in the darkness before he turned onto the highway. Just beyond the village a white car approached from behind, overtook him, pulled over. A squad car. The Mountie got out, looked back at him, obviously waiting for him to catch up and stop.

Shit.

"Jackson." Trevor Townsend took off his cap.

Jackson stopped, balanced there with the bike leaning between his legs, and looked into the darkness where the river would be. Didn't this guy ever sleep?

"Where's your truck?"

"It's frigged."

"Where are you headed?"

"W-work."

"Who are you working for?"

"Uh, Lloyd Harris."

"That's four or five kilometres. You better hop in the car." He opened the trunk. "Put your bike in here."

Jackson did what he was told and climbed into the cruiser.

"I wanted to talk to you. You know you can press charges against your brother, Delbert, for assault."

"Eh?"

"He punched you. It's your right."

Jackson shook his head, stared at his knees. Townsend eased the car out onto the road.

"Assault is a serious matter."

He shook his head again.

"Well, you think about it."

They sat in the stillness. Jackson glanced over and took in Townsend's profile. The dashboard lights highlighted the Mountie's five o'clock shadow. Maybe he had been called out of bed tonight. Jackson chewed on a fingernail. Gathering his courage, he asked, "Wh-what happened to, um, Douglas?"

"Your nephew? The Children's Aid brought him back to his mother. Didn't you know that?"

"No."

"That's all I know, really. He'll have to testify when the case comes to trial."

"Oh."

Jackson saw the Harris's kitchen light switch on just as Townsend turned into the laneway. Jackson wanted to tell him to stop the car, to let him off here, he would walk up the lane. But you can't tell a cop what to do. He wasn't even sure that he was going to get the bike back. Townsend drove all the way up the long, long lane, turned around in the circle drive, lighting the farmyard with a sweep of his headlights. He stopped the car and got out to open the trunk.

"It's not safe to ride without a light, without reflectors even. And there's a bike helmet law in Nova Scotia now. You need a helmet and a roll of reflector tape, at least. Get Mr. Harris to drive you home if you're heading out after dark, okay? Give me a call if you change your mind about the charges."

The cruiser wasn't a hundred feet down the lane before Lloyd appeared at Jackson's side. "I don't appreciate the hired help arriving in squad cars. I don't like it one bit. I have neighbours, you know. This isn't a prison farm." He stomped back to the house muttering. The only word Jackson caught was "Bigneys." He wished he was at home finishing his scroll. Or perched on the stool in Albert's little room in his workshop, easing colour into a fiddle, listening to Albert talk about his varnishes. First light began to spread across the eastern horizon. He headed to the barn to start the milking.

Jackson spent most of the day pounding fence posts, stringing wire and thinking about Halifax. He tried to recall every aspect of his evening at Folkard's. So many people looked the same that it was hard to remember names. But there was Jim and Carol and the little boy was Stuart. And there was a guy, older than himself, who had looping black curls and a gentle rolling laugh and who shrugged his shoulders in a way that made you feel everything was all right. His name sounded like Dez. The salad had olives in it, dark, rich and tangy. He would buy some for himself, he decided, just as soon as he got things paid off, as soon as he had a bit extra.

Jackson set down his fence-post maul and covered his face with his hands. "Albert says you don't play the violin. How did you come to start building them?" Carol had asked him. "I dunno, just started." That wasn't the sort of thing other people said. Words rolled out of them. Words, sentences, stories, laughter. They all seemed so sure about everything. They all knew where they were going, what they were doing the next day or next week or next month. If only he didn't have to open his mouth. He did okay, listening. If he could just sit and listen he would be okay. Everyone else had so many friends, knew so many people. Albert talked to everyone. Jackson wondered if anybody knew that Albert's son had been gay.

It took Matthew two and a half weeks to get Jackson's truck back together. Jackson worked every day from five in the morning until after dark and handed almost all of his pay over to Matthew. At the end of it he still owed Matthew three hundred dollars, but he had his truck back. Sunday morning it rained, and Lloyd sent him away after morning chores.

He changed his clothes and headed for Albert's. It had been three weeks since he had been there. His palms sweat so much the steering wheel kept slipping in his grip. Some days he was convinced that Albert liked him, but then he would think of everything he had done wrong, and he wasn't so sure. He knocked at the door of the shop, his third fiddle and the plates for his fourth in the plastic bag in his hand.

"Where the hell have you been?"

"I-I-I had to work. My truck . . ."

"Your fiddle's sold, you know. And you left your other one in my drying cabinet. Jim wanted to . . . well, you didn't leave your number or anything. You could have called!"

Jackson fidgeted with a button on his shirt, bit his lip. When he glanced up into Albert's face, Albert's eyes clouded over, he stepped back and cleared his throat. He looked out the window, saying nothing, then returned to his chair, poured a mug of coffee, stared hard at the cup. When he spoke his voice sounded pained. "The coffee's hot. You take milk, eh?"

"Yeah."

"Come on, come on. Sit down."

"M-my other fiddle . . . I'm s-sor . . ."

"No, no. Here you go. Drink this. I've got your money, how's that? Jim sold the fiddle, like I said. Here, now." He picked a screwdriver off a work bench and stepped over to a light switch by the door to the varnishing room. He unscrewed the plate and pulled out a tight wad of bills, then replaced the plate.

"You didn't see a thing," Albert said.

"I do that, too."

"Yeah?" Albert thumbed through the wad, counting it. "Great minds, eh?" He handed it over to Jackson.

"I owe you . . ." Jackson pulled a scrap of paper out of his shirt pocket. "I-I made a list. I owe you for all this. And I need more wood and strings and . . ."

"Let's see the new fiddle first." Albert reached both hands towards Jackson's bag.

That Sunday slid easily into the same pattern as the Sunday three weeks earlier. Albert played Jackson's new fiddle and checked his plates, and they retired to the next room, where Albert helped him with his varnishing. The time melted away. At the end of the afternoon they cleaned up and drove into the city together for dinner at Jim and Carol's.

Everything was easier this time. He stuck close to Albert, kept his ears open.

Carol sat beside him at dinner. "Your fiddle went to a girl

named Sandra Ennis. Her mother's a great friend of mine, and she says Sandra's playing all the time. She just loves it."

Jackson nodded. He wasn't too nervous, just a bit, but he still didn't know what he was supposed to say.

"They'd love to meet you."

"Eh?"

"If you're able to come next Sunday, I'll ask them over."

He turned scarlet.

Carol smiled. "They just want to say hi. It's part of the fun of having a handmade instrument — knowing who made it. You don't need to worry." She patted his leg and whispered, "I'll tell them you're shy."

Shy didn't seem like quite enough. "Y-you could tell them I can't talk." Jackson blinked in surprise at the sound of his own voice.

Carol laughed. "Will you be in next Sunday, do you think?"

"Uh, I guess so."

"Well, good. Because we missed you the last couple of weeks. We didn't even know where to find you when Jim sold the fiddle. He thought Albert would have your phone number."

"I don't, uh, have a phone." He could have left Kate's number or Matthew's, but he didn't want anyone from home talking to people from Halifax.

The man called Dez, with the curly black hair, wasn't there this time. He must have been part of the band from out of town. This time there were new people who talked about a television series that was being shot right in Halifax. Jackson could hardly believe it was true. But these people were playing a bar band in the series, and then they got other jobs as extras. He had never known anyone who had been on TV before.

When they left Jim shook his hand. "You give me a call and bring those fiddles around when you're ready to sell. You drop around, now, when you're in town."

Jackson sat beside Albert on the way home and stared out the window, feeling happy but also relieved to have escaped the crowd. The laughter and music hung in the air around him. Albert whistled.

"Come on in," Albert said when he slammed the car door and headed for the house.

"I've gotta go home tonight. I got work in the morning. Five o'clock." Albert turned and stared at him, a funny look stalled on his face as though Jackson had just called him a filthy name.

Jackson stammered, "I-I-I got to. I owe everybody m-money."

"Well, come have a coffee then. You'll need it for the trip." It was an order. Jackson followed Albert wordlessly into the house. Albert made the coffee. "So," he said after a silence, "you been trying to play, been practising?"

"Nah, it's hopeless."

"Hmpf. You just need a few lessons."

"No, I, well, when I gave up bootlegging, people came around and I'd play and they'd leave."

Albert laughed. Jackson knew he hadn't told the story very well, not like the people at Folkard's, but he made Albert laugh. He had made Carol laugh, too. It gave him a funny feeling — scary, but good.

"Can I, uh, Carol said, um, can I come back next Sunday?"

"You come whenever you want."

When Jackson drove up to his cabin, walked in and switched on the light, Albert's look came back to him. Lonely was the word he was looking for. Jackson sighed and slumped against his wall. He swallowed a lump in his throat and poured himself a glass of water. But how could Albert possibly be lonely? He knew everybody. People were always calling out hello to him. Jackson had two hours before he had to get up for work. He set down the bags of wood and fiddle parts he bought from Albert and lay down on his bed.

Jackson knew they were coming to the end of planting and wasn't surprised when Lloyd grunted out over dinner that he wouldn't likely need him again after tomorrow. Not until the hay was ready to bring in.

Elsie pushed a jar of sweet pickles in Jackson's direction. "Help yourself, for heaven's sake, Jackson. You've been such a help around here, hasn't he, Lloyd? Through the chores in just a whiz. Not much more than two hours, really. Such a good worker. Isn't he, Lloyd?"

"Hm."

"I'm sure there's lots of work to keep you both going out there, once planting's done. I made a pie for dessert. I hope you like coconut cream, Jackson." She leaned over and took his plate. "We're not as young as we were, you know. Never hurts to have a bit of help. We're not as young as we were, are we, Lloyd?"

"We're doing all right." Lloyd pushed his empty plate towards his wife, avoiding her eyes, looking at Jackson. "You'll get a call when the hay's in the field."

Jackson sneaked a peak at Elsie, who pursed her lips but said nothing more.

Jackson was relieved. He had barely had time to work on his fourth fiddle at all. He needed a few days to settle down with it. True, he wasn't out of debt yet. And there was his vehicle inspection next week, and his insurance was due soon, but he had two fiddles at the varnishing stage. Soon he would have money from them.

He glued the back and belly to the ribs and began the intricate process of inlaying the purfling. The inlay, made of three strips of veneer, two black sandwiching a white, ran around the edge of both the back and the belly to prevent splitting. When the fiddle was done and varnished the white strip took on the colour of the fiddle, leaving the black inlay looking like parallel lines painted on as a decorative border. On the very cheapest of fiddles the stripes *were* painted. He cut a thin trough one-eighth of an inch from the edge, hollowed it out to a perfectly uniform width and depth all the way around, with no raggedness. Then he fit the strips tight into the slot, bevelling the ends where they met at the corners.

Friday evening Ronnie knocked and walked in. Ronnie always knocked. He even tried to get his girls to knock. Jackson liked that more and more. And he liked Ronnie for it.

"Hi-how-are-ya."

"Hi."

"Kate says you're looking for work."

"Oh."

"There's this guy I know in New Glasgow. He's building a garage, just on the weekends, eh? He wants to get it done, so he's paying a few guys to help out. I'm going in on Sunday. I told him you'd come, too. All cash."

"Sunday? I don't think so."

"Oh. Gee. I thought . . . Kate's been . . . Kate said . . . oh. Okay then. And, uh, you know, Rosie and Matthew are doing barbecue tomorrow? I'll see you then." He leaned over the table to look at the fiddle body. "Boy, that's really something. I don't know where you get the patience."

On Saturday Matthew's Troy barged in and recited his message. "Mom says we got a movie so come down and see it 'cause you'll go funny up here by yourself." He was gone. Jackson didn't even look up. Just thinking about going to Halifax the next day made him happy. He smiled, remembering Albert and the Folkards' older son. When Albert walked out onto the deck the kid had swung off the porch rail and landed beside him. "Hey-hey-hey, it's fat Albert!" Albert had clamped his hand around the back of the boy's neck. "So your parole board let you out again. I guess they didn't get my note." Later the boy had been laughing himself sick, trying to teach Albert a video game.

Matthew's Jason arrived next. "Get your ass down there! It's dinner time. We're not friggin' waitin' anymore!" He pulled on his arms. "Come on, stupid. Mom's making us wait for you. Come on!"

Jackson found himself dragged outside before he came to his

senses. He turned himself sideways. His balking startled the boy, and he shook himself free. "I may be down later," he said, stepped back inside his cabin and locked the door. He stood there trembling as the boy pounded on the door, then gave up and ran off. Jackson's fingers lingered on the lock. He knew he should unlock it in case someone wanted in, but he didn't. He returned to his work. He tried to regain the feeling, thought about working side by side with Albert, hunched over his fiddle, but it was hopeless. The physical resistance had left him drained.

Two hours later, when Emma arrived, she had to rattle the doorknob until he got up to let her in.

"Mom's really mad. She found out you wouldn't work with Uncle Ronnie tomorrow. And you were supposed to go to Aunt Rosie's tonight and you never. But you know why you were supposed to go? Know why?"

"No."

"'Cause Rosie's sister, April, was there with her friend Shauna, and Mom said they're pretty girls and it wouldn't kill you to sit in the same room as a pretty girl every once in a while. I hate that. I don't know why they don't just shut up. Everybody always wants you to have boyfriends or girlfriends all the time. Why don't they just shut up?"

Jackson looked up from his work. She sat slouched in the chair across from him, sucking on a strand of brown hair that fell across her face. Acne had broken out on her fat cheeks. Her dull green turtleneck stretched in wrinkles across her body, puckering at the seams. She sat in silence, chewing her bottom lip.

"Are you going to get married?" she finally asked.

"Are you?"

"No." She answered hard, as if the question was unbelievably stupid.

"Me neither."

"Yeah. Me neither."

They sat quietly for a while. Emma held a length of purfling between her thumb and finger, examining it. "You gonna get this skinny stick of wood into that little tunnel there?"

"Hope so."

"It looks like it could be made of licorice, eh? If shoestring licorice was square. And striped."

Jackson remembered the bag of licorice pipes he bought the day before. He crossed the room to fish them out of his jean jacket pocket, tipped the bag onto the table.

"Have one."

"Nah. I hate licorice."

Jackson clamped one between his teeth like Sherlock Holmes. "Just as well. Smoking's bad for you."

Emma smiled at him and he smiled back.

Every Sunday Jackson slipped his bracelet on his wrist and drove to Albert's, where they worked on fiddles together all afternoon and then went to Folkards' for dinner. Then they returned to Eastern Passage, and Jackson spent the night in the little bedroom that once belonged to Albert's son and then to Albert's younger daughter. Soon he started driving into the city in the middle of the week, on a Wednesday or Thursday maybe, just for the day, because he felt like it. He looked forward to seeing Brenda in Folkard's Music Store and having her call him by name. He smiled at her, being careful not to show his crooked teeth. He walked up and down the streets, guessing to himself what was around each corner before he got there. One day he stood in line with other people and bought french fries from the chip wagon outside the library. He crossed the street and sat under a tree to eat them. When he sold his fourth fiddle, he bought a magazine whose cover had a shirtless guy wearing what looked to be a police cap. He should be saving more of his money for winter, not wasting it on gas and tossing it around in the city. But he wasn't saving. Every time he went into the city he walked around the fort on Citadel Hill. He never saw any gays. Maybe it wasn't true that they met here. Maybe it was a rumour or a joke. He didn't want to meet them anyway, just see them. Before he drove home he might nip out to Albert's and put a coat of varnish on a fiddle he had left there to dry. Albert had showed him where he kept the keys to the house and the shop.

He helped Lloyd Harris get his hay in the barn, but after that Lloyd had only the odd day's work for him. Most days Jackson worked on his fiddles.

One Monday morning in August, when he returned to his cabin, Jackson found Emma sitting at his table, reading a book.

She looked up when he came in. "How come the Harrises want you sleeping over on Sunday night all the time? Do they go away or something?"

"No."

It hadn't dawned on him that whenever he drove off, everyone assumed he went to work at Harris's. No one ever suspected him of doing anything other than hucking bales or milking cows or shovelling shit. And since he always had a couple of fiddles under construction, they probably didn't even know he had been selling them, that he was getting better and faster.

The following Monday Jackson arrived home humming to himself. He opened the door and found his sister Shirley shifting a baby onto her shoulder and patting its back. What was Shirley doing home?

"Hi, Jackson." She shrugged, smiling. "I just got here yesterday. Yours was the only empty bed."

"Oh."

"Kate said you'd be gone all night."

"Uh, hi."

"Yeah. Hi. I couldn't believe it when Kate said to sleep in your cabin. I thought, well, you know what it used to be like. But it's great now. Even mostly clean. More or less. I couldn't believe it. Kate said, Jackson doesn't drink anymore, doesn't sell, nothing. He totally straightened out. I couldn't believe it. You cut your hair, too, shaved your beard. Boy, you look really good. I'm serious!"

"What . . .?"

"Don't worry, don't worry, don't worry. I won't disturb you. I'll just put the kettle on."

He stepped into the room, cleared a handful of tools off the table, stowed them in the drawer of the sewing machine. The neck he was carving he placed on the shelf.

"Oh, don't worry about the table. I'll get that."

A stack of clean Pampers poked out of one of the bags on the table, and beside it sat a single dirty one. "I was just changing her, just as you came in. I'll just clean up here." The baby squawked when she shifted it suddenly. "Oh, gee. Here, could you . . .?"

She passed the baby over to him, set it in his arms and turned her attention to the clean-up. He stared at the baby, then back at his sister.

"It's yours?"

"What? Oh yeah, of course she's mine. Three months old. Born May twentieth, four-sixteen a.m., Moose Factory, Ontario, six pounds, two ounces. Tara-Lee Gertrude. After Mom, eh?"

"Moose Factory?"

"They don't make moose there, you know." She laughed. "That's just the name of the place. I wasn't spending another winter there, that's for sure. One was enough for me. You bet."

He stroked the baby's head. Her hair stood straight up, black and shiny, and her eyes, as dark as the hair, searched his face. He touched the end of her nose with his forefinger, and she gurgled and waved her fist. Shirley set a pot of tea on the table.

"I'll take her now. Come see Mommy. I'm sick of all this running around. Now that I've got her I want to settle down. I just want to settle down. I hear Donny's married." She nestled herself into the chair with the baby.

"Yeah."

"Oh. Could you get her little duck toy? It's in on the bed."

Jackson got up to get it. His bedroom looked funny with someone else's things lying around it. He bent over the bed to pick up the squeeze toy. No, it wasn't just the luggage that looked strange. He reached out and touched the sheets: clean, crisp, white. They weren't his. His heart began to pound. His magazines! There were three: the little newsprint one with the stories and the two glossy ones with all the pictures. He leaned down beside the bed, tried to peer under the mattress. It was hard to manoeuvre with so little room, barely a foot between the bed and the wall. They were still there, all right. But they had been moved. Not accidentally brushed up against and ignored but pulled out, looked at and replaced, one glossy placed perfectly on top of the other in the dead centre of the bed, the booklet directly below it. He was supposed to be picking up the plastic duck. He was taking too long. He forced himself back to the main room, handed over the toy. Tried to calm himself enough to speak casually.

"Y-you changed the sheets?"

"Yeah." She laughed. "They were a bit skanky, you have to admit. What's wrong? Kate took them down to her place to wash them, that's all."

"Kate?"

"Well, Emma. Kate sent Emma up after I got here to check the door was open, change the sheets and that. She's a great help, that girl."

"Yeah. No. That's great. I should've washed 'em. S-s-sorry they were dirty."

"It's gonna be hot today, eh?" Shirley said.

"Yeah." He walked out of his cabin and stood there, unable to think. Just when things were going perfectly. Perfectly. His head throbbed and his stomach ached. How could he have been so stupid? How could he! He closed his eyes so tightly they hurt. When he opened them Emma was standing there, staring at his truck. He didn't move a muscle. She turned and saw him, stepped back as though he had threatened her, then looked down and away before she spoke.

"Mom said tell Aunt Shirley to bring the baby to our house."

Then she raised her head and pierced him with a look of blatant accusation, turned and ran. She knew. There was absolutely no doubt.

He grabbed a plastic bag and returned to his bedroom. He

closed the door. Think! He drew the magazines out from under his mattress and folded his clean jeans around them. He placed them in the bag and stuffed other things, T-shirts, underwear, socks in on top, beside them, behind them. He concentrated on his movements. Making sure he didn't run, he stepped out of the bedroom, crossed his cabin and nestled the fiddle pieces he was working on, back, belly and neck, in around the fabric. Don't run. Don't run! He felt as if he was walking through water, every movement artificially slow and exaggerated. He knew his cheeks were flaming, and the knowledge only made him more exposed, more vulnerable. Shut up, shut up, shut up! He left the cabin, set the bag on the seat of his truck, returned.

"I, uh, you can stay on here. I'm, uh, going. Out."

He needed money. He glanced around the room, mentally checking his hiding spots, but Shirley was sitting right there cooing at her baby. He shut himself in the bathroom and pulled forty dollars from underneath the toilet tank.

Shirley called to him, "So we can stay till you get back?"

"Yeah." He walked back into the main room and looked around, although he didn't know what for.

"Great. It's not bad here, really. Except for the bedroom. Sheesh. You can't even turn around in it. I can hardly fit the baby in there with me. And the smallest bathroom in the world. Why make everything so small? Kate says you'll likely be building on . . ."

The end of the sentence disappeared behind the cabin door as he pulled it tight behind him. It hadn't rained in two weeks. On the road his tires threw up a wall of dust so thick it obliterated everything behind him.

Jackson let himself into Albert's shop. Albert would be working all day at the music store. Jackson had seen him off that morning, so when Albert got home he would never even know Jackson had been gone. It was nearly one o'clock. He sat by the window with his bag, stuffed with his clothes, his fiddle pieces and his magazines, between his feet. And waited. For three hours he sat there, then finally he pulled the fiddle head he was working on out of the bag and, with Albert's tools, set to work.

Emma knew. How could there be any doubt? There couldn't be, the way she had looked at him, accused him. But she was only fourteen. Maybe . . . maybe what? Maybe she wasn't sure? Maybe she wasn't going to tell? How could he have been so stupid? He should never have brought those magazines home. What was he going to do now? He concentrated on holding his hands steady on his work.

In grade six Mr. Scarth began letting him stay in during recess. Sometimes Matthew fought in the school yard, and sometimes his victims took revenge on Jackson, who didn't fight back. Mr. Scarth always asked what happened. I fell. How did you get this bruise? I fell. What happened to your eye? I fell. Mr. Scarth said he didn't have to go outside if he didn't want to. Morning and afternoon recess, Jackson would sit at his desk with the piece of paper Mr. Scarth set in front of him. "I want you to answer this question for me. I'd like you to be finished by the end of the week." Every week a different question was written across the top of the sheet. If you could live under the sea, what would your house look like? If you were as strong as Superman, what would you do first? If you could have any job in the world, what would it be? On Monday and Tuesday he would sit at his desk through recess and stare at the page. Wednesday he began a drawing. Thursday he chose a colour, maybe two, and shaded in the picture to make it stand up on the page. On Friday, like Mr. Scarth asked, he wrote a sentence or two, always printed, small, straight up and down so it would look like typing. Every Friday afternoon Mr. Scarth would squat down beside Jackson's desk, pick up the sheet and say, "Thank you, Jackson. This is beautiful." All week Jackson would wait for this moment when Mr. Scarth hovered at his side, large and quiet and smelling of oranges and chalk and aftershave. Jackson stared at the floor, at the faint cross where the tiles met, chewed his fingernails and waited. Waited for Mr. Scarth to stand up and walk away with the drawing, wait for his heart to start beating again.

Mr. Scarth kept all those pieces of paper. He put them in a

bright green Duo-Tang and kept them in a drawer in his desk. In the last week of school Mr. Scarth asked him to stay in at lunch hour. Mr. Scarth pulled a wooden chair up beside his own at the teacher's desk and called him up. Mr. Scarth's hand burned on the back of the wooden chair, inches from his shoulder blades. The book sat between them on the desk.

"Your recess book is finished, and I'd like for us to go through it together," he said. "You don't have to say anything if you'd rather not. It's a beautiful piece of art. There isn't a single page that doesn't express something strong and poetic about you. I hope you'll be very proud of this work. Very proud. Page one. If you had a car and you could drive anywhere, where would you go? Down the beach, into the black ocean. The salt would eat the car away. The way you've drawn the ocean here gives a feeling of vast expanse. And the way you have the ends of the tire tracks lapped away by the waves is a brilliant touch. It leaves me with a lonely feeling. Page two. If you could have anyone in the world as your classmates, who would they be? Crows would be in every desk, sitting on the backs of the chairs. I love the way you make the black feathers look so realistic here. It's easy to imagine them cawing back and forth to each other. That's very evocative. Page three . . ."

He should never have tried to keep that book. Never. He should have thrown it in the fire. No he should have dumped it in the trash at school. He should never have hidden it under his mattress. "Page eighteen. If you could take one person to the moon with you, who would you take and what would you do? With Mr. Scarth, and we would leap into a crater to be safe. I was very touched to be mentioned in your book. We look as if we're having a great time, holding hands and leaping over the edge like that. We know that we're not going to be hurt, don't we, because there's so little gravity."

At the beginning of the summer holidays, Matthew had to be dragged out of bed in the morning for his turn at chores. He was pouting in front of the TV when Jackson came down for breakfast. Vernon was there, too. His crushed leg had nearly healed, and he was walking with a cane but still resting it after chores. Jackson passed through to the kitchen, heard Matthew speak up behind him.

"I can show you something funny, Dad."

"What? Your face?"

"No, really funny. Wanna see? Wait here."

He listened to Matthew's bare feet pounding up the stairs and a minute later pounding down again. "Look at this page, Dad."

"If you were a bug . . ."

Jackson froze. His spoon clattered into his bowl of Shreddies. He remembered how the milk had splashed up and landed in tiny droplets on the table top, the complete paralysis that shut down his body, then slowly released its grip, leaving him quivering, trembling all over. His throat dried to paper and couldn't produce the "No" that squeaked out of his brain. His stomach cramped. He wished he really were a bug and could crawl off across the floor, under the door and away forever.

". . . where would you choose to live? In a yellow sunflower far away. Jesus!" Vernon's laugh shook the walls.

"Yeah, look, he's a bug. See here?"

"Who did this? That one, I bet."

"Yeah." Matthew laughed.

"Lemme see." Vernon howled. "Jesus, he's kissing a fish!"

I am not. I am not kissing a fish. I'm holding it, listening to it. Can't you read? His father could just barely read. He and Matthew lurched through some of the sentences, reading them out loud. If the sentences were long or had hard words, they didn't bother.

"Delbert! Look at this," Vernon crowed when Delbert stuck his head in to see what the noise was. Everyone in earshot poured in to see.

Instantly Jackson hated Mr. Scarth more than he had ever hated anyone or anything before. He hated that he had eaten all those lunches, all those stupid little cans of pudding and fruit. He wished he could puke them all up. Maybe if he could puke and puke and puke he could get rid of them. The new pack of coloured pencils that Mr. Scarth had given him when his own started to wear down to stubs were going into the fire. He didn't care. He hoped Mr. Scarth wouldn't even be at that school next year. He hoped he got fired. He never wanted to see him again. He was the stupidest teacher in the world. Jackson slipped off his chair silently and ran for the woods. He didn't care about the mosquitoes and the blackflies, he just kept running until he tripped, fell heavily, and lay there weeping his humiliation into the under-brush. He knew he should never have answered those questions. Every question made him weak with fear, but he answered them anyway because stupid Mr. Scarth asked him to. Why did he tell Mr. Scarth anything? He never should have, he was so stupid. Why did he try to keep the book, hide it under his and Matthew's mattress? Stupid!

Jackson got up and, carrying his bag with him, shut himself in the little varnishing room, where he felt safer.

Albert didn't come home. Jackson waited until six, then seven, then seven-thirty. He walked up the road about half a mile to a corner store and bought a pack of cigarettes and a bag of Doritos. He returned to the shop and waited some more. It was nearly eleven before Jackson heard a car in the yard and a hand on the doorknob.

"Oh. I thought you'd gone back. Thought I left the light on in here by mistake."

"No."

"You staying?"

"I guess."

"Well, what are you doing in here?"

Jackson picked up his bag and followed him over to the house.

"Monday night's my babysitting gig. I get my granddaughter while my daughter goes to her dance thing. I'm beat. I'm going to bed."

"Yeah. Me too."

All day to think, and Jackson was no further ahead than he had been. What was he going to do? How could he have been so stupid? He set his bag down at his feet again, stared at the bit of folded denim peeking out the top. Those magazines were still there. He should have tossed them in a ditch somewhere. Shit. He stretched out on the bed that had once been Albert's son's, then his daughter's, and stared towards the ceiling in the dark. Emma probably hated him now, probably told everyone. He imagined her in Rosie's kitchen, in the yard with Margie. "Men," she'd whisper, with her face all scrunched up. "On every single page of the magazine. And they're naked!" They would go check his cabin, but it wouldn't matter that the magazines were gone. Once people started to think about something like that, it was too late. He remembered how Delbert's eyes had sliced through him when Ian's letter had arrived, how even when he turned away Jackson could feel them boring into the back of his skull.

But Emma never told anyone about his breaking the windows in the cabin. He thought maybe she would, maybe by accident, or maybe she would get mad at someone and tell, or maybe she would get tired of keeping the secret, but she hadn't told a soul. Maybe, but this was different. But not that different. No one at home would understand. They would all think he was like the faggots. They wouldn't know it was a different thing from the queers on TV — waving their arms around and wiggling their bums and lisping, you can tell they want to wear dresses all the time, even if they aren't wearing them. The guy who lent him and Ian the room in Halifax, who had cut his hair and shaped his beard, whose voice was so girly anybody would know right away, he was like the TV queers. Exactly like them. Jackson didn't even know why Ian was friends with him. Ian wasn't like that. And neither was he.

They would never understand the truth back on MacIntyre Road. At home they probably thought "gay" was like being a woman in bed, putting up with it. But it isn't like that at all. It's like another body grows up inside you, so big and strong it's hard to believe it's still you, but it is. You can't stop it. The more you want him, the more he wants you back, and the more he wants you, the more powerful you get, and the more powerful *he* gets, and the more you want him. It's not like with faggots and queers. It's a different kind of gay. Gay is that thing he and Ian had before Ian went away.

He tried to beat back images of Douglas abandoned in the driveway, Douglas in Delbert's grip waiting for the punch. He tried not to think about his cabin. He had money hidden there, he had tools, his brass fiddle planes and his mould with the ribs in it. He still had clothes there and his razor and his father's suit. He had a bed and a table and his sewing machine stand. If it wasn't for Shirley sleeping in his bed right now, he could drive back, collect his things and be gone. He could be back here before Albert woke up. No one would ever know. But Shirley was there.

He sat up in bed, wrapped his arms around his knees and rocked himself. Shit, shit, shit.

CHAPTER THIRTEEN

ALBERT DIDN'T RUSH OFF to the music store in the morning. He didn't work on Tuesdays or Thursdays. So he slept late, and when he got up, he moved slowly, leaned back in his chair.

"You got no work today?" Albert asked.

"No."

"I've got a job to look at later, if you want to come along."

"A job?"

"I still do a bit of renovation work. Small jobs. I'm semi-retired now — I only work on my days off." He laughed. "A few jobs a month keeps the wolf from the door. That's the only problem with the store, the pay's not great. But I don't need so much now, eh? Not like when the kids were all home. And an old guy like me is better off sitting in a shop than running up and down ladders all day."

Jackson made himself a cup of tea and, at Albert's urging, a piece of toast. "What kind of job is it?"

"Bathrooms, bathrooms, bathrooms. Men come and go, civilizations rise and fall, but bathroom renovations go on forever." Albert winked at him and opened his *Chronicle-Herald*.

"Sure. I'll come." Jackson sat back like Albert and pretended this was the only life he had ever known.

After they looked over the bathroom and left the estimate, Albert had several other stops to make, errands to run. They had lunch at Tim Hortons, then Albert suggested they catch a movie.

"That Eddie Murphy kills me," he said.

"Sure." Jackson had only been to a movie theatre once before in his life. It had never occurred to him that you could just go to a movie. In the middle of the afternoon. For no reason.

Jackson had seen Eddie Murphy before, on video, but he was way funnier in a theatre. He and Albert laughed about the movie all the way home.

They spent a couple of hours in the workshop together, Jackson carving a scroll, Albert designing a set of cupboards for a customer. Eventually Albert set down his tools and picked his fiddle off the cable spool where he had left it. Jackson stopped carving to listen as Albert played something long and languid that Jackson had never heard before. When he finished the piece Jackson looked at him expectantly, urged him on. After half an hour Albert set the instrument down.

"This is the life of Reilly, eh? Too bad nobody made us dinner while we were busy."

Jackson felt so good he spoke before he thought. "I c-could make dinner?"

"Now you're talking!"

Albert clapped Jackson on the back and steered him towards the house, into the kitchen. Albert disappeared. Jackson heard the armchair in the living room groan and the TV click on. He stared around the kitchen in panic. He searched the cupboards, found a row of canned beans and canned stew and a few boxes of Kraft Dinner, the real kind, not Co-op brand. There was soup and soda crackers. Gradually he caught hold of himself, made tea and focused his mind on the project.

It's okay. Albert eats the same things you do. It's okay. His heart thumped like it did just before he began a new piece for a fiddle, before he bent a rib into shape or before he stroked the initial curls of wood from a plate or sunk a blade into a scroll. He could do it. And even if he couldn't he was going to try. In a cupboard under the counter he found a pot and set water on to boil.

Jackson stood at Albert's side, holding out a plate to him.

"What? Oh yeah. Oh, great." He straightened his recliner and accepted the plate. Jackson crossed to the couch with his, set it on the coffee table, kept his eyes riveted on the TV news, waiting for Albert to speak, hungry but too nervous to eat.

"So you're a chef, too?"

"Y-you like olives?"

"Yeah. I just never had them in Kraft Dinner before. Never thought of it, I guess."

Jackson had sliced them thin and on the diagonal like Carol Folkard did, so you could see the slice of pimento in every one. He hadn't been sure if it would be better to add them to the macaroni or to the canned peas, but he figured they would show up better against the orange-coloured sauce than the dull green of the peas.

Albert tucked in. He winked at Jackson. "First rate," he said.

Jackson only had to push his dinner around his plate for a couple of minutes before his stomach settled down. It was good. Anyone would have to admit that. He picked a few olive slices out of his dinner and tried them with a forkful of peas. He had made the right decision. Olives didn't work with everything. After dinner he watched Albert closely as he made coffee so he would know how to do it in the future. They shared the end of a bag of Chips Ahoy and Albert told him about the first fiddle he had ever made.

Jackson knew on Wednesday morning that Albert would be driving off to work at the store. He wanted Albert to ask him to go, too, to help out maybe. He got up and sat at the kitchen table while Albert rushed around.

"You're working at the store today, eh?"

"Uh-huh." Albert leaned over the sink, his mouth full of toast, a mug of coffee poised, waiting its turn. He crossed behind Jackson on his way out and squeezed his shoulder. "Lock up, eh? If you go out."

Jackson listened to Albert's retreating steps, the sigh of the bungalow's back door, Albert's car door slamming. Jackson wandered down the hall to Albert's bedroom and peered out the window. He watched Albert back down the driveway and drive off. Jackson turned and sat down on Albert's unmade double bed. The sag in the mattress tried to pull him in. All the furniture in the room was crowded together, as if everything had slid to one side in a storm. There was one nightstand, one dresser and a closet. He stood, looked around, rested his hands on top of Albert's dresser, stared at the jar of pennies there, the comb, the nail clipper, the two ballpoint pens. There were three scraps of paper. He unfolded them — store receipts Albert had pulled out of his pocket — Canadian Tire, Tony's Convenience, one with no name. Jackson put them back the way he found them. His fingers slid down the front of the dresser to the drawer handles and pulled open the top drawer. He patted the wild tangle of underwear and unmatched socks, ran his fingers over the small pile of folded handkerchiefs. One by one he picked up the tight little jewellery boxes lined up along the right side of the drawer and popped them open. Three pairs of cufflinks: one with red gems, one gold, one silver with fiddles on them. Tie clips. A watch stopped at ten past three. A plain gold wedding band, which he picked out of its box and slipped onto his finger. It twirled around, it was so big. He tried it on his thumb, but still it didn't fit. He put it back in its place. None of the lower drawers held anything of interest, only T-shirts, turtlenecks and sweaters.

The closet held a surprisingly large collection of clothes. He pulled a blue and white striped shirt off a hanger and slipped it on over his T-shirt. It fit him like a tent, so getting the buttons done up evenly was tricky. He unbuckled his belt and tugged it out of his belt loops, fastened it around his waist over the shirt. He wanted to use a pair of the cufflinks but couldn't figure out how they worked around the buttons. So he just buttoned the cuffs and turned up the collar to make himself look like Robin

Hood or a musketeer. He stepped into the bathroom to check himself in the mirror and smiled. He removed the costume and returned it to its place in the closet. He flipped through shirts and trousers, through progressively smaller suits and sports jackets, stopping every now and then to try something on. Out of the very back of the closet he pulled a red woollen high school jacket. There was a crest on the front and tabs on each arm. "Albert," said one tab. The other said, "Defensive end." Jackson slipped it on, zipped it up and stuffed his hands in the front pockets. It was way too roomy, of course. Albert had never been nearly as skinny as he was. All the same, it was hard to believe that Albert had once fit into it. He had been a different size and shape, a different man altogether. Not the same person at all. He probably hadn't even met his wife then, and now he was married and divorced. Maybe he couldn't even play the fiddle back then. Maybe he tried, but his family laughed at him, so he played football instead until he got his own place. How could one person live through so much change? How would you know you were still the same person?

He pushed all the hangers in the closet back where they had been, smoothed out the clothes so everything looked undisturbed, but kept the jacket on. He padded down the hallway, the linoleum cool on his bare feet, and stepped onto the living room carpet, warm and soft between his toes. He stood there a moment looking around the room. His eyes settled on the piano, Albert's younger daughter's piano. He approached it and poked at a few of the keys. The notes would have scared him, he knew, if it weren't for the comforting weight of the jacket on his shoulders. He walked his fingers up and down the keys like a Yellow Pages commercial, then played a few notes at random, pretending they made a tune. He tried out Albert's chair, switched the TV on and off with the remote. In the dining room there was no table or chairs. There was only the cabinet meant for dishes but holding an odd collection of things: five tumblers that may have come from a gas station, several plates with flowers painted around their edges, a few fancy glass dishes for candy or pickles, and a few little statues with different animals playing fiddles. Jackson picked up the family photograph and carried it over to the couch, where he sat and studied it. What kind of gay had Albert's son been? He looked pretty normal, but it was hard to tell. Maybe he was real fruity. There was probably something wrong with him or Albert would have liked him better. He returned the photo.

Jackson stood in the centre of the nearly empty room, tilted his head back and looked up into the frosted globe of the light fixture. Dead flies had collected inside it. Keeping his eyes fixed on it, he turned around five times until the room swirled. He stuck his arms out straight, planted his legs apart and held his position, waiting for the spinning to stop, his body tumbling over and over inside the football jacket.

He pulled on socks and boots, poured himself a cup of tea and carried it out to Albert's shop. He let himself in, strolled around the shop picking up every tool, examining it, setting it back down. He flipped through a pile of papers, but they were only measurements for bookcases, stairs, drawers, receipts for lumber and hardware. He picked up a slot screwdriver, leaned against the wall and stared at the switch plate beside him. He hesitated a moment, bouncing the handle of the screwdriver off his palm, then he stepped forward and unscrewed the switch plate. It offered up nothing — no money or any other secrets. Neither did any of the other wall plates. In the varnishing room he opened the doors to the old wardrobe and poked through the jumble of cans, brushes, paints, sandpaper, tools and all sorts of odds and ends. Then he pushed a chair over to the wardrobe and climbed up to check the top of it. In a dusty cardboard box pushed way back against the wall he found an odd-shaped chunk of wood, and he pulled it out into the light. It was the block that would be left over when cutting out a fiddle mould. Precariously tacked to the fiddle-shaped chunk of pine was a stick of two-by-two spruce meant to represent the fiddle's neck. The scroll of the fiddle head had been drawn on the stick with a felt-tip marker, a couple of freehand swirls that didn't even try to match. The sound holes were also drawn on sloppily, different sizes and in the wrong place. The remnants of two elastic bands, now rotted, clung to the crooked finishing nails, two in the neck and two at the tailpiece. He turned it over in his hands. On the back, scrawled in over-large, ungainly letters in black marker, was the inscription, "To Dad from Christopher age 12." It was more like the work of a six-year-old — hopelessly awkward, ugly and ridiculous. Jackson dropped it onto the end of the work table. What had Albert kept it for? It was pathetic.

He lifted his own fiddle out of the drying cabinet and admired it. He and Albert had experimented with the yellow colouring, and he was pleased with the bronzy effect. Now that it was done he was anxious to see how it polished up. He picked the rottenstone, spray bottle and polishing paper off the shelf, chose a clean rag and tried to settle in. Albert's jacket was far too hot, so he took it off and stowed it under the bench. Whenever he thought of that fiddle-shaped thing behind him, his back teeth ground together.

By the time he heard Albert drive in at the end of the day, Jackson had finished his polishing. A rich gold shimmered up through the varnish. Without a doubt this was his most beautiful fiddle yet. He could hardly wait to show Albert. Jackson sat still, waiting for Albert, listening to him slam his car door, open the shop door, approach the finishing room. Jackson looked up from his work and over his shoulder.

Albert's eyes fell to the crude model of the fiddle lying there on the table. His face froze to an impenetrable sheet of ice, dead pale, every feature rigid. "Where'd you get this?"

"I was looking for the linseed oil." Jackson held out his gleaming fiddle for Albert to see, but Albert never even glanced up. He just picked that wretched chunk of wood off the table and stood there with the hideous thing in his hands. Why wouldn't Albert look at him? Jackson tottered on his stool, desperation clawing at his gut, shredding it.

"I f-f-finished m . . ." He couldn't go on.

Albert never lifted his eyes. He backed through the door with the thing tucked under his arm. Jackson wanted to grab it, yank it away.

Jackson stood to follow, but the weight of a horrible desperation, hard and heavy, pushed him backwards. He made it to the finishing room doorway and watched Albert pull the shop door tight behind him. The beautiful bronzy yellow that Albert had shown him, that they had mixed, the two of them working together all one Sunday, getting the colour just so, had come out perfectly. Jackson stared down at it, sick with grief, fear and that hopeless anger. Why wouldn't Albert look? To Dad from Christopher, eh? Well, Christopher was useless. He was pathetic. Albert said they didn't get on that good. Maybe if the boy hadn't been so friggin' hopeless they would have. Maybe if he hadn't been such a useless, worthless fuckin' faggot they would've got on just fine. That fiddle thing was garbage, it was shit! And Albert could just go fuck himself if he didn't know it. He lurched over to the house hugging his own fiddle. The racket from inside the bungalow stopped him dead with his hand on the aluminum door. Albert was playing something on his violin. Not an ordinary song, but a piece with lots and lots of noise in it, screeching and crashing. Jackson leaned his back against the siding, rocking himself gently from shoulder blade to shoulder blade, the back of his head rolling along the vinyl, side to side, his fiddle clutched to his chest. Albert's piece made him dizzy, as if he were the lookout on an old wooden ship, all alone up at the top of the mast. The weather blew and stormed and tossed him around, then got calm and warm and sparkled all over, but still he was alone up there, and all he could do was hang on to the mast and watch. If he fell, there were only the sharks to catch him.

The music came to a crashing end. Jackson opened his eyes. What was the point? What was the point of even trying? Albert could go fuck himself. And so could little Christopher. He didn't need Albert. Albert began to play again. Jackson walked right into the house and down the hall to his bedroom. No, to Albert's son's bedroom. He made no attempt to be quiet. He stuffed his few things back into his bag around the porn magazines, turned and walked out again, back to the shop to collect his fiddle pieces.

He was going home. There was nowhere else to go. Forget Albert. Forget him. Maybe it wouldn't be so bad at home. Maybe

Emma hadn't figured it out. Maybe Shirley and the baby had found their own place by now. Suddenly he remembered Albert's jacket. He wasn't going to put it back now. No way. He pulled a plastic bag from the collection on the back of the shop door, stuffed the jacket in it, and divided up his clothes and his fiddle pieces, trying to get them to hide both his magazines and the stolen coat. It was hopeless, of course. The secret cargoes were far too bulky. And what's more, he couldn't block the rising dread that this was only the beginning, that soon there would be bags and bags of things that he couldn't let out of his hands, leave unguarded. Soon he would be too weighed down to move.

He dug in his jeans pocket for his keys. Fuck this. Fuck all this. He left the shop door swinging behind him, settled his fiddle on the seat of his truck, tossed in his bags, slammed his truck door hard and gunned the motor on his way out. Albert never appeared in the driveway or at the door, never rustled the curtains.

CHAPTER FOURTEEN

JACKSON PULLED UP TO THE PUMPS at the River Road gas station. He didn't see Delbert's car, parked behind the Everett brothers' truck, until it was too late, until Delbert stepped out of the little store and stared right at him, started for him. Jackson shrank into the seat, felt Delbert's bulk looming on the other side of his window, blocking the light. Delbert pounded on the glass. Slowly Jackson rolled down the window.

"Where the hell have you been?"

Jackson opened his mouth but nothing came out.

"Lloyd's been looking for you, you know. You lazy bugger. Kate thought you'd fucked off and got pissed and drowned or some fucking thing. She was going to call the cops, for chrissake!"

The boy sauntered out of the garage to pump the gas. "He'll take ten bucks of regular," Delbert called. The boy nodded. Delbert stuck his head inside the window, forcing Jackson back against the seat. The thin red veins in Delbert's eyes bulged. "Look, you. I got enough trouble without cops crawling all over the place on account of you, ya scrawny fucking faggot. Got that?"

Delbert's pores, his nostrils, his breath filled the cab. Jackson sat rigid while sweat trickled down his neck and back. Then Delbert was gone. Jackson's neck hurt from pushing back into the seat. Suddenly the face at the window was the pump jockey's. "Ten dollars," he was saying. Jackson's hands fluttered over his pockets, trying to locate money his brain could not place. He found a five-dollar bill in his wallet and three loonies in his pocket with four quarters, two dimes . . . he was going to be short. Coins slipped through his shaking fingers onto the floor. He had to get out of the truck to search for them.

Another car pulled up behind him, waiting for the pumps. The boy bent to pick a quarter out of the gravel. He clicked his tongue impatiently. "Oh, forget it. Pay the rest next time you come. Just count your money first next time, would ya?"

Jackson's hands shook so hard he had trouble turning the key. The worst thing was, he still didn't know. Delbert called people faggot all the time. Did he mean it this time?

When he reached MacIntyre Road and turned off the pavement onto the dirt road, the truck bounced into a pothole and he bit his tongue. He struggled not to cry.

Matthew was setting up a birch pole tripod over the hood of a car in his yard. He glanced up at Jackson's truck, turned, wiped his hands and walked into his house. Did he turn his back on purpose? Because he knew and wasn't going to talk to him? Or had it just got too dark to work?

Shirley met him at the door of his cabin, bouncing her baby on her shoulder.

"You're back. Kate's spitting mad at you, boy. You better get down there."

Jackson set the kettle on to boil. Shirley was looking at him funny. He was sure of it. He couldn't stop thinking about the plastic bags stuffed behind the seats in his truck, the magazines and the stolen jacket. It would look suspicious if he locked the cab.

"Some guy was trying to find you, ya know."

What did she mean by that? Some guy? Why did she say it like that? Jackson made his tea.

"I'll have a cup of that, too. Kate wants you down there. I'm serious." The baby whined, fussed a bit, Shirley bounced her up and down, she quieted a moment, then made a face and started the cycle again. "Oh, come on, settle down."

Jackson finished his tea. When he stood up Shirley handed

him a little duffle bag with a long strap and bits of pale terrycloth hanging out.

"You can carry this for me, okay? I'm going to rock her at Kate's for a while. Maybe she'll fall asleep."

Jackson slipped the strap over his shoulder, realizing instantly how faggy it looked. Shirley snorted. He knocked the strap off as if it had burnt him, picked the bag up by its handles. She knew. For sure she knew. And now they were on their way to Kate's. He hadn't said anything, hadn't agreed to go. It was always like this, swept along. Kate met them at the door of the bungalow.

"Where on earth have you been?"

He shrugged with one shoulder, looked at the ground, waited for the axe to fall.

"Lloyd was looking for you. What was I supposed to say? I had no idea where you were. Three days! We hear nothing! You wouldn't be the first one in the family to die drunk in a ditch."

That's why she was standing so close. She was trying to smell alcohol on him.

"You've got work to do here. Responsibilities. That garden of yours is a mess!"

Emma ran past them, heading for the door. "You leave him alone! He can go if he wants! Maybe he has his own stuff to do. He makes fiddles, you know! And he sells them, too. And they're beautiful — the only decent thing anyone in this family has ever done. Ever!"

Kate grabbed her wooden spoon and hauled back for a strike, but Emma slammed the door in her face and pelted off across the lawn. Kate marched to the porch, brandishing the spoon. "You get back here! Don't you talk to me like that!" Anyone could see it was pointless. Kate returned, red-faced, to the kitchen.

Charlie got up from the TV and lounged in the archway. "What's wrong with *her*?"

"Maybe the Lord Almighty knows, but I sure don't. I've been at my wit's end with that girl all week. I'd as soon raise five boys as one girl, I swear."

Shirley was trying to settle herself and the baby into the rocking chair. "Oh, come on, Kate. It's probably just her time of the month."

Kate's mouth dropped open. Her eyes darted to Charlie and Jackson before she glared at Shirley. "You just wait!" She pointed at the baby girl in Shirley's arms. "You just wait."

Jackson set the baby's bag on the floor and backed along the wall towards the door, making his escape. He climbed into his truck and drove down MacIntyre Road, headed nowhere in particular. Just past the first turn he saw Emma striding through the dust towards the paved road. Jackson stopped to pick her up. She climbed into the cab and slammed the door but didn't look at him.

"I don't know why you'd think I'd want a ride from *you*!"

Jackson tried to think of something to say, but he couldn't.

"You think I'm just a little kid, don't you?" Emma made it sound like the worst crime he could commit. He hadn't thought about it at all, one way or the other.

" I, I don't know."

"Yes, you do. You think I'm a little kid!" She sat there with her lower lip stuck out, her jaw set and her arms crossed in that final way that reminded him of Kate and also of his mother.

"Where are we going, anyway?" she demanded.

"The ocean?"

"Fine!"

Jackson concentrated harder than he needed to on his driving. Emma sat rigid while he drove out towards the water and parked the truck by the beach. They both climbed out.

"You figure, what's the use of letting Emma know anything? She's too young. She'll go off blabbing everything to all the little kids. But I *never*!" Her voice cracked, and she had to stop to swallow. When she started again her voice lowered to a whisper. "I never said a word about you breaking your windows and that. But then you lied to me and said you were sleeping at Harris's all those times and you weren't."

"No, I . . . *you* said I was sleeping there."

"You never said you weren't! It's still a lie!" She was crying now. "Or it feels like a lie, anyway."

Jackson was scared he might cry, too. He crouched in the sand, his cheek on his knees, looking away from her.

"You're a liar. You know that?"

"Y-y-you saw the, um, books?"

"It's not my fault Shirley showed up out of nowhere. It's not my fault I had to change the sheets. I only said your bed would be empty, that you sleep at Harris's on Sunday nights, 'cause I thought it was true! I didn't know!"

"D-d-did you t-t-tell anyone? About the books?"

"No!"

They sat side by side in the sand but at an angle, nearly back to back, looking away. Exhausted from the tension, they let the rhythm of the waves fill the space around them.

Finally Emma said, "That's why you said you're not going to get married, isn't it? 'Cause of men. Instead of women?"

Now Ian knew, and Albert and Emma. He shifted a bit, glanced over at her. She looked older and taller. He bobbed his head in a nod.

"You think Mom's going to find out?"

"Hope not."

Neither of them made a move to leave. They both sat poking the sand with the broken stems of dead reeds, drawing lines and circles and letters, smoothing them over, writing again until the darkness grew so thick they could barely see their marks.

Finally Jackson stood and brushed himself off. "We better get home."

Shirley looked up from her magazine when he arrived back at his cabin. She was sitting in his chair, her legs crossed, bouncing a foot up and down. One hand was wrapped around a mug of tea, and the baby was nowhere in sight, probably in his bed. Shirley pushed the magazine away.

"Know what's funny about coming home? Everything's the same. You go away and it's like you're a whole different person. You don't even notice it, really, till you get back, and everybody's having the same argument they started before you left. Know what I mean? Well, you don't, 'cause you've never been away, but it's weird. It's like, you go to a place, right? And nobody knows who you are, so they don't expect anything. I mean, as far as they're concerned, you could be anybody, do anything. They don't know. If you want to change, you can just change. Nobody says, oh, that's not like you, Shirley. I don't know how you can stand it, actually. Living your whole life stuck in this cabin, everything exactly the same. Thanks for letting me stay here, eh? It's really great. I'd be screwed if you kicked me out. My unemployment's supposed to come this week. I hope it gets here soon."

Jackson slumped into his old chair in the corner where he used to sit and whittle, and he lit a cigarette. He wasn't used to looking at his cabin from this corner anymore.

"I can't believe Mom is dead. Nearly two years now, and I still can't believe it. I kept thinking I'd call, you know? And tell Mom this or that. Like when I had her, eh?" Shirley nodded her head towards the bedroom door. She didn't say anything for a few minutes. When Jackson looked up she was wiping away a tear. "I guess everybody else is used to it by now, eh?"

"No."

"I had to come back to get my head straightened out. I gotta get back on my feet again. Sometimes I gotta be alone so I can think. I'm like that, a thinker. Sometimes I gotta just get some time to myself. That's how I am."

Matthew walked in, nodded at Jackson. "So you're back, boy. Kate was snorting like a dragon the whole time you were gone. Christ! You'd think it was my friggin' fault if you fell off the wagon! I told her you had business to attend to. What's her name?" Matthew planted himself between Shirley and Jackson, his back to his sister, and pumped an imaginary erection. He laughed, jostled Jackson and pulled a chair up beside him. Jackson turned away.

"Hey, guess what? You know Old Wank, eh? That pervert who

lives out past Thompson's? Well, me and Johnny Everett were in that joke store in the mall, and they got this inflatable sheep for fucking, you know, with the hole in its arse like those inflatable woman dolls? So we buy it and blow it up and tie it to Old Wank's mailbox, ass end out, so it'll be real convenient for him, eh?" Matthew roared.

"Hey, Shirl, Rebecca wants you down in Digby for a visit. I said I'd take you to the bus. She said okay." He cradled his arms and rocked them as though he were holding a baby. "Say, when do we get to meet the father?"

"Never, that's when. Now quit asking me that."

"Come on. What's the story?"

"Mind your own business. You're as much of a brat now as you always were, know that?"

"Remember that time you said that girls could drive as good as boys, so you hauled Rebecca into the truck, and you backed out of the yard, right straight into the ditch? Straight in! Just like that!" Matthew dissolved in laughter.

"I was fourteen friggin' years old, okay? Give it a rest."

"Dad comes storming out of the barn ready to whale away on somebody and sees you two climbing down out of the cab. Remember that, Jackson? For chrissake, he says, the next time you ladies go off shopping for new bonnets, you should ask for better directions, eh?"

"Of course *you* never put a car in a ditch."

"Not sober." He laughed again. "Hey, boy, any chance you could spare me a couple of bucks? Rosie's got a frigging padlock the size of your head on her purse, and I'm dry as the road."

Jackson glanced up, met his brother's eyes. It was only a matter of time. Even if Emma never let it slip, it was only a matter of time. Sick with sadness, he got up and disappeared into the bedroom, where he pulled a ten-dollar bill from a cache cut into a floorboard. He returned and handed it to Matthew.

"Right on!" Matthew jumped up and darted off.

Kate sent her Peter up to the cabin with his camping mattress and sleeping bag.

"Here, Mom said use this." He dropped them at Jackson's feet.

Shirley looked up. "Oh, that'd be great. 'Cause it would be such a pain to move the baby out of the bedroom, eh? I'll just keep sleeping in there with her, okay? I'm beat. I'm ready for bed now, actually."

Jackson made up his bed in the corner, longing for the dark solitude of night. Shirley took forever getting ready for bed, but finally she switched off the light and silence descended. Jackson lay there with his eyes shut tight, trying not to think about Albert. Finally, he drifted off. A cry erupted. He sat bolt upright. In the next room little Tara-Lee wailed for her midnight feeding. Eventually Shirley switched on the light, prepared her bottle and finally plugged the noise. They all slept again until nearly five o'clock, when the baby woke once more.

Jackson figured he might as well get up and drive over to Lloyd Harris's to see what work he had for him. Lloyd liked his help there before milking, no matter what the work was. Lloyd muttered all through milking about how you couldn't get reliable help. How you could spend all day on the phone calling people who never bothered to stay home so they could get a bit of work when they had the chance. Lloyd wanted a few calf pens built. That was all. One day's work, and then nothing more until the grain was ready.

Shirley packed up her bags and her baby to spend several days in Digby visiting with Rebecca. Jackson cleaned off the table and began to assemble his fiddle. Now that he wasn't terrified every second about the magazines, he had nothing to distract him from that angry weight on his shoulders, the wobbly rage burning over a sadness. Albert. He couldn't get it sorted out. He needed to lock his door, immerse himself in his work. He had already glued his fiddle pieces together and set them in clamps. Now he had to inlay the purfling, back and belly. His hands took over, his fiddle lifted him away, and his life shrank into the distance until it was small enough for him to see and poke at, examine without the fear that he would fall apart.

In school he had had to do a book report. Mr. Scarth had given him *Tom Sawyer* to read. The funeral scene was the best part, where Tom returned home to find his own funeral in progress, everyone convinced he had been swallowed up by the river. Jackson had tried and tried to imagine his family seated at the front of the church, sorry and silent at his drowning, but in his mind they all kept jostling each other and asking what there would be to eat after the funeral. The thought of Vernon pulling off his cap, shaking his head and looking grief-stricken struck him suddenly as funny. He remembered the weight of Vernon's body as he carried it down MacIntyre Road to the farmhouse, how the journey had left him breathless and empty, and how he had rolled the body off his shoulder, sloughing it onto the car seat on the porch.

He couldn't put his finger precisely on why Albert had made him so mad, but he was fairly sure that Albert had tricked him somehow. They had worked together, side by side, Albert talking away about varnishes and the fiddles he had made and about the days when he used to play professionally. And they always went to Folkards' together on Sundays. Albert knew he was gay. Then all of a sudden Albert hadn't wanted to talk to him, hadn't wanted to even look at his fiddle.

Jackson had snooped in the shop. He had hated that stupid, ugly fiddle-thing Albert's son had made. Now Albert hated him. Jackson concentrated on his purfling inlay. It had to fit perfectly into the slot he carved for it.

Ronnie knocked on his cabin door. When Jackson answered, Ronnie held out a little plastic container.

"Margie made a pot of beans. So you've got supper."

Jackson bobbed his head, took the container, stood back and let Ronnie in.

"You finally got a couple of days' peace. Nothing like a bawling baby in a small house, eh?" Ronnie grinned.

"Yeah." It astonished Jackson to realize that he and Ronnie

shared this experience. True, Ronnie was a father and he wasn't, but they both felt pretty much the same about the noise. In fact, this could be why Ronnie was sitting here right now. His infant daughter was probably raising the roof off his trailer. Ronnie could have sent one of his older girls up with the beans if he had wanted to.

Jackson sat back down to work. "Y-you know anything about football?"

"A bit, yeah."

"What's a defensive end?"

"You know how the players line up opposite each other on the field? Well, that's the guy on the end of the line. He makes sure nobody gets past him, that the team doesn't lose any ground. He has to protect whatever ground they've got."

Jackson was cutting out the notches to attach the neck to his fiddle body when Emma dropped in to tell him his peace and quiet were over. Matthew had been sent to the bus depot to pick up Shirley and the baby. She sat awhile, watching him fit the neck into place, and then wandered off.

Shirley lugged her bags into the cabin, plopped everything on the floor, laid the fussing baby on the bed and closed the bedroom door. She set the kettle on to boil and collapsed into the captain's chair.

"Oh my, what a trip!" The baby howled in the next room. "I've got to change her now. I just need five minutes." She held five fingers up for Jackson to see, as if that were some sort of proof. She pushed his tools to one end of the table and began sweeping shavings and sawdust off it with one hand, catching them at the table's edge with the other.

"Rebecca hasn't changed a bit. Still a pushover. I wouldn't let that man of hers get away with half the things he does. Sheesh." She noticed Jackson's nearly complete fiddle. "Did you make that while I was gone?"

"I put it together."

"It's nice. Can you play it?"

"No."

"Oh. Rebecca should just put her foot down with that guy. He doesn't do a thing around the house except make a mess." She turned and addressed the bedroom door. "All right! I'm coming, I'm coming."

Jackson had to forsake his bed again for the mattress in the corner. In his dream he was a boy, playing with Matthew in a rowboat. But then somehow Matthew was on the shore, running off to play with someone else, and the oars were gone, too. Jackson tried to stand, his young legs quaking, trying to steady the rocking hull. Knuckles white on the gunnels, he leaned towards shore, willing himself onto the beach, but he only floated further away. There were lots of people there, running up and down the shore, but not his mother. He couldn't see her anywhere, kept hoping she would appear to save him. Delbert laughed, shoved the boat out further into the water with the oar. Vernon leaned against a dead tree trunk, picking his teeth with a stalk of grass, watching him flounder, watching the water swirl around the boat, tug it further and further out of reach. Vernon pushed himself upright, spat out the stalk, turned his back and ambled off, his long legs bending and striding over the bank and into the distance. Vernon stopped to talk to Albert. Jackson was sure it was Albert up there, so round next to Vernon's lean figure. The outgoing tide grabbed the boat and tugged it, swirling, out to sea. He woke to a scream, but it wasn't his own. He lay blinking in the dark, waiting for his heart to stop racing, while in the next room little Tara-Lee wailed.

Emma showed up after breakfast. "I can't believe summer's almost over. School starts next week."

Jackson climbed down from the planking on the rafters where he kept his fiddles out of harm's way. In one arm, packed in his homemade plywood carrying case, was his beautifully polished

golden fiddle, the one Albert wouldn't look at. He gazed at
Emma, who had taken the baby on her lap while Shirley went to
the bathroom.

He hesitated, then spoke, "You want to come to Halifax?"

"When?"

"Now."

"Today? Right now? How long will we be gone?"

"For the day. I gotta sell a fiddle."

"Really?"

He nodded.

"I gotta go ask Mom." She thrust the baby at Jackson's empty
arm. He had to set the fiddle down to catch her. "Don't go before
I get back, okay? Wait for me!" She flew out the door.

Jackson wondered if he might get a little more for this fiddle.
Maybe seven hundred dollars? He wondered if he should ask. He
would have to find Jim Folkard when he got to the city. Emma
burst back into the cabin, puffing, wearing different clothes and
trying to stuff a folded bill into her front pocket.

"I can go!"

Shirley emerged from the bathroom. "Why did you make the
bathroom so small? It's ridiculous. You going off again?"

Jackson handed her the baby, picked up his fiddle and
motioned Emma to follow him.

Emma sat with the golden fiddle in the case on her lap and
chattered through most of the two-hour drive. Jackson didn't
mind, in fact, he felt stronger with her there. He felt in charge,
knowledgeable, competent. She followed him timidly into Folkard's
Music Store, and his chest swelled with pride when Brenda called
out to him.

"Hi, Jackson!"

"Hi. I need a set of strings."

"Finish another one?"

"Just about." Emma hovered at his elbow.

"Who's this?" Brenda asked.

"My niece. Emma."

"Hi, Emma. I'm Brenda. Your uncle . . ."

Jackson backed away, leaving Brenda chattering at Emma. He moved towards the fiddle supplies at the back and found himself hesitating, staring down the hall towards Albert's room. He knew it was Tuesday and Albert would not be here.

"Albert's not in today," Brenda called out. She joined him at the back of the store and leaned into his ear. "He was in a pretty black mood yesterday — called Jim twice to see if he'd seen you."

Emma stared at the tools and supplies displayed in the cabinet. Jackson paid for his strings, and they left.

As soon as the door shut behind them, Emma started up again. "Wow, everybody knows you! You're supposed to call Albert. Who's he? That woman said everybody loves your fiddles. Who's Albert? Who's Jim?"

"There's a park up here," he told Emma as they turned onto Spring Garden Road. They walked by the stores and restaurants through the crowds of people, Emma looking in all the windows.

"Aunt Rosie and Aunt Margie would love shopping in here, eh, Jackson? Aunt Margie would want to buy one of everything."

When Jackson led Emma through the iron gates of the Public Gardens he felt as if he was showing her his own private territory, his flower beds, his trees, his ducks. "Look, the signs tell the names of the different kinds of trees. Sometimes they have problems because there's too many ducks living here."

They walked around the park, then back down the opposite side of Spring Garden Road. Noon-hour traffic packed the restaurants and the sidewalk café tables. Jackson peered nervously into the restaurants. He would have liked to take Emma into one, and if he had ever been in one himself, he would have. They bought their lunch from the chip wagon by the library.

"They got good fries here," he said.

"Do you come here all the time?"

"Yup."

Emma told him about the other time she had been to Halifax, and how a boy she knew spent all summer here every year because his parents were separated and his father lived here.

Jackson had to see Jim about his fiddle. He had never been

inside the Journeyman's Joy, but he walked by it a lot, stood outside on the sidewalk and stared at it from across the street. He would have to get the truck and drive down so Emma would have somewhere to wait.

"There was a guy murdered here last week, you know," Emma was saying. They finished their lunch and dropped their garbage in the trash can on their way back to the truck.

Jackson parked outside Jim's pub and sat quietly for a second, smoking a cigarette, gathering his courage. Emma looked at him expectantly.

"What are we doing now?"

"The guy who sells my fiddles owns this bar. You wait here. I'll be back." Jackson picked up his fiddle case and headed across the street.

His eyes took a moment to adjust to the dimness inside the pub, a moment when he stood blinded, vulnerable and afraid. He hadn't been in a bar since he had given up the drink. But if he left he would have to explain to Emma why he was back so soon and still with his fiddle. Tables came into focus. The place was about a quarter full, but many people were leaving. A couple of men in sports jackets brushed by him on their way out. A waitress was clearing tables. He glanced around, hoping to find Jim sitting alone somewhere, but he didn't see him. He stepped forward towards the bar. He recognized the bartender instantly. It was Dez, the man with the looping dark curls and the comfortable laugh that he met on his very first Sunday night at Folkard's. Dez smiled and nodded.

"Hi," Dez said.

"H-hi. Jim here?"

"He's just stepped out. Shouldn't be too long if you want to wait. Can I get you something to drink?"

"Oh, no, I, uh, don't drink."

"A Coke or something?"

"Uh, yeah, sure." Jackson eased himself onto a barstool, set his fiddle on the bar in front of him. Jackson imagined himself like Jim, coming in with a big smile and his hand out, calling Dez by name, asking how he is, leaning back on the bar and looking around. Jackson groped for his cigarettes and pulled one out of his case slowly and studiously, keeping his eyes on them as if they might float off otherwise.

Dez rang up a customer's bill and returned with his drink. "I'm Dez." Jackson nodded once, noticed Dez's hand extended over the bar, waiting for a handshake. He struggled to get his pack of smokes back into his pocket and reach out for the hand before Dez gave up.

"Yeah. Hi."

"We met at Jim's once. Several months ago. Sorry, I've forgotten your name."

Jackson jerked his head in a nervous nod.

"It's not James, is it?"

"J-Jackson."

"That's right. I remember you brought Jim a fabulous violin you'd made. So is this another one?"

Jackson nodded.

"I'm not a player, myself."

"I u-used the yellow this time. To try."

"What?"

"On the fiddle. Yellow colouring." What a stupid thing to say! Dez didn't care what colour his fiddle was.

"Oh, excuse me." Dez left to ring up some more bills.

Jackson's eyes followed him to the other end of the bar. How much longer would Jim be, he wondered. He scratched at a bit of dirt on the fiddle case with his fingernail. The wall of the pub just to his right was covered with people's photographs, different sizes and shapes, some on an angle, some straight, all overlapping each other in a great jumble. Lots of the people in the pictures held musical instruments. Jackson's eyes passed over the faces, seeing them but not seeing them. Suddenly he found himself staring into the smiling eyes of Ian Sutherland.

"That's the Fiddlers' Wall. All those people have played here at one time or another."

Dez was back. Jackson couldn't tear his eyes away from the photo, even though he knew Dez was staring at him.

"You know him?" Dez asked.

"He's from Scotch River."

"No, he's from Halifax. That's Ian Sutherland."

"Y-you know him?"

"Sure. We dated a couple of times. Nice guy."

"Dated?"

"Yeah. Went out with. Oops. Ian's not keeping family secrets, I hope. He never told me if he was."

"You and him?" Jackson turned to Dez, too shocked to hide his embarrassment. "So you're . . ."

"Gay? Loud and proud. How do you know Ian?"

Jackson's mind raced. What the hell was he supposed to say to that? Ian went out with this guy who would say it right out loud to a stranger? Ian wasn't even trying to hide it in Halifax. And Ian claimed he was from *Halifax?* Ian wouldn't admit he was from Scotch River? How do you know him, Dez had asked. He was waiting for an answer.

"I-I dated him a couple of times, too."

"Oh yeah?" Dez beamed. "That's the best news I've heard today."

Jackson blushed crimson.

"Jackson!" Jim walked in the door, his hand extended. "What have you got for me?"

Dazed and flustered, Jackson pushed the fiddle case along the bar towards Jim. Jim opened it and picked up the fiddle with reverence. He began examining the construction. Jackson had been going to mention money, see if there was a possibility of getting a little more, but now that he was here he couldn't bring himself to.

"This is a real beauty. Albert's looking for you, you know," he said, not taking his eyes off the instrument. "He sounded a little ticked off. There's a phone there if you want to give him a call."

Albert must be furious with him. Everyone knew. His stomach hiccupped. It was going to start cramping.

"I-I gotta go."

"Sure, well, I'll check my . . ." Jim looked up and saw Jackson had backed halfway to the door. He raised his voice. "This is great!" We'll see you on Sunday?"

Jackson bobbed his head in a way that could be interpreted as a nod. He headed back to the truck, where Emma sat waiting for him. The sight of her steadied him. He could think everything over later. Right now she was relying on him, the one who knew all about the city, who knew what to do in the city.

"Wanna see a movie before we go?"

"Oh yeah!"

He turned the key in the ignition and checked the traffic.

"This is so cool."

Shirley told him she was looking for a place to live, but there was only one house for rent near Scotch River, and it was way too expensive. There was a cheap apartment outside New Glasgow, but it was too far away, she said. And she couldn't live there alone without a car. She had begun arguing with Delbert, wanting to know why he had a right to the farmhouse.

Jackson couldn't work in his cabin with Shirley there, couldn't bring himself to begin another fiddle. Every morning he drove his truck up the road and sat there in Albert's football jacket smoking cigarettes. The old emptiness that used to push in on him began to settle between his ribs, and he wanted a drink worse than he could remember. There was no sharp craving that he could identify and fend off, just a slow, gnawing hopelessness. Albert would never see the yellow fiddle now. It was going to be sold. Albert hated him for rummaging through the shop, hauling out that fake fiddle, sneering at it. He probably knew by now that he had been through the house, too, probably discovered his jacket missing. Several times on Wednesday, when he knew Albert would be working at the music store, he drove to Scotch River and dialled Albert's home number from the phone outside the Quik Mart. He let it ring and ring, imagining the sound filling the empty bungalow.

Albert's next work day was Friday. Again, Jackson pressed himself against the Quik Mart wall, dropped in his coins and dialled. In his ear the comforting trills of the phone had begun. Jackson leaned into the receiver, listening. Suddenly the line clicked, and Albert's gruff "Hello" filled his ear. He held the phone frozen to his head while Albert called out, "Hello? Hello!" Hang up, his brain told him. Hang up the phone! But he couldn't move. Soon the buzz of the dial tone replaced Albert's voice. He held the receiver, listening, then after a while set it gently back onto the cradle. His hand quaked.

Shit. It was Friday morning Albert worked. Monday, Wednesday and Friday morning. This was the afternoon. He wrapped his arms around himself, felt himself shrinking inside Albert's oversized jacket. His fingers ran over the tabs, following the stitching. Albert. Defensive end. He was losing ground.

He drove back up MacIntyre Road past Margie and Ronnie's trailer, where Margie and Shirley were sharing the front step, talking and watching the kids on the grass. They would be swapping complaints about Delbert and Darlene. He went through his cabin, pulling his savings out of every nook and cranny. Two hundred and five dollars to get him through the winter. He stuffed his wallet, collected his newly completed fiddle and headed out.

CHAPTER FIFTEEN

JACKSON STOOD AT ALBERT'S shop door with his knuckles poised ready to knock, hovering. He bit his lip, lowered his fist, leaned against the door trim. He slipped around to the back of the shop, hiding while he worked up his courage. He had never walked around the building before, never seen it from this point of view. The back was really the front. The three large windows looked out towards the sea. There was Albert sitting with his head in his hands, looking old and tired. Jackson jumped back, startled by how clearly he could see Albert, how easily Albert could see him if he raised his head. But Albert didn't look up. Shaking, Jackson retreated to his truck, grabbed hold of the truck's door handle. He stood there, sick from the sadness that welled around him. He stepped back, returned to Albert's shop door and placed his palm flat against the wood, held it there. Then quietly he turned the doorknob and let himself in. Albert looked up. Jackson chewed his lip, looked away, waited for Albert to yell, ask him what in the hell he wanted.

"Look what the cat dragged in."

"Hi." Was it possible that Albert wasn't mad after all? He was something, but not mad.

"Jim said you'd been around to see him. With the fiddle." Albert stalled as though he wanted to say something else but couldn't. "The colour polished up nice."

"Y-you saw it?"

"Jim showed me. I figured you were busy. Couldn't drop by with it. Working, were you?"

Jackson scuffed his boot on the floorboard.

"Well, you gonna stand there all day?"

Jackson shuffled forwards, slipped into the chair across from Albert. The chunk fiddle sat there between them on the cable spool table. Albert wasn't looking at it, though.

Albert had a six-pack on the floor by his feet, three empties on the table. He sat back and crossed his legs, pulling an ankle up to his knee. Jackson fumbled for his cigarettes. Albert pulled another beer out of the box, went to unscrew the cap, then hesitated, watching Jackson light up the smoke, shake out his match, toss the smoking sliver onto the table.

After a moment he said, "If I start to smoke again and you start to drink, we'll both catch hell."

Jackson looked up. Albert grinned a little.

"Yeah."

Albert slipped the beer back into the box, fit the empties in beside it. Jackson took a deep drag from his smoke, then butted it out carefully on a scrap of spruce, returned it to his pack. He tried not to stare at the fiddle chunk sitting there between them, but it kept pulling him in. It was so ugly.

"My son Chris made that. When he was little. I'd forgotten about it until you found it. I made a mould that year, and Chris asked for the cut-out. I was surprised because he wasn't interested in violins. We fought with him over his lessons for a couple of years, finally gave up. He never came to the shop. He didn't know the shop had a door." Albert laughed, but Jackson could see he wasn't happy. "But he made that. Gave it to me."

Jackson wanted to say the right thing. If someone would just write it out on a card and pass it over, he'd say it. Anything. "It's n-nice."

"Yeah."

The smell of beer and tobacco smoke hung over the piny smell of wood chips. Albert picked the thing up and wiggled the stick-neck back and forth. "He never could pound a nail. Not that he ever tried that hard. I'll tell you something, from an old man: you never know how things are going to turn out."

Albert glanced down at the six-pack, then stared out the window. Jackson was afraid he was going to stop talking, wasn't sure how to keep him going. "Wh-when did he die?"

"Two years ago now. It was quick as hell. He'd been sick a few times, but nothing that serious. Then he got this pneumonia they get. A whopper of a case, I guess. Still, he was strong, nobody expected . . . they just couldn't get ahold of it. It was a miracle they even called me. He didn't want me to know. They only told me about the virus a year before that. His mother had known for years. He didn't want me to know. The last time he was home he stayed with his mother. He always stayed with his mother. He wouldn't come here. They invited me over there, to her place, like a goddamned dinner guest. Then they told me. Together. It's not so bad as it used to be, he said, new drugs coming out. Working as waiter, he said. Doing fine. Didn't need any money. Doing fine. Maybe if we'd known Morse Code we could've clinked out something on our dinner plates, I don't know." Albert caught his faltering voice and said nothing more. He heaved himself out of his chair and picked his fiddle and bow off the bench behind him. Albert must have been playing earlier. Albert walked around the shop with it tucked under his chin. He zipped up and down several scales. Over and over, his fingers racing up and down, but no tune, only notes, one after the other.

"M-maybe he th-thought you'd be mad? You know, if you figured out he was gay?"

"Gay? I'd known that for years. Overheard him talking to his mother when he was still in high school. They were in the kitchen, didn't know I was in the basement, coming up the stairs in my sock feet. Don't tell Dad, he said. I didn't have to hear him say it. I knew what he'd told her. He was begging his mother, don't tell Dad, he said. You know what he's like. That's what he said, you know what he's like. He took off for Toronto the day after his graduation. Not much you can say then."

Albert sat back down. Jackson picked at his fingernails.

"How about you? You tell your father?"

Jackson looked up, startled and afraid. "Eh?"

"Or did you know what he was like, too?"

"Uh, no. Well, he died." He struggled to regain himself, felt Vernon's talons clamped on his shoulders, trying to shake an answer out of him. Until your teeth rattle was the expression, and they really would rattle unless you got your jaw clamped shut early, before the shaking started. No use talking to That One. "Uh, no," Jackson repeated. "I told *you*."

"Yes, you did. You did that."

Jackson followed Albert's gaze out the window and down to the sea. There was nothing special to look at. Albert's face settled into something soft and sad. He raised his fiddle to his chin again, and Jackson waited for the music. But Albert played only a single note.

"This is a G. The first string played open. If you hold the string down here, about an inch from the end, with this finger, you get the next note, A. Another inch gives you B. Then a half tone, the D string open, an inch down the D string, another inch and another half tone." He played each note as he explained it, then played them in a row, singing very softly, "Do re mi fa so la ti do ti la so fa mi re do." He set the fiddle down on the table between them, still staring out the window. Neither of them spoke. Finally Jackson reached out and picked up the fiddle and the bow. He played the open string, then pressed his forefinger against the fingerboard, felt the string digging into his skin, the glossy smooth wood behind it. He drew the bow over the string.

"That's flat. Up a bit, towards your chin. Too much, back a bit. There. Keep your bow at a ninety-degree angle to your strings."

Twice up and down the scale and Jackson was fed up. He set the fiddle back on the table.

"It's hard when you're just starting out," Albert said and tapped his fingers on the arm of the chair. "I got this set of cabinets to build. I was going to go to the lumber yard today, but I've gone and drunk too much. What do you think of that?"

"Well, I could drive."

Albert lifted one bushy eyebrow and looked at him sideways. "Yeah, I s'pose."

"Course I can't help load. I've, uh" — Jackson coughed and thumped his chest — "I've gone and smoked too much." He sneaked a peek at Albert, watched the lines fall from his face, his teeth catch the light, heard the chuckle rise up from somewhere deep in the centre of the mountain and spill over, filling the workshop. Jackson felt himself grow lighter.

"Well, let's go then, before they close." Albert stood up, disappeared into the finishing room for a second. When he came back, Jackson's jean jacket was swinging from his forefinger. "Did you know you left this here?"

Jackson didn't sleep well that night in the bed that was once Albert's son's and then Albert's daughter's. For hours he leaned on the windowsill staring into the streetlamp twilight. Traffic never seemed to stop for long. For hours he stared at the little trailer on the other side of the driveway where Albert used to live when his daughters were in high school, the one he meant to fix up and rent out but never got around to it. Jackson squeaked his fingernail across the window. If Shirley paid him a bit of rent for his cabin on MacIntyre Road and Albert didn't charge too much. If Albert didn't mind him being around a bit. But what if he made Albert mad? Albert would toss him out, and he would have nowhere to live. He winced at the thought of the football jacket balled into the plastic bag stashed under the seat of his truck. There wasn't enough profit in the fiddles for him to pay rent, keep a truck, buy cigarettes and food. He would need some kind of job, not much work but a little. Where would he find work out here? He didn't know anybody. How would he ever manage? He wouldn't have Kate to borrow from or Matthew to fix his truck. He wouldn't be able to manage. It was impossible.

Jackson was already sitting at the kitchen table when Albert got up the next morning. Jackson's stomach cramped with the same numb fear he felt after Ian walked off and left him. He fiddled with his teaspoon, kept dropping it on the table, picking it up again. His hands shook. Three times he opened his mouth but nothing came out.

"Gotta get started on those cabinets today," Albert said.

"H-how m-much, if you wanted . . .?"

"What's that?"

"It's okay if you don't want to . . . j-just if you still wanted . . ."

"Eh? Spit it out there, lad."

"If you wanted to rent out your trailer . . . would it be dear?"

Albert's eyebrows shot up, a tiny smile crept across his lips. "You looking at leaving home?"

Jackson nodded.

Albert swallowed his grin, knitted his eyebrows. "Well, you won't find a better deal than that trailer. I'll guarantee you that. Two hundred a month. You can't beat that. And fifty bucks a month off if you make my dinner for me twice a week. Don't try serving up the Kraft Dinner without the olives, though. I only like it the fancy way now. And the first month's rent is free if you clean it out yourself."

Jackson's heart pounded against his ribcage. "Okay," he managed. "Th-that's good. Okay, that's good."

ACKNOWLEDGMENTS

I would like to thank the Canada Council for the Arts for the financial encouragement which got this project underway. A version of the prelude appeared as "Jackson" in *Wayves*; a version of chapter four appeared as "The Still" in *The Antigonish Review* and the 1999 *Journey Prize Anthology*; and a version of chapter five appeared as "Passing On" in *Descant*.

For her editing zeal and expertise, thanks to Laurel Boone, and thanks to all the folks at Goose Lane Editions for their help and patience. Special thanks to the members of the writers' circle, Hazel Felderhof, Alex Keir, Pat Nelson and Marion Kearns, who sat through each chapter and offered their critical eyes and ears as well as friendship and enthusiasm. Thanks also to Jessie Chisholm, who read and commented on the manuscript. For insights into the art of violin-making, thanks to Lloyd Tattrie. Thanks to all my friends for their forebearance in the face of obsession, and especially to Joel for his unflagging support.